Baelfire: Innocence Lost

A Novel By
Jade Jesser

Current eBook Edition: 2014

Published in the United States of America
By James Mace and Legionary Books
http://www.legionarybooks.net

I dedicate this first book to the loving memory of my sister, Kari. You were the first person to truly make me feel supported and loved, sis. Thank you for giving me the strength to pursue my dreams!

This series, however, I dedicate to my son, Collyn. With it, I pass on my sister's advice to me: Always follow your dreams, do what you love, love what you do, and take care of the people around you!

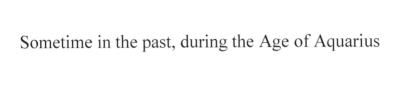

Sometime in the past, during the Age of Aquarius

You Dirty Rat

It had been exactly four minutes and seventeen seconds since the four men entered the building: two from the west, two from the east. Each man dressed in all black, each man masked, each man armed to the teeth with the best weapons and technology money can buy. These men were not military, however, nor were they part of some terrorist organization. For these four, it was just another day at the office.

Charles DeRon Jackson was a beast of a man. Some would say a genetic mutant. He stood nearly seven feet tall and had shoulders to match. If it weren't for a bum block from a jackass of a fullback, he probably would have gotten the sack and kept his knee. Fate doesn't always handle things your way, though. So here he was, running a two-by-two formation as a cover man for his team leader. He hated using guns, they felt so small in his hands, and they just didn't have the same sense of gratification as did the feel of a crushed jawbone. But come what may, Jackson always did what was needed. Besides, Jackson's fully-automatic shotgun would not appear small in any hands but his own.

No one knew much about Caine other than the corporation hired him out of some fallout with the military. There wasn't much to debate, he was a ruthless soldier, a superb team leader, and carried out orders with precision and accuracy. Unlike his cover man, Caine was a bit smaller than average, which deceptively added to his lethality. His target acquisition and combat accuracy scores were off the charts in training, and his multiple tours had given him experience that most men would argue a curse.

Jackson and Caine moved quickly down the hallway, Caine's weapon leaving a red mark of death on walls and doorways as they approached. Caine paused for a moment as they approached an intersection, making a fist with his left hand. Jackson did his best to press his back against the wall while searching behind them. Adrenaline swam through his system like the moment before a hike, and he pressed his thumb into his earpiece to better hear the chatter coming from the other team.

"Alpha team, this is beta, do you read?" The transmission was clear in both Jackson and Caine's ears.

"We read. What is your situation?" Caine whispered.

"No sign of the package. There does appear to be some lab coats working late. They are sitting in the break room."

"Fuck'em. This was the wrong day for overtime," Caine replied.

"Roger that."

Caine and Jackson could not hear the sound of the other teams' weapon fire through the suppressors, but they had done enough missions with the pair that they knew they would be happily thorough.

"Jackson, let's move." Caine's whisper was harsh and demanded respect.

The two rounded the corner and there, facing them, was none other than Rodney Jerome Miller. Rodney had retired after many good years of service working for the city in the sanitation department, more specifically, the public school sanitation department. Budget cuts required of him an early retirement. The reduced monies forced Rodney to seek part time employment to supplement his income. Before today, Rodney had considered himself lucky to find a job like this. His boss even let him listen to his jazz through his headphones while he worked. Now Rodney was falling to the floor. A bullet shot through his brain that he never heard coming. Neither man paused for Rodney. They stepped over him silently, looking for the room that held the package.

"Strike team, this is Night Watch, over."

"Night Watch, we read you," Caine replied.

"Step it up, guys. Looks like a fire alarm has been triggered somewhere in the building. You got about 4 minutes before someone comes to save you."

"Ain't no one gonna save us." Came a response from the com.

Rounding another corner, Caine and Jackson noticed a large double door. The sign on the door read "Authorized Personnel Only". Bio hazard symbols on both doors, as well as a key pad on the wall, indicated they were in the right place. From the opposite hallway, they could see Ortiz and Williams approach.

Caine used his hands to order Williams to check inside the room. The soldier quickly glanced through one of the door's small windows and sat back down quickly. Using hand signals, he motioned that there were four people inside, none of them armed. He pointed at Ortiz, then the keypad. Nodding in understanding, Ortiz reached into a leg pocket to retrieve a durable plastic case. Inside the case was an electronic device capable of overriding the security code on the keypad. In a few short seconds, the steady red light on the keypad turned to a flashing blue, and the team could hear the mechanical lock open.

Caine held up three fingers, then two, then one.

The four men burst through the door of the laboratory. The occupants never stood a chance. Short bursts from Caine, Williams, and Ortiz' weapons did their jobs quickly and efficiently. In a few seconds, the only motions in the room were the beams of red light cutting through the remnants of the muzzle fire, as they scanned the room for movement.

"Clear," shouted Caine.

"Clear." Came the others' replies in sequence.

"Jackson, keep an eye on the hallway. Smoke anybody dumb enough to come down this way."

"I got this," said Jackson as he moved towards the double doors.

Caine moved towards the back of the laboratory. In it were several cages holding a variety of rats. Large, small, male, and female, all of the rats looked oblivious to the goings on around them. The occasional sniff in the air or standing on the hind legs to check the security of their confinement, told Caine there was nothing special about the rodents. They appeared nothing more than rats.

Reaching into his pack, Caine pulled out what looked like a cross between a touch-screen tablet computer and a handgun that could fire some unknown type of ammunition. It took him a moment to assemble it into its apparent functional shape, and he began pointing it at the various caged animals. Each time he pointed it, a detailed cross section of the targeted rodent displayed its entire structure, its age, its weight, the density of its bones. Pressing some selections on the screen enabled Caine to select any particular attribute he wished to examine. In this case, he was trained in the device's use to look for pathogens in the bloodstream. He had no idea what type of pathogen, but he knew that it was important. So he went from rat to rat, searching as he was instructed. He was having little luck, however. All of the rodents came up with a negative.

A certain cage caught his eye, and Caine moved over to it. It was not a plastic cage of a standardized size and shape as the others; rather, this cage resembled a pet transport, complete with a name tag on the front, "Nym". Caine carefully looked inside and there, sitting

9

quietly with its beady red eyes, staring back at the soldier, was a rather large, white, but seemingly normal rat. Like most rats, this one was not afraid of human presence, and this one seemed more friendly than usual. The thought entered Caine's mind that this was someone's pet; certainly the name seemed to articulate a specific sense of unique affection compared to the other specimens. In any case, Caine was not paid to think but to do his job, and time was running out for the team. He scanned the rat. The cross section appeared: weight, age, sex. Caine tapped on the side of the scanner, thinking there must be an error. He then began the process of reinitiating the scan. He paused for a moment, looked at Nym, then back at the scanner.

Ortiz noticed the pause. "Sir? What's going on?" Quickly, Caine finished the scan. He stared at the positive results of the pathogen. Again he looked at the rodent that stared contently at him. He could not help thinking the rat knew exactly what was going through his mind. There was an eerie, unnatural intelligence about it, and Caine did not like it one fucking bit. As he snapped out of his short trance, Williams approached.

"You're shitting me, right?" Williams asked.

Caine shot the soldier a warning look. Quickly, he folded up the scanner and retrieved a second case from his pack. Inside was a small tube, some sort of aerosol can with medical jargon on the outside and a convenient, rat-sized face mask. Neither Ortiz nor Williams could deny the revelation of the mission as Caine began to assemble the device. Confirmation was solid when the squad leader produced another device that resembled a fancy tube with two smaller canisters attached. Digital readouts appeared on the side of the tube that could be sealed on both ends.

"We came here for a god-damned rat?" complained Williams.

"We came here for a package," answered Ortiz.

"I just smoked five people over a fucking rat? That is definitely a first for me."

"Shut the fuck up!" hissed the squad leader.

Caine had put the scanner away. His hand was shaking as he opened the door to the cage. Both Ortiz and Williams, confused by their leader's trepidation, brought their weapons to bear on the rat, partly expecting the thing to burst out of the cage and attack them like some mythological predator.

Caine cautiously reached inside. Nym sniffed his glove, and as he turned his hand over, the animal nonchalantly climbed onto it. He retracted his arm from the cage, and the rat stared at him, as if it expected what was to happen next. Carefully, Caine affixed the face mask to the rodent, a task that did not seem to bother Nym in the slightest. A slight "hissing" noise could be heard coming from the canister as Cain proceeded to press a few buttons. In a few short seconds, Nym was asleep in his hand. Caine handled the sleeping mammal as one would expect a demolitions officer to handle a live explosive. He inserted the sleeping Nym into the transportation canister and, after sealing the end, pressed a few more buttons on the side. Coolant flooded the canister as designed and left Caine holding a sleeping rodent in cryostasis.

"Let's move," ordered the squad leader.

"Yes, sir," spat Williams. He started towards the door and, as he passed Ortiz, added, "Can't believe we came here for a fucking rat."

Ortiz, Williams, Jackson, and Caine all began moving towards the extraction gate. They could hear the sirens howling in the distance, getting louder as the approached the exit.

"Night Watch, come in. What do we have? Over." Caine's message held little sound of concern, just a question based on the expectation of a factual response.

"We have one squad car pulling in at the moment, followed by one full size fire truck. Looks like they are here to save you assholes."

Jackson's response was not over the radio. "All those childhood dreams of saving lives are about to go right out the window…"

"I don't have a problem wasting a copper, but my uncle back home is a fireman. Seems a shame to do that over a…package!" Williams' statement was half to himself; none the less, the squad leader abruptly spun on the soldier, slamming him up against the wall.

"One more word about the package and you won't leave this place. Am I clear?" Caine's threat was as much in his eyes as it was in his words. It was clear that whatever the squad leader had seen on the rodent's scan results had freaked him out.

"Clear, sir," Williams answered the man directly, but as the squad leader moved to continue down the hallway, Williams' body language reflected nothing but rage. Williams did not like being intimidated, no matter how successful the effort.

As the four men approached the exit, they could see two officers moving cautiously towards them. The policemen were scanning the building above them, looking for smoke. Behind the parked squad car sat a fire engine, and a half dozen men suiting up around the outside of it. Parked behind the fire truck was the squad's van, with their final member inside. This posed a terrible problem, not for the team, but for the officers and firemen that had inadvertently obstructed their escape path.

Caine looked at Jackson, who dipped his chin in acknowledgement. Williams closed his eyes, clearly angry at the squad leader's decision. Ortiz checked his firearm and nodded alongside of Jackson. The four men burst through the exit door. The officers barely had a chance to draw their weapons. The thunderous sounds of Jackson's automatic shotgun echoed across the courtyard between the doorway and the fire truck. Fanning out behind the large man, the other members of the squad came, targeting the men suiting up to search for perilous flame. Small red dots spelled death as bullets spit to their precise location on chest and helmet alike.

Jackson's hand-held cannon released resounding booms as its payload tore into the parked squad car, ripping the metal, glass, and interior parts asunder. The concussive blows shook the vehicle, sending shrapnel out the other side. This destruction was minimal, however, when compared to the demolition of any poor man the fire arm bared upon. The strength of the weapon was such that a mere graze would send a man spinning through the air, and a direct hit could nearly tear the target in two. In just seconds, the thunder of the weapon had ceased, and eight men lie dead or dying on the ground outside of the laboratory. The team continued and moved quickly towards the van parked behind the fire truck, pausing only to finish off fallen targets that had not given up on the fight for life.

Ortiz moved to the driver's side, Williams to the passengers, while Jackson and Caine joined the wily "Night Watch" in the back of the van, which was outfitted with all manner of surveillance and communications equipment. Williams, visibly frustrated, hurled his helmet into the back, past the squad leader, smashing it into one of the many instrument panels.

"Holy shit! You guys are ruthless! Damn!" The electronics expert could not contain his excitement regarding the squad's swift and decisive maneuvers.

"I can't believe this shit!" Williams was in a rant. "We just iced over a dozen people over a stupid rodent! This whole thing is…"

Caine's knife finished his sentence. The squad leader's blade entered Williams' neck below the left ear, behind his jawbone. Death moved in quickly, and Caine did not hesitate. He pushed the body of Williams out the passenger door and casually took his place. The others stared at him with both shock and awe.

"Damn, bro," stated Jackson. "You just killed Williams!"

"That's right. I did. We don't get paid to assess the nature of a job. You all best remember that shit." Caine's tone was ice. "Not like it matters, we are all dead soon enough anyhow." The latter statement was made to himself, barely audible to the others; however, if they had heard it, none of them would have made mention of it given the passing of recent events.

"So did you get it? The rat? Did you get it? Did you? Did you?" The communications guy was definitely energetic, and such personalities in the face of these circumstances rarely made the situation better.

Ortiz shifted the van into gear. He was not in a rush. One of the benefits of leaving no one alive as a witness, was that one did not know when a disturbance would be escalated or reported. They had several minutes, at the least, before dispatch reported anything wrong. As they drove off, the squad leader reached into his pack and handed the tube holding the comatose rodent to the all-to-eager communications guy.

"Awesome. Crazy shit right? Did you even look at the scans?" asked the wily fellow.

Ortiz looked at Caine who stared straight ahead. He remembered the squad leader's strange reactions to the scans taken in the lab. The squad leader did not reply. The communications guy hooked the tube into a laptop mounted on the side of the van. As he did, a read out appeared not dissimilar to the one from Caine's scanner. Watching over his shoulder, Jackson looked puzzled at the information on the screen.

"See that right there, big guy? That's why this rat was so God damned important. That's why your orders were to leave no witnesses. Crazy, huh?" Each time he made a point, the man flicked a number on the corner of the screen.

Jackson squinted his eyes. He stared at the man with confusion. "Does that say what I think it says?" His question was a child's first step onto a tightrope.

"Sure does. Wild, huh? Yes-sir-ee! That rat you got there is nearly one hundred and twenty years old!"

Caine didn't seem to notice Ortiz nearly driving the van off the road with his sudden surprise at the news. He merely looked ahead and then out the side of the window, watching all of the fellow travelers going down the road. It didn't matter. They would all be dead soon anyway.

Present day: The Age of Sagittarius

A Nest of Ants

The damp dirt squished around his fingers, knees, and toes, as he crawled behind the bug snake. The late morning grass was much taller than the crawling boy and still carried the remnants of last night's drizzle of rain, a common characteristic of this particular moon's placement with the constellations. This particular placement held the moon in the grip of the Hunter; festivals across the land would praise the passing of spring into summer, good harvests, and good hunts.

The dirt-covered boy cared nothing of festivals; Ronin had seen more than nine winters, three of which were longer than most, and the winter of his own birth was legendary according to his mother. Hunting, however, was a favorite past time of the boy and, during the month of the Hunter, the boy was off on adventure from dawn to dusk. Every morning he sprang from bed, obediently yet restlessly ate his breakfast, completed, often halfheartedly, his chores, and dashed from his mother's arms into the hills behind their simple home. This day had been no different, and the adventure had led the boy to following a peculiar, yet regular visitor to the Asperii household's garden: the bug snake.

Shawna Asperrii's garden was well known to the local villagers, not because of the name associated with it, but because of the product that came from it. Shawna and her son Ronin lived alone on a secluded hillside two days south of a small village known as Balanced Rock. She dealt only with one merchant from the village, Filius Max, trading the well-grown garden crop for the goods needed for her and her son's survival. The merchant would meet Shawna at a midway point twice a year for early and late-season trade. The man always getting the better of the deal. Shawna suspected that as long as Filius continued to profit in this manner, he would have reason to keep their biannual meetings secret. Secrets are often the key to becoming successful in the world of trade, and Shawna hoped the merchant kept that key as close to his heart as she did. Every morning as Ronin bounded off on his cheerful adventures, Shawna reinvested in the hopes that her presence in the South Hills would remain off the topic of the local townsfolk's gossip tables. She counted on the fact that Filius continued to attribute his one- sided trade profits to the feigned ignorance of a woman, rather than that of a protective mother paying for tightened lips with blistered hand. The Asperrii's presence in the South Hills had to be kept a secret at all costs and, for the past eight seasons, no whispers had leaked from the merchant's mouth. Shawna's seasonal meeting place had never been compromised by accompanying stranger or delay, which was a blessing for both parties. After all, Shawna and Ronin's anonymity was worth killing over.

The garden was large enough that Shawna had to employ the service of Brown Dog, an old mare traded to her from Filius a few seasons past. The horse was aged significantly more than the merchant had claimed, but with that age came the patience of putting up with an adventurous child that had the habit of using the hair of the horse's mane to scramble onto her back. Ronin spent almost as much time with Browndog as Shawna did and had given the horse her unfortunate name as he had the other members of the farm. There was Ruckus the rooster who was married (affectionately) to Clucky, Pecky-Mecky, Strutty-Putty, and Miss 'Tute, the latter of which often chased Ronin around the chicken coup, complaining the whole time. There was Rocky and his wife, Mudface the pigs; Knothead and Sliver, the goats; and Bird the cat. The only residents of the Asperii farm not named by the youth were a pair of large wolfhounds named Cretus and Celestte that often accompanied the boy on his daily adventures. This time of the year, the pair was often away from the farm on their honeymoon as Shawna called it, returning when Celestte was full with litter. This worked out well for Shawna, because the pups were of good breeding and fetched a fair trade with Filius in the late season after weaning. Cretus was a protective beast, strong and loyal, with a nose for tracking and a fearsome growl for curious would-be predators. Matched easily by his mate, the pair had thwarted many of the forest's interlopers over the years, their place as farm protectors not at all taken for granted.

The farm itself was not a grand villa of the countryside. Nonetheless, the structures were built on a stout foundation of dwarf-mastered stone. The wooden frames of the buildings guided a strong mixture of mud-and-straw brick which, in turn, was carefully plastered both inside and out. Shawna had already repaired the thatch on the winter-worn roofs and was currently in the process of cleaning the large atrium area, in the center of the main home. Built on lintel and post, each building was not built for grandiose size, rather for quaint necessity and durability.

Shawna and Ronin's home was of modest size compared to other rural habitations with a large living area and columned porch. Both Shawna and Ronin had their own chambers and a third chamber built specifically for the Asperrii's only frequent guests, Solam and Sherium. The home also had the unique addition of a dwarven-cast iron stove in the center of the main living area. This near priceless gift boasted a large chimney that radiated heat in the home throughout the winter. A kitchen area with a large pantry allowed for easy preparation of meals cooked on the magnificent stove. Shawna even had an underground cellar constructed on the side of the house near the large garden outside. Tapestries of beauty and craft accented each wall, both for decoration and insulation, and shelves held trinkets of Shawna's travels from lands far removed. Had Filius seen the interior of their home, he would have no doubt grown suspicious of Shawna's dealings with him. The tapestries, trinkets, and iron stove would be reserved only for Sabrinian royalty, and the wealth attributed would surpass the most successful Merchant-Lord of Balanced Rock, easily making him appear a beggar in contrast. Ronin's chamber also had a shelf, and upon it, magnificent trinkets of his own. His mother's room followed suit, though in her room rested certain items as sacred as the pairs' anonymity.

The Barn was a bit larger than the house and situated in simple fashion. Ample space provided Brown Dog a comfortable area, as well as Rocky, Mudface, and the two goats. The chicken coup nestled indoors for nesting, and each of the animals' relative stalls had outdoor access to a well-built pen. Dry grasses and wild alfalfa were placed in a large pile at the far end of the barn, left over from the winter's store. Bird, the cat, made his home here, and the expert mouser rarely went without a meal in either summer or winter months. A small portion of the barn functioned as the farm's tackle and tool shed, housing all of the tools needed to work the farm and large garden, as well as a shoeing station for the Asperii mare.

The location of their farm was near perfection, nestled downhill from a small pond conveniently crafted by beaver-rats. Shawna had a clay pot noria constructed at the mouth of the small waterfall, leaving the pond to provide drinking water and irrigation for the farm. Winter freezing of the pond rarely affected the small waterfall, and so fresh water at the farm was usually abundant year round. The clay pots of the noria had to be removed before the first freeze, however, and replaced with less efficient wooden versions. Springtime usually required a significant amount of maintenance to the waterwheel, but its small size made the daunting task fairly manageable. Ran by nothing more than gravity and the flow of the water itself, the noria dumped the life-giving substance onto a raised wooden flume that directed the water to a canal system that provided irrigation for the garden, and then into wooden pipe that led to the underground basins that filtered, before filling the impluvium in the courtyard between the house and barn. The stone courtyard in between the home and barn was simple in appearance, yet elaborate in design. A square impluvium gathered rainwater and the water from the plumbing system designed with an ingenuity more often reserved to the palace towns and wealthy villa of the land. Several underground basins filtered the water before it reached the storage facility, a few pipes insured the impluvium did not overflow and fed into a waste water canal. The sewage system was crafted with equally careful planning, allowing for a clean little latrine to be placed a short distance down the hill. Waste water then flushed down the hillside below, far from the normal activities of the farm.

Ronin knew nothing of the engineering that went into building the farm, the ample size of the barn, or the presence of year-round irrigation. Nor was he aware of the wealth that the stove and decorations inside represented or the relative life of simple luxury he lived. There were no neighboring farms where the boy could go to play, no children around for him to relate to, no place to compare to his own. His only companions were the other members of the farm and, in many cases, like today, the critters that made residence near his own, like this bug snake.

Ronin loved snakes. In actuality, the boy loved all animals, but snakes were always so different! Snakes were fearless and patient. Ronin could watch a snake slowly stalk its prey or even set motionless for hours, waiting to strike; then, at the precise moment, the snake strikes, sending its victim to its place within the Great Circle. Bug snakes were just like any other snake, really, with the exception that they would sometimes get on a trail of bugs and snap them up, one after another, sometimes for hours on end. Their tongues shooting out to zap up dozens of unsuspecting victims with lightning speed. Ronin would follow a bug snake all day if he could, as was his current task, giggling in joy each time a tongue snapped up another meal.

Shawna smiled as she heard Ronin's giggles in the grass above the garden. She had very little to worry about. The boy had no real boundaries around the farm. Cretus and Celestte were never far away, and a shout from the boy always caused the hounds alarm, sending them running in the direction of the boy. Even without the added security of the hounds, the main reason for Shawna's lack of her concern for the boy's immediate safety was the same reason Shawna had to be concerned about the farm remaining hidden from travelers and authorities. Shawna was *mangmu lieren*. In the old tongue, this meant simply: "aimless hunter". Far from an accurate description, the *lieren* are individuals whose vision is locked in a world different than the physical world surrounding them. They did not see the different shades of color associated with the springtime, blossoms of a blooming tree nor colorful feathers of a hopeful male songbird. They could not see the soft hues of a lake or the reflections of the sky upon it. For both Shawna and Ronin, the world they saw was one of energy and interaction. Living things whose life force flows throughout, the world around them appeared in brilliant waves spanning the spectrum of all visible light, intermingling with one another as different hues of paint would on a canvas. Unblocked by the dull-grey shapes of all things unliving, the life force, or *joa*, of all living things fills the vision of the *lieren,* allowing them a sight that penetrates the physical world, transforming it into a multidimensional painting consisting of those key pigments of creation. No living thing can hide from the vision of a hunter, and a being's *joa* is as unique as its physical appearance, recognizable and distinguishable from all other beings in but an instant. Ronin could no more hide from his mother, than she him. No rock or barn crevasse can detour the presence of the flowing life force of someone hidden behind it.

She need but glance in the direction of her son's last position to see the trails his *joa* left. In fact, the skilled woman knew the boy's exact position, as well as both hounds, the mare, and any other living thing for miles around. The magnificent sight Ronin inherited from his mother was both a blessing and a curse. A trained hunter can

21

track down any individual over any distance. They can see through any disguise. Such a blessing can be invaluable to those requiring it, especially if the hunter can be trained to the whims of a master. Shawna knew this, her past had been a tiresome life of avoiding exploitation; a life she had no intention of allowing her son to live. She leaned upon her garden hoe for a moment, took a look around, and smiled in comfort as she turned back to her work.

Zap! Another bug disappeared into the snake, its small flash of *joa* quickly blending into the snake's own. To Ronin's delight, the bug snake was on a trail of ants, a particularly stingy kind that the long-haired boy was none too fond of. The bug snake was on a buffet of glowing delight, and the young hunter did his best to keep up with the ravenous serpent. One after another, vibrant blue flashes of life force blended into the icy blue of the reptile; each flash making the snake's own color seem a bit brighter.

His long hair, maintained by a loving mother, snagged the grass as the boy crawled behind the snake. He had not the foresight that his mother's brush would be, seemingly, tearing at his very soul later as consequence.

Ant after ant disappeared into the body of the serpent, so quickly were the snaps and zaps that Ronin didn't notice the hundreds of blue lights approaching the snake from all sides.

The snake continued forward, pulling along the curious trudging boy, both parties oblivious to the ambush laid by the stinging little warriors. One by one, a small blue light moved into the flowing movement of the bug snake. Ronin watched as pincer and stinger attempted to penetrate the scaled hide of his champion. Two came, then three, then four, then ten, no, twelve. The snake moved forward, unimpaired by the freeloaders attached to its back, snapping the attackers that came in forward arc. There were twenty now, no, thirty at least; still the snake moved forward, its sinuous movement not slowed. Ronin was amazed at the snake's resilience to attack! The stinging little ants stood not a chance against such a foe! Fifty now, at least fifty attached to the serpent, unable to find a niche in its armor. So many blue flashes disappeared into the snake's mouth that it could not eat them all. Ronin hooted in victory for his companion, convinced that the impenetrable defenses of the beast would be the end of the stinging vermin.

He did not notice it happen at first, when the snakes own *joa* was substituted by the blue of the hundreds of ants that now surrounded it. It wasn't until the bug snake's smooth slither turned into a violent spin that the boy realized his champion's armor had failed. In a violent convulsion the snake spun itself into an unnatural ball, still with small swarms of blue attaching themselves to it. The serpent twisted into what Ronin imagined was a miraculous defensive maneuver, using its body to propel itself off of the ground. Thrashing, the serpent attempted to shake off its attackers, to the desperate extent that the now puzzled onlooker struggled to keep view of it. Ronin watched as the reptile twisted in on itself, using its own body to attempt to dislodge the stinging insects. More and more they came, half dozen for every one that was dislodged.

Then the thrashing and twisting stopped. Little blue lights glowing a bit brighter as the *joa* of Ronin's companion faded away. There was no more icy blue. No more snake, no more-

"Ouch!" yelped Ronin as he felt a violent pinch on his knuckle. "Yow!" he said as his hand slapped instinctively at his foot.

Then the boy began to scream.

Cretus and Celestte, hunting burrow-rats nearby, both shot their heads into the air, ears alert at the sound of the most beloved of their pack. They paused but a moment before darting selflessly into the tall grass towards the boy. Shawna, with all of her past experience in battle, could not begin to imagine controlling the fear that shook her spine at such a sound. The terrified mother bounded into the tall grass with the determination of legend.

The frantic screams continued for what seemed like a lifetime but, in all actuality, the big male dog bounded into the boy only moments after they began. Cretus, not known for his caution, began barking at the boy, as if to ask him what was wrong. The ants attacked the hound instantly. There was a frenzy of the warrior insects as the dog leapt several feet in the air filled with adrenalin. When he landed, the big male began chomping large quantities of the things as they swarmed him. Celestte, blessed with the instincts of a protective matriarch, ignored her battling mate and moved quickly over to a now thrashing Ronin. When she reached him, she grabbed the boy by the scruff of the neck and began dragging him away from what appeared to be a small mountain of crawling, biting, stinging ants.

She ignored the attacking ants as they stung her mouth and tongue. She growled as they crawled into her nostrils and stung her. She focused only on dragging the boy away and drag she did. She used the scruff of his tunic to shake his small body as she went, attempting to shed the layer of insects that covered him. Her ears twitched at the yelps of her mate, as the brave male continued to offer distraction to the tenacious vermin. Still she dragged the boy, twisting his body this way and that, trying desperately to dislodge the poisonous creatures that had now found her an equal threat. She tugged, and pulled, and shook, dragging Ronin further and further away from the nest.

Shawna approached like a gazelle bounding through the grasslands; her former life of combat and chaos springing forward from the back of her mind to overtake this new one of labor and routine. Her *lieren* vision immediately picked up on the two hounds' fight and flight response, their life force glowing with the rush of adrenaline, rapidly pounding with their heartbeats. Ronin's own *joa*, clutched in the protective jaws of Celestte's rescue, seemed masked by an unwelcome shade of pixilated blue. Cretus yelped and leapt in the air, little flashes of blue falling off of him like dozens of falling stars. Fleet of foot, she closed the distance between herself and the savior bitch, who gave Ronin another shake like a dog would a captured rabbit. Like a wet rag being whipped through the air, droplets of glowing ants flew from the boy.

"Celestte!" she screamed. "Drop him!"

The dog did not listen, she continued to drag the boy further away from danger. Ronin was no longer screaming.

When Shawna reached the mongrel, she began to understand the situation. Her life-long friend was doing exactly what needed to be done, albeit with the only tools provided for her. Shawna grabbed the limp figure of her son and began swiping his body clean of ants, a method much preferred to the violent shaking the animal had used. Celestte relinquished command of the boy and began to chomp and scratch the ants that attacked her. Cretus still assaulted the nest, bounding and leaping in the air only to land and aggressively chomp into moving piles of the stinging adversaries.

Ronin did not move, and fear grabbed his mother like a giant plain's constrictor, squeezing the breath out of her in a near nonexistent moment of panic. There wasn't a spot on the boy's bare

24

skin not red and swollen with ant wounds; the little beast's venom causing countless swollen mounds on the little hunter's skin. His eyes were already swollen shut, and he wasn't breathing. She snapped to her senses and opened his mouth. It was filled with the flashing colors of the stinging insects and, towards the back, the corpses of them. She used her finger to clear his mouth and shifted him to his side. With a firm hand she slammed his back, trying to force a cough. Nothing happened. She looked in his mouth, mucous covered skeletons of invading ants now filled it, and she scooped them out. Time stood still; Celestte barked at her. She turned the boy over on his stomach and jerked him so his mid-section was over one knee. With Ronin's head towards the ground, she again sharply pounded his back.

For a moment there was nothing in the world but the sound of her hand striking his back. She could not hear the hound dog barking encouragement to the boy, nor the yelping soldier-dog in the background. For a moment there was no sound at all.

Ronin began to cough.

"That's it, baby! Get 'em out! Come on, baby!" Tears that filled her eyes now freely swept down her cheeks. A sensation the warrior-woman had little recollection of.

She used a finger to help clear the ants the boy had coughed up. Ronin began to cry, and cough, and sneeze, sometimes all at once, which seemed to cause more of the same. To Shawna, it was the most wonderful sound in the world. She picked him up. The crying boy was too weak to hold onto his mother. As she ran towards the house, his arms and legs flopped lifelessly. The sound of his sobs assured Shawna of his presence, and Celestte trailed closely behind as the two protective mothers rushed their injured boy home.

Shawna burst into the kitchen and used a free arm to clear off the preparation table. The sounds of breaking clay bowls and pots rang in her ears as she laid the wounded child on his back. His cries were turning to gurgling chokes, as the swelling in his tongue and throat increased. She was, as the wise ones would say "still tip-toeing around a flock of sleeping Razorbeaks". If the swelling was too severe, it could block his airways. Ants had nearly made their way into the boy's lungs, stinging the whole way. Shawna was not a healer. In fact, the majority of her younger years were spent perfecting quite the opposite, but her years of adventuring had given her old habits that die hard. One of these old habits was packing light and carrying things with you that had multiple uses. The papaya fruit, for example, was one such item. Not only a food and a handy tool for seasoning your stew, the papaya can be used to help with small cuts, rashes, and insect bites. Shawna only hoped that it would help Ronin's condition and that she could get some down her son's gullet in time. She grabbed one of the fruit and smashed it on the table. She mashed the fruit up in her hand and gave it a quick scan for the seeds. She squeezed the paste into his mouth and then tilted his head up. The boy gagged and choked, but his worried mother could give him no quarter. She repeated the process again and again. Careful to keep a finger in his mouth to prevent his tongue from blocking his airway, she cradled her boy. She held back the tears, giving in to resolve.

It would be a long night.

The Wagon Wheel

Baylee's knuckles whitened with strain as she struggled to carry the two full buckets of milk from the barn to the house. She gritted her teeth in determination and defiance of what would surely be never ending torment from her two older brothers should she drop one. The thought seemed to spur her on with added anger, because she knew the big buffoons would probably hog one of the buckets to themselves, thereby forcing her father, herself, and her younger siblings to share the other.

The house was too small for the six of them, but Baylee's father had been unwilling to move since the death of her mother, an all too common risk of childbirth in the region. The youngest of her family had survived despite the odds, and his eldest sister had gladly taken on the role of surrogate mother. Her father took the death with great difficulty; and as a result, had nearly let the dairy farm fall into ruin. If not for the encouragement of his spirited daughter, it very well may have, but Baylee was as naturally stubborn as her departed mother and had no intention of allowing anything to happen to her family. Her father had been amazed to discover the house in order when he emerged from his grief stricken state several weeks after burying his beloved on the hill. He cherished and loved the fine children she had given him.

Eelia was over two winters now, and so was given his name, especially since it appeared that he would be following in his brother's footsteps in size and stature. He had the fortunate, and sometimes unfortunate, pleasure of being ever closely watched by his older sister, Clara, who on more than one occasion had him adorned in her own outgrown dresses. Baylee was always quick to rectify these unfortunate predicaments, but not without first taking the time for a much needed giggle. The older twin brothers, Jacin and Jacob, were the muscle of the family. At fourteen winters, they would soon be ready for service and would leave the farm for ten years in the military. Baylee would take the head of the farm, as was customary, and find herself a husband in good standing with the Capitol. She imagined her father could not await that day, where he could return to a much more simple life of hard work and good supper, without the painful negotiations of business best suited for a woman.

Icomus always made sure his family was provided for, but it required long hours of travel back and forth from Balanced Rock. Milk had to be delivered every other day, and cheese and butter as often as it was ready. Icomus' grandfather had established the farm decades ago, a move that had been a sound one since dredge-goats were scarce in the region. The lumbering beasts produced ten times more milk than a common goat could, but also required ten times the upkeep to properly maintain. Their shaggy coats even had the basic properties needed to make clothing, and blankets, and the like, though the refining process was slightly more difficult than common wool. Icomus' children hated having to wear the rough clothing made from the giant goat, but he had always taught them to live humbly and with honor. The fact of the matter was, the name was nearly the only thing that the dredge-goat had in common with its much, much smaller cousin. The dredge, actually derived from the aggressive Torian Dwarven Ram, was a beast ridden mercilessly in fearless charge against the enemies of the Grandfather. The Dwarves merely slaughtered the less aggressive beasts for feast and festival or, sometimes, offered them in trade to what the dwarves viewed as soft, weak, dung-headed merchants. Icomus' grandfather had been one such merchant who, for a few gold coins, a Man'Antian slave girl, and the relentless mockery of the "much wiser" dwarven tradesmen, set off to make his fortune in his homeland.

Baylee plopped the buckets of milk on the dinner table, as she unconsciously wrested Eelia up into his high chair. "Clara," she ordered, "Take the bread out of the fire. Mind your hands, girl!"

"I know, I know," mocked the little girl, as she tromped over to the iron tongs next to the fireplace.

"Put them here." The older sister deftly spun around Clara, a master in her own kitchen, all the while cleverly placing a burn matt under her sister's targeted drop off point, and setting a cup of milk in front of the gleeful child in the high chair.

The iron pan smoked with the heat of the fire. Baylee spun like a ballerina around her sister once again, using another burn matt to pop the top off the rolls' heated tomb. The wonderful smell of the pancake filled the room, seeping outside like a creeping fog. She knew as soon as it hit the barn, her brothers and father would come running. Lid in hand she casually dropped it by the fireplace. With the same expert motion, she used another matt to wrap the handle of the serving ladle that had been warming in the large pot of stew cooking over the fire. She stirred the stew carefully, smelling the aroma with, unbeknownst to her, the exact likeness of her mother.

"No, Eelia. Hot!" Clara over-articulated the words to her little brother as she slapped his hands.

Eelia frowned in fearless defiance and tried to slap his sister back. The constraints of the highchair were too much for the little farmer, and he set about grunting and whining while trying to reach the monstrous scorner. When this failed, he reached again for the iron pot.

"I said no, Eelia, that's…"

"Let him touch it," Baylee interrupted Clara calmly, as she added a pinch of salt to the stew. "It will only happen once." She closed her eyes, taking in the wonderful aroma of her creation. "Set the table and bring me the bowls, the boys will be coming in soon."

Clara was obedient to her older sister. To her, Baylee could do no wrong, and so she left her careful watch on the younger brother. In just the instant it took her to cross the small kitchen, grabbing a bowl from the pile, Eelia screamed like a cave cat stuck in a barn full of hellhounds. He had reached far enough to grab the heated iron pot.

"I told you!" Clara reminded him. "Hot." She approached her older sister with one of the bowls and Baylee filled it. The two repeated the process until all the place settings had filled stew bowls and then again with cups of milk.

Eelia, not much for crying, was nearly recuperated when Baylee set his bowl in front of him. Steam poured from it.

"Careful now, Eelia, this soup is hot…" Baylee's voice was soothing and yet full of warning at the same time.

Eelia pointed his injured finger at his sister.

She smiled. "Burn." She spoke the word. "Hot things can burn you." She looked at the wound, it was not severe. "Here, let me kiss it better." And so she did, making the pain go away.

The two boys slammed into the doorway at about the same time, their square shoulders nearly lodging them into the wooden frame. They struggled to get ahead of one another before their father, bigger than the two boys combined, came bashing through the door behind them. With a booming laugh, he knocked the twins asunder, sprawling them across the floor with a playful roar. Jacin would not be so easily dissuaded, though, and pounced on his father from behind. Jacob, seeing the opening in the front, charged the big man's midsection. The three, laughing all the while, tumbled into the wall, bouncing back and forth until crashing into the small table by the doorway. Out of breath and laughing, the three looked up to see the woman of the house standing over them, fists on hips.

"This," she gestured to the fragments of the broken end table, "is why we cannot have nice things."

"This is why we cannot have nice things!" Jacin made a silly voice that was supposed to mimic his sister's.

Baylee did not think it was very accurate.

"Stew again, sis?" Jacob teased as he got up and moved past his sister towards the kitchen.

"You two will wash first before you touch that pan!" Baylee shook her fingers at her brothers, but she was too late.

"Ouch!" the two ogres snapped in unison. The burning pan only partially prevented the invasion as they stuffed their mouths with the pan fried bread.

"Hot!" Eelia shouted, pointing at the pan.

Everyone began laughing, even Baylee, who was trying to be stern.

Baylee's father lay on the floor, propped up on his elbows, admiring his family. Here was his daughter, apple of his eye, standing there as her mother had done so many times, trying to keep the family in order. How proud would she be to see this. The thought split the man's face in two with a smile the sun shows a summer field. On his knees, he engulfed his daughter in a hug, joining in with his family in the laughter.

"Boys, wash up." Icomus' order was a statement of fact, and not to be questioned.

Jacin smacked Jacob hard in the back of the head and raced for the door. Jacob nearly plowed Clara over trying to reach his brother, revenge spurring him on.

"Is the wagon loaded?" Baylee asked her father, who was making himself comfortable at the head of the table.

He broke a piece of his bread and dipped it into the stew.

"Not until we say grace, father!"

"You're right, of course, daughter." Icomus smiled as he plunked the moistened bread into his mouth. Either he was terribly hungry or his daughter was becoming a marvelous chef. The boys returned from their hand washing all too soon and Clara plopped up next to Eelia. "Who will say our blessings?"

Most of the children were quiet, that was except for Clara, whose fanciful notions often had her playing Valley Priestess and the like.

"I will say grace. Please join hands." The little girl was now decades beyond her age and calmly sat in reverence, hands open, awaiting compliance.

The others stared at one another, smiled, and then complied with Clara's request.

"Dear Motherly Priestess, we thank you for our meal and how my big sister made it; also how my daddy and my big brothers helped. We thank you for teaching Eelia what 'hot' means. Please make sure daddy has a safe trip tomorrow, and that he gets good deals at the market. And, please, tell my brothers to take a bath, they smell terrible! Oh, yes, please, tell mommy I said hi. We all miss her. Peace and good will to your children. No mercy to our enemies. Amen."

"Amen." The family echoed the last word together. It was a word Eelia was proud of.

The meal began as usual, the twins shoving the whole bowl into their stomachs without seemingly needing to utilize the actions of breathing or chewing. Icomus was no better, a hard day's work spurring his appetite on.

"First thing in the morning, I want you boys to hook up the two males to the wagon. They have a hell of a bad temper so make sure you have an apple in one hand and a club in the other. Each one will take both of you to manage. Do this and you can come into town with me next trip. Baylee, you are going to come with me tomorrow. I need you to trade for whatever we need around the house. I don't know if Filius has done his trading yet, but he'll need to know what to get if we are low on anything."

Baylee nodded in acceptance, trying to be reserved about her excitement of going into town with her father.

"Can I come too, daddy?" Clara's voice was full of hope.

"No, Beebottom. You need to help out here. With Baylee gone, who will watch out for Jacin and Jacob? Eelia is far too young!"

"I'll do it!" Clara's voice was full of pride for her new responsibility. Jacin and Jacob smiled at their dad and Clara.

"Clara has to watch you, 'cause you might get a boo-boo!" Jacob teased his twin.

"Clara may have to clean snot from your nose!" Jacin returned.

Jacob retaliated with a fist to the shoulder.

"Ouch!" Jacin's fist went to a thigh.

"Ouch!" Jacob barked.

"Enough." Icomus finalized the scuffle. "Do you boys understand? And you'll be in charge of the place for a night. This is serious. Do you hear me?"

"Yes, father." The simultaneous response caused two more fists to be thrown, this time with the added attempt of stealth.

Icomus merely raised an eyebrow.

The family went about the rest of the evening. They sat by the fire and sang songs while Jacin played his lute, and Jacob his flute. Icomus bounced Eelia on a knee as he kept rhythm with his sons. Clara and Baylee sang and laughed. Today was a good day, and one by one the children of a simple man fell asleep by the fire. One by one he carried them to their beds.

Icomus threw another big log in the fireplace and stepped quietly outside. He slipped on his boots and walked around the house. Ranger, their faithful hound was waiting for him. Their nightly ritual had formed a bond between the man and dog, and both knew it. Icomus grabbed his bow and quiver, and the two walked out into the still of the evening. The sounds of the night were clear, as insects and the like began their nightly search for food. Ranger sniffed the air. The nightly walk was more than just to check on livestock and watch for signs of predators. Icomus and Ranger always ended up on a small hill behind the house. It was on this hill where Icomus had buried his grandparents, his parents, and his loving wife. It was here, where every night Icomus secretly longed to join them.

* * *

Baylee woke up to the tugging of her curly brown hair, something Eelia had done since he could walk. In a half asleep state, Baylee rolled out of bed and walked her little brother towards the kitchen. Baylee was amazed that her brothers had already risen and were, no doubt, in the process of wrangling the two male dredge goats into position on the yoke of the wagon.

The difficulty of the task could not be understated. Icomus' wagon was scaled to the gigantic man. Even so, each of the four wheels came to his shoulder. The weight was such that the wheels were of solid wood, a necessity to bear it, and had been cut from the trunk of an Eastern Greatwood. The build was solid and had had no need for mending since its construction; a nice oiling and a little pride in ownership maintained the massive wagon that his father had built decades before. None the less, when the wagon was empty, it was twice again as heavy as the largest covered wagon. Today, full as it was with the delivery, Baylee struggled to imagine its weight.

Dredge-goats were suited animals for the job; the brutish beasts shined under burden, if a skilled handler could overcome their stubborn nature. Though there was always the possibility of hitching a team of horses, Icomus' thought about the beasts were that they were just too fragile. The farm with its tall barricade-like fencing, the enormous barn, and the sturdy wagon all reflected this.

Icomus just simply refused to own a horse. He often joked with his children when they saw one swiftly running down the road: 'Aye, they are fast,' he'd say, 'but how are we going to make you a winter coat out of that little tuff of hair on its neck? We'd have to use the tail, too, and you know what comes out from under that.' Icomus always took reliability and size over speed.

Eelia climbed precariously onto his chair as his older sister threw a log on the fire, poking the still hot coals into flame. Yawning, she moved towards the water bucket, filled a pot, and hung it over the hissing wood.

"Clara!" called Baylee. "Clara! Wake up! I need you to run out to the barn and get some milk for breakfast!"

"No! I'm sleeping!"

"You couldn't have answered me if you were sleeping. Now be swift!"

She could hear Clara's feet land on the floor in the loft above her. Then the stomps as she moved towards the ladder and, finally, the creaks of the rungs as she moved down into the kitchen.

"Well, I would be sleeping steal if you would have just let me!" Clara's tone amounted to the imaginary load of bricks she carried on her shoulder.

"Still," Baylee corrected. "You would *still* be asleep, not *steal*. To steal is to take from another, and it is not honorable. Now, kiss your brother, it is a new day."

Clara complied and then moved over to her boots. As the little girl was about to exit the house, she heard her big sister clear her throat.

"Did you forget something?" Baylee asked.

Clara rushed over to hug and kiss her big sister, who was measuring cups of oats to put into the rapidly heating water pot. Baylee hugged Clara, and thus set the little girl's day in motion. Baylee had no idea that these small acts of affection were the staples that held the family together. She only knew that everyone always seemed to have a bit of a brighter day if it started out with a hug and a kiss. It was wisdom that her mother had taught her, and such a gift should not be squandered by any one person.

Oatmeal wasn't the most grandiose of meals, but nonetheless, it provided what energy was needed throughout the day. A little added butter, cinnamon, and sugar, topped with some fresh milk, and one had the staple of any day full of hard work or, in Baylee's case, long travel. It would take her and her father most of the morning to travel into town, and they would not be returning until well past sundown. Baylee would need to pack some vegetables and cheese and fill some water skins with milk, so they could have something to snack on for their journey.

Clara returned with Icomus, Jacin, and Jacob in tow. The two boys each carried a bucket of milk and set them on the preparation counter. When the table was set, the family sat down for breakfast.

"Smells good, daughter!" Icomus boomed.

He plopped down in his chair and took in a hearty breath of the sweetened meal. The twins did the same and, not wanting to be left out, Baylee's youngest sibling joined in. Baylee filled the milk jug from a bucket, and Clara took it to the table. The three men emptied it in moments, pouring it in their cups and on their meal. Clara, defeated, returned to her sister for a refill. Obliging the request, Baylee followed her sibling to the table.

"You boys make sure you boil the rest of that milk, use the vinegar from the strawberry wine we traded for last season. Make sure you separate everything completely; we don't want the whey making the cheese too soft. Dump it into the soggy grain for feed. Damn goats love that." Icomus had given the speech before, almost every other day. Each time the boys exchanged glances but, wisely, never reminded their father of the fact.

With breakfast over, the family went outside where the twins had the loaded wagon waiting. The two dredge-goats pawed at the ground. Huge blinders caused them to swing their heads towards the sound of the approaching family. The rams' horns were large round stumps, characteristic of their breeding; these beasts lacked the curving hooks of their slightly smaller more aggressive cousins. Baylee carried Eelia in one arm on her hip, her food pack slung over the other. She took a wide breadth around the goats as to not startle her little brother, or rather, to not startle the Dredge Goats. Eelia feared nothing. She propped the boy up on the steps to the wooden bench, and tossed her pack of food up between the footrest and the uncomfortable driver's seat. Remembering this, Baylee hurriedly ran towards the barn to retrieve some old blankets to pad her bony bottom.

"Clara, watch Eelia," she hollered over her shoulder to the distracted child.

Clara was mindlessly staring at the Dredge Goats wondering why her father never called them by any name, well, at least not any names she was allowed to repeat.

Icomus had Jacin and Jacob following him around the cart, as he did every day before departure. Check all wheels, make sure there are no cracks or weak points, check the ties straps, and test the security of the tail gate.

As the three approached the tail gate, the sound of a ratchet mechanism released. Right away, Icomus recognized it as the wagon's powerful brake calling out retirement of its duty. Icomus moved to look and see why Baylee had released the brake so early, his mind forgetting her running to the barn moments before. He was moving to tell her to be careful, because that brake release has a nasty habit of pinching ones hand if it isn't released just…

Eelia screeched like a stuck pig as the brake release lever snapped onto his hand.

His cry was so startling to everyone around him that Jacin and Jacob nearly jumped out of their skin. Icomus moved forward instinctively as a father protecting his young, and the Dredge Goats, who now had no heavy break holding them back, jerked their heads into the air at attention. Mistaking the boy's cry out for an order of haste, the two goats jerked the wagon into action, rearing on hind legs for added thrust. The well-oiled wheels responded in kind, and Icomus had to leap sideways to catch the step. The wagon had only moved forward the distance of a single man, perhaps two lying down when Icomus hopped onto the bench area and pulled the brake tight. He swept his scared and wounded child into his arms and began checking for missing fingers.

Sure enough, the boy's little finger on his right hand was nowhere to be found. The pinch had nearly closed the wound but the blood was beginning to flow.

"Damn it, boy." The father muttered with teeth closed.

The wound was not fatal, and age would turn it to jested tale but, none the less, the boy would be shy of that wagon for the rest of his days.

"FATHER!" Jacob and Jacin screamed in unison, coming around from the opposite side of the wagon.

Icomus jumped down from the wagon, holding Eelia's hand so tight he knew it hurt the boy. His eyes were locked onto his cradled child, and he started toward the farm house.

"FATHER! FATHER! FATHER!" the two twins called out in terror, their voices quivering like the child in his arms. Urgency of voice caused him to look up at his boys, and to the worst sight the master of the house had ever seen.

Clara was on the ground behind the first wagon wheel. Jacin, on his knees behind her, covered his mouth with both hands. Jacob stared at his father, trying to mouth his sister's name. Both were quivering, tears welling in their eyes. Icomus sat Eelia down, who still screamed of the end of all days. Icomus rushed to Clara, whose plain woolen dress had a growing darkness in the midsection that forced sand in throat and stone in stomach. His world spun around him as he fell towards his daughter, hoping somehow his feet would carry him the rest of the way. Stumbling he landed on his knees in between the two boys as his shaking legs gave way beneath the weight of shock. He cradled his youngest daughter in his arms and went to pull her close. Her body moved towards him, her legs did not.

Clara groaned; choking blood spilled from her mouth.

"Oh! Great Mother! Clara!" There was so much blood! Icomus meant to roar, but it came out a whisper.

Rounding the oddly moved wagon, Baylee zoned in on the screams of her younger brother. She was the mother now, and the chills of what made the fearless lad sound such an alarm sent shivers down her spine. She saw him there, and Eelia saw her. He held out his bloody four-fingered hand for his sister to make the pain go away. She picked up her brother and examined the wound. It was a bad one for certain.

"Father, Boys, what happened to Eelia…" before she finished her sentence, she turned to see the three men huddled on their knees. Was that Clara between them? She rushed over to them carrying Eelia on her hip.

"Clara? Oh, Great Mother….CLARA!" Baylee's shout snapped Icomus out of his trance.

"Baylee, take the boy away!" Icomus tried to say; again a whisper.

More blood spurted from Clara's mouth. Baylee was frozen.

"Baylee," Icomus stuttered, "take Eelia away." His words were measured, and they caused Baylee to take a step back from the gruesome scene.

"Baylee, he shouldn't see this!" Icomus turned back to Clara, who was beginning to shake unnaturally. She stared blankly at her father.

"It's okay. Clara. You're fine." Icomus pulled the words from his heart with the ease of pulling the darkness from night. "Just don't try to talk. Just close your eyes, Beebottom." The last sound of Clara's pet name kept Icomus' bottom lip curled over the top quivering with despair in a vain attempt to show his little girl strength.

"Baylee," Jacin turned to his sister, "take Eelia away. Listen to father. He shouldn't see this." Jacin had tears rolling down his face. None of them should see this!

Baylee did not move. Her hand moved to turn Eelia's head into her shoulder, which the boy did gladly, burying his pain into his big sister. 'None of them should see this,' she thought. 'None of them!' She was scared for her sister, scared for her family. The fear caused a flame to ignite somewhere deep inside her. Still she did not move, the warmth of the flame filled her.

Jacob took a turn to order Baylee, but he was in a rage.

"Baylee! Damn you! Take our brother…" He stopped in mid-sentence, the anger on his face transforming into awe as he stared at his sister. "What in Mother's name?"

37

Baylee stared at Clara. She could not watch her sister die like this! No! She would not allow this! She thought for a moment that Clara's body began to glow. She began to wonder if this is what happens when the Valkyr come to take away the dead. No! She would not die!

Baylee did not notice her brothers and father shielding their eyes from her. Baylee did not notice that Eelia had stopped crying. There was just a fear, a rage, combined with a love within her that kept growing.

She felt weightless. She felt warmth from the center of her forehead.

She felt weightless. Then Baylee collapsed to the ground.

One Chance

Kurg used his mighty arm strength to slowly pull his body forward, carefully using a leg to push himself forward, belly to dirt. The tall grass in the plains may hide him from view, but his movements had to be slow and methodic, else he could put the herd into a panic. Twice, maybe three times of the sun's travel, he was able to move in such a manner, as did the other members of the chief's tribe, each in unison, each closing the trap bit by bit.

The hunters had scouted the herd two days before, and knew quite well they would graze without bias in the area. The Toenuk were full with calf and on high alert, and the gigantic animals could stomp the entire body of a Plainsman into the very ground with but a single hoof, not to mention the constant threat of swinging tusks from the young males who were readying for challenge to mate. Kurg had chosen for his son, Teegan, to bring down the oldest bull of the heard: Halftooth.

Halftooth was a huge male, big even for a Toenuk. His size over the years had granted him victory over many challengers despite his one tusk, broken by his predecessor a decade before. Kurg had chosen Halftooth for his only son for two reasons: the first being that a Plainsman Chief had to be strong and demand more of his children than he did of others; secondly, he knew the boy would become a legend if he struck the beast down. Teegan would only have one chance to do so, just one chance to bring the big bull down and honor to his family.

The hunting party formed a horse shoe around the gigantic animals and had done so slowly over the last two days, sleeping in the very field with the grazing beasts the night before. They were lucky this day, for the various predators of the plains were nowhere to be seen; more specifically, the main flock of Cocktchya had downed a calf three days before and was still full from the kill. This fortune meant that none of the flightless birds, big enough that some tribes use them as mounts, would be there to scout out the crawling warriors with keen eye and razor sharp beak. Not much was more troubling to find a young brave torn apart in silence to avoid ruining a hunt, but such is the way of the Plainsmen. Mightiest of the races, death is a part of life, but a coward's burden is bore by his brothers, an unimaginable fate worse than being eaten alive.

Everything in the great plains of Sabrina was grandiose. Even the Plainsmen stood half again as tall as the sickly humans that lived in the cities to the east. Kurg could not believe the shaman's tales of how the Plainsmen spawned from the puny beings in the times before the Cocktchya and Toenuk, but he did have respect for their ruthlessness. Humans sometimes came down to the plains to take Toenuk calves for their war machines and Plainsmen children for their fighting pits. The thought reminded Kurg of the dangers Teegan must face if ever he met up with the tusk-less, mane-less human folk. His son must be wary of any creature that must smile to bear its teeth, for those types of creatures were deceptive to the core. A Plainsman's pride was in his tusks, and like the Toenuk they hunted, symbolized status. But unique to the Plainsmen, the tusks are the place where a warrior displayed his magick. They etched spells in them, hung a shaman's trinkets, and soaked them in the blood of the fallen. Some tribes used herbal mixtures and fruit dyes to uniquely color them for battle, hunts, and raids.

The sun's travel demanded another movement from the hunters, and this time Kurg risked a dangerous motion. He slowly pulled his body upward, careful to sway with the blowing grass. He inched upward towards the air above the grass. He had to take a look at the positioning of the herd. That was certain. The risky maneuver had nothing to do with concern over his only son. He told himself he had no fear that the boy was out of position or that a sow had misplaced a step and broken the youth's back. No, his son was fine and in no way lying in agony in the field, biting down on a stick to avoid crying out. No. His son was fine.

Fear is always the worst enemy during a Toenuk hunt. One wrong move, or merely bad luck, could mean instant death. Not only are Toenuk as large as a small farmhouse, they have a temper passed down from their aggressive ancestry. Any Toenuk perceiving a threat could swath clean an area with its massive tusks. A stampeding herd, the size of the area Kurg's warriors crawled, could easily level a forest, shaking the very ground like an earthquake. Their ferocity makes young Toenuk a valuable resource for the humans of any land, who used them to pull wagons or charge the lines of their enemies. They were so valuable that some tribes had even turned to capturing and trading calves for human profit. These Plainsmen had taken to human ideals like slavery and property, and to Kurg, had become as rotten as a termite-infested fallen Great tree. Kurg despised the humans' lack of respect for the freedom of all things; for the gifts the Great Spirits have given. The ways of their war lead to an amount of death that made Kurg shiver, and his tribe sang the Long Song for the stolen children dying in human fighting pits; for the tribes long lost to human blades, tribes that would never go on a first hunt again.

Rising to full height, he stretched his neck upward to observe the herd. Six sows in all, four young males, probably two or three winters at most, another half dozen calves from last year, and Halftooth, the bull. Herds in Kurg's youth had numbered nearly twice this, but nowadays, this was one of the largest remaining. Kurg made a practiced chirp, so practiced that it was not unlikely to get a response from actual Burrow Dogs that shared the plain's bounty with the Toenuk. The chirp snipped through the tall grass, across the herd, and into the keen ears of the hunters.

***

Teegan's arms trembled with each pull as he moved into position. He had practiced his movements for years with the other boys, but had not factored in the effect the rumbling footsteps of the Toenuk would have on his mind and body. His heart hadn't stopped pounding for what seemed like hours. Waking with the herd and the dawn had taken a toll on the young hunter's endurance; he was simply exhausted. Unfortunately, he also had not factored in the long last pull he'd taken from his water skin. His groin ached with each passing moment with a natural call he simply could not ignore. He tried to fight it off by clenching the spear to his side.

The spear was passed down from chief to warrior during the time of the first hunt. Blessed by only the greatest of shaman, all tribes that hunt the great beasts of the plains had one for just this purpose. The spearhead, carved from the tusk of the very prey it is used for, was etched with such precision that the sharpened tip had to be covered with a cone-shaped wooden sheath. The spear tip's length was easily that of a Plainsman's forearm, and it was sharp enough to pierce the thick hide of any beast, Toenuk or no. And still, its extreme length, and a point likened to a Quill-Rat's favored defense,

41

did not serve to correctly articulate its craftsmanship. The spear head was hollow and chambered. Inside, the vicious tool held enough poison to kill an entire tribe or, after a few days, one mighty Toenuk Bull.

The valuable toxin came from the Jungle Tribes to the south east, yet trading with the clan of Plainsmen that lived there had not happened in many snows. Teegan was too young to remember the last time a Bloodthorn had ventured down there, regardless of the lack of sources to resupply the deadly substance.

Fighting his bodies need for release was a battle of will Teegan was rapidly losing, and defeat in such a battle could very well cost him his life. Teegan knew that Toenuk had a keen sense of smell, and any odor other than their own could send the herd into alert. And though he was prepared to lose his own life in his first hunt, he had no intention of endangering his brothers or uncles. He gritted his teeth, his small tusks barely protruding from his lips. Anger swelled within him, but the call of his bladder would not abide. Teegan was forced to let it go, and warmth spilled about his thighs and stomach, and cool wetness down his cheeks signaled his surrender.

A distinctive chirp came across the field of grass, one that required the hunters to respond with deceptive mimicry of their own. Teegan froze. A response from his position may cause a shift in the herd. If just one of the mighty beasts detected his newfound shame, it would certainly cause a thunderous panic. He prayed to the Sky Father. He begged to the Earth Mother. He cursed the Spirit of the Hunt. If his father had heard him, his last worry would be the swinging tusks of a Toenuk. He simply could not announce his position right now, he was desperate and in a near panic. His lack of response could also mean the end of the hunt; after all, it was *his* first hunt. If his brothers or uncles feared the worst, another type of chirp would sound, and the hunters would retreat from position. His dilemma was great indeed.

Problems will always be. Solutions come where least expected. Remember always your place in the world around you, and any problem will find itself undone. His father's words were always a riddle and always ended up ringing true.

Teegan wondered what his father would say about this particular problem. His son, soaked in his own piss and stench, nearly in striking distance of the most dangerous beasts in the Great Plains. Teegan was so close he could smell his prey.

He could smell his prey.

Teegan took a moment to think. He had but a moment. What he smelled could very well be his saving grace, a large pile of Toenuk dung. There was no other thought in his head, no warning from his brain to his body. He began to crawl towards his ironic savior.

As he moved, Halftooth popped his wide head upward toward the sound of the original chirp. His small cupped ears perked towards Kurg's position, twitching wildly as if to refocus their direction. The huge bull snorted a warning at the camouflaged Plainsman and popped his head upwards tossing his one good tusk in the air, as if to display the wielded instrument of doom to whatever dare challenge him. He stomped a massive front hoof into the ground, sending a vibration felt in all directions. The rest of the herd responded in kind, causing the ground around Teegan to rumble. Halftooth was nervous, and this meant the other members of the herd were nervous as well. He stomped again, another tremor that Teegan felt rattle his insides.

Halftooth's ears shot backwards opening to the sound of the crawling boy behind him. His massive head half-turned to enable a beady eye to catch a form wriggling towards him. With a guttural grunt, the beast spun round on his hind legs, opening nostrils to take in the scent of the interloper. His front legs pounded into the ground with a resounding boom.

Teegan was out of time. In a last move of desperation, he coiled his hind legs beneath himself and sprang through the air, landing square into the side of the freshly dropped remains of the bull's day of grazing. He drove forward, pushing himself into the damp warmth until his entire body was covered, sheltered spear still in hand. If the ruse did not work, Teegan's young life would quickly come to an end.

The troubled Toenuk moved towards the dung pile taking in deep breaths through boulder-sized nostrils. The rumble of the Toenuk's hooves made the dung settle around Teegan as the boy dared wipe his eyes free of the burden so he could see his fate approach.

Teegan's blood was ice. The warmth of the dung pile covering him was aided by the equally warm snort of air coming out of a hair-filled hole larger than the boy's head. Halftooth was close enough for Teegan to touch. The Mighty Beast took in a deep breath before blowing out a recognizable scent along with juicy goop that only added to the sticky filth the young hunter already took refuge in. Halftooth took several smaller samples of the air before pausing and then stomping another hoof into the ground.

The restless herd, picking up the vibrations, knew the one-tusked bull meant to calm them. One by one, Toenuk heads went back towards the ground doing what they did best, filling the endless hunger of the giants' stomachs. Halftooth turned from the hidden boy and slowly began to move to rejoin the rest of the grunting, feeding behemoths.

***

Kurg's entire body went into a heighted sense of alert as soon as the big bull turned round to see what was in the grass behind him. He could see a swift sway of grass as what he assumed was a hunter moved rapidly towards the bull!

'What a damned fool.' Kurg thought to himself. Halftooth moved towards the shuffling grass and then stopped sniffing at what the chief determined was a large pile of Toenuk droppings.

Or maybe not so dumb. If the hunter had done what Kurg thought he had done, then the decision to drown himself in shit just put him in striking distance of the bull. That was if the hunter was his son.

Kurg was not one to take risks or make guesses, but if that hunter was his own son, and if he had just saved his own skin by covering himself in Toenuk crap, then he was probably frozen solid with fear. So Kurg made another chirp, this time it was the one that alerted the hunters to the imminent strike the boy would deliver to the bull.

For every bull the Plainsman brought down or had seen brought down, the strike had different effects. Sometimes, it was a mere shrug, a pesky bite from an insect leading to three or four days of tracking until the eventual fall of the beast. Sometimes it was much worse. Those hunters, still on bellies in the grass, had to prepare for a thunderous charge of the rampaging colossals and get out of the way if possible.

The chirp was answered across the herd by invisible stalking Plainsmen.

Now Kurg just had to hope his assumptions were right.

Dung dripped across his eyes as he blinked in dismay. Had he not already emptied his bladder, at this point he surely would have. The big bull, king of the plains, battle scarred from years of protecting his herd was there, just inches from where Teegan hid. The beast could have crushed the boy if he had chosen to root in the stench that protected the boy. Teegan gave thanks to the Sky Father that he hadn't. Instead, the Toenuk sniffed the pile of excrement and simply turned away, unworried.

The young hunter took a deep breath, his body trembling.

A second chirp came across the small valley, piercing Teegan's ear. It was followed, as before, by chirps around the herd. The young warrior swallowed hard. It was a chirp that meant he was about to strike, normally started by the hunter carrying the spear.

He closed his eyes, searching behind them somewhere for strength. His hand quivered, moving to remove the wooden sheath covering the deadly instrument. The action seemed to last forever, adrenaline coursing through his already stressed body. But to his dismay, when he opened his eyes, his shaking arm held a spear with head of ivory, carved with shaman magic, and filled with a poison deadly enough to give him his *one chance*.

He breathed in, this time holding the breath that filled his lungs.

Teegan stood, now just a few body lengths from his target. He knew he had just seconds to strike the vital area behind the Toenuk's massive front leg. This spot, the only one thin enough for the spear head to breach. This spot, where timing had to be just as precise to catch the beast in stride. This spot was his target for his first hunt.

There was nothing but his target as he raised up from the muck, yet Teegan could see everything. There was no sound in his ears, yet he could hear the flicker of grasshoppers as they scattered from Halftooth's hooves. His hand relaxed around the haft of the spear as he prepared for the throw. His legs pivoted into position to allow for his hips to add to the attack.

He exhaled, and in that moment his spear took flight.

The throw was perfect.

Halftooth roared when the spear struck home, a half squeal that deafened the ears of the young hunter. The bull spun round again, so close that a massive tusk swung menacingly towards Teegan, forcing the boy to dive sideways in order to avoid being crushed by the blow. The Toenuk was not finished with the boy and reared up on hind legs, meaning to smash the hunter beneath massive hooves.

Already prone, Teegan scrambled to avoid certain death. The hooves slammed into the ground just missing Teegan by less than the length of the young hunter's spear haft. The thunderous slam sent earth, grass, *and* hunter flying through the air, knocking the breath from the boy as he hit the ground. Halftooth zeroed in on the hunter, and lowered his head for a finishing blow. Lurching forward, the bull moved to end his assailant.

Breathless, the boy became the stone in his chest, his wide eyes staring down his maker.

Halftooth barreled forward swinging his head backward to take the hunter with his one good tusk, but before his blow could strike home, a flash of movement whisked his target out of range; another hunter had come to Teegan's rescue.

Older than Teegan, Morgal was one of the tribe's best runners. He was swift, and in this moment, no other hunter could have pulled off the maneuver. Teegan and Morgal tumbled to the ground away from the mighty swath of Halftooth's attack, the older hunter's momentum carrying them both past deadly hooves but far from danger.

The big bull spun again, staring now at two targets, and this time, with no unseen saviors coming to their rescue.

As the massive Halftooth reared up on hind legs, beady eyes targeted the two helpless Plainsmen with a sinister glare. As he descended, Morgal shielded his eyes with a single arm, a futile defense indeed. Teegan's eyes widened at the inevitable.

Whoops and shouts from other Plainsmen rose from the bull's left as a massive sow slammed into the stomping bull. The sow's momentum caught Halftooth under the front shoulder, the female's own tusks driving deep into her protector's side. The collision caused Halftooth's attack to miss his target, as well as release a pain-stricken squeal. A mist of blood hit the air as the sow's tusk dug deep. However, it was the weight of the falling bull that would prove fatal to the startled female. Stumbling, the mighty bull continued downward, twisting the massive neck of the sow in an unnatural manner; one that ended with the sound of lightning shattering a tree trunk.

Morgal unshielded his eyes, astonished, then leapt to his feet, grabbed a startled Teegan by the scruff of the neck, and jerked the younger boy to his feet.

The herd was in chaos. A horseshoe of hunters had sprung up around them, tossing spears and shouting battle cries. The confused Toenuk began to search for a way out of the trap, and one by one began to run towards the opening that was free of the annoying insects. Most of the herd began to rumble away, shaking the ground like a volcano about to erupt- all except for its enraged protector.

Halftooth was injured. Adrenaline pumped through the Toenuk's veins, a wiry mane stood on end as he shook his massive body free from the fallen corpse of the sow. With a powerful plume of dust and sprayed blood, the big bull spun to look in the direction of the fleeing pair of hunters that would not escape retribution.

Kurg began to shout to the other hunters, still whooping out directions for the trained ears of the hunters to pick up. The herd was in a stampede, running from the hunters' target and the fallen sow. The chief had to strain his commanding voice to be heard above the rumble of the rampaging herd. The wounded bull was still far from helpless, and the seasoned chief's words could spell the difference between life and death. So far, not a single hunter had perished, and Kurg expected to keep it that way.

"Focus," he ordered. "Close the gap! Hit the bull!"

The hunters moved in to create a full circle around the bull, all the while tossing javelins into the flanks of the moving mountain of rage. Each strike caused Halftooth's muscles to twitch, but little more. The gigantic Toenuk was focused on the still running forms of Teegan and Morgal.

"Stop running and face him!" Kurg's voice rang out clear, his orders were to be heard and obeyed.

Teegan and Morgal slowed in a turn and faced the recovering bull, gathering resolve all the way.

"Prepare for his charge!" yelled the chief. "His anger will take him past you. Time your movement and leap away together!"

Halftooth pawed the ground as Teegan and Morgal created distance between one another. If they spaced themselves correctly, the bull would commit to crushing them both, thus giving each a chance to make the dodge. But if the hunters moved too far apart, the bull would commit his charge to either one or the other, making the dodge impossible.

The rumble of the stampeding herd could be felt through Teegan's feet as he stared at the adversary in front of him. He used his arms for balance, carefully crossing one leg in front of the other as he stepped away from Morgal, who mirrored the boy's movements. His knees were bent, ready to spring into action after the bull reached full speed. He wasn't certain if it were the shaking ground or fear making his body quiver like a soaked child shivering from a cold river bath, but he remained focused. Timing was everything.

Halftooth lurched forward as his huge mass went into motion, even though his vast form required two hooves on the ground at any given point, the length of his stride allowed him to cover ground quickly. He lowered his head, and beady eyes on either side strained to focus on his intended targets. The world around them beginning to groan under the weight of the beast, the Titan of The Plains began to swing his head from side to side to keep track of the tiny assailants.

Luck favored the hunters yet again as the big beast chose to trample them both, timing their leaps perfectly, both Teegan and Morgal leapt to safety. As his father surmised, the momentum of the Toenuk Bull carried him well past the two hunters, and the bull took a long turn in order to make a second pass.

"Form a line!" The order was loud and clear, booming from the Chief Plainsman's chest.

As the big bull rounded for another pass, the hunters followed the instructions, spacing themselves out in order to repeat the acrobatics displayed by their kin. As they moved into position, Kurg began to whoop and holler whilst waving his mighty arms, the rest of the Plainsmen following suit.

Halftooth charged again, another failed attempt between two hunters, as he did, more javelins whipped into his flanks, inspiring another frustrated roar. Again the big bull rounded in a turn, and again the skilled hunters formed a line of war-calling annoyance. The process repeated a second time and a third. Each time, the tribesmen managed to stay out of harm's way.

On the fourth failed attempt, the big bull, whose wiry-haired flanks now carried with them a dozen or more javelins stuck in each side, continued to run past the line of hunters. A combination of blood loss from the sow's wound and exhaustion from the failed charges had taken their toll. Reaching a hill at some distance, the big bull stopped, turned towards the hunters and bellowed a curse. Even if mighty Halftooth survived the deep wound given to him by his own mate, the poison in his bloodstream would soon reach his brain; a result that would eventually cause confusion, disorientation and, ultimately, the cease of vital organ function. The King of The Plain's fate was now sealed, and the Plainsmen needed only to track the beast until the inevitable result occurred.

The group of hunters answered the Toenuk's curse with a cry of victory. That is all the Plainsmen but Teegan and Kurg. Teegan only stared at the insulted titan now disappearing over the hill. Kurg studied his son. Pride had swollen a lump in the leader's throat, and he did not dare allow emotion to surface. One by one the hunters gathered around Teegan, still gazing toward where Halftooth once stood. The boy could barely feel the pats of congratulations nor hear the shouts of admiration.

"Teegan." His father's voice snapped him out of his trance. "You smell like shit."

Laughter sprang up around the young hunter, who very quickly found himself taking suit. His knees were shaking, and it was hard to tell if the little Plainsman was laughing or crying. Excitement and adrenalin often had such effects, and there was no loss in pride for it. His father's hand on his shoulders sent a stabilizing jolt through his body, as if the chief's touch itself were strength.

"Morgal, Korent, run to the shaman. Tell him it will soon be time. The rest of you, harvest the sow. No reason to leave her to the vultures."

Kurg took his son, arm over shoulder, towards the sow as the two runners darted off towards the direction of the shaman. Teegan paused and turned to the swift moving hunters.

"Morgal! Thank You!" Teegan shouted.

The runner did not stop, merely raised an arm in recognition.

Father and son travelled towards the fallen sow with the rest of the hunters. Kurg paused at her corpse to recite the Long Song, and Teegan joined in with the other hunters in reverence of a fallen sister. After the song was completed, Kurg retrieved his spear, lodged to the shaft in the sow's right eye. The perfect shot that had no doubt sent the beast stumbling in pain and panic into the big bull.

Kurg stared down at his son. Teegan could see what no words could convey properly. The man was proud of his son. Though the large Plainsman did not smile, for that was not his way, he nodded several times in approval.

The boy would surely do many more great things in the many snows coming to pass.

The Chamber Maid

The full moon shone down upon the lake capitol of Anon. Patrols marched up and down streets lined with artificial crystalline lights powered by the city's central pyramid. Nestled not far from this was the mighty palace of the High Priestess, whose marble statues and columns reflected the majesty of Sabrinian philosophy. The beautifully crafted structure housed the country's leader herself, as well as her two daughters, twins, produced in accordance with Sabrinian law. The palace was actually a part of a larger building that housed many priestesses of varying class and nobility. This was the Temple of the Gospel, the heartbeat of the Holy Doctrine, and the lungs of Her Own Voice.

It was customary for all citizens capable to do so, to take a pilgrimage to the impenetrable fortress city in order to view the Temple of Wings in all its majesty. The enormous, statue-laden structure actually utilized the southernmost side of the great pyramid as its foundation, and the giant female figures of marble seemed to motion onlookers to behold the solid golden pinnacle of the Great Pyramid. The building was so vast that its lower levels housed the Learning Grounds, a clever name for the dormitories and libraries that served as living quarters for the Acolytes and Priests for as long as the city had been a city. It was a place of worship, servitude, learning, and enlightenment. It was in this grand structure that Sabrinians could seal themselves in marriage, bless their children in the light of the Goddess, and as many proclaim, hear the very sound of song coming from Her Own Voice.

It was also in this structure where the Keeper of Doctrine stored the knowledge of the world, cut off by the truth of the Scriptures. This knowledge often meant secrets, and keeping them close to all but a few select devotees. These were secrets that only the powerful and privileged dare whisper. Truths behind both legend and miracle. Truths that spoke of the flesh and of the hypocrisy of the very society the palace temple represented.

The High Priestess was, in fact, Her Own Voice. The only person in Sabrina in touch with the Goddess herself. The Goddess could speak through her to let her subjects be aware of her will, a holy gift reserved for very few. Second to the High Priestess was the Keeper of Doctrine, whose charge was to ensure the written will of the Goddess be observed at all times, even during times when pleasures of the flesh demanded interpretations of the Holy Scriptures for validation.

***

The guard thrust himself over and over into the young maid on her hands and knees in front of him. Her acolyte gown was pulled half way up her back, crumpled up, and used as a handle for the man behind her. She whimpered between closed lips as to not allow the onlookers the satisfaction of her discomfort. The guardsmen was not at ease in the situation either, despite the male's more physical road to ecstasy, it was well known that the daughters of the High Priestess had no problem in ordering a man flogged for not performing to their expectations. It was once said that the little daemons had sent a guard to the monastery to be removed of his manhood, a fate not deserving of anyone, anytime.

The twins, properly perched as ladies, lay on their klines, lounging chairs elongated for comfortable stretching of the legs, and symposium that had been placed in such a manner that they could watch these little 'demonstrations'. The spectacles had grown more and more frequent to attempt to cull the insatiable appetites of the heiresses. At thirteen snows, they would soon be choosing a *mangmu lieren* of their own. Tradition in Sabrinia defined it as a mandatory bonding for any priestess, including the daughters of the High Priestess herself. The bonding of hunter to priestess served two functions, the less important being the protection of the priestess. Though it is this façade that overshadows the union's true purpose, to breed more hunters into the Sabrinian ranks. Excitement for breeding and pleasure obtained during was a birthright for any Sabrinian woman, though very few had the means to explore it the way these two did.

Nonetheless, it was the twins' prestigious mother that had set up the special chambers, and it was her orders that demanded that whomever, or whatever, the girls wished to observe mating would do so without question. "Women must understand their lesser, both in class and sex", so say it in Aphosia chapter six, verse four. The majestic leader of her people would dare not leave loyal subjects to the mercy of offspring uneducated in the Scriptures.

"Sister, I do believe she is starting to enjoy this one."

"Yes, sister, I do believe you are right."

"Perhaps it is because he is smaller than that last one."

"Yes, perhaps. It appears that the larger it is, the less comfortable it is."

"True, but the red district woman seemed to enjoy the larger one."

"And yet, she was equally...oh, what is the proper word...equally conducive to this one here."

"The red district woman was quite proficient in her manner with the men."

"We should request her again. The things she did with her mouth!"

"Shocking to say the least!"

"Do you think that this girl here can do those same things with her mouth?"

"I don't see why not. Guard. Stop pumping her. Girl, turn 'round and use your mouth on him."

As the two began to change positions, the twins began watching the inexperienced chamber maid, not much older than the twins, trying to navigate such unfamiliar territory. The fumbling and confusion was noticed, as the guard began to grit his teeth with the sharp tinges of pain brought about by the Acolyte's lack of practice.

The twins began to laugh.

"How strange, sister, it doesn't look very complicated, does it..."

"Yet she cannot seem to move at all without hurting him."

"We should definitely request that red district woman again."

"Yes, most definitely."

The chamber maid had begun to cry, but the twins had not noticed. Instead, turning towards one another to begin a new conversation, bored with the performance of the makeshift actors. The guard tried to warn the girl with raised brow and widened eye. He shook his head quickly as to caution her that both can be punished for lack of performance. Despite his self-concern, he could tell his fellow actor would never be the same after this day.

"Sister, what do you think of mother's *mangmu lieren*?"

"What do you mean, what do I think?"

"If we are going to have to choose, shouldn't we choose one like him?"

"I suppose. Mother says his skills on the battlefield are very impressive."

"Which battlefield do you think she is referring?"

"I am almost certain she means both."

Again the twins laughed together. One began to remove the necklace off of her neck, brushing aside the wavy platinum locks, given to both girls by their mother. Holding it above her own head, she rolled upon her back on her daybed and held the pendant above her as to allow the reflection of the chandelier to bounce off the precious jewels and shiny metals. She held it there, staring at the griffon-head medallion, and let her vision become *open*. The other watched as her sister's iris and pupil swirled together and slid across the milky white surface towards her skull, as if the newly formed color was a sentient worm with a mind of its own and needed to hide from the light.

Her eyes, now sheets of glowing white remained fixed on the pendant, slowly she opened her hands, but when the pendant should have fallen to her blossoming bosom, it remained floating in the air. The other twin giggled as the first moved her hands around the floating pendant, making it spin round and round, causing small reflections of light to dance across the walls and intricate tapestries that decorated the room.

"I'm so jealous! I wish I could hold air like that!" Her twin laughed.

"Whatever, you can see fire! Who wouldn't like that?" Her tone was marked with concentration as she controlled the energies around her.

"I suppose you're right, as usual, sister..." Though some of the words of her last statement lingered with a sense of distain, she, too, rolled onto her back, allowing her eyes to shift as her sibling's had done just a few moments before. She pointed a finger towards the ceiling, and as if there were an invisible candle wick growing from the tip, a small flame appeared.

"Shall we try again?" Excitement trumped concentration as her hand snatched the eagle head medallion from the air.

54

"Yes, indeed!" the small flame jumped with the same inflections of her voice.

Facing her sister, she formed a ball of air around the flame, pushing it into the shape of an egg, fire swirling inside as if it was trying to escape. She moved her hands to begin to guide the glowing orb through the air, as if she were a seductress beckoning a lover. The orb moved in a circle above and between the two twins.

Again a flame appeared atop the finger of the first, and again the second formed a ball of air around it. With one hand beckoning and the other hand directing, the second glowing orb joined the first in a strange merry-go-round above the young priestesses. Soon came a third, and then a fourth.

"How many do you think we can do, sister?"

"Shall we try for six?"

Another flame appeared at her finger tip. "Nonsense. Let us try for eight."

She smiled in response, concentrating harder with each additional orb. "Always pushing the limits, sister. That is why I admire you so."

"Flattery will get you everywhere, my dear twin."

"Make them say the prayer of battle, sister."

"Yes. Say it!"

The floating flames jumped towards the two performers that had stopped after the first dancing egg appeared. They both had been staring at the floating lights in fear and awe. The guard could feel the chamber maid tremble, and she him, neither ever imagined such things possible, and neither knew that to witness such would ultimately mean their demise.

"Say the prayer!"

The flames caused the two to cower to the floor; trembling, they began: "There shall be no use of the daemon's power for any seeking the Light of The Goddess. There shall be no life for those spawned with it, or by it. Let it be known that the fires of Her Wrath will burn the world free of such heathens, and we shall carry the torch."

"I love that last part, sister."

"As do I, as do I."

***

55

Maesma sat up in the bed, staring at an angle down at the floor. The High Priestess sat up behind him and entwined her legs around him. Her hands danced over his shoulders, excited explorers of a bountiful land.

"What is it, my hunter?"

"Your daughters, my Priestess. They *weave* indoors again." He spoke through his teeth, a dog growling at an unwanted hand near precious bone.

"Relax, *shui nan'de*. Are they in their own chambers?" The woman did not have the gifts of a hunter, and so could not see through the floors of stone like panes of glass. Maesma, on the other hand, knew the position of every living being in the palace, from rat to servant, festering termite to sleeping guard; nothing escaped his vision.

"No, Priestess. They practice in the 'educational' chambers you set up for them." The hunter did not mask his disdain for the bedroom the twins had been spending more and more time in.

The high priestess let out a disappointed sigh.

"I know you do not approve, my love, but it is the way of things. They must learn all the trades of a woman that will lead armies to victory. You do trust that I will make the best decisions for *my* daughters, do you not?" There was a warning in her voice that seemed to transcend the concept that Maesma had been involved in the creation of the twins. Sabrinia was a woman's culture, and men had to be constantly reminded of their place.

"Of course, Priestess." He took one of the explorers and kissed it in reverence.

"I like the other one," she said with a sneer.

"Of course, Mother."

The sneer became a smile with his compliance.

"Still," she continued, "I must have a talk about their discretion. If they keep showing off in front of servants, then some of our most sacred Scriptures will come into question. The last thing we need is for rumors to poison the minds of our loyal citizens."

"Rumors?" The Hunter masked the daring inquiry with another taste of her hand.

"Yes, rumors. The Doctrine forbids the manipulation of *joa*. A priestess does no such thing. Her gifts are divine." The priestess' hands led to a southern bounty that made her snared prey straighten with the natural reactions of a man. She, too, could not help but release a small moan into his ear through the gated lips of a mischievous smile.

"Would you agree that my gifts are divine, *shui nan'de*?" Lips barely parted for the whisper.

"They are, indeed, High Priestess." With that he turned into her like a plains lion making a meal of helpless calf. He went for the throat, passion leading the way. He did not stop until he had consumed her.

Sometime later, they lay staring at the canopy of the bed.

"You'll leave with the obelisks tomorrow," the matriarch began. "We will need to place two on the southern front, then a third in the small town of Balanced Rock."

"Balanced Rock?"

"Yes, I have promised it to the Keeper Raen. She is..." there was a pause, searching for the proper continuation "...aging well beyond her usable years here in the capitol, and I owe much to her tutelage." The statement held many hidden meanings, as though the High Priestess had forgotten her company cared nothing for politics.

"That old goat will have the whole town groveling with every breath."

"My fondness for you would not save you if Raen ever heard you call her an 'old goat,' lover." The priestess propped her head on one hand and drew imaginary scenes on Maesma's chest with the other. "But you do speak truth, and that is why she will reside out there for the time being."

"You think there are 'riches' yet to be discovered in the south?" the hunter cared little of the answer, enjoying the bliss of recent exertion.

"Truthfully, I do not know. But it has been over a decade since we have performed a Cleansing of the area, and it is unknown what manner of our enemies may lie hidden in the shadows of the south. Raen will see to it that there is no stone left unturned and that our subjects there are well versed in The Doctrine. These delusional rumors of a "true messiah" returning have flowed into every border city and coastal port in my land. We cannot show weakness. Balanced Rock is an oddly strategic location for such a manner of...religious query."

"True messiah?"

"Yes. Some sort of apocalyptic second coming if you will. Nothing we have not felt or heard before."

"I understand. This young sergeant I will hunt for, what is his name again?"

"Cabot. His name is Marcus Cabot. He is quite the vicious dog. Reports of his ruthless devotion to The Doctrine have captured my attention. You are to assist him in any way he requires, and you are to observe him. If he deems a worthy role model, he will soon gain his own permanent command."

"I do as your politics deem I must, my priestess. No matter the depth of my lack of understanding."

"That is the beauty, *shui nan'de.* You don't have to. You are a man, and a man is a dog, and dogs must be trained and rewarded with treats. It keeps their little tails wagging and little teeth sharpened."

"Yes, Mother."

She pushed her lips forward in childish placation.

"Oh, but you are the finest of the breed, *mangmu lierne,* loyal guardian and my personal death dealer. My fondness for you could not be replaced by three lesser men. Believe me, I have tried."

Maesma took the compliment with a grain of salt. Being humble in the presence of any Sabrinian woman (regardless of the observable fact the High Priestess's curving hips and porcelain skin could create such a reaction) was a must for men of any class-let alone a slave like himself. Even in the high circles of Sabrinian nobility, men were trained with eloquence and humility; their status lower than all women save the nameless servants. Based on the laws written in the Scriptures, people like Maesma were often referred to as 'Untouchables', and interaction with them, aside from barking orders of servitude, was strictly forbidden. Even touching one was a great dishonor, and being caught in a romance with one could send a man to the priesthood for castration. Untouchables like Maesma were nothing more than property; fortunately for him, he was the property of the most powerful woman in all Sabrinia and, arguably, the world. This, of course, being likened to the shiniest toy admired by all the other spoiled children.

"So we will be taking a full squadron for the test of the young sergeant's leadership?"

"Yes. Cabot has been briefed on the particulars of the mission. You will obey him to the very word."

"Of course I will, my priestess.

"Once the southernmost obelisks are up, we can begin sending supplies to the fronts, while I send the rest of Raen's belongings to Balanced Rock. Her villa is nearly completed, so she will be relocating shortly."

"Her *mangmu lieren* will no doubt be arriving with her." Maesma did not guess at the assumption. He knew Bo'Ah well and quietly hoped for the chance of reunion- perhaps the years were making him soft.

"Yes, and you will give our young sergeant a message for him to open upon your arrival in Balanced Rock. It will be in your personal belongings tomorrow. Do not give it to him beforehand." A yawn slowed down the last of the woman's words. She shifted to her side, back facing the Hunter.

Maesma was somewhat relieved at the well-known foreshadowing of the woman's rapidly approaching rest. He knew better than to pull himself up close behind her, her back to him was no invitation this late in the evening. He crossed his arms behind his head. He was a dog to her, a well-trained one at that. Sleep began to take him.

"Oh, before I forget, my faithful beast, go downstairs and take care of the twins' little problem. I will address the situation with them tomorrow. Replacing these servants is getting expensive and taxing on my time, I shall have to take it out of their clothing allotment if they continue."

She smiled as Maesma got out of bed. His stature was a masterpiece of carved perfection, one of the many reasons he had remained at her side for many, many seasons.

"Shall I return after, priestess?" His head was half turned to her as he tied his loincloth around his waist.

"I don't see why," she answered. "Your duties here are complete as well."

***

The cold stone beneath Maesma's feet cooled the rage in his heart as he descended to the Dark Beneath; a name given to the living quarters and dungeons beneath the Temple of Wings. It was not the thrill of the hunt that got him to this point this time, it was the reason for his predation. The chambermaid had all but thanked him as his hands twisted the air from her neck. The guard had not even heard him approach. It was the reason behind his latest prey that fueled an anger inside him. It was the calling of his station. The laws of a nation that demanded he end the lives of two humans not unlike himself. They had not been born of privilege. They had not been privy to the knowledge that two spoiled girls' games would end their lives. He focused on the cool floor beneath his feet and the two mighty Sabrinian mastiffs tromping happily beside him, able to see what he could not. Soft panting and light padded footsteps told Maesma where his Hellhounds were, which was never far from his side. If he could see with normal vision, he would not need the panting to assure him of their presence. Hellhounds' eyes reflected light in the darkness with a near unnatural blood-red glow that gave them their name.

Normally, the seasoned hunter had no difficulty in killing. The nature of things had not taught him to be anything more than what he was, a predator. The hunt drove him to gain what little satisfaction he could find in this existence, but stalking a traumatized maiden in her youth, whose only crime was to see what should not be seen, gave the heavy load on his shoulders no remedy. As for the guard, the man had barely held a sword in combat, let alone be sent to this particular type of hangman's noose, because of the whims of children too young to grasp the situation.

He had killed them both with the same difficulty as one would step on unwanted spider, and no thrill had fueled him to view his actions as honorable. Still he continued downward, barefoot on cold stone, into the depths beneath the city where all hunters trained to become what he was, a murderer.

Maesma had no memory of life before the depths. For that matter, he had little memory before the bonding of himself to the high priestess. His memories fused into his body and mind in the scars of battle and death, like a mark a rancher places on valued livestock. He had long since lost count of the people he had slain, the lights his *joa* had taken from cooling corpse. He had trained here, like those before and after him, in the darkened depths beneath the palace where all secrets could remain buried with the dead.

He did have some luxury, however, a small dormitory, nearing some thirty snows or more, had been granted to him. In this place he

60

hung many trophies of those more worthy than the victims that had fallen to him this night. He was allowed this room without hellhound or bunkmate, a benefit unseen for someone of his stature, though his pair of vicious canines slept by his side by his choice. He did not need to see in the realm of normal vision to know his way to his chambers, he could walk there in his sleep. It was the one place where he felt solitude, the one place where his identity remained hidden in the trophies of his fallen foes.

It was here where Maesma would rest and regenerate for upcoming tasks.

It was here where the three well-trained dogs would sleep, for he gladly counted himself as one of them. He would wake tomorrow, purposely forgetting a defenseless chamber maid and the guard that watched her tremble.

An Adopted Cub

Shawna awoke to the sound of her son's raspy breath. One hand folded over his, she used the other to brush away the hair fallen over his face. The last two days were a struggle for the young boy, but he was doing better. Her heart had been so heavy until he managed to take his first drink of water, a turning point that allowed her to fall asleep. Warrior or not, the Asperii woman had no idea how she would continue on, had her son not made it.

She had made a call to her dearest friends, Solam and Sherium. The two lynxen were well-versed in medicines, and she hoped they could ease some of Ronin's pain. Using soul crystals was not Shawna's forte, but the necklace Sherium had given her was linked to those worn by both of the big cats, and she hoped that she had followed the instructions properly. If so, she would hear the jingling of jewelry outside the door any day now, a weakness the huge felines are known for. In some places, where the huge felines are worshiped as gods, they are often given treasure troves full of gold adornments and the like.

Shawna had met the mated pair several seasons before the birth of her son. The friendship with the horse-sized cats had continued through the many changes of both season and strangers, including the one that left Shawna alone with a newborn son.

It had been Solam's watchful eye and Sheriam's skillful use of *joa* that helped bring Ronin into the world safely, and now the boy had become accustomed to the visits of the mystical beasts as any other boy would a loving aunt and uncle. Solam and Sherium had named Ronin *Diyi You'Shou* or first cub in the old tongue. Sherium had never been able to conceive, a problem growing amongst the prides of Torian Lynxen where the pair were from, so her friend's child had filled much of that chasm of loss.

Times were changing for the big felines now. Once revered as sages sought world-wide for the generational knowledge passed down since the age of the Sea Serpent, they were now hunted for pelt and claw, not to mention the king's ransom of jewelry each adored. Shawna was not surprised that avoiding traps and the like would delay their arrival. Nonetheless, the dearest friends would come and know what to do for the little treasure, more precious than anything the cats could wear.

Shawna took a moment to pour more water on the boiled herbs near her son's bed. The steam from the mixture seemed to relax the boy's air flow and allow him some relief from the effects of the hundreds of insect stings he'd suffered.

"Mom." His voice was slow and labored, remnants of a body fighting unknown invaders to the point of exhaustion. "Mommy. I'm hungry."

"Oh, baby!" Tears rolled down Shawna's cheeks as if the statement were made from the glory of the Goddess herself.

She pulled her child close, mother's affection both comforting and healing.

"Let me get you some soup, baby." Her words were joy. She wiped her eyes and, reluctantly, let her hand smooth her gown as she stood to move into the living area where she would heat the boy's broth.

As she entered the living room, Celeste's ears twitched towards her, though the bitch's head did not move from paws. Shawna, whose vision was locked in a world of life force and energies, could not see the sad eyes of the hound looking up at her. Cretus, hero of the farm, had not survived the insects; his body had been lost in the swarm. Seeing the sad eyes or no, Shawna knew exactly how Celeste felt with the loss of will to carry on. Had Shawna not been with child years ago, she too might have given in to despair, though the loss of her mate was due to betrayal and not death. Ronin's mother knew the hound may very well never leave that corner of the living room, the corner that still held the smell of her beloved mate.

Shawna began to prepare her son's dinner, memories flooding into her mind of a time long past. Chicken, fresh herbs, and spices with bread to soak and swallow. She was sure the stings inside his throat would still be tender, and so she was careful not to make it too hot. Thank the Goddess he wanted to take in some nourishment.

The woman paused, a smile growing on her face. She could see the shapes of her friends loping from the hills above the house. The big cats moved with grace and awe, their own *joa* flowing with the landscape around them as if they coexisted in absolute harmony. Solam and Sherium had arrived. They rounded the barn, their presence making Browndog a bit uneasy as always; after all, Solam had made point to mention how fine a meal horse was.

Shawna hurried to fill a bowl, then paused in regards to the dispirited hound. Normally, Celeste and Cretus would be shouting their hellos to the Asperii guests as they approached, but the female again declined to so much as raise her head.

Shawna propped open the front door to the atrium, then spun round to take her boy the much needed nourishment. She knew the lynxen would feel comfortable entering the home and had no concern of the normal formalities of greeting, given the circumstances. She moved with grace and swiftness to her boy's room and sat on the edge of his bed, helping him prop himself upright with a strong arm forged by long days in the family's garden.

Once the boy was in position, his small arms shaking with both excitement and lack of sustenance, she took a mother's breath to cool the contents of the spoon held with calloused hand. Her hardy son opened his mouth to take in the warm offering, and he winced as he swallowed it down.

"Tastes good, mom." the compliment was labored, and poised in such a manner of kind sincerity that Shawna teared with pride.

"Such a good boy, you are. Here, let's try another." Again they repeated the process, and again Ronin did his best to take down the soup.

Jewelry jingling in the doorway announced the appearance of the mystic felines in the living room. Shawna looked over her shoulder then back at her son.

"There is someone here to see you, my brave little hunter." Her words held a sort of reverence, and it was if the entire tension of the room had lifted slightly.

If Shawna could see as the lynxen did, she would have seen the weakened boy light up as if it were a birthday morning. His large swirling blue orbs, unique even among *mangmu lieren*, enlarged with as much excitement as one pinned down by exhaustion could muster.

Solam stood in Ronin's doorway, his mass filling the entire space. He had large eyes and white muzzle, surrounded by silver fur with black stripes. Long ears were tufted with black hair, and he boasted a majestic mane gifted only to males. His mouth was framed with nothing less than what could be considered a long white goatee on a man, with whiskers that rested to form a comical looking mustache.

64

His headband was made as a gift from the Highbreeds of Tyria and held jewels worth more than any thief could imagine. Equally as valuable was the lynxen's necklace that housed the invaluable soul stone Shawna had reached out to him through. Earrings of pure platinum finished the big cat's adornments, crafting a strange mix between man and beast from a time long forgotten.

Sherium pushed her head into the doorway, her own massive head lacking the beard and mane of her mate; but where the female lacked in hair style and coloration, she made up with in decoration. Her headdress was a complicated web of delicate chains with precious stone at every intersection. She even bore a piercing in her nostril that connected to those in her left ear and bracelets on both paws.

"Out of the way, you big oaf." Sheriam's thoughts were made available to all in the room, a talent the lynxen often used in a manner of respect for those that could not communicate through the same means as they did. Speaking 'Without Words' was complicated at the least: a combination of a waking dream of images, smells, and sounds mixed with perceived descriptions. Something often quite difficult for first-timers to fathom. Neither Shawna nor Ronin were new to this; in fact, the young boy had grown up knowing the pair of surrogate relatives and was quite adept at understanding their thoughts, as well as interpreting their silly descriptions.

"Sherium! Solam!" The boy's voice was the croak of a sickly toad, excitement even causing audible croak.

"Do not speak with your voice, You'Shou, save your strength!" Sherium moved across the room, her body taking up the majority of free space aside the two humans and the meager furnishings.

"He appears to have beaten most of the poison on his own," Sherium exclaimed.

He is strong. I told you he would be fine. The second thought was easily decrypted as a reassurance for Solam himself, as well as the females in the room that the big male addressed. His entire body seemed to let go of tension, relieved by sight of his loving mate with their first cub.

"May I?" Sherium asked Shawna for unneeded permission to channel the flows of *joa* around the boy.

Sherium was a weaver, blessed to be able to see and alter the natural energies around her. When she did so, her eyes took on a

65

form similar to the hunters, opening themselves to the energies of the worlds around them.

For beings other than hunters the Vision is intoxicating, and pulling them through one's own *joa* released an unexplainable and invigorating excitement. Sherium, and others like her, see all the dazzling forms of energy, but, in most cases, can only manipulate certain types. In cases such as the queen lynxen's, manipulation of the very energies of fire and water can be used to help seal wounds, start seized hearts beating again, and even remove the remnants of poison brought about by thousands of ant stings. One's *joa* is the key to altering any type of energy, but when it comes to soul to soul contact, the life force energy must be intermingled from being to being, from weaver to recipient. This contact is invisible to anyone not able to see the flows of energy, making weavers very dangerous. After all, a weaver like Sherium could simply extend her *joa* into an unsuspecting target and stop their heart beating, causing death without mace or blade nor the bloody evidence to render guilty judgment.

Mangmu lierne, like the Asperiis whose vision is locked in the world of energy, can see this weaving of energy and avoid the whip-like tentacles that extend from *joa xin* or the heart of life force. Skilled hunters even learn how to attack these hearts, rendering a weaver harmless. This ability to see, but not manipulate energies, makes *mangmu lieren* wanted bounty hunters, guardians, and in some cases, assassins. Many nations employ the hunters, some even revere them. Other countries, like Sabrinia, enslave them.

Sheriam's *joa xin* was located in her forehead and was amplified by an attunement jewel housed in her ornate headdress. Jewels, crystals, and crafted totem were all common tools for weavers and can come in many different varieties, as unique as flakes of snow from the heavens. Some work like a magnifying glass, boosting the size of the *joa bian,* extending like a whip or tentacle from the heart of the energy. Some worked as a prism to fracture the tentacles into multiple targets and some, like Sheriam's, could be used to narrow and pinpoint *joa bian* to the precision of a fine thread sent through needle's eye. The big cat allowed her vision to become open, the iris sliding away into the back of her eye.

Ronin could see the energy rising in the gentle queen as her *joa* began to flow through the crystal. The narrow tentacle tickled the boy as it entered his chest and expanded into his veins. Sherium moved her energy through him, wrapping it around his own like a rapid growing vine. Within moments her own life force flowed through every inch of the young boy's body, causing the boy to squirm and giggle.

"Get ready, You'Shou. This will get a little warm, just close your eyes. Everything will be fine."

Sherium began to channel little flows of fire that emitted from the candle, and water from the bowl of soup. Weavers could pull energy from any source, but the ease of having the related element often made the task easier.

What would have been nothing more than a big cat staring at a resting boy to anyone else, was an orchestra of flowing light for Shawna. She quietly watched her friend channel reds and blues from flame and bowl into her own body. Sheriam's body was a magnet, pulling the other energies into it, using her will to add them to her own *joa*. The flows of fire and water wrapped around her own and danced down into Ronin's body; a process of little discomfort for the boy due to the healer's years of expertise. Poison removal was, fortunately, something Sherium was quite used to, due to the fact that her gluttonous husband had a fondness for the taste of both Fringed Serpent and Arrowfish.

Ronin smiled when the hot and cold sensations entered him, riding along the queen's carefully placed whips. As the energies passed areas of the body where the ants' poison had taken hold, Sherium caused them to flare, energizing the boy's already impressive defenses. Like an athlete in a sweat room, Ronin began to push the foreign elements out of his body. Sheriam's weave worked with the systematic precision of a Dwarven Steam Forge. In a few minutes, the boy, damp with sweat, lay in soft slumber, body free from the remnants of the ants' poison. The lynxen pulled her *joa* back into her, and allowed her vision to return to the normal world. The boy would be just fine.

"Thank you, Jiejie." Shawna's thoughts were of deep sincerity with just a hinge of regret. *"I panicked. I'm sorry for the wasted trip."*

Shawna might have laughed if she could have seen the expression on Sheriam's face. A giant cat staring at a human as if they were completely insane was a comic play for the greatest of stages.

67

"Nonsense. Some creatures leave deadly mark, and even one blessed with your sight cannot see how deeply it has been etched. Besides, the winds of the plains have drowned gentle voice and child's laughter for far too long." The female lynxen was the embodiment of compassion.

"He will sleep through the night and wake with a hunger of a starving Pride Seeker." Sheriam's thoughts were a soothing flute in Shawna's mind.

"Sister, we must talk." Solam's voice was the base drum adding into his mate's more delicate instrument. *"Our travels have brought with us a fortunate warning of events to come."*

Shawna did not hide her bewilderment. Solam must find it important, indeed, to cut short such an intimate reunion. The big tom turned and headed out into the living area, his mate lingering then falling in tow.

Shawna paused for a moment, staring at her sleeping boy who entered his dreams with a comforted smile. Whatever Solam had to say, at least Ronin was safe. The Asperii woman followed her friends, who had made their way into the main room and were finding suitable locations to sit. She passed them to head to the pantry to retrieve the serving bowls and a dusty jug of Highborn Wine reserved for such occasions. As she returned, both lynxen stared patiently at the sorrowed hound curled up with the scent of her lost mate. Celeste didn't even acknowledge the audience, rather, sad eyes casually lifted brow to rise toward each of the big cats, then drifted off into the distance.

Shawna sat the bowls in front of her guests and poured a hearty amount of wine to each before giving herself proper portion.

"It won't be long for this female. The Sorrow has her." Solam's thoughts were not filled with pity, rather a deep understanding.

"How did she lose her male?" Sheriam's question was halfhearted; whatever the cause, the three knew darkened outcome.

"Cretus was lost saving Ronin." Shawna was monotone in her thoughts.

The brave dog had given the swarm a second target, one that seemed a more direct threat to the nest, and it had cost him his life.

"Well, this female will follow her mate soon enough. Once they give into The Sorrow, it is just a matter of time." Solam's thoughts

tugged the two lynxen into a shared gaze. They knew that they, too, would be powerless to The Sorrow in similar circumstances.

"So." Shawna spoke aloud, somewhat startling at first, but a sufficient way to dispel the murky tone of the conversation. "You have an announcement for me I see?" Her pale white eyes drifted towards Sheriam's midsection, where several new pulsing balls of energy now resided. Her sipping from her wine goblet did not hide her smile.

"We are with cubs!" Sheriam's thoughts swelled with happiness and joined with her mate's. Emotions swirled into Shawna's mind and brought warmth into her heart. The energy was more intoxicating than the wine.

The three shared in what could be nothing short of laughter and tears of joy expressed in communal feeling. For years the mated pair had tried to conceive and been unable to do so. The Prides of Tor had been on a rapidly spiraling decline in numbers and long gestation periods made having offspring even more complicated.

"I'm sure Ronin will make an outstanding older brother." Caring mother pictured her son wrestling with playful cubs, allowing the image to fill the minds of expecting parents. Shawna rushed across the room and threw her arms around her sister's nape in loving embrace.

Sherium let out a prideful purr to show her verbal satisfaction.

"About time, big brother! I was beginning to doubt your choice of diet!" Shawna pressed her cheek into Solam's, petting his ears playfully. She placed a memory of the sickened cat covered in bones of gorged-upon fish for all to see like a proud owner of priceless painting.

He, too, purred with contentment.

The moment lingered. Solam and Shawna had seen many battles together, and the bond between the two caused the hunter's eyes to come to uncommon tear.

"You shall stay here to litter! I will prepare the common room to accommodate the cubs! It will be everything we..." Shawna's excitement was cut short, not by her use of open voice but rather by the feelings of concern now surrounding the room. The big cats stared at her, room filling with a thick fog of trepidation and fear.

69

Celeste, not immune to the nature of lynxen presence, rolled somberly to her side.

"What is it?" The Asperii woman was truly taken aback.

Her friends had been sharing a sacred moment, filled with rays of love and joy, then pulled the dark feelings into a room like a storm cloud drowns out the sun. The big cats exchanged concerned looks not visible to the hunter, but their heartbeats increased noticeably, sending *joa* from heart to muscles as if they expected an attack.

"We did not have time to fill droughted lake with water," Solam began, *"but conversation with the Tai'gong Lang helped to cause dry stream to flow."*

"The wolves have kin in nearly every land, and some still can translate words from hounds like your own." Sherium added the common knowledge into the room as one would unsuccessfully attempt to make light a gory tale of war.

Solam's stern look silenced his mate.

"The Tai'gong was very concerned about reports from his kin pack here in Sabrinia. A lot of voices can no longer be heard on the night winds, and those that can still be heard speak little of fat slow-running goats." The big male lapped at his empty wine bowl resulting in a full, obnoxious sounding spin that caused Shawna to move to refill it.

Solam continued: *"Understanding kin speak can be difficult for us sometimes. They use...simple...thoughts."*

"Simple and vulgar." Sheriam's second interruption prompted Solam to twitch his ears in noted irritation. She stared at him, apparently wounded by another signal of silence.

"None the less, the Dire Grandfather took great care to warn us of paths to take that would steer us clear of new places where they see the Food-Takers now hunting. In these places they clear vast areas of Windblockers to build rows of giant thorn and above-ground den."

"Forts are a norm, why is this so strange?" Shawna asked, still poised to take more terrible news.

"That's what I thought!" Her sister agreed quickly.

"That is not what you thought at the time." Her mate obviously remembered things differently than she.

"Oh really? I suppose you can read my mind now?"

Both Shawna and Solam looked at the queen, clearly lost at the question. Sherium, aware that she had just made herself an open target, pulled back ears, daring her mate to challenge her. Carefully, as an unknown cub passing a sleeping Pride Seeker, Solam continued,

"As...I...was trying to describe, the forts, other than their position, were of little consequence to me. After all, it is always difficult to decide which to compare humans to: rabbits or fleas. Both images accurate to a degree though the latter, a disease carrying nuisance and the former, not armed with spear and sword, need labored polishing for proper reflection. In any case, no matter where one travels in this world, do not be surprised to find them nesting and breeding."

Shawna was not offended, she was *mangmu lieren,* and thereby disconnected from the materialistic world of most men. In fact, she managed a bit of a chuckle and tried to imagine a bunny carrying a spear into battle. The visualization was a punch line to Solam's joke, and all in the room took part in verbally acknowledging such.

After the three took a moment to return to more serious tone, the big male continued his tale, forming the memory in his mind as Shawna needed, allowing for additions from less than patient pregnant female in the room.

"The Grandfather Wolf agreed to take us to one of these locations, helping to camouflage our life scent from the hunters he said were in the area. We moved as quickly as possible without drawing attention to ourselves. As we approached, it was Sherium that first took notice of the change in the earth."

Sherium added her own thoughts to the story, visions of the Great Mother's own life force, so powerful that it seeps from deep within her to form a vast network of energy. This, if seen from atop the tallest peak, would resemble an erratic spider's web, making dancing light similar to that viewed in the sky from the frozen wastes of the North. Unlike the Dancing Spirits of the Far North, these lines can only be seen by those whose vision allows it. Weavers, like Sherium, can even use them to enhance their own manipulations.

In every land they are known by a different name. Shawna, often falling back on her Sabrinian heritage, had always known them as Angel's Yarn, taught from legend that they were used by the Goddess herself to stitch the lands together. The lines' beauty is a marvel to hunters and weavers alike, shimmering like sheets of water slowly fading into the sky.

Solam continued with dire tone. *"The change was a subtle one, like a clearing fog that makes one question the clarity of one's vision. Something had been placed in the intersection of two lines."*

The male's vision showed a spear-like object pierce the earth, causing energy to seep out from around it like blood from arrow's wound. Images of the fort soon formed protective a barrier around the lance of stone and the wound it created.

It was Sheriam's turn to take over the tale. *"There, in the center of the fort, pointing like a spear into the heavens, was a stone obelisk with golden pyramid on atop."*

The female cat shivered.

"A horseless chariot, complete with soldiers and their fashioned fangs and horn, flew in slow patrol like soaring buzzard around the unnatural nest, pausing over areas of construction. One of the soldiers upon its back must have been the Greatmane. Barking orders from floating perch."

Shawna sat forward, as her friend's thoughts formed images in her mind, unwelcome fear causing hair to stand upon bumpy skin. She found herself clutching her wine goblet. Thoughts and feelings associated with a world she was blind to were always difficult for her to translate.

"Did you open yourself to the energies to see what aid granted these soldiers gift of flight?" Shawna hoped Sheriam's memory of the energy would better help her to understand the imagery.

Solam answered for his mate. *"She did not, we dare not risk gaze of hidden eyes if there were any hunters nearby. But The Tai'gong told us of what he heard upon the winds. The buzzards are held aloft by energies stemming from top the obelisk itself. We lore keepers have always known that the Pyramids of Anon powered the city, a marvel limited to proximity of the structure itself: lights without torches, carriages without horse or wheel, and weapons that can set entire forests ablaze."*

"I have never seen the capitol nor the marvel of the buildings that power it." Shawna's thoughts were filled with a slight regret. *"Fear of chains has always prevented such a venture. Though from a distance, I once saw its shining lights like a sunrise on horizon, and*

rumor has never sufficed to slate curiosity as to what makes it function so."

"We too, sister, have not dared to approach any Sabrinian city, knowing that the chain would be abandoned child's dream of royalty for us. The humans' love for lynxen pelt is known throughout the lands." Again Sherium could not protect flank from invading tremble.

"Still, the Pyramids' power only adds to city defense and comfort, attributes not undeserved for any being, including the clouded souls that follow the mighty priestess." Solam added an audible sigh. *"These smaller versions, however, add not to protective shell, but rather sharpen an already elongated tooth."*

Shawna's fingers tapped on the side of her goblet to the rhythmic hammering of the soldiers in the shared vision, as they brought up yet another portion of the fort's outer wall. These obelisks were an issue, yet far removed from the reclusive Asperii villa, if one could describe simple living as such.

"I understand how this raises hair on withers, but why the urgent turn from rejoice of rescued cub and discovery of more, to schemes of woodland flea?"

"Brace for storm, sister, and I shall bring cold winter." Solam's stare searched for proper diction in his bowl of wine. *"The fleas have infested the lands not far from here and have made a village thriving in production of livestock and wheat. This place is named from the heavy stones defying wind and water to remain upon delicate stand, is it not?"*

"Balanced Rock bares name as such and, too, swears fealty to the Goddess," answered the woman aloud.

The large male looked up from his bowl, a practiced glare wasted on the woman whose vision was forever locked in a different world.

"Take warning, sister. For it is not accident that precarious boulder refuses to budge."

"I don't follow?" Shawna did not deceive.

"What my oaf of a husband is trying to say, is that it is the natural energy of the place that gives cause to keep the rocks from falling. Three lines cross there. It is a powerful place."

"And if these fleas are tapping into these crossings..." Solam did not have to pause for long.

"They will find great cause for placement of fortification and cursed stone column into such a place." Shawna answered.

Her friends had indeed brought dreary weather.

"The buzzards will circle far and wide from this nest you call Balanced Rock, and if shrewd eye catches view of our sister's sheltering bones, you can bet they will pick clean any remaining morsel." Solam's eyes again searched wine in bowl, this time looking for refuge from the dreadful thoughts all three shared.

"Solam?" A scratchy voice from the doorway of his room snapped all three to attention.

Ronin, still rubbing his eyes, began to plod towards the prone tom, legs apparently lacking any bones and mind still halfway lost in fog of dream.

"What is it, Diyi You'Shou?" Solam used soothing thoughts as the child fell in between paws big as the boy's entire chest. He crawled up into the big cat, nuzzling in the safety of mighty limbs and covered in the warmth of majestic mane.

"I had a nightmare." The response was drawn in a raspy whine that's usual reprimand would be removed in light of recent events.

Solam began to respond, but gave pause. The boy was already again fast asleep, snuggled into the mighty beast, whose very presence banished all sense of fear lingering from pestering vision.

Both Sherium and Shawna stared at the two, taking heed to not let the legion of worries remain unchecked, lest this oft forgot influence of Speaking Without Words affect the boy's much needed rest a second time. Both saw the loving pair in their own way, yet whether carried across back or with arms, the burden at hand would inevitably reach the same destination. The Asperiis would have to leave their home or face the fate of chain and cage.

The Little Witch

Jacin's pitchfork plunged into the soiled straw, the boy was careful to not drop the contents short of the wheelbarrow. He hated changing out the dredge goat's stalls. His words to the Goddess that all the lumbering beasts do is eat and shit. He could hear his brother hollering at the big male outside, attempting to goad the stupid beast into a corral while the deed at hand was tended to.

After a few moments, Jacob joined his twin. Neither of Icomus' oldest children were strangers to hard work, but both would have given a chunk of Dwarven Steel to have someone less fortunate take their place at this task. Nonetheless, complaint does not stand to accomplish task, and their father would have their hide if they didn't get these pens cleaned.

The pair had the cart filled in no time and, as soon as the pitchforks became obsolete, Jacob darted towards the flat shovel, knowing that his brother would have to go for the broom if he did not get there first. Jacin was aware of this as well and had no intention of being stuck in the barn for another second. Jacin had a problem though: dung-and-straw filled cart obscured path to chosen tool. He had but a second to decide, in order to best his brother, the young farmer had to leap the filled wheelbarrow.

Jacob was just steps from the hanging flat shovel when his twin set himself into motion, as such he did not set as fast a pace as he could have: after all, who would have thought his brother would set into motion such a desperate feat! As one twin rounded the cart, the second leaped over it, driven by determination. Jacin's trailing foot brushed urine-soaked straw off the top of the cart, a tell-tale sign of the close proximity to calamity the boy had just ventured to, but the wheelbarrow stayed upright. He landed safely on the other side, momentum carrying him towards the hanging tool in a more direct path than his sibling's, whose eyes now widened with dismay.

Four hands reached the shovel at the same time, four arms strained with all might, and four eyes glared across wooden shaft at one another.

"Let go, goat cock!" cursed Jacin.

75

"You let go, shit eater!" Jacob yanked the shovel towards himself, causing his brother to stumble. Seeing his twin off balance he shoved quickly forward, solid handle striking Jacin in the mouth.

Jacin let go of the shovel and checked his mouth for loosened teeth, there were none, though his hand shown evidence of the taste of blood rapidly filling his mouth. If looks could kill, the one Jacin gave his brother would have brought plague to bare on small village.

"I'd rather be a shit eater, than a goat cock!" taunted the unwounded brother.

Jacob began to back up and was forced to drop his prize as his growling twin shot in at him, looking to hook a leg in one of his father's favorite wrestling maneuvers. Both boys had won many matches during the yearly festivals, and Jacin's expertise from such showed. He pulled Jacob's leg into his armpit and drove forward until both boys slammed onto the ground. Jacin could hear his brother's well timed exhale to prevent wind from unnaturally blasting from lung. The fight was on and, in this barn, there were no rules or referees to spoil the fun.

Immediately, Jacob formed his hand into a cup and smacked his brother in the ear, forcing air to spiral inside, striking his ear drum like a gong mallet. The blow rattled his brain and twisted his head to the side. At the same time he struck, Jacob arched his back and pushed with all his might to dislodge Jacin from position of dominance.

The assault was successful and dazed twin soon found himself being spun onto his own back. Jacin gritted his teeth, causing more blood to seep into his mouth. The fluid seemed to fuel the boy with vigor, allowing him to push Jacob's right knee down and away while he slammed a fist into his target's left armpit. The combination caused Jacob's reversal to carry over beyond control and allowed Jacin to once again come out on top. Jacin grabbed his brothers loose tunic and crossed it tight over the others neck, a tactic that would certainly choke his fraternal enemy into submission.

Jacob was no slouch, however, and privy to most any attack his brother could scheme up. He reached up and grabbed a full handful of hair, wrenching Jacin's head backward. With his free arm, he hacked the braced arm holding tunic at the elbow, breaking the effective lock. Craftiness as ally, as the elbow collapsed, Jacob let go of pulling hair, strategically allowing Jacin to win tug-of-war. As the dominant sibling's head snapped forward, Jacob thrust forward his own, resulting in the forehead of one smashing into the nose of the other, opposing force aiding in the attack.

Jacin growled again as he staggered to his feet off of his brother. His vision blurred, and his eyes were already filling with tears, a surefire sign that blood would soon flow from nostril and mouth alike.

Jacob, too, regained his feet, gasping for much needed air and repositioning his tunic. He shook a finger at his brother, who now cupped hands beneath a nose that had begun dispersing blood like a village water pump.

"That's what you get! What in Goddess name were you thin..."

The warning was cut short, given to a charging bull bellowing with rage.

Bloody twin moved in, pausing prior to a second lunge. There would be no more wrestling today. Two straight left jabs came where another take-down might have been. They were square shots that were prelude to a strong right cross, a combination taught to both boys by Icomus. Jacin placed the right perfectly, and his twin stumbled backward into a barrel of oats. Boy and barrel both smashed into the floor.

Jacob pushed himself onto all fours, now bleeding and coughing up bits of oats he had inadvertently ingested when he smashed into the barrel. Jacin propped his head sideways, fists still up, dancing in defense.

The prone twin looked up and wiped his lips clear of oats, dust, and blood. Eyebrows struck together, lighting fire in narrowed eyes.

"Didn't know you liked eating oats, too..." Jacin was not above his brother's insults nor was Jacob above anger-spawned battle cries.

From a crouch came the downed twin, his stance adding to strength of leg and speed of charge. His entire mass slammed into his sibling so quickly that another swing from waiting fists hand no time to land properly. Both Jacob and Jacin, as one, flew backward.

Two sets of hands, two sets of arms, and two sets of eyes, in fact, all the parts that two boys contained in sum, smashed quite heavily into a filth-filled wheelbarrow. Wet, piss-soaked straw, clumps of goat dung, shards of broken cart, and two bloody siblings sprawled across the floor of the barn.

Groaning, the twins rolled slowly from side to side, repeatedly spitting straw and whatever else out of their mouths with what seemed to be little success; futile efforts were interrupted when the barn door flew open with a resounding thud.

"What in the Great Mother's cunt is this!?" Icomus' voice was a boom sent into the thick rafters, silencing moaning twins and ceasing pathetic movement. Even the remaining dredge goat, whose constant munching had not been slowed by the scuffle, pulled its head up to stand at attention.

Both boys rolled onto their backs, propping themselves up to stare at the loving man turned executioner. Icomus' hands were folded across his chest, possibly to help contain the boiling rage his massive chest heaved to keep at bay.

The farmer stared down at the twins, lying there in a pile of broken cart, soiled straw, and each other's blood. If a mouse had been brave enough to scurry from nest, size and weight could have been guessed by sound of foot treading on wooden floor.

Icomus opened his mouth, but no words came out. He instead snapped it shut, muscles in his forehead drawing teeth together with visible force. His eyebrows pulled folds of skin on his forehead together: two draft horses dragging heavy loads. A long sigh announced they could go no further.

The three awaited signs of scurrying mouse.

Again, the big farmer's lips parted to speak, but again no words came out. A big hand came out from its hidden cave of muscle to attempt to straighten crooked eyebrows.

Eelia, who had followed his father into the barn, stepped out from behind one of his father's legs. He stared, open mouth at his older brothers. He looked around, eyes absorbing every detail, his young mind filling in the blanks with story book explanations. Icomus moved hand from brows to chin until he realized the presence of his youngest child. Tool of many tasks, the loving father scrubbed his calloused mitt through the little boy's hair.

"Eelia. Go to the house"

Kind intentions held anger at bay, and the two twins squirmed with anticipation. Their little brother, at that moment, was stronger than the Greattree beams supporting the oversized barn.

"House."

The boy nodded and obeyed his father, leaving the barn.

Icomus watched the door shut behind Eelia.

"Get up." The man growled.

The boys stood, apparently healed of all injury if speed of attention was any valid indicator.

"Sir, I..." Jacin began as he scrambled to his feet.

"Shut it." Icomus had to forcibly keep his fingers from clenching into a fist as he approached the two. The farmer wasn't just a big man, he was hardened by a working man's life. His day began at sunrise and often ended when head struck pillow. He had no time for this foolishness.

The twins shuffled as the moving tree rooted in front of them. The end was near.

Icomus had a brother growing up. Fever had taken the twins' uncle well before he had the pleasure of introducing the man to them, but this father had no doubt that if his brother stood there in his shoes, he would see the same reflection Icomus now observed. How many times had he and his brother torn up something, busted something, or made a mess in this very barn? The answer was irrelevant and, at the very least, would have brought a smile to a face now stern with discipline.

"You will clean this up."

"Yes, sir." An answer that hit each ear in unison.

"You will mend this cart."

"Yes, sir." Again both voices as one.

"You will finish your chores."

Spontaneous affirmation.

"You will bathe before you enter the house. I don't care if you have to leap in the fucking creek bare-assed and come home with frozen peckers! Take a washboard, too, I won't have your sister paying for your fool actions."

The boys looked at each other. Could they be getting off this easy?

"Yes, sir." The answer was a bit uneasy but Jacin, hoping to avoid the belt, pressed advantage.

"Are we going to talk about it father?" Jacin asked gingerly, but not without merit.

It was true that there had been an uneasy air about the farm the last few days, the last few days since the incident. It wasn't every day when your little sister created a blinding light from the center of her forehead that in a moment mended mortal wound. Both Clara and Eelia had woke up the next day as if nothing had happened. Their savior, however, had not.

Baylee had slept for two days, waking only to eat, drink, or go to the outhouse. Other than the exhaustion, she complained of no ailments. This morning she had risen to make the family breakfast as she would have any normal morning. Unfortunately, she had apparently invited a giant pink dredge goat to join the family for the meal, what with all the odd looks and squeamish actions of the three men at the table. The young woman had finished her bowl with blushing cheek and salted her food with crushed frustration.

Icomus let out a big sigh, one that did not allow his shoulders to return to position to the sheer weight of worry upon them.

"There is little to talk about."

Hollow words were apparently read in the wood grain of the floorboards. The boys did not believe him.

"Father." It was Jacob's turn. "We've never seen anything like that. Right before the light got bright, it looked like there was a glowing...a glowing eye in her..."

"I said there is nothing to talk about!" The farmer's voice was pushed through clenched teeth.

"Sir, I know, we both know it's not easy but..." Jacob looked at his brother.

"Father, it's like that tale mom used to tell us." Jacin finished.

"Our sister has powers...just like..." Jacob felt foolish to even bring it up.

Icomus looked back and forth at them, eyebrows raised, waiting for a foolish response.

Jacin did not help his brother this time and left Jacob to be the courageous one.

"Just like the story 'The Little Witch'." The revelation lacked conviction.

Both twins looked at each other, then stared at the floor in front of them, awaiting the inevitable proclamation of their stupidity. It never came.

"That... was... your mother's favorite story." The big man took in a deep breath and a sigh that opened the flood gates of memory.

"She used to tell it to us all the time," Jacin said.

"I loved the part with the trolls in it," added Jacob.

There, inside the barn, the three men shared a memory. They could all hear her voice, watch her hands turn the pages, they noticed the changes in her voice as she added a smile.

***

The Little Witch

Once upon the time there was a little witch with long, wild hair.
She liked all kinds of things, like skipping and dancing in the woods.
The Little Witch had lots of friends: squirrels, birds, bugs...
And even the trolls!
She liked to play games with her friends.
Most of all, the Little Witch liked to help others.
The Little Witch was very magickal and could do amazing things.
She could heal broken wings...
She could fix broken teeth...
She could mend a cracked shell...
She could even fix a bad funny bone!
One day the Little Witch found a sad boy in the woods.
The little witch tried to help him get better, but her magick didn't work.
This boy had a broken heart.
When the townspeople came to find the boy they saw the Little Witch.
They thought she was the one that hurt him.
She showed them that she could not hurt anyone! She could only help others.
Her magick scared them, and the townspeople chased the Little Witch away.
The Little Witch was sad and alone.
But soon her friends came to see her. The missed her.
They reminded her that she was good, and it did not matter what the townspeople said about her.
Soon they were all dancing and skipping and playing games.
Even the boy came to play!
And they lived happily ever after.

The End.

"I thought the townspeople locked her away in a dungeon before the trolls dug her out?" Jacob's question was open for either to answer.

"I think mom just added that part in there for us," Jacin stated "She was always doing little things to make it special, you know, more boyish. It was just a stupid story anyway."

"Was it? Why did she tell it to us, Jace? All the time?" Jacob looked at his brother intently, then diverted his gaze to his father.

"She just wanted us to remember that people can be dicks and to not care what they think."

"Language, Jacin." Icomus put in.

The twins were definitely on edge. This was a broken axle on the cheese wagon.

"The truth is, boys, that story has as many different endings as your mother wanted it to, mainly because it had been told to her by her mother and her mother before that. Who knows how many mothers passed it on, but one thing is for sure, the original ending was somewhat more...gruesome...than the endings she told you two." A big hand rubbed across Icomus' face, making an abrasive sound that reminded the farmer that it would soon be time to shave again, and that the twins had many years to come before they obtained the wisdom of their father.

Jacin and Jacob exchanged open looks, complete with shrugs of bewilderment. They had never before known of a "gruesome" ending; in fact, they were not even sure that their mother had been capable of telling anything containing as much. In fact, the whole concept that the story had been passed down generations was fascinating and did nothing to help repair the broken axle.

"When your mother first told you boys, you were too young to remember, but it was this first telling that prompted me to ask her if she could think of something a little less dreary." A slight smile touched the corners of his lips as he continued "Course, her being a woman, she made up an ending that had a beautiful wedding between the witch and the boy. You know, mushy women crap."

The big man was lost in memory and had led his children into the maze with him. "I told her to add some heroics for the boy to rescue her, but she'd have none of it. She said it made the witch too weak if

82

the sad boy saved her." His sigh parted lips to a full smile. "Your mom did let the trolls come save the girl, though, she said at least that was more believable than some boy doing all that digging." He chuckled, clearly he had lost sight of his planned destination.

Both boys wanted more but, given the situation, neither dared remind their father he had gotten off track. Silence took a breath that seemed to last an entire evening. Finally, Icomus came to.

"The point is the original tale was nearly the same up until the witch met the boy." Four eager eyes stared up at the looming figure, intensity helping their ears absorb the new content.

"First of all, he was a man, not a boy, and the witch was a woman, not a girl. The man did have a broken heart, for he was married to an ambitious, conniving woman, but the witch was able to heal it. Not through magick, but the way any woman can heal the broken heart of a man." Icomus wisely did not slow to explain. "She showed the man her world, and they rapidly fell in love. He had not known such feelings from his estranged wife. Soon, however, it was the man's past that caught up with them. When the man's wife tired of her own games, she found out about the two of them sometime later. For reasons I cannot explain, a woman that doesn't want you usually doesn't want anyone else to want you either." Luckily, the concept went over both young men's' heads, and the farmer went on. "The wife was outraged at the affair and hired men to capture the witch and her 'spelled' husband."

Icomus was never a story teller, he had never been in battle with anything other than a stubborn dredge goat. He had never spent a lot of time in the taverns listening to bards paint pictures with their tongues, but right there, in that barn, he had a captive audience; and he understood how intoxicating telling stories could be. He licked is lips so that he could continue and stepped towards the boys for effect.

"The little witch and her 'boy' ran from the men for days, evading them at every turn with the help of both the witch's friends and her magic. For some time it seemed they would win, that was until one day the little witch had a baby."

Jacin and Jacob were a bit thrown off, but none the less continued to listen intently.

Their father kept going. "With their baby, the little witch and her boy could no longer run and hide, and soon the men caught up with them. They killed all of the girl's friends. And the little witch, exhausted from using much of her magick, could only cast one last spell. The spell hid the man and her baby within the heart of an old oak tree, but it made her weak, and the men caught up with her. They did awful things to her and then took her back to the jealous wife. Enraged, the wife tortured the witch, trying to find her husband. The witch did not break."

"What happened next, father?"

"Yes, what happened?"

Both boys were leaning in, waiting. Icomus moistened his mouth to help him finish his story. "The wife rallied the town folk, told lies about the witch, and had her...burned at the stake."

"They burned her alive?" Jacin swallowed hard.

Jacob shook his head: "Her friends, or the man, no one rescued her?"

"No one could, son. The men had massacred them all. You see, in real life, not many stories truly end happily."

Neither boy liked the tale's finale.

"Who cares anyhow? It's just a stupid story mom used to tell us at bed time." Jacin was always the skeptic.

"I care! Jace! Didn't you hear what father just said? Mom's mom's mom told it to her. And who knows what that means!" Jacob was excited despite the grim clouds gathering around their punishment.

"It means nothing!" Jacin closed his eyes and slowly shook his head.

"It means our sister is a witch..." Jacob mumbled the revelation.

For the third time, Icomus drew in and let out a deep breath. Both boys looked at their feet before curiosity took over and led their gaze upwards.

"What it means, boys, is that we all wish your mother was still here to answer some questions, and she is not." With one motion, the big farmers hand pushed his wide-brimmed hat backwards so he could scratch a balding head.

"I've been thinking about this for days. Not the story mind you, but it does stir up the muck, doesn't it?" Neither boy answered. Icomus moved calloused mitt from forehead to chin. He rubbed it slowly, but in such a manner that the boys thought he may pull off his own lips if he were not careful.

"Boys." The big man took a step forward on one knee. The giant man used to do this to get closer to eye level, he was painfully aware now that the years had gone too quickly. On one knee, he looked up at them, hat still balancing on the crown of his head, his eyebrows curved upwards in a look the two had never seen. Their father was scared.

He pulled both of the boys closer still, his hands knew the filth that clung to hard work. His eyes moved slowly back and forth, and in a low voice that was nearly a whisper he spoke.

"What happened the other day, no matter what, cannot go beyond this circle of trust. The two of you must swear to me and to each other that you will never EVER speak of what happened. People would not...understand."

The boys were tearing up. Partly because their father never spoke to them this way, and partly because they had never seen him this afraid.

"Father are you saying..." Jacin started, but Icomus squeezed his shoulder gently for silence.

"Swear it to me, boys. Never joke about it. Never tease. Never tell your wives or your children." He was a man chiseled from a piece of Greatwood again.

"I swear father," Jacob chimed, he was always the believer.

"Jacin? Son?" There was a sense of desperation in the delivery.

Jacin looked around, clearly confused, and clearly on the edge of a breakdown. He did not understand why this was even a conversation.

"SON!" The farmer's voice cracked like a whip somewhere between a whisper and a scream.

"Of course, father. I swear. I swear." The boy was crying but trying to do so as he thought a man should.

"Then we are agreed." Despite knees that bade otherwise, the big man stood, now towering over the twins, he extended his right hand. It was a farmer's deal that would be sealed with a handshake. It was everything the man stood for, and the deal would be kept forever.

"I strike this deal with you both." Icomus spoke. "Until the final sun sets, and the dust of my bones feeds the next harvest, or my name isn't Icomus Gladus Coreni."

"I strike this deal with you both. Until the final sun sets, and the dust of my bones feeds the next harvest, or my name isn't Jacob Marrus Coreni."

Jacin looked at the two of them as if they were mad. Then after a brief pause, he spoke aloud and clearly. "I strike this deal with you both. Until the final sun sets, and the dust of my bones feeds the next harvest, or my name isn't Jacin Hypion Coreni."

The three shook on the words. Icomus, hands now on hips, surveyed his sons. They would grow to be fine men, if they were not already. He turned and began to walk out the barn door.

Watching in silence, the twins held their breath, hoping the man had forgotten the mess they had made, and not really recalling what had gotten them there in the first place. The big farmer stopped at the doorway.

He did not turn around.

"And clean this fucking mess up." His hand was on the door, to close it behind him. "I swear to god if so much as a pebble of goat shit gets on the dinner table, I will peel the Goddess cursed skin off of BOTH your asses in front of your baby brother and sister, just so they can watch you wail."

The boys did not notice the door slamming shut. They looked at each other.

"You want to use the shovel?" Jacin asked his brother, holding the tool like an offering of peace.

***

Clara had rolled over onto her back in the loft above the boys. She could no longer hear them when her daddy had knelt down anyhow. All she knew was that her sister was a witch! A real witch with magicks and everything!

Her mind was racing! Did her older sister know how to fix a bird's broken wing? She no doubt could do so! Could she turn Clara into a bird!?! Oh, how grand that would be! To go flying around like a bird could! But she wouldn't eat worms, although Clara did suppose that if she were a bird and got hungry enough, maybe she wouldn't know the difference.

She stuck her tongue out in the air at the thought of it. No she would definitely not eat worms; though, she reckoned that she could talk her little brother into trying it out, and see how he liked it. After all, it was easy to talk him into doing things, and she wasn't about to try it out herself first.

She began to formulate a plan to get Eelia to do her bidding and spread her wing-like arms open as she lay on her back in the hay. She imagined the ceiling as the ground and that Baylee had transformed her into a beautiful pink, and yellow, and blue, and green, and red bird (with a blue beak like the color her lips were after Goo Toffee at the summer fair).

Just as she had found an imaginary morsel for her sibling, the barn door slammed shut, snapping her out of her fantasy.

Shoot! She thought. *If dad thinks I'm not helping out sis, I'll be in deep duck muck!*

Deftly, and with the expertise of a barn cat, Clara hopped out of the hay shoot and onto the outside pen roof. She held her arms straight out, not with the intent of balance and speed, but rather because she was once again the bird in her daydream.

From the roof she hopped to a stack of barrels, then an old crate, then a nice solid fence post. She ran along the top of the fence like an acrobat would a tightrope, an action that would have inspired just as much awe and fear had her father been watching, until she had to hop onto the ground. She did so, the entire time with her wings spread out wide.

As she came up from the landing she took a second to smooth her skirts and pin her hair back behind her ears. Her father had not gone straight into the house; rather, he appeared to be going on a walk with Ranger, which was even better for the little eavesdropper.

Her walk towards the house turned into a skip. How wonderful it was that her sister was a witch! Clara was so happy! She couldn't wait to tell the whole world!

Of course, no one could know what she knew, not just yet.

So Far Away From Home

Teegan sucked the blood out of his thumb for what must have been about the thousandth time. After a few seconds and several repeated oral clean-ups, he went back to chiseling away at the piece of bone. Focusing on his work was the only way the boy could avoid embarrassment from the way the rest of the tribe had been treating him. He had become nothing short of a hero. He had felled the biggest Toenuk on all the Great Plains in his first hunt, a huge beast known by not just his tribe, but by many tribes, as Halftooth.

His bravery and quick thinking had spread like a swarm of locusts on the plain; before he could even open his mouth, his remarkable camouflage tactic had become an intricate plan he had devised all along. According to the other hunters, it was the only sure-fire way to get close enough to strike down the legendary beast. In truth, the young warrior had wet himself right there on the field, and the only way to save his own life was to dive head first into a pile of shit.

He was ashamed, and he could tell no one.

He had tried to tell his father, Kurg, the truth behind his actions, but the chief merely interrupted the young man with a hearty pat on the back. He explained that the nature of the hunt itself was the important part, and the 'tiny' details should be kept between the hunter and the Sky Father.

Nonetheless, Teegan had been more than surprised when the chief ordered the entire camp to be moved to the place where Halftooth took his final breath. The shamans had come from several mountain tops for the blessing: three ravens, two vultures, and an eagle had arrived when they had heard the spirit's call. None in the boy's tribe could recall such a gathering. The chief ordered a great celebration, and decided to move the clan to a location close to the fallen sow and Teegan's big male. Processing the two beasts could feed the entire tribe for several months, not to mention the hides and bones the hunters would have had to leave behind had the tribe not shifted locale.

On a side note, many of the tribe's women had taken the death of both male and female beasts as a sign from the Earth Mother that their own relationships had to come to an end; thus, most of the hunters arrived at the newly placed camp to find their belongings packed lovingly and sat outside of their wives' tents. This recognized sign of a divorce wasn't too much trouble for the tribe, and breakups like this were not uncommon. However, like the gathering shaman, the sheer quantity of those participating in this 'rebirth' was not remembered by a single elder in the group For the most part, braves and newly available wives alike did not fret as it merely meant that new marriages would surely follow the upcoming festivities. In the meantime though, many a mother's tent had become a crowded mess of her sons that had yet to marry and her sons that were no longer labeled as such.

Possibly due to the fact that there was a mass of shaman and a crazed amount of marriage disarray, the young hunter found that he could not get a single moment alone. Either someone wanted to hear the story again, how the great Teegan brought down the mighty Halftooth or they had a question about another hunter's part that was played. Teegan would find himself surrounded by the young and the old alike, wanting to learn more about the arm that threw the spear.

If it weren't the story telling, it was the shaman. Strange fellows, always talking about this and that. Things that most of the Plainsmen did not understand. Many of the hunters joked about how the shaman spent too much time in the form of their totem and could no longer accurately speak the message of the tribe. Most hunters joked that was, except for their chief, Kurg. Kurg revered the wise men, revered their ability to transform hair into feather and hands into wings. Whispers and mockeries ceased well before earshot of the leader, for all knew that he was a true believer in words wrapped in riddles that the shaman spoke. Teegan was different. He found himself, literally, nauseated around them. They would prance around him, examining his ribs or legs. Poking or prodding with their sticks, chanting and dancing, these wise men appeared to the youth as crazy. One even jammed both his hands into Teegan's mouth, stretching his mouth open so wide the boy thought the old man would try to climb inside his mouth. The only shaman he had yet to meet was the Eagle. The Eagle had come the furthest into the plains to bless the kill. It was a rarity, indeed, to see one so far down from the high forests of the frozen lands to the north, but the wise man had kept himself to the fallen bull, apparently in order to bless the horn.

Neither the crowd waiting for repeated recollection nor the twitching avian movements of the wise men's' magick could compare to the strangest thing that happened to Teegan since his first hunt, and that was the behavior of the tribe's women. Girls ranging from eight winters to many winters now doted on the tribe's young champion. They brought him everything from honey sweetened treats to crowns and wreaths of flowers, warm blankets, and even warmer smiles, eyes measuring him up and down, and giggles dancing into his ears. Even some of the they newly available women-adult women-congratulated him on his hunt, taking far too long to give praise whilst standing far too close and leaving their tops far too loosely laced. Teegan's cheeks flushed warm with blood on more than one occasion when full hips and breasts stood in front of him in a gentle sway, speaking a voiceless language he had just begun to discover. The effect had crept to southern regions as well, causing an even deeper reddening of his cheeks. It wasn't until this second coloring that the women-adult women-would walk away contented in his reaction.

Morgal had happened upon one such instance and did nothing to aid his younger hunt-brother. He had been one of the unfortunate or, in his view, fortunate men to come home and have his things waiting outside his wife's tent. His arrival was after the plainswoman had left, and young Teegan had turned as red as a brave three days in the sun.

"Be careful, bull killer. Putting one foot in front of the other can be no easy task if one's spirit travels from his mind to his trousers." Morgal laughed.

"Morgal, I...I don't understand?"

"Understand what, bull killer? Why all of the women give you so much attention?" His smile continued, one that split his head in half, tacked up on each side by tusks much larger than Teegan's.

"Before my first hunt not a single tribe daughter looked twice at me. Now..."

Morgal laughed from deep down, his own memories of similar times: "Women are always a mystery! You take Tauka'Aun for example. She ran for two days to meet me under the moonlight once and now shoves me back to my mother's. There was a time when being the fastest runner meant having the fastest woman. Tomorrow, who knows, maybe she will bring you a blanket!"

"Brother, I..."

"No worries, bull killer! I'll find another! Just make sure you get that one on all fours, you won't have to work as hard!" Morgal gave Teegan a hearty slap on the back and strode away. Laughter taking time with each stride.

Sure enough, come the following day there was Tauka'Aun, blanket in hand, standing all too close to Teegan. When she handed it over her hand lingered, barely touching his. She stared deep into his eyes, the champion several seasons younger. She was so close her tusks almost touched his own. He could smell her breath, the sweetness of fresh tobacco tucked between her teeth and gums. Her large eyes swallowed him, and he could tell she would eat much, much more. When she left, his knees could barely support the rest of his frame for the way they shook.

Morgal's ex-wife had not been the only one. Girls his own age brought him gifts and jewelry, so much so, his mother and sisters had jokingly told him to pitch his own lodge tent. His bed roll now had necklaces, crowns of flowers, pouches of tobacco, blankets, skins, and clothing, all gifts for the returning brave that was now considered an eligible man. The entire affair was so embarrassing, it had the boy-warrior wishing he was covered in shit, staring at a bull Toenuk trying to trample him.

His mother would choose a wife for him soon, but until then he was fair game to any unmarried woman, and that would make the upcoming festivals very uncomfortable. So uncomfortable that he now spent several hours carving bones from his fallen claim to sudden fame to avoid dwelling on the thought. How hungry her eyes were!

Teegan sucked the blood out of his thumb for the thousandth and one time. His distraction too easy to come by.

Carving the bones of Halftooth was important business, and Teegan understood almost as little of that business as he did about women. Of his many forgotten lessons, however, Teegan did know that every bit of bone kept some part of the mighty beast's spirit. The shaman made sure of it, they called the ritual 'Keeping the Spirits Close', and it was performed as the fallen took its last mortal breath. Forever would the ferocity of the King of the Plains be present in the trinkets and totems carved out of his bones. A Plainsman made his armor, his spear heads, and his jewelry from the Toenuk killed on their first hunt. Even the etched clubs carried into battle were made from the massive tusks of the beasts; those held the most powerful magick of all. The warrior and his first kill were one until that warrior's Long Song; only then would both spirits be released to roam the clouds with the Sky Father.

Teegan, like all of the members of the tribe knew the stories of the shamans trapping the spirits. He knew there was a dance and chanting. There was special paint and special smoke. Teegan knew what they did, but he did not know *how* they did it.

Truth be known, he didn't want to know, however, lacking the desire for knowledge did not mean that sometimes it was not thrust upon him. There was so much chatter around the camp that he could not deny that there were unusual circumstances at work. On more than one occasion he had overheard the shaman talking about the unique circumstances surrounding the death of Halftooth, but their explanations were always referenced to tales the old told at campfires. Ever since he was a small child, well before the times of young warrior training, Teegan learned stories about the great spirits, primarily the Sky Father, the Earth Mother, and the Trickster. The latter of the three was known for causing most of the mischievous things that happened in the world, not denying his name tendency to be expressed in action. Things like convincing the Makers to create the Plainspeople, giving the Makers fire stolen from the Sky Father, and the concept of property were all foolish deeds of the Trickster.

As the story of one such deed goes, one day the Trickster had stolen the Skyfather's mighty hatchet as a prank. He had goofed around cutting down entire forests, breaking down natural damns and carving out canyons. The Skyfather, using the time of distraction to his benefit, ran off with the Earth Mother to a special place where they could finally have some privacy. Soon, the Trickster became bored of chopping and carving things, and complained that the hatchet was too heavy. He searched all around for the Skyfather, dragging the hatchet in the dust, leaving great lines across the land. These lines, called Mother's Yarn by the Sabrinians, Dragon Trails by the Tyrians, and Ley Lines by the Man'Antians, were places of extreme magick. Teegan's people believed that the Sky Father's hatchet, drug by the lazy Trickster, made these lines and the wandering sprit created areas of vast power where two or more lines crossed. Many tribes revered and even worshiped these crossings. Totem poles, statues, and temples all marked these sacred places. But not all of them had been marked, especially in the wilder parts of the world, and it was this important point of fact that made the young hunter recall the childhood tale of the Skyfather's hatchet.

Halftooth had died on the exact spot where three lines crossed.

Teegan knew this was significant, but he had no idea just how significant it was. Not even the mighty Kurg, chief of the tribe, knew how unbelievably rare such an event was. Even the Ravens and the Vultures were constantly bantering, and sometimes bickering back and forth, as to what the outcome of such a Last Breath would be. Only the Eagle Shaman, so far from home, remained silent and in a constant trance over the body of the fallen bull Toenuk, the King of the Plains. For the last two days, the shaman had neither slept, ate, or drank, constantly repeating the binding ritual over and over.

So far the shaman had only allowed a few bones, the meat, and some of the organs to be harvested from the carcass. Halftooth's mighty heart had been wrapped and put into the river, and much of his blood stored in clay pots for the upcoming feast and rituals. The hide was being processed as well, but the larger bones had to be left in place. Even Halftooth's one good tusk, which Teegan would someday carve his weapons from, was still attached to a skull the size of a Sabrinian covered wagon. Carrion birds waited with respect, perched in branches of nearby trees, making the wooden guardians seem more alive. Ravens and vultures barked at each other, yet had formed an unnatural alliance that no doubt was due to the presence of the shaman representing the animal spirits.

All in all, the picture painted on this canvas was an odd one; an entire camp bustling with activity, hunters harvesting the body parts of two mighty beasts of the plains, each as big as a small house, hide sections being tanned, entrails dried, and blood bottled. The kills had caused two short trails to be worn in the earth as men and women moved to and fro from camp to carcass. Children played with one another, fueled by the lack of worry that such abundance of food lifted. Women of age decorated the camp for the upcoming festivities, placing strings of flowers and wind chimes of wood and bone all about. The old and wise watched over them, eyes fogged over with memory of days when it was they who played, decorated, and harvested the things they needed. Their role now one of the most important; teachers, keepers of history, and living libraries of reference-all traits whose value had been rashly disregarded by many of the more 'civilized' cultures of the world.

There was more hustle and bustle going on in Teegan's camp than he had seen in, well, ever.

Yet there he was, sitting on a small tree stump sucking his thumb. Trying to etch his tribal symbols into bone, each slip of his hand was a bit of revenge dished out from the fallen Toenuk. Working on the trinkets he would eventually use as jewelry to hang from his ears, nose, or tusks, was also practice for his etching of his war club. It would take time for him to finish the shape of the club, and his practice would allow him to decorate it as the years went on, a custom for warriors of his tribe. After each hunt, after each battle, for each foe vanquished, carvings would be made. Someday his club would look like his father's. Etched from head to handle and wrapped with leather straps for better grip, Kurg's club had been carried by the mightiest of his clan since he was Teegan's age. The chieftain had installed four thick metal rings into the weapon's head and added to them many etched claws, fangs, and bones of the beings he had felled with it. When the boy's father stepped on the battlefield, his enemies trembled, fear of becoming a part of the malevolent club that would see their end. Kurg had named the thing Bonerattle, a twisted joke from a child's toy.

"Teegan?" Came a small voice, it was another girl's, and it caused him to flinch so badly that his knee took a gouge instead of his thumb.

Teegan grunted, a bitter mixture of pain and disapproval. He turned to face the girl.

"Sorry, Teegan. I...I wanted to give you this..." The voice was attached to Lu'Kall, a girl a season or so younger than the young champion. In her hand was a very poorly crafted flower-wreath. Her face was flushed with embarrassment at the crafting, yet nonetheless, she thrust the thing in front of her, a portion of the wreath breaking apart and falling at Teegan's feet.

"Thank you..." Teegan was holding back a chuckle.

Lu'Kall turned yet another shade of red. She turned to storm off, forcing Teegan to rise.

"Lu'Kall! Wait!" he said, hustling to catch up to the girl.

94

She did not stop.

When he closed on her, Teegan grabbed her arm to turn her around, an action that was borderline taboo due to the ages of the pair.

"I'm sorry, I did not mean to laugh." His insult was reflected in her glare.

"It's okay. You are just a stupid boy. I should know better than to make stupid things for stupid boys." She was clearly upset.

Teegan regarded her clothing, fresh flowers in her hair, and spotless of mud and dirt. Lu'Kall had always been one for hunting and fishing, or playing stick ball, not weaving crowns of flowers.

"You look...nice!" Teegan complimented his friend.

"Oh shut up, you ass feather. You know I'd rather split your head open with a cricket stick than wear this crap, but my mother insisted." She stared at the boy for a second, giving away something hidden that he did not understand.

"Has everyone in the tribe gone mad? Why would your mother insist on such a thing?"

"Listen shithead! You are *the* bachelor of the tribe, in case you haven't realized, and your mother has made announcement that you will be married by the end of the festivities. Every available female will be pining for your hand." She stared at him, not immune to whatever plague infected the other women at the camp.

"But why?" Teegan was as lost as a shaman with a fishing pole.

Lu'Kall smacked Teegan on the side of the head, a blow intended to jar some sort of memory that the young man did not yet possess.

"You felled the King of the Plains and on a crossing point none the less. Not only is everything we harvest from the beast filled with magick, so now is your name." The girl was disgusted that the explanation was needed.

"I feel the same," said Teegan. "I don't feel filled with magick..." His tone reflected his secret, the humiliation he still felt by wetting himself during the hunt. Maybe he could tell Lu'Kall. The girl would understand, he had built mud forts with her since he could remember and he knew that, barring a few insults, she would keep his shame to herself. If he could only figure out why she looked at him so strangely!

"You are no shaman, bone brain. You aren't supposed to *feel* any different."

There it was, that hungry look similar to what he had seen before in Tauka'Aun, though much less apparent. But hadn't she just called him a bone brain? She had definitely gone mad.

"Don't you think this is all crazy?" Teegan whispered. "I mean, I know that Halftooth was a big bull, but it is customary for all boys to fell a bull on their first hunt. And come on, invisible lines that were made by a lazy spirit-lines we cannot see, supposedly crossing at the point that he died? That's just crazy talk!"

"You don't believe in the significance?"

Teegan shook his head, and Lu'Kall sighed. Any observer could see her non-verbal indecision to slap him aside the head again or not.

"I know we cannot *see* the crossings, meat tusks! But again, *we* are not shaman. Why do you think there are so many here if it were not true? And even if it were not true, the Earth Mother has seen fit that during your first hunt, the entire tribe would be fed for an entire snow! That in itself, is great magick!" She looked away from his eyes, apparently hoping that she could find a better way to explain things to him written on the laces of his moccasins.

"Stories will be told of you, Teegan Bloodthorn." Her eyes rose up once again to meet his. "And you will know your children, for you have powerful magick."

"Woman, are you mad?" His tone very much resembled the generations of foolish men that had made the same remark.

"You are an idiot, Teegan, but even an idiot must marry, and you *will* choose me as one of your brides or I will be carving my initials into your broken forehead. Am I clear?" She was a field of dry grass set ablaze.

"Wa...wa...one of my brides?" He would definitely rather be staring down the nostrils of the angry bull again. Had he known how things were going to turn out, he sincerely questioned whether he might have stood up to pat Halftooth on the nose rather than making the spear throw.

Lu'Kall over-exaggerated a sigh and a grunt, a well-practiced response for a girl her age and one that made Teegan feel several years *younger* than she.

"Cocktchya wouldn't use your bones for a nest, bull killer, but I'll see you at the ceremony anyhow." She spun on her heels and left him there, more blind and deaf than ever before.

96

The ceremony, the returned brave had not forgotten but rather wished he had. He was not looking forward to eating a meal made of the eyes and heart of the fallen beast, let alone washing it down with its blood. He stared at his shabby carving. It looked like it was carved by a tuskless child with two left hands, and he had to give this to his father.

Could things really get any worse?

***

The boy, swimming in an oil of unwarranted fear and worry, started back towards his stump, transforming the shabby carving into a bonecrafter's masterpiece with intent stare and wild imagination. His focus was so strong that he did not see the feather-garbed figure standing in his path.

Teegan walked head long into the shaman and bounced backward onto his own backside without so much a sway of movement from the living obstacle. When he looked up, he froze; fear, awe, and shame turning into one big rock in his stomach. Not only had he stumbled into the figure without respect or regard, his now-seated position allowed him a perfect view, up close and personal, of the reclusive Eagle.

The eagle-feathered cloak had a hood crafted out of the head of the raptor. The beak was open in a petrified screech that allowed the shaman's face to be seen from below, as though the wearer had been swallowed whole and now peeked out from the inside of the great bird's throat. As if the stern look the shaman gave him were not enough, the delicate features inside the hood, framed by petite tusks, were most definitely belonging to that of a woman.

A very attractive woman with full lips.

A very attractive woman with full lips and large breasts.

A very attractive woman with full lips, large breasts, and two fists on hips that sent Teegan's spirit racing from his brain, just as Morgal had warned.

Necklaces of bone were thick about her, but stopped before they could cover the ample breasts that were pierced with small long bones of some sort of animal. There was little more than a strap of leather covering the shaman's garden. A loose chain of silver hung just below her smooth naval, the muscles framing such could be seen in great detail despite the thick, patterned body paint cracking off in places like a dried mud. Her leather moccasins were laced in the back, and climbed all the way to mid-thigh, meeting the base of the colored designs.

He found his vision hard to focus, as he was certain he had not seen a woman hold that much beauty in her hands in, well, ever.

"Come." The shaman spoke, reaching out a hand to help the boy to his feet.

Teegan looked around, the hustle and bustle of the camp had stopped. The entire tribe stared at them, enthralled by the young hunter's embarrassment.

He did not move. He could not, though his mind strained visibly to order any part of his body to do just that.

"Come," she repeated the word, this time speaking directly to Teegan's hand, which quickly shot upwards and grasped her own.

In the blink of an eye, Teegan found himself being all but dragged out of the camp by the Eagle Shaman. No one said a word, they just watched him leave, nearly a hundred sets of eyes tethered on him. She was only a bit taller than he, yet her strides were difficult to match. They marched (well, the woman marched while Teegan struggled to maintain balance) out of the camp towards the body of Halftooth. Passersby stopped whatever they were doing to watch the two travel out of view, then silently went back to their business as if they had not just seen a boy being abducted from his home.

They passed the body of Halftooth. Soon, the two had hiked out of view of the camp and up the slope of a nearby mountain. The shaman no longer held the young champion's hand, but he still struggled to keep up. In no time at all, the camp was no more than slight streams of smoke in the distance seen by quick glances over the boy's shoulder. Teegan and the woman walked the rest of the afternoon, and the sun reached its western nest. Darkness was a blanket on this side of the ridge and, slowly, the Sky Father would pull that blanket over soon, tucking in the rest of the world.

Teegan could see very little, focusing on the woman's light footsteps for direction. Abruptly the beacons stopped, and the tribe's champion found himself once again on his backside, staring up at an immobile obstacle.

"We are here." Feathers rustled on the cloak as she spoke. With one arm she pushed aside an overhanging bush that covered the entrance to a small cave. Teegan got up, ducked under the patient doorstop, and went inside.

The cave was pitch black for a moment until the shaman entered, muttering a command word, a fire jumped up in the center of the room, nearly blinding the boy, who shielded his eyes long enough for them to adjust. The cave was covered in paintings; herds of Toenuk and flocks of Cocktchya grazed on stone walls. Plainsmen hunted all types of game across mountains, plains, forests, and even from boats, spearing animals in the water many times larger than the Toenuk. On one wall, Plainsmen fought with one another, on another they warred with the humans. Out of the mountains they fought short, sturdy figures with flowing beards. Deep in the forest they squared off against long, slender folk, nearly as tall as the Plainsmen. A mother gave birth, a chief showed his children how to fish, and an old man was put to rest on a burial spire. On the ceiling was a giant eagle, seeming to watch over everything beneath it. The paintings were elaborate and glorious, vividly colored in the styles of his tribe. Teegan's mouth fell open at such beauty and detail; he had seen cave paintings before, but none filled him with pride like this. He swore that the shapes moved, acting out the scenes they depicted, but when he blinked they would be still, accusing stares pointing guilt towards an overactive imagination.

"This is a sacred place." Came words from behind him. Her accent was thick and unlike any in his tribe. "This is for the Eagles to take shelter in these lands. This place will provide you warmth, protection, and even nourishment."

A small trickle of water ran down the cave's southern wall, pooling in a convenient outcropping before draining away to some unknown location. She guided Teegan by the shoulder and cupped her hand in the small pool. When she did so, the water seemed to sparkle with unnatural energy. Her gentle hand moved from shoulder to neck as she filled the boys lip's with the strange water. Right away, energy drained from the hike seemed to creep into his bones, heading to the extreme ends of his limbs and back into his troubled mind, soothing it. She smiled at him, lights from the fire dancing in her eyes. She did not break his stare as she, too, drank from the pool.

That look again! This was another woman-an adult woman, who looked at him as though he were a roasted chunk of roasted Toenuk fat. Tauka'Aun could take lessons from this woman, who had to be nearly old enough to be Teegan's own mother. Still she was a far cry from that, her muscles were like a warrior's, lined and edged better than Kurg's bonerattle. Age had only begun to touch the edges of her eyes but did not line her lips; a sign the woman found little to smile about in the way she was smiling at him right now.

She stood up straight, remnants of her drink running down her lips, droplets splashing on ample breasts. She wiped her mouth as an afterthought and took a step towards him. Teegan stumbled backwards. He nearly fell into the fire, but managed to divert himself onto a pile of very soft and inviting animal skins. He had not noticed the bedroll, at first, due to the wall paintings. He sat there, just as confused and uncomfortable as he was hours earlier in camp. The shaman took another step towards him, one leg in front of the other, accentuating her hips. The lights of the fire framed every curve of the woman's body, as her shadow danced on the wall.

She stood up straight in front of him, unclasping the feathered cloak that covered her. She peeled off the hood and let the drapery fall to her feet. She reached up to the bun of hair tied at the back of her head and slowly shook it loose. Her hair was wild and twisted in muddy locks; it clung closely above her slightly pointed ears and forehead, still tricked into thinking the bun held it captive. She drew her hands slowly backward, eyes closing with the relief of freedom, lips parting with the longing for more.

With hair down, she lowered her gaze. Teegan visibly quivered, parts of his body were responding to her that he didn't ever realize could respond in such a way. He was dizzy and almost sick to his stomach. She slowly pulled the leather strap that was keeping her most personal space free from view. Teegan watched it fall to the floor and thought for a brief moment that his stone sling was quite a bit larger than that, and the object was really of little use for hurling rocks at small prey animals.

His distractive thoughts were shattered as the shaman crouched down, her hand drawing a line from her knee towards her own garden, taking a slow path along a sculpted thigh. His eyes followed her hand, as it seemed to find a strange way to search for that hidden place. As her hand searched, the shaman made the slightest of soft

100

cries, not unlike the muffled moans no one dared discuss. Her eyes once again told the story of freedom.

Teegan's hands moved up to slap the vision from his eyes, but his fingers, the fools, slowly parted so he could see in between them. The shaman was crawling towards him, her hand reaching his ankle.

"What are you do-doing?" Teegan did not stutter, it was a high pitched crack that caused him to start the word again. She crawled up him, her hands inching towards the tops of his thighs.

"There is something we must do while the magick is right, young hunter." Her fingers attacked the laces of his trousers like an orchestrated machine.

He was exposed in an instant, his body pounding with affirmation.

"The magick is right? I don't under..." He could not finish his statement, he had never felt a tusk used quite like that before.

She continued to crawl up his body until they were aligned.

"We must keep our spirits close, young Teegan."

His name sounded odd in her accent.

"The spirits need me to guide you." She pressed against him, her wetness so warm and inviting. Teegan's lower half dared his heart to explode, dared him to take his hands away from their forgotten task of protection.

She licked his tusk and continued, "The spirits say you will need my help to do what must be done. They say we must...keep...our....spirits....close." Between each word she let forth a labored breath. It was music to his ears. His body twitched in rapid convulsions with the final word of her reply, a whirlpool of pleasure replacing the dizziness he had felt before, but the whirlpool did not stop, he was spinning and spinning until...

***

"Come." The shaman spoke, reaching out a hand to help the boy to his feet. Teegan looked around, the hustle and bustle of the camp had stopped. The entire tribe staring at them, enthralled by the young hunter's embarrassment.

He did not move. He could not, though his mind strained visibly to order any part of his body to do just that.

"Come." She repeated the word.

He reached gingerly for her hand, eyebrows not certain how to reflect his confusion. She helped him to his feet, and he took in his surroundings. Everyone was there, staring at him, waiting for him to move but saying nothing. Weren't they just..?

"Where are we going?" he asked the shaman.

"Where have you been, young Teegan?" His name sounded odd in her accent.

"I...I do not know." He was confused. Had that just..?

There was a smile from under the hood that only he could see, a smile that knew too much, yet revealed not enough.

"I suppose that does not matter, Thorn of Blood. I suppose it only matters where you go from here." She stared at the hand he still held, and he quickly let it go.

"Come. It is time we begin." With that she turned towards the fallen bull and began to walk, it was a strange mixture of poses and dancing, ruffling up the feathers of her cloak as any eagle would.

Ravens and Vultures watched her, heads twitching and tilting just like their feathered animal totems.

Teegan cautiously trailed her at a distance as other members of the tribe stopped what they were doing and fell in tow. All of them following the chanting and dancing of an Eagle Shaman, so far away from home.

Welcome to Balanced Rock

The day was a hot one. The sun stared down on the countryside unhindered by the sheets of clouds and light blue sky. Spring was gone, unable to hold back the promises of a long summer.

The Priestess Raen stepped gingerly from her floating carriage onto the sturdy set of steps beside it. She had been preceded by two well-dressed chamber maids and an all too thin clerk whose shrewd eyes and shapeless hips made her look like a serpent. A silent monstrosity of a man held Raen's left hand for added stability as she lifted her long robes with her right. His garb was the color of fallen snow, a loose fitting tunic and wide-legged trousers tightly cuffed at wrist and ankle. A white bandana covered a hairless head, protecting the skin beneath that was nearly as bleached as the clothing. The man seemed to function despite the impairment of a white leather blindfold that covered both of his eyes. A huge black dog stood next to him like a carving from a master sculpture. On all fours the beast stood to the man's waist. The pair were difficult to behold, frozen in time, yet waiting to spring to life at a moment's notice.

Raen wore the robes of a Sabrinian Matron, a priestess whose rank nearly rivaled the Mother of Doctrine herself. Attired in a grandiose garb of embroidered silks of rich purples and whites, her breasts were pushed out and up to near exposure, then covered with a diaphanous veil originating from a long hat with draping tassels at its highest point. Her waist length hair was braided into spirals on the back of her head, customary for the style of the times. A Sabrinian priestess was more than a religious figurehead; they were the idols of the public, the trend setters, the epitome of beauty and grace. She wore earrings of tear shaped jewels and necklaces that carried more wealth than the small town had ever seen in one place, and her gaudy bracelets clanked together as she stepped off the stairs onto the long carpet rolled out from the doorway of her house.

Servants lined the carpet on both sides, dressed in the formal bleached white, down on all fours with hands crossed above their heads. Foreheads rested on the back of their palms, the servants breathed as slowly as possible as to appear unmoving for their newly arrived mistress. Armed guards, with armor freshly polished were placed at every entrance of the newly constructed villa, also stood motionless and would do so despite provocation unless ordered otherwise.

Town folk gathered around the entrance to the villa in a wide half-circle. Balanced Rock was not a big place, and its people had never had the privilege of seeing a Goddess Carriage nor a detachment of palace guards. Like any construction project, people had gotten used to walking by the villa while it was being built. Now it was complete and surrounded by soldiers in shiny steel helmets with tall plumes of violet-dyed horse hair that made them resemble more of a house decoration than the battle-hardened field warriors seen riding into town in the past. Servants existed in Balanced Rock, of course, but not bridled with the formality seen here. Slavery was a right every woman in Sabrinia had, and it was practiced more and more the closer that one got to the cities.

Ambrosia Moria Max, formally known as the wealthiest woman in town, had several servants. But this far away from civilization, she had allowed them to wear their own clothing and even gone so far as to give some of them names. She owned the town tavern, a bakery, a tailor shop, and a large cattle ranch on the northern edge of town. She was the head of her estate. Her husband Filius, who had proven himself a shrewd and beneficial asset, took care of many of the less important dealings of her estate; but none the less always managed to put a significant amount of coin in her coffers. This pattern of behavior allowed him a significant level of freedom for the typical Sabrinian husband. Ambrosia waited with other members of significance at the base of the Goddess Carriage. Ambrosia had never before seen one of the luxurious floating carriers outside of the bigger cities and had forgotten how majestic and awe inspiring they were. Like a long extended version of a regular horse-pulled carriage, this floating version had no wheels. Its operation was a complete mystery, said to be carried by the hands of the Goddess herself. Ambrosia remembered her first ride in one as a girl. No bumps or jarring, rocking motions, just the sense of floating on the clouds. She remembered seeing the man walking outside the drifting marvel, guiding it with a single hand. She remembered the luxurious pillows inside, the gold trim, and the velvets. Years later, she had learned the Sabrinians use similar floating wagons to transport the enormous base stones of the pyramids, fully crafted obelisks and statutes, or even several support pillars at once; all carried by the ever present hands of the Goddess.

Like Ambrosia, the other women standing at the base of the mounting steps sat on the town council. All of the women had several things in common, all had land and businesses in Balanced Rock, all maneuvered for position within the circle for magistrate status, and all were deathly afraid of what a Matron Priestess would do to upset the political balance of the small town. It was not an unfounded fear. Raen was literally given Balanced Rock, a gift for her years of service, from the High Priestess herself. The council women were about to find out just what that meant. There they stood in their finest gowns, made from materials less expensive than Raen's servants'.

"Welcome to Balanced Rock, Matron." Ambrosia did not raise her head from its forward position.

Raen let her gathered robes fall to the ground and leisurely released the supportive grasp from the blindfolded man. He stepped to the rear of her and stared straight ahead, somehow giving the feeling he was able to look at all of the council members at once. No, he didn't look *at* all of them, he seemed as if he looked *through* all of them.

"We thank you for your hospitality." The answer came from the clerk, her analytical mind calculating the value of the items worn by the people in front of her, and the potential value of the people themselves.

The Matron remained speechless. She looked around, waving at the town folk that had gathered around, smiling as the crowd began to cheer, a crowd that grew bigger with every passing moment.

"Matron, welcome." The greeting came from Herminia Camdania, owner of the town's blacksmith and a small ranch of her own. She was a beautiful woman, known to enjoy the company of all of her workers regardless of the presence of wedding vows; she was easily weakened by a set of broad shoulders often associated with men in her trade.

"Welcome, Matron." This was Otillia Mialka. She owned a storage facility for coin and belongings. She had acquired a large amount of Man'Antian dogmen in a game of cards and their loyalty had allowed for the venture.

Dana Travenore, Tanya Daisee, and Geneeve Luena followed in suit, each greeting the priestess and each being ignored by all except a growingly impatient clerk, who tapped on what appeared to be an oblong book with wooden covers and strange bindings.

The carriage guards, who wore grandiose engraved armor and visored helms that covered the entire face, stood at attention. They had oversized pauldrens protecting their shoulders, polished bracers defending arms, and shin guards to the knee. Flowing cloaks, covered mostly with holstered shields, rippled slightly as they leaned upon their pilum that were thrust slightly forward. Oddly, they were bare-chested. Sexes almost indistinguishable due to borderline grotesque physiques, the two men and two women had stomachs etched in stone. They formed a square perimeter around the group, facing outward. Hidden eyes shifted about, taking in every detail.

The clerk took a step forward, opening the oddly shaped book, the cover opening all the way 'round to lock together with the back. It had perfect recesses carved into it for a specially designed ink pot and quill. After a second or two of brief assembly, the thin woman had a mobile desk, perfect for taking notes. Another special recess in the now-assembled desk appeared to be a drawer filled with a velvet padding. Inside were a pair of reading glasses that the shapeless woman put on her hollow face. She skewed her face in an attempt to wedge the glasses into position, aiding the inadequate muscles with a push from her index finger. The spectacles seemed to enlarge her already viperous eyes, giving the woman both the appearance of vulnerable prey and menacing predator at the same time. Her cream-colored robes were pressed to perfection. Ambrosia would have surmised that the woman spent hours straightening her gown after her journey had she not witnessed her slither from the carriage just moments before. Pristine as the garments were, a single wrinkle would have stood out as if an entire goblet of red wine spilled on the plain gowns. Unlike the flamboyant fashions of the capitol, these coverings did not have the purpose nor the cut needed for exposing any flesh, instead the only real patters of note were the Sabrinian griffins that were embroidered on small lapels near a too-thin neck. Her hair was pulled back so tightly, Ambrosia thought it may tear out at the scalp.

Priestess Raen continued to greet the distant onlookers, but did not make eye contact with the women around her. She had no need. Everything that would need to be said would be done at tomorrow's town address. There would be a lot of changes coming to this community so fallen in its way. It would be up to Raen to set everyone straight. She motioned to the thin woman, who cleared her throat. A hush came from the many sets of lips in the crowd that awaited the new policies that the Matron Mother would bring to their small rural town.

"The Matron Mother, Keeper of the Doctrine, and First of the House Nona would like to thank you for coming to her arrival today. In the many glorious days to come, the Matron Mother hopes to see and get to know each and every one of you. For the time being, you may leave any and all tributes to the Matron Mother here at the front gate, Goddess be praised. Tomorrow, you kind folk of Balanced Rock shall hear from Her Own Voice, as she will address the entire town in the Village Square after breakfast. May you walk with the Goddess; peace and good will to your children; may you show no mercy to our enemies."

When the clerk concluded the speech, Raen refurbished her appearance to the crowd as if the words had ridden on breath propelled from her own lungs. The people of Balanced Rock responded with a roar of approval, though not a single member of the crowd was truly aware of the last time someone addressed the whole town in the Village Square, let alone what a proper tribute to leave a Keeper of the Doctrine would be.

Raen looked at the clerk and, with a coded nod, began to walk towards the center of town. There was a slight bustle as the entourage formed into rows behind her. The blindfolded man flanked the priestess, seeing nothing and everything all at once, his giant hound by his side. The four honor guards moved in perfect form, maintaining a perimeter around the religious leader. Six council members awkwardly fell in tow with the two chambermaids bringing up the rear. The crowd parted for the soldiers, everyone trying to get a closer look at the group as they passed. Ambrosia could not recall the last time she had felt embarrassment like an awkward schoolgirl, but she was certain that this moment topped it.

Balanced Rock was nothing special as far as size or location. It was a modest town whose inhabitants were hardworking and driven. They were nestled far enough from the Plainsmen to the northeast and Cliff Peoples of the Southern Gorge to be of little threat to either, and so had been able to live in relative peace. As such, it had grown slowly and in much disarray. There was no real sense of organization when it came to street and building construction, leaving inhabitants to navigate an asymmetrical hedge-maze of both residences and businesses alike. This was of no concern for the people of Balanced Rock, it was the way things had always been, and they liked it that way. Most of the townsfolk also stayed out of their country's odd political games. Strict integration of doctrine law and civil law had very little use out in this remote of a location. Many of the men, like Ambrosia's husband, held almost as much weight in town matters as the women. Though, ultimately, final say almost always fell to the decision of the women's council, as tradition dictated. None the less the naming of slaves, popularity of monogamous marriage, and lack of castrations was something this priestess would not allow. This small town was destined for greatness, and Raen would see that those conspirators that removed her from the capitol would rue the day they chose sides against her. Her villa here had not been a gift, it had been a prison sentence, and she planned to make a feast of whatever those butchers had carved out of her life.

Parting rows of people, moving while they talked amongst themselves, shielded children from potentially getting run over by the protective honor guard as they passed. The group wound around a building as they got towards the center of town. Abruptly, the high priestess stopped. The soldiers, the blindfolded man, the chambermaids, and even the clerk who was taking notes in the book must have had some sort of foresight, because all stopped with the perfect precision of a well-rehearsed dance troupe. The same was not so with the council women who bunched up like an accordion, Ambrosia's arms spread wide to avoid further conundrum. The clerk looked over her shoulder in a flash of disgust.

The Matron still had not spoken since getting off of the Goddess Carriage, a fact that made all of the counsel women's' skin crawl and raised hairs as they passed. They awaited a word, just any word to assure them that change would not be too drastic, that the small town of Balanced Rock would be the same. Raen began to tap her fingers on her arm, now crossed in quiet contemplation. She stepped toward the village well, located in the center of town, surrounded by businesses and houses. She looked back towards her villa, where the view was blocked due to a two story building. The priestess looked at the building, past it towards her villa, and back again to the town well. Her fingers tapped rapidly, creating a sound that pierced the ears of the six council members, driving tension into the center of their minds.

One word would stop all this, if the woman would just speak. One word to convince the women that the town would be fine. Just one word to drown out the incessant tapping. Raen paced back and forth a few more times, eyeing both the center of town and her villa, and the building in between. She moved her tapping hand to her chin, an action that somehow made the situation worse. She stared at the clerk, who approached her and began to mimic the priestess' observations, pacing behind her in what appeared to be an odd sort of child's game. Again, and without warning, they stopped. The priestess folded her hands and began casually walking back towards the group. Her smile did not touch her eyes. Still she did not speak.

"Whose building is this?" Again the clerk, not the Matron Mother, broke the uneasy silence. It was agonizing for Ambrosia and the others.

"It is my building...errr..." Dana Travenore responded, not quite sure who to address.

"You may speak to Her Own Voice." The serpent-woman made a face that was more of a sneer than a comforting grin.

"It is my building, Matron. My bakery. We have made bread there for generations. Would you like..."

"The building must be moved." The shapeless woman interrupted Dana's offer.

Ambrosia imagined that the clerk actually drew out the "s" sound in the way a serpent would, if one could talk.

"I don't understan..." Dana began but again was cut short.

"The Keeper of the Doctrine is here by the will of the Goddess. That will we must all follow."

Ambrosia was not certain the sound was in her imagination after all.

"What shall I do, though?" Dana genuinely did not know the answer.

The clerk looked at Raen briefly, then turned back to Dana with the same sneer.

"The will of the Goddess is mysterious, councilor. Nevertheless, the building must be moved by the week." She looked at Dana absently, then beyond her in a manner of thought before making notes on her notebook.

"How will I move my..." This time Dana was interrupted by a hand on her shoulder, it was Ambrosia with a look of both understanding

109

and warning. She was certain she had seen a forked tongue shoot from the clerk's mouth, further argument would only bring fangs to bare. Dana, defeated, nodded to Raen in compliance, who in turn smiled lovingly at her, a proud councilwoman turned beggar lacking arms and legs.

The priestess began walking again, and the council members dared to exchange glances as they once again fell in line. This had been the first stop in the tour of Balanced Rock, and already one woman would be tearing down her family business to relocate it. Ambrosia did not think for one second that the rest of them would escape unscathed; in fact, as she watched the woman jotting notes down in front of her, she knew it would be quite the opposite. Ambrosia closed her eyes and bit her lips, praying to the Goddess that the tapping did not start near one of her buildings and secretly dreading it might start near her home.

Ambrosia and the other council women had chosen to stay away from the capitol for many reasons, each unique to a woman. All knew one thing was for certain, law was written in the doctrine. Ambrosia and her husband had a son, and the Scriptures said he must join the army for the majority of his years. Only through blind luck did boys like hers turn into men, and both she and her husband Filius would be doing their best to make sure that happened. On top of it, she loved her husband. He was not a perfect man by any means; in fact, he had more problems with rolling dice and drink than most, yet he was a good man. A solid provider of trade and a shrewd business man, Filius was more than influential in the success of her business. Who was to say that he wasn't allowed to drink and play dice until all hours of the morning like the women?

Otillia had her dogman slaves. Obedient soldiers and guardians procured from Man'Antas. Four men whose odd features did not abstract their virtue. They had become, over the years, accepted members of the community. Running errands, helping out with needed labor, and doing whatever else their master needed of them. In return, she had given them their own names, their own housing, even their own allowance. Any one of these went against the Goddess's will.

Herminia, Geneeve, and Tanya also had reasons for doubt and had long ago started meeting with Otillia and Ambrosia out at the Maxs' home. It had been Genève's bold tongue that had gotten them interested in the movement years ago. Oddly enough, the only councilwoman that was on the fence about joining in on the secret

110

meetings was Dana. Now that she would be tearing down her shop and moving it at the whims of a pampered priestess, her choice of sides may have been made for her. Ambrosia knew, now that they were united in disbelief, they could make more happen than the occasional slave rescue or jail break, she just did not know how much more.

Helping a slave escape here and there was small time and of little risk due to the town's relative isolation. Now the citizens of Balanced Rock's very way of life could be in jeopardy due to the presence of the villa and its unwanted fanatic. If the Keeper of the Doctrine was even half as stringent as her reputation preceded, then the councilwomen would all be in for a painful adjustment, if there were a place left for the council at all.

The Red District Woman

The day was a hot one. The sun stared down on the countryside unhindered by the sheets of clouds and light blue sky. Spring was gone, unable to hold back the promises of a long summer.

"...I heard they nearly caught him this time." The bald man said as he approached his only audience.

"Oh, Yurri. Who cares? He's a criminal. He will have his days on the gallows. What do they call him?"

"The Treesnake." There was a sense that he was describing the sun rising from the darkest night in the history of darkest nights.

"Goddess, you say it like he's got Herrodius' strength and a Valkyr's wings." The woman smiled at the cobbler, obviously a great deal more than storeroom banter had exchanged between these two.

"Valkyr are always women, Aggy." Hands on his hips only helped the tone condescend her.

"Well, I'm sorry, but seriously, Yurri. What kind of a 'hero' calls themselves the Treesnake?"

"A hero with a huge, glorious, cock."

"It's always about sex with you..."Agytha was talking out the side of her mouth, the other side reserved for her signature grin.

"Not, always. I like to suck them, too..."

He cringed a bit right before she hit the man playfully, and they both laughed. She took a minute to finish lacing up the shoe maker's latest creation.

Agytha ran both of her hands up one of the well-oiled boots. They were absolutely magnificent! Every time she ordered a new pair, Yurri simply out did himself. The craftsman was the best bootmaker in the country, and arguably the world. This time he had created another masterpiece, boots that went past the knee with designs cut out in the back to expose her thin calf and lacey stockings. The heels were nearly twice the length of her thumb adding over a hand's height to her own, all the while accentuating her calves and curvy backside. They smelled of leather, and the wooden heels shined magnificently, the entire package warmed her cheeks and other areas of her body. This was an elation that took the place of physical touch, a necessary desensitizing aspect of her particular line of work. Agytha held her leg straight forward with agility and grace, cocked her head to the side as she took in the sight. Goddess, these boots were amazing! They complimented her high slit skirt and tightened corset to perfection, and Agytha even surmised they would go well with her floppy wide-brimmed hat that hung up on the shop's coatrack.

"You like?" Yurri knew the answer, but a not-so-hidden vainness demanded a compliment.

"Oh, I like!" Agytha spoke to the boots as if they were her favorite lover.

"I took the liberty of adding in your...signature...touch of...class." Yurri purred out the phrase as if he were a house cat getting a perfect scratch.

Agytha reached down to the heel, finding a perfectly hidden lever in the finished wood. When she pressed it, a blade sprung forth, extending out nearly the same length as the heel. Agytha squeaked like a child on Gift Day finding a new pony tethered outside.

"Yurri, you are the best! Simply the best! I would like to order another pair...in white."

The man raised an eyebrow, halfway thinking that his best customer had forgotten the cost of this pair, let alone the cost of..."White?" he asked.

"Yes, white. Thank you so much! They are amazing!" She tossed the cobbler a pre-counted bag of coin, then another of the same. Yurri did not have to ask for the final piece of steel flipping end over end towards him, he just had to react fast enough to catch it without dropping the rest.

"Agytha, you know I have never put my nose where it doesn't belong..." Yurri knew this to be untrue, and his grin deceived his words, nevertheless he continued, "...but you have a lot of extra coin lately. Do you have a new best customer? Some new type of Lord from the Nine Kingdoms come through town that you have cast your spell on? If so, do tell! And does he have a brother?"

"Oh, Yurri, you flatter me!" She feigned innocence. "And you know that if I ever needed a shieldman in my exploits, you would be the first to know. Unfortunately, no Sailor Lord or Pirate King has fallen victim to my wooing." She paused, calculating the hidden price she was paying for her new boots. Yurri did not miss this. She nonchalantly stood, and examined her entire outfit in one of the man's many expensive mirrors.

Yurri was nearly a decade older than Agytha, and the years, though not vast in number, had long since stolen his hair. Aside from this, and a rather hooked nose, he was a handsome man, and an expert in his field. His flair for the extravagant made him popular amongst the wealthy women of Sabrinia, and his comfort on his knees made him popular amongst many of the men. Agytha was his best customer and his best friend. Working together, they had been able to circumvent many of the obstacles presented by the Sabrinian idea of proper breeding; especially with Yurri being a man, and Agytha having a profession that was decidedly distasteful in higher circles. Of the many tools they developed, the two had a near miraculous ability to get on the same mental wavelength, finish each other's sentences, and know exactly when the other was trying to hide something, especially when it came to tastes in men. Right now, Yurri knew Agytha was trying to hide something.

"Speak, sister, or I'll be forced to cut half an inch off your left boot heel and leave you there to wobble like an old woman." His hips were offset and used to balance one hand while he pointed at her boots with the other.

Agytha looked visibly wounded. In fact, one of her own hands pressed against ample bosom as if something deep inside her chest had been attacked.

"You wouldn't dare!" She exaggerated.

"I would. Now out with it!" His arms were crossed in a parent's practiced pose.

"I have taken on two new clients." A bit of embarrassment leaked towards the surface of her cheeks. "Unlike any clients I have taken on before."

"This sounds like biting into a passion fruit! Go on! Dog men? Wanderers? Don't tell me....you're fucking one of those savage Plainsmen..." Yurri was clearly not waiting for a response.

Agytha thought that she may be able to walk right out of the shop and leave him to his artist's mind, but her escape route was cut off with a stern look.

"They aren't that type of clients, when I say they are unlike any clients I had before, I meant it." She struggled with the statement. It was hard for her to explain.

114

"Oh, you had me at 'they.' Go on! Go on!" He took her seat, leaning in with his shoulders as if it would help him hear better.

"It's these two young ladies. They..."

"Wait...ladies? Boring! You were never into ladies..."

"I was never *not* into them either." Agytha corrected. "Do you want me to tell you or not?"

"Yes, yes." Yurri had admittedly lost a bit of interest. Who cared about a tussle with a couple young noblewomen? Such things were nothing new.

"They are the High Lady's daughters." Agytha's head was down, but she looked up to her friend, wincing for an expected blow.

"What?! The twins?!" Yurri was exasperated. So much so he nearly fell over the chair clamoring up to get to her. She held her hands up, an awkward cross between a defense and bracing her clumsy friend.

"You fool girl! You cannot bed down with those two witches! No matter how good the coin! They'll turn on you when it suits them and everything we've worked for will be for not! If something were to happen to you, I..."

"Oh, Yurri. I know how much you like the parties but, if anything, we are just party favors. We do not approach with introduction like the other guests; we are the bringers of debauchery. The late night arrivals for the truly depraved. Nothing more." She rested a hand on her friend's cheek to calm the plea in his eyes.

"Well, that's easy for you to say, you strumpet! You have a vagina! I am cursed in these lands!" Yurri's hands motioned to his branding by birthright.

"That is exactly why I have to play this game. It's not just for the coin, it's for the camaraderie. There is no higher voice in Sabrinia than the High Priestess herself, and that woman is only reachable through whatever is most precious to her." She walked across the room to the ornate bar in the corner, pouring herself and the cobbler a glass of wine. She sauntered over to him, a somber look in her eye.

"My brother has been locked in the temple for nearly a year now. I am fortunate that these two vixens have developed such a staunch appetite for voyeurism."

"Wait, they only like to watch?" Yurri finished the question with a face that could have meant the wine had gone sour.

"For now, though every week their curiosity grows like a vine." Agytha pursed her lips.

"Do you really think that this...exhibitionism will get you closer to your brother?'"

"I can only hope. If not, being close to them is the next best thing...."

"For what?" Yurri was baffled. Did he even know the woman in front of him? He tried to search for the answer in a sip of wine.

"Revenge." The voice came from behind them. Yurri spit the swallow of alcohol in a wide spray, startled by the unexpected intruder.

Yurri turned to see a man in common clothes holding a straw workman's hat in one hand and the shop's bell in the other. The man was the same age as Agytha and frightfully handsome. He was not overly tall, but his eyes were such an emerald green they belonged in a crown for the Goddess herself. He was unshaven for a week, dark stubble only framing a smile that moistened lips and unlaced trousers. His dark hair, shaved closely on the sides, was disheveled, but almost as if it had been done on purpose. He released the bell to scrub his hand through it, snapping it into position. The man was covered in dirt, as if it too could not get close enough to a youthful body framed by hard work and too-perfect breeding. Yurri would have been jealous had his heart not been pounding out of his chest.

"Lover!" Agytha said, as she moved in to kiss the man, oblivious to the cloud of dirt he now tracked into her best friend's shop.

"Goddess, Koll'Ynn, you scared my dick off!" Yurri still held his chest, checked his manhood to verify he had indeed made a joke, and moved to retake a safe position on the stool.

After some time he regained missing breath, only to see the two still in heated embrace. It was a fairy tale picture of a lady kissing her servant-love. Yurri found it both beautiful and enviously disgusting.

"Oh, goat cock! Get a room! And not in here, you're filthy!"

Koll'Ynn approached the seated bootmaker, and gave him a kiss on the cheek, and a hearty pat on the back. Yurri smiled and took his arm in order to help himself up for a proper greeting.

"What brings you in here, besides trying to give us...well me...a heart attack?" Yurri asked.

"Well, I was working on that special project we started a few days ago." Koll'Ynn walked towards Agytha who shook her head so her hair fell down her back, preparing for another kiss. Even though the boots made her nearly as tall as he, she somehow shrank down so that he could tilt her head back for the embrace. Right before his lips touched hers, he continued, "I needed a bit of a break..." a small kiss "...so I went upstairs to the tavern for a drink..." another, this time longer than the last, "turns out, you had a message. Oenrus said you were going shopping. So here. I. Am." Each pause meant another kiss. Each kiss meant another sigh from a deprived boot maker.

"Seriously, you two. You're killing me." Yurri could not help but watch the pretty picture painted before him.

"What is the message?" Agytha rubbed her hands together before turning them into a wiggling receptacle for the rolled up parchment. She unrolled it, it was written in careful hand:

Red District Woman

Please attend us at the Temple this evening. We are in need of your expert tutelage. We so appreciate your skills and hope that our prior cost arrangement will suffice.
Thank you for your valuable time.

"The twins." Agytha began tearing up the note. She looked at Koll'Ynn, who widened his eyes and tilted his head towards Yurri.

"He knows. I told him," Agytha responded.

"So you made your decision?" Koll'Ynn was matter-of-fact.

"We need him, Koll. He can help us." Agytha was making a case to a man who had already heard the argument. Koll'Ynn put his hands out wide in surrender.

"*He* can know what in the Keeper's Grave you are talking about."

Yurri was concerned and finding a courage forged in decisions being made without his choice.

Agytha looked at both men before continuing to address her lover. "Servants pick up their master's orders. What better way to pass information than through a box of shoes?" She was still undecided.

"You don't have to tell me. Tell *him.*"

"YES!" Urged Yurri. "Tell *him!* I mean, tell me! Wait! Tell me what?"

117

Agytha looked at Koll'Ynn. It was hard for her to ask her friend to do what she was about to ask him to do. Her lover patted her on the shoulder and stepped back to the cobbler. He took the empty wine glass and turned towards Agytha, motioning for some refilled lubrication for the upcoming exchange.

"Sit, Yurri." Koll'Ynn guided the man to the stool, then pulled up another to sit in front of him. Agytha brought the refilled glass of wine to Koll'Ynn who passed the baton off with dirt-crusted finger nails.

"You really do need a bath," Yurri said, accepting the drink with only two fingers, as if the grunge would somehow be contagious.

Koll'Ynn smiled. That smile. Whatever he was about to say was going to be good.

"Yurri. Agytha and I have gotten ourselves into something." Agytha approached her lover, put a hand on his back. "It's something more important than any one of us." He held her hand.

"Oh, Goddess! You're pregnant." Yurri finished the wine in a single gulp and beckoned Agytha for a refill.

"No. Nothing that bad." Agytha joked as she went to retrieve the wine bottle.

"Thank God!" Yurri was puzzled. He did not know how the pieces of the puzzle fit together.

"There is an unbalance here, Yurri. For men. For slaves. An unbalance that is blindly followed due to words written in ancient fictions." Koll'Ynn had clearly given the speech before.

"And...?"

"And some of us don't like it too much." Agytha interrupted.

"There are a lot of people that feel this way, Yurri." Koll'Ynn pressed the sale. "The way some of us are treated. The gladiators, the servants. The Otherbreeds. Men." He paused. "How much do you pay in taxes?"

"Excuse me?" Yurri was totally confused.

"Taxes, how much do you pay for them? For your use of this shop you had to build?"

"I don't know...I guess a fair amount...I..."

"Do you want to know what Agytha pays for the tavern?" Koll'Ynn knew exactly how the business man would respond. He shook his head, somewhere near anger and disgrace.

"There is an unbalance here, Yurri. For us." His hand gestures where a rapid sewing of the two men together.

"And some of us don't like it too much." Agytha refilled the wine glass yet again. She looked back and forth at her two favorite people in the world, and they both could see it in her eyes. A hand on Yurri's shoulder sealed the deal.

"Oh, I get it!" Yurri sipped his wine and chuckled. "Yurri gets it alright. But what exactly are you planning on doing? What can the three of us do to a thousand year old machine of brainwashing religion, military conquest, and systematic genocide of entire peoples that have tried to bring them down?" He sipped his wine, a perky bird waiting for a response from two people that had obviously gone mad.

"Seriously, you two? What are the three of us going to do, ruin the entire country one blistered foot at a time?" Yurri spoke too fast, his friends' looks were stern resolve, if this was a joke, the punch line wasn't coming out anytime soon. Even an entirely uncomfortable laugh did not aid in cracking the facade the bootmaker only wished existed.

"I mean really, Agytha. Koll. Look. What can we do? We don't have an army. Look, I don't like things any more than you do. I mean I once saw some guards do...unspeakable things...to a Tyrian girl and then leave her for...I just...look. Oh, Goddess! I keep saying 'look.' I mean, it's not like we are going to start a revolution here, are we?"

Koll'Ynn and Agytha did not openly answer, they just looked at each other and then back at the stuttering cobbler. He looked at them both, his mouth opening for words and head shaking back and forth, but there were no strings attaching his movements to theirs'. They just stared at him, giving no quarter. He went to drink from an empty wine glass, and Agytha moved to refill it. Yurri pulled the bottle out of her hand and drained the rest. When he finished, he looked at the pair of them.

"Goddess' cunt. You want a revolution." The bootmaker sighed. "Well, I seem to have run out of wine. If we are going to talk blisters, then you two fucking love birds can pick up the bar tab."

"So you're in?" Agytha asked him a question that was more of a second chance for her best friend to back down.

"Of course I am, you whore." The same friendship that allowed the name calling forced him into service, despite the perceived choice otherwise.

"Alright, I'll fill you in on what we have done so far." Koll'Ynn again helped the craftsman up. Turning to Agytha he nodded in understanding: "You have work to do."

"That I do." She responded with an embrace that said so much more than the simple acknowledgement. "Take Yurri to the baths, tell Cera to put them, and as many bottles as you two need, on my tab. You need to clean yourself up, you dirty boy." Those words meant so much more as well.

"Oh! Can I help bathe you, Koll?"

"No, Yurri." Agytha answered, consciously defending her mate from unwanted awkwardness. "Though I'm sure he would be very appreciative of such a cleaning."

"Oh, he has no idea, girl." Yurri was saucy with his jest, and both he and Agytha smiled at Koll's obvious trepidation.

Koll'Ynn exited the shop first, leaving the two best friends to linger inside for a moment while Yurri locked up. The pair stared at each other.

"I hope you know what you are doing." Yurri said with a worried flavor lingering on his tongue.

"So do I, my friend. So do I."

The two embraced, a hug that twisted them in a tangled sway for a long moment. They knew what one another were thinking when they parted and looked into each other's eyes. They were about to take a tremendous risk, to what ends, neither was certain.

They were, however, certain of the cost of failure.

Agytha and Yurri caught up with Koll'Ynn outside, the two men heading opposite her to the direction of the baths, while she strolled down the cobblestone street towards the Great Lift. Rarely did she take a Goddess Carriage or Sky Chariot to see the twins, the cool summer wind after her visits helped her to think. She looked back over her shoulder at her departing lover and best friend as they disappeared into the crowd. Yurri had his arm over Koll'Ynn's shoulder, chatting about something of obvious grandeur. Koll'Ynn laughed with him, entertained by the shoemaker's flamboyant and intoxicating pizzazz. How she loved him for putting up with the bald fellow.

120

Koll'Ynn was willing to risk anything to make the girl happy, and some of those risks were far more dangerous than sharing a bath with a friend who actually enjoyed watching him undress. Agytha knew that he was her chance to see her brother again, she knew that he was the one that won a game of stones before any of the pieces were played.

She stopped at the town crier, passing out drawings of a wanted criminal. She smiled as she examined the "wanted" sign for the notorious Treesnake. The vile criminal known for smuggling slaves and stealing money. She thought the likeness of a clean shaven man with a wide-brimmed hat was not very accurate at all.

Well, maybe it would be a bit closer after he took a bath.

Beast of Burden

The day was a hot one. The sun stared down on the countryside unhindered by the sheets of clouds and light blue sky. Spring was gone, unable to hold back the promises of a long summer.

Maesma sat in the tree above the hill like a falcon. The spot offered a vantage point from a safe distance that even the actual raptor would have difficulty with, but not Maesma. His vision was locked into another world, one estranged from that of normal men. If there was one thing the seasoned hunter had learned in all his years, it was that Plainsmen were not the savages most humans took them for. The people of the plains were keen survivalists and had an appreciation for the land the man had never seen in another race. He respected them; he respected their passion for life and freedom, mostly because it was a passion he never developed. His years of murder weighed on him, and these ideas like passion seemed to put a sharp pain in his spine that reminded him of a price he paid living without it for all this time. There was never anything but the hunt for *mangmu lieren*; the sweet rush of the kill, the moment when the prey gives its last breath and the predator breathes it in. This was not passion though. This was just the kill, and the only thing it was good for was slating the hunger for a short time before the next.

Beneath him, obedient as stone statues, lay his two hellhounds. The males, Jove and Romule, were Sabrinian Mastiffs, bred for size, ferocity, and obedience in such a meticulous manner that even the Man'Antians respected the long-haired canines. This pair of hellhounds augmented Maesma's weakness in the physical world. Their tools were that of their ancestors, using the scent of their prey and unbridled endurance to run them down for days on end if need be.

Though both Jove and Romule could smell the camp fires in the adjacent valley, the scent of roasting meat, the drying of thick hides, they could not see what their master saw from his perch above them. Maesma was *mangmu lieren*, aimless hunter in the old tongue. His vision was locked in the spirits of all things, and so he could see the energy of any being no matter how small or massive it may be. Experienced hunters could see how the energies of air and fire blended with smoke, they could see how water heated and cooled in cycles, they could even see the mist-like Veins of the Earth, flowing above the ground like a river turned on its side, and known by many different names in many different places. Yet for all of this vision, *mangmu lieren* were literally blind to all things un-living; a brick wall, a bridge, even something as simple as a rope were bane to a hunter.

Maesma had never before seen such a gathering of the Pigbacks. Mostly women and children, the large group had nearly 30 warriors, and among those, he counted five weavers. These five were no doubt the shaman of the tribe, and their life forces shone like the moon in a sea of stars. To slay one of these would be a challenge, but five at once? That would be nearly impossible. The last two kills he had made had been a chambermaid and a guard; two spiders he had to step on for fear of a slippered foot being soiled. Spiders. Not a challenge suited for the most experienced hunter-killer in all of Sabrinia.

He dropped down from the tree and, like a fog creeping across a lake, disappeared into the woods without a sound. Jove and Romule followed him, crouching down, their black coats blending into the shadows.

***

Teegan rolled over. Mostly, this was due to the sharp pain in his groin caused by a kneecap from one of his new children. The assailant now bounded away from the wounded Plainsmen with intoxicating laughter as only a youngling can possess. Adjusting to being married had been difficult the past few days, and it wasn't just because his two new sons where at the perfect height for a square punch to sensitive areas. Nor was it the fact that they somehow found those sensitive areas despite the presence of bedding. The difficulty wasn't found with the discovery of what that look that a woman gave a man meant. Fact was, that 'adjustment' had ended up being a huge plus. The change wasn't even awkward due to the arguments his two wives, Tauka'Aun and Lu'Kall, constantly had over who would be his third. The adjustment to being married was tough because of the decisions he was now expected to be a part of.

123

His marriages had been the final rites of his manhood, as such, they were performed on the final day of his First Hunt Ceremony. His mother had deemed him worthy of the great honor of having three wives. An honor that sent nearly every man in the tribe giggling behind his back as he walked away. Hearing the men chuckle was a behavior he had yet to understand. Tauka'Aun, whose previous marriage made her masterful with both her hands and her hips, kept his mind spinning in a whirlpool of pleasure nearly every time he entered his teepee. His second wife, Lu'Kall, was even younger than himself, yet still would not allow age or experience to detour her vigor and drive for being a 'dutiful' wife. The two had made the days pleasant and the nights even more so. And because of this, Teegan could not understand why the other tribesmen mocked him. Yet muffled laughter or no, and with or without his full understanding, he was now considered a man. This meant that he had to sit and discuss for long hours those things that the men found important.

Today, the men of the Bloodthorn Tribe would decide where best to travel for the summer. There were many options and each tribesman, or rather each tribesman's wife, had their favorite place to spend the warmer days. One thing that was different this year, as opposed to previous years, was the abundance of new hides they had collected from the fallen Toenuk sow and her mighty bull, Halftooth. Two young braves were also rapidly approaching time for their first hunts. So not only would the men debate about a destination, they would determine the best route to take to accomplish the first hunts along the way. Not many Toenuk herds remained due to the way the humans hunted them to capture newborn calves. Teegan also knew the majority of the day would probably be spent complaining about wives, and bragging about children, and without fail, the other men making fun of the newest member among them.

Teegan's mother was married to the tribe's chief, Kurg. The mighty warrior had lead the tribe for many snows with a shrewd, forward thinking that carried a wary regard for the weaker humans to the North. Kurg called the slavers Roosterheads, a name given for the ridiculous plumed helmets they wore. Funny names or not, Teegan often felt his father was actually somewhat afraid of the tuskless beings, primarily due to the great lengths he took to keep the tribe away from them. The young brave had not been the only member of Bloodthorns to notice, and anything even resembling fear was a sign

124

of weakness. Kurg had planned for his son to take down the biggest bull on the plains to dissuade some of this chatter, but soon the hunt stories would grow boring and repetitive, and the war stories and old glories of the tribe would be told once again told at the fires. When that happened, the mighty Kurg would once again find one foot in front of the other, walking a precarious social tightrope between safety and losing his people's support.

Even though he had none of his father's burdens, Teegan still had a bit of trouble being called "father". Tauka'Aun had two children from her previous marriage with his friend Morgal, who was now affectionately known as the boys' uncle. This was the way of the tribe, and it kept the group together.

"Father, father!" called Ruggy, the older of the two boys. "We made you breakfast!"

"It yum!" Grine was a bit young to make a full sentence, but still managed to waddle around nicely.

It was a nice gesture that the boys brought Teegan breakfast, even if he wasn't exactly certain what it was they brought. It was wrapped in leaves steaming, and Teegan was certain it was still wiggling. They boys offered up the meal as if he were the great Sky Father himself. Grine wiped snot from his nose and Ruggy smiled. Both had eyes far too large for refusal. Teegan's two wives stood behind the boys, each stifling a laugh with a loosely-cuffed fist.

Teegan closed one eye as he peeked inside the steaming leaves. He gathered up enough courage to unwrap whatever it was in there.

Suddenly, with a wild screech, something jumped from the leaves and on to Teegan's chest! Surprise caused him to fall over backwards, while the leaves flew up in the air and something very hot, very angry, and very loud screamed its way around the teepee.

Teegan was yelling, a combination of fright and confusion. Ruggy was yelling because Teegan was yelling, and Grine was chasing the squealing what-have-you around in circles!

Laughter exploded from Tauka'Aun and Lu'Kall, who were nearly doubled over watching the catastrophe.

Whatever poor creature the boys had caught and partially cooked finally managed to make its way under the edge of the teepee and out into the safety of the wilds, despite the efforts of a hard-working Grine. Teegan and Ruggy's yelling subsided long before the snickering from the onlookers did. Teegan had nearly died of fright for the brief moment, and all the women did was laugh at him! How could they?

The tent flap opened, allowing an inquisitive Kurg to peek inside. He had no doubt heard the shouting well before he had arrived at the tent. The laughter from Teegan's two wives rekindled with smiles shot to them from their tribal leader, who, after a brief assessment, gave in to a slight chuckle.

"How was breakfast?" the chief said, looking at his recovering son. Making room for Grine to duck through his legs to get outside to look for more.

"Not dead." Teegan answered dryly as he walked over to the much larger man. Kurg took the startled Bloodthorn under a massive arm and pulled him close before stepping outside of the teepee.

"Is it always like this?" The younger man sought wisdom from one more seasoned. "Marriage? Kids?"

"How do you mean?" The big man smiled down at him awkwardly through tusks adorned with magic totems and trinkets.

Teegan had turned back to wave goodbye to his wives and now brought that same grand smile to the man who walked beside him.

"Is it always so much fun?" Teegan continued, "the joys, the laughs, the..."

"...night time?" Kurg finished the question with memories of his first few weeks of union.

Teegan flushed red at the thought of his wives after dark, and his father knew he had struck the proper note.

"It is always...an adventure...bull killer." Even his father had adopted the name, and he said it with a hearty pat on the back and that charming, pride-filled smile. "Come, we must meet with the others today. Then we will talk about the joys of marriage, and the pitfalls of having to have a wife to run it."

Teegan tried to puzzle out his answer as the two walked towards the center of the temporary village where the other Bloodthorns were gathering. They both took in the simple joys of their lives, Kurg's arm draped over his son's shoulder, and both looked forward to seeing what else this amazing day had in store.

*** *** ***

"Why not just hit them in their own stinking camp? We can send a runner back to Macival Post, he would return in less than two days' time with an entire contingent of troops." The sound of the heavy leather bracers Lucavion wore creaked as he pounded his fist into an open palm for point.

"They may be gone before then, first sergeant." Cabot outranked the man, albeit barely. He was still trying to discern the reason why the High Priestess had seen fit to place the two men on the same mission, let alone why she sent her personal protector along for the ride. So far, the entire mission had been a boring delivery of two Great Obelisks to two different forts. The last one was now to be taken to some Goddess-knows-what of a village for Goddess-knows-why of a reason. To make matters worse, their path required he bring the deliveries by beast and wagon. Cabot had always hated the smell of Thanadonts, they shit almost as often as they ate, and the fact one of the overgrown pigs was the only thing big enough to pull the massive trailer nearly made his head hurt. How he longed for a Goddess Barge to float the Obelisks over the land like a leaf on the water, but alas, none of the needed lines of energy known as Angel Yarn aided him with his route. Without the presence of this source of power, a Goddess Barge was nothing more than a hearty-made wagon lacking wheels and having a very heavy stone base. No yarn meant no mystic barge, so a wagon built sturdy enough to bear the weight and pulled by a giant boar had to be used. As if on cue, the lumbering brute outside bellowed, followed by a series of low-pitched grunts. Cabot rolled his eyes.

"Then we take the Pigbacks now! We have fifty trained legionnaires. Even with such numbers as they have, they are but savages. Mostly women and children, and that's good stock!" Sergeant Lucavion was a strong, handsome man and, like all Sabrinians, had olive skin, almond eyes, and dark hair. His breeding had funneled him into service and now he raced the man next to him for rank.

"True. We could use many of them to replenish some of the game's stock. I'm certainly getting tired of watching Irgrot the Ugly crush every purse thief in Anon." Cabot was not nearly as handsome as Lucavion, but being the homely boy at the dance always allowed him to dodge attention, sit back, and see just how people worked. His rival loved the thrill of battle.

"Aye, he does need some new heads to bash! He's got nearly twenty kills under a tenth cycle! There hasn't been a score like that since..."

Cabot paced, tuning out Lucavion's expert rambles as the man carried on about the games. He couldn't believe that someone so easily distracted could actually be threatening his rank. Two other men stood in the room, the hunter Maesma, who had provided Cabot the intelligence on the Pigback tribe and the advising Warpriest Gallus. The hunter was silent during the two sergeants' discussion, just as quiet and obedient as the two hellhounds sitting outside of the officer's tent. Priest Gallus, self-proclaimed scholar of the "Plainsmen" people, agreed with everything either sergeant said, interjecting only pointless affirmations of either man's suggestions.

Cabot continued his trek around the center table. A makeshift map of ink wells and crumpled up parchments created a rough representation of the terrain and the surrounding area. Cabot's dagger stuck in the table to represent the Sabrinian camp position, while one of Maesma's hooked blades marked the area where he had spotted the savage Tuskers.

Master Sergeant Cabot's first instinct was to leave the Pigbacks alone; they did not pose a direct threat, and losing even a single man on a delivery mission would be seen as a complete failure; failing would be something Lucavion could, no doubt, capitalize on. These Tuskers did, however, present an excellent opportunity to bring home an added gift for Her Eminence, not to mention the possible commission from the sale of even a small amount of the sought-after slaves. It was too juicy a steak to let go to the flies. As his rival continued to babble on about this brilliant combat move, and that he was now recalling some long-dead hero of the coliseum or the like, Cabot feigned both interest and wide-eyed admiration for the man's statistical knowledge. The master sergeant nodded and smiled at Lucavion, secretly thinking that maybe the loss of one soldier may not be such a failure after all. When he finally paused for breath, Cabot interjected.

"First Sergeant, I agree that we need this stock, but I do not know if a frontal assault is a proper approach. You are absolutely correct about these savages, but remember even the most savage of beast attacks with abnormal vigor when it comes to protecting their young.

As you have said before, we know, historically, that even a camp protected by only women can be quite an oppositional force."

Lucavion looked to the corners of the tent for memories of saying such wise words, but nodded with a winner's smile in dismissal to the fact that he must have had forgotten speaking them.

Cabot continued. "With the Pigbacks, the Goddess has seen fit to grant women the strength of any one of our legionnaires and their men the strength of two." He crossed his arms, and with one hand checked his chin for the length of his beard stubble. He walked a bit, pretending to be at a loss.

"We need to separate the warriors from the women and children," Lucavion said with conviction after a lengthy pause.

"But just how do we do that, first sergeant? What is it we have that they could want?"

The first sergeant was not following, so Cabot led him further. His plan needed to be the handsome man's idea.

"He has fought them before." He looked to the hunter then stared for a long time at the table.

Lucavion, apparently, was trying to move the representations of enemy positions with his mind, what with all of the strain on his face. If it were possible, Cabot would have rubbed the stubble off of his chin by now.

"They have a passion for, what was it, life and freedom?" The master sergeant squinted his eyes in a prayer that his rival would become just a tad less daft.

Maesma nodded quickly in response. Still nothing from Lucavion.

"What do they call the Thanadonts again, eunuch?" Cabot turned the inquiry to the priest.

"Um...Toenuk sir. Yes. Toenuk I believe it was." Gallus replied with a slight grin.

"That's it! I know what we can do!" Lucavion had a plan at last. Now it was just up to Cabot to twist it so it would work. Hopefully, he could do just this before it was time for lunch.

***

Kurg and Teegan laughed with the other men as the day fought for its last bit of life. It was the general consensus that the

129

Bloodthorns would go south to trade with the Cliff People, and maybe search for a safe path to the coastal tribes, for it had been many snows since the Plainsmen had traded with them. The meeting had not been a grueling one, rather a lighthearted gathering of lighthearted people. Kurg could feel the evening sun waving a farewell, and it seemed to fill him with the Sky Father's magick. He closed his eyes for a moment, it had been good day.

Kurg's thoughts must have spurred the entrance of irony, for as soon as they trickled into his brain, Morgal came bursting into the circle.

"Humans! Nearby!" He panted. Clearly he had run at a high speed to carry the news. "They have with them a Bull Toenuk bound with clinking straps of steel!" He bent over, resting his hands on his knees to catch his breath.

Kurg and Teegan moved rapidly to the man. "Are you certain?" Kurg's question was a grunt.

"Certain, chieftain! No more than a dozen. The beast pulls a mighty wagon longer than the biggest bull with tusks outstretched."

Excited shouts began shooting up all over the village as Plainspeople started crowding around the runner, the chief, and Teegan.

Kurg put a hand on Morgal's shoulder. "Did this wagon look like a small version of one of their forts with what looks like small housing on top? Maybe even a tall, skinny house on top?" His gestures were very specific, Kurg had seen a war wagon before, and the mobile fortress had nearly brought an end to an entire war party.

"No, chieftain. It was flat with short sides and a giant spear of stone strapped to it with their funny ropes." Morgal was regaining his breath.

Kurg was puzzled. He had seen the spears of stone before, but only stuck into the ground with the shiny golden spearheads pointing up at the Sky Father. He had always assumed the humans grew them from the ground, but what Morgal saw was either something different entirely, or it meant that the humans had to move the stone spears by hand.

"How many humans?" Kurg asked him again.

"Not more than a half-flock. Their chief was barking orders at them in their squeaky tongue. The round legs of the wagon were swallowed by the Earth Mother, and they could not move. Some of the Roosterheads yelled back at the chief, too. I thought they would battle."

Nearly the entire tribe was gathering around by now. Kurg did not like this, not one bit. The Crow and Vulture Shamans were forcing their way through the crowd as well, perhaps their wisdom could help the situation. The chief knew the tribe would want blood, and this target was a Cocktchya with one leg and no beak-or at least it appeared as such.

Teegan cringed, the crowd was growing restless and asking heated questions. The presence of the shamans only fueled a growing bonfire sparked by happenstance. He had no idea what to say or how to respond to the situation, let alone how help out. The rest of the tribe told him he was a hero for the result of his first hunt, but deep down inside there was no hero. The rest of the tribe considered him a man now, yet he did not see one of those in his heart. He was on the plains again, standing in a circle of grunting Toenuk, all of which could smell his piss.

"What is going on here, chieftain?" asked a vulture, apparently the high shaman in the circle.

The others moving and behaving like their totems all began to squawk similar questions as soon as the first finished his. There was no sign of the strange Eagle Shaman that had led the others in the Binding Ritual several days before. The vulture rose his arms in silence at both the other wise men and the crowd that nearly burst into an uproar of shouts and questions.

Kurg bowed his head with respect, an odd visage to see such a large man show submission to such an oddly built one.

"There are some humans a few hours from here. They are small in numbers and vulnerable in position," Kurg spoke to the ground, as the shamans inspected him like he was infested with mites they would soon pluck from his wire-haired mane.

"These humans-what threat do they pose to you and your Thorns of Blood?" The shaman asked the question shrewdly, and it preceded more squawking repetitions of the same question from the other interlopers.

"None, Taker of the Dead. They move past us, heading the opposite direction of our journey." Kurg's reply was the first drop of rain before the thunderstorm. Humans were never 'not a threat' to any Plainsmen, and everyone listening to him knew that fact.

"None?" The shaman's question was repeated by the other vulture, then mimicked by the three crows, who altered it slightly by pitch.

"None?!" This time the lead shaman drew out his guttural sounds, making the question as much of an accusation as one simple word could possibly be.

The crowd rumbled in disapproval, something else that Teegan did not yet understand. His father had kept the tribe safe for as long as the boy could remember, and part of that safety was due to the idea that the Bloodthorn leader had stayed as far away from the Roosterheads as possible. Surely they knew that!

"Shaman, I did not mean that humans pose no threat to us. I meant that this group of humans poses no threat. It is not nec..."

"The humans are there, why?" Any other member of the tribe interrupting Kurg would have prayed for death rather than feel his wrath, but the shaman was safe from retribution. This protection had nothing to do with the shaman's status, but because the chief believed in their magick.

"They are taking a stone spear somewhere. One of those that stand out from the middle of their fortifications." Kurg still spoke to the ground.

"They thrust these spears into the ground." The vulture educated a quickly-silenced crowd.

The other shamans mimicked the last word, making Teegan's skin crawl. "It is the way they steal the power from the Earth Mother. They stab the spears into a place where the Spirit Lines cross, and then bleed her slowly." Again the last word sounded eerie in the silence of the now attentive crowd.

"Tell us, chieftain," the second vulture spoke. "How do they carry the stone spear?" The first vulture cocked his head sideways at the second then, in a strange neck movement, pivoted his head towards the chief to wait for his response.

Kurg's shoulders sank in a bit, knowing the response of the question would lead to blood. Humans were vile, and Kurg despised them, but they were also a viper in the tall grass with poison enough to fell the entire tribe.

"They have lashed a Plainsbrother with steel rope. He drags the spear behind him on a huge wooden wagon as they mock him with their painful words and sharpened poles."

Morgal had not told Kurg this, but he did not need to. The chief remembered all too well the way the Toenuk looked pulling the Sabrinian war wagon years ago. It was the very picture of sadness and despair. That day, many Plainsmen would also end up roped in steel and be dragged away tied to the very brother they had tried to rescue. Kurg had been lucky that day, he was left for dead by the Roosterheads, stuck by an arrow he never saw coming that marked him with a scar he now rubbed with the salve of memory. The crowd was transforming into a nest of wasps, and Kurg had just grabbed a hold of the branch that anchored it.

"And his tusks?" The shaman knew the answer, as did Kurg. Nonetheless, he looked towards Morgal who had seen the atrocity first hand.

If the humans had left the tusks on the beasts, it could be a sign of respect. This could give the leader of the Bloodthorn a small chance to argue a quick southern retreat rather than an altercation. The runner shook his head. Though the movement was left-to-right, might have well been the up-and-down nod to an executioner. Kurg closed his eyes as the Taker of Death folded his arms. The crowd ignited.

The wasps stormed from the nest, shouts and blood demands erupting all around Teegan. The energy was so intoxicating that Teegan found himself joining in. They screamed and jumped up and down! They followed the cries of the shamans. They all screamed for death.

The chief, eyes closed and head down, could hear his son's shouts. His head turned slowly, and his eyes crept open, orbs that had been filled just moments before with nothing but pride and joy for the boy. They took Teegan into them, those eyes. They stopped him from chanting with the other Plainsmen, they drowned out the sound from those that continued. Teegan had never seen that look before.

His father was scared.

***

"They are watching us right now," Cabot said.

"Are you certain?" Gallus was nervous.

Two men below their hiding spot on the bluff walked around the wagon with torches. Some of them, led by the fearless Lucavion, feigned sleep underneath the wagon, waiting for the sounds of the charging Tuskers. Despite Cabot's recommendation of caution, the other sergeant had absolutely insisted on being a part of the bait. He applauded the courage.

Sergeant Cabot, the eunuch Gallus, his horn blower, and some twenty men lie in the darkness of the surrounding ridge. They hid on the sides of the hill in small pits, then camouflaged the openings with cut foliage in order to become seemingly invisible to the keenest eye.

The High Lady's hunter had told them to make sure they could not be seen from the skies above since enacting the plan, but other than a few crows, there had been nothing but some very thin clouds and now a very bright moon and countless twinkling stars. Cabot had thought the hunter mad, yet followed his instructions. There was a reason the Light of the Goddess herself had chosen the blind assassin, and Cabot was not fool enough to lack the wisdom that would be refusing the 'recommendations' of one so close to the Head of State.

"I'm completely certain. I have read much about the Pigbacks. They are not as dumb as they look by far. In fact, they are known for their trickery and battle prowess. They are waiting for the perfect time to strike. They are strong and ferocious, and completely opportunistic-all very desirable traits. Even with all of this I'd not take any ten of them over any one trained Sabrinian Legionnaire." The sergeant was serious, however exaggerated. Yet it was not overconfidence that spilled his words. Where the Tuskers had strength and ferocity, the Sabrinians had discipline, organization, and dedicated combat training. He had a good reason to assess the situation as he did, the soldiers around him were full-time professionals, trained from days shortly after they could walk. Only after coming of age and ten years of continued service was a man allowed to apply for exodus from the army which, shy of a medical discharge or the favor of a noble, was rarely granted. These factors doubled when taking account the technology of well-crafted steel.

Sabrinian theology did have a way to motivate its fighting force. The priestesses in charge of policy were quite aware that all soldiers had one thing in common; they could be motivated by the dangling objects between their legs. A good soldier, seasoned and decorated in combat, was allowed to marry after only three years of service. For many young men, the idea of a honeymoon was well worth giving that extra effort in battle and standing ground against seemingly unbeatable odds. Merit badges from that point on allowed paid times of leave to visit home and loving wife. Sometimes, after a great battle the officials would order acolytes, entertainers, and priests to visit the camps for victory celebrations. Usually, these were nothing more than drunken medications to ease the pain of loss, but sometimes they became orgies of legend. Parties so grand they were named after the battles where they were held and talked of in taverns with much greater frequency.

Reward wasn't the only focus for a legionnaire. The opposite side of the coin meant there were harsh penalties for failure, and even worse for desertion or betrayal. Flogging, denying rations, and extra mess duties were all punishments for basic disobedience. However, if a man were convicted of something considerable, he could find his ten year tenure reset, lose his marriage rights, be sent into the pits to fight, or even end up a eunuch in the priesthood like Gallus. All in all, it was an effective machine, and it created fighting men very, very motivated to achieve glorious victory.

"Where is the hunter?" Gallus inquired with a harsh whisper.

"Gone looking for meaning, or some such business. He did not explain. He has too much free will for a slave." Cabot did wonder where the assassin had gone, taking his dogs with him. Those three, no matter how free willed, made his job all the easier; it was no wonder the priestesses always kept them around.

"The hunters fascinate me. Always have. I wonder how..."

Cabot cut the man off with a touch on the shoulder. His eyes peered out of his hiding place to the opposite side of the shallow ravine. There was movement. Shadows that were deceived, ever so slightly, by beaming moon on this cloudless night. The savages were indeed coming, crawling towards his troops on the flats above their side of the slope. The chosen position made his ten men below him into pluckable passion fruit, ripe for the taking, and lacking thorny vine. The Tuskers would attack downhill, using the momentum to their advantage, and right after they reached the wagon, he and the rest of his men would spring the trap. This would not be a good night to be a Pigback.

Yes, Cabot was confident in his plan. It was well thought out and soundly engineered. His men below would only have to hold out for a few seconds after the savages dealt with his little surprise. He would then sound the horn, and it would be all over for those below and those at the Pigback Camp

Even though he truly believed this, the sergeant's breath stopped for a moment as he tried to discern the growing rumbling sound in the distance. To his dismay, he recognized it from written accounts of past battles he'd read about in the academy. Drums began pounding from the Tusker's flats. The sound of the instruments troubled him. Cabot knew only what Gallus had briefed about on Shaman magick, but knew everything about the effect the pounding beats had on his men's morale.

He turned to his horn blower with a forced grin. "Looks like you'll have a rhythm section to play to after all..."

The man did not return the smile.

***

Kurg crawled on his elbows and knees to Teegan and Morgal with an intensity in that would have terrified them had they not been on the same side. The Crows' drums had begun behind them, and the chieftain had only moments to explain.

"You two," urgency vibrated in his throat, "you will wait for a count of 20 before following us in. Yulger, Mreggan, Heldgo-wait with them."

"But the..." Mreggan began to object, only to be interrupted by Kurg punching the man in the jaw. It rocked his head sideways and silenced him.

There was a reason why Kurg was the chief, and the power behind the prone right hook proved it. Mreggan was visibly dazed.

"Count to twenty. Then follow us in." No one opened their mouths to disagree.

The leader of the Plainsman stood up and yelled a war cry that pierced through the sounds of the drums. His blood was hot, and his heart pounded with anticipation, his bonerattle thrust high into the air, its magick winding its way down his arm. The decision to attack the humans had not been his, but he would lead his people regardless. His senses were amplified by the thirst for battle, and he and ten of his warriors charged down the slope towards the Stone Spear and shackled Toenuk that grumbled slight acknowledgement towards the sound of the Chief of the Plainspeople.

There were two men with torches that came running towards the sounds of the charging braves, led by the howls that demanded death. The lust for combat had taken Kurg. He heard the shouts of the other warriors as distant howls, replaced by blood flowing through his ears. The shaman's drums pounded in sync with his heart spurring his footsteps to speeds he normally could not obtain, his legs felt lighter, his skin felt thicker, the wind in his face felt cooler. This was the way of shaman magick, and Kurg knew it would help him crush his enemies.

One foot in front of the other, blurring terrain passing by, Kurg barely noticed the men throwing torches over the heads of himself and the charging warriors, but he did notice what happened when they hit the bushes to both sides of the charge. The bushes exploded into flame, no doubt coated in the human oil used for their lanterns; this was not intended to harm Kurg's troops, if so the throws were grossly lacking proper timing. His thoughts of the bushes did exactly what the humans wanted, took his eyes off the ground in front of him.

The blinding distraction offset the cool light of the moon and made the ground in front of charging Plainswarriors hard to navigate. It was as if the ground was not stable somehow.

The voice of warning in his head came too late, as his lead foot struck the ground and pressed through. He did not hear the faint snapping of the twigs that covered the spike pit, the rush of the air went from running to falling. The wind became dirt as his face, planted into the base of the pit, the impact rattling his head.

Kurg spat out the dirt and, along with it, a hefty amount of blood. Drums still beat from the flats above them and now helped to fill his soul with rage. He went to stand before realizing that there was a spear through his midsection, and another through his right thigh. Pain wracked his body, causing him to cough up more blood. He could hear shouts of the Roosterheads as they rallied out from under their wagon. Looking to his right and left, he could see shadows of several of his battle-brothers that had fallen into the pit with him; some were moving, some were not. There were no words in his language for the anger that consumed him. He reached under his own belly and snapped the spear that had skewered him, and followed the procedure with the one that had pierced through his thigh.

"Toenuk Shit!" Yulger yelled as the first wave of braves fell into the pit.

Six of the tribes best warriors had fallen in, one of them being the chief.

Morgal was off like a plains lion starting a chase, despite Teegan yelling at him to wait. They had not quite made it to the twenty count, but as Teegan glanced to his companions, he soon realized that he was the only one not charging down towards the pits.

Those warriors that did not fall in found themselves outmatched, two to one, as the humans crawled out from underneath the wagon. They had not been sleeping at all. Frustrated by his lack of conviction, Teegan readied his spear and charged down the hill towards his ill-fated brethren.

***

Waves of reds, oranges, and yellows emitted from the area around the campfire. Maesma was always fascinated by shaman magick, and how it flowed on the waves of sound coming from their drums. Each of the wise ones called upon a different attribute to both enhance their brothers, and take away from their enemies. No one could see these waves of course, no one could know their wonder and beauty, unless they had the vision of a hunter.

Maesma did not have time to let the colors mesmerize him, for he knew that as the waves reached the battle, they would have very real effects on the combatants. This could turn the tides no matter how sound of trap was lain. He approached the group of shaman from the shadows, his sun-starved skin painted with thick stripes as black as the two dogs that crouched beside him. This odd opposite to his pale bareness helped him to blend in perfectly with the surrounding terrain that was doted upon by the cloudless moon. If the wise men were to turn his direction, the fire would reflect three sets of eyes. Two pairs were red, and one was as white as a corpse. All glowed in the darkness, all with the most vile of intent.

There had been sentries, of course, but only four. They had never seen Maesma coming, far too confident in their hiding places. The assassin almost pitied them, mostly because he held such an unfair advantage on those that thought themselves safe. Four silent sentries were made permanently that way and now lay in pools of their own blood.

Three shaman stood round giant drums, the gorgeous glow of their *joa* flowing into the mallets and transforming into waves as they pounded on the drums. These shaman were weavers, and their life-force was enhanced by the powers they channeled. Two more shaman danced around the fire, whip-like tentacles called *joa bian* extended from their chests, from areas of power known as *joa xin*, into the heads of those that played the drums. The chanting from these two made Maesma's heart race, pumping adrenaline into him. It had been many winters since the assassin had seen so many weavers in the same place, working in unison for the same purpose.

The two dancing and singing were much more powerful than those playing the drums. Their *joa* was a beacon in the pitch black, and it dwarfed those next to it. He could almost taste it. It was so bright, he thought he'd have to cover his eyes; as if each one of them were a living obelisk in and of themselves. The forces within them were extended to the drummers, amplifying them as they pounded away. But it took concentration to maintain the trance and the connection, and that concentration meant they were unaware of the monster stalking them from the dark.

His attack had to be swift and sure, the dancing men were opposite him and the three drummers equally spaced around the flame. No matter how fast he was, or how he used Jove and Romule, he would be attacked. The object would be to hit them fast enough to cause the others to startle. If they hesitated, he could hit a second target before they reacted, this left a third open. His hellhounds were trained with death holding their leash, they were more than ready. They would be his distraction. They would be his moment of hesitation.

He sent the beasts in, silent until the moment of attack, each going for the throat of a different unsuspecting drummer.

Jove went in hard and fast, his large canines guided by a deep snarl. The black shadow sunk its teeth into the soft throat of the Shaman, knocking the man onto the ground.

Romule was a bit less fortunate, his target hearing the assault on the other drummer. A forearm barred the way of jaw to tender flesh, but did not stop the weight of the mastiff from sending the foe to meet the hard-packed dirt, hellhound joining in on the one-way ride.

The life-force of one of the dancers snapped back, the tentacle rearing backwards like a frozen whip waiting to strike. He focused on Jove, not knowing that it was already far too late for the man whose head was now being thrashed back and forth by the mongrel. The whip never struck home. Rather, a pair of blades made their way through the back of a feathered cloak, invasive and not at all cordial in their penetration into the Plainsman's lungs. Maesma did not have time to remove them. He kicked the man towards the third percussionist, aided by shock he floundered forward with such ease that made it appear that the stuck shaman had intentionally made the attack himself.

Maesma leapt forward into a crouch, staring up towards the second dancing Wiseman. A targeting whip of pure *joa* was already coming at him. He tumbled to the left and towards the shaman as another tentacle struck out from the same spot. Maesma dodged sideways in the opposite direction, landing on his stomach nearly at the feet of his intended victim. A third *joa bian* was already descending on him, and if it struck him, the weaver could do any manner of destruction. He rolled into the shins of the shaman, tripping him forward so he landed on top of the prone assassin. Normally this would be a position of power, for the Pigback was much larger and heavier than the human, but this was not the case when Maesma was that human. He was almost as deadly on the ground and weaponless, as he was with one of his blades already stuck in his victim. The big Plainsmen soon found two legs, seemingly made of wood and ropes rather than flesh and bone, wrapped around his neck. Maesma squeezed, sinking his legs into the space between chin and shoulder.

Running out of time, the shaman struggled to his feet, grabbing for his assailant's throat. But the human was the quicker, and both his hands clamped around a thick wrist. He pulled the captured arm across his chest, twisting most of his body towards the outside of the shaman's elbow. The motion also tightened the vice his stronger limbs had 'round the tusked man's neck. Unfortunately, it also left his head open for a mighty hammer punch from his grappled foe. Luckily, the first hit the hard part of his skull and did not dislodge him, as did several repetitive blows.

140

Air was almost gone from the beast-man, and Maesma knew it. There was one last-ditch way the Plainsman could possibly dislodge him, and Maesma has seen the attack a hundred times. He would slam the hunter on his back and attempt to drive his tusks into his eyes. It was a favored move for the larger humanoids. They loved the taste of the dying's blood on their lips. And here it came, the Pigback rising to full height, then kicking its own legs out from under its body.

Maesma hit the ground hard, but his training allowed him to exhale as to control the placement of his breath, rather than have it blasted from his lungs. The blow dizzied him, but he kept his vision. He still held onto the Pigback's arm with all his might, this time, steering the mass to prevent the tusks from reaching him. The shaman used his full strength and weight trying to fold the hunter's body in half, trying to press his tusks into Maesma's eye sockets.

Closer they came, urged on with airless grunts.

Maesma squeezed his legs and pressed up with his arms.

The shaman used his free arm to push against his immobilized one, sending the tusks closer.

Maesma squeezed his legs.

Closer they came. So close Maesma turned his head, a drooling tusk leaving a dampened trail across his cheek.

Maesma squeezed his legs until he heard a resounding pop. The shaman's body twitched with the spasms of death, then shit itself as it fell limply to the side.

The hunter rolled the opposite direction, onto his knees, panting with exhaustion. He felt the *joa bian* hit him from behind. It was the third drummer, fully recuperated after Maesma kicked the dying dancer onto him. He floated upwards, flows of air coming to life around him. He spun around in the air, arms and legs frozen in a vise tighter than any torture rack. With his special vision, he could see the flows of energy wrapping around his wrists and ankles, each pulling in an opposite direction. Energy from the fire began flowing into the shaman and winding its way up the whip of *joa* towards the helpless hunter. When it reached him, it would heat up his insides. It would boil his very blood.

The shaman cursed victory at him in is his guttural language, spit flying off the ends of his tusks.

Maesma forced a smile against the constricting forces of air holding him. Not because it would be a good day to die, but because the elaborate, time-consuming method the shaman had chosen to end him did nothing to dispose of the black shadow of doom leaping through the flames to bring him down.

Hellhounds were very protective of their masters.

***

Lucavion stepped forward, his shieldman at his side.

"Two wolf formation!" he shouted.

As his men moved into paired formation, squaring off on the startled Tuskers in front of them, he and his own partner moved in behind. Only four of the Tuskers had managed to avoid the spiked pit that was dug and covered in front of the flat wagon. Though he had hoped for more, this number was satisfactory. Sabrinian soldiers trained to fight the Pigbacks two on one. It allowed for a defense that constantly tired the larger opponent, stabbing at vital areas with patience and defending frenzied onslaughts with solid Sabrinian steel.

He moved to the side of the first pair and stabbed his sword deep into the back of the Tusker that fought with them. The wound caused the beast-man to lurch forward and fall to one knee. The original pair made short work of this weakened foe, sending it to whatever gods it worshiped.

"Strong defense!" His order was clear and concise. It let his legionnaires know that he, his shield man, and the newly freed up pair of soldiers would soon have their opponents from behind. No risky offence was needed. Patience would safely lead them to victory.

A second savage spilled blood from severe lacerations from several sources. It's twitching body freeing up another pair of troops to move in on the remaining two Tuskers. The final two, now being backed towards the pits they had barely managed to avoid, were pressed again towards spiked death by a half circle of trained Sabrinian Legionnaires.

The Pigbacks grunted and snarled, gathering their courage for a final attack.

"Resolve!" Lucavion's voice boomed into the air. "Push them back!"

"Ah-roo!" The nine men to his sides shouted in unison, ducking behind their shields and clanking their blades on the top in the ready. The perfectly coordinated sound was like a single slam on an oversized cymbal.

***

Morgal bellowed in rage as he leapt the pit, he did not look down as he jumped, he did not want to. He used the momentum of his jump to add strength to his shoulder as he slammed into the shield of one of the Roosterheads. The maneuver knocked the human backward onto his back and carried Morgal awkwardly into one of the circular legs of the wagon.   As he turned to recover, he saw three of his other brethren hop the chasm and follow his lead.

Heldgo had leapt into the air sideways, using the length of his body to level three of the shielded humans. He rolled like a log for a bit slowing down underneath the wooden wagon. Yulger and Mreggan hit the line hard, too, effectively equalizing the odds.

Teegan slowed as he approached the pit, the sight inside demanded it. His blood froze instantly at the sight of his father forcing himself to stand, a sharpened stick protruding from his lower back, with what could be nothing less than some of his father's insides stuck to the end. He was so horrified he did not see the one that pierced through Kurg's thigh until the man reached down and pulled it out. Kurg's scream shook the boy's core, snapping him out of the trance. Kurg then punched the end of the remaining spike in his stomach, forcing much of it further through his back. He doubled over, vomiting blood, but did not fall. Through tears, Teegan watched open-mouthed as his father reached behind to pull the sharpened stick through his body. Kurg growled and let out a roar that could be heard above the battle and above the...

Teegan realized the drums had stopped. What happened to the shaman?

He looked towards the now silent drummers, then back towards the battle. Kurg was making his way out of the pit, as was another one of the braves. The others that had fallen in no longer struggled for life. Tears were running down his face as he saw them fighting for their lives. He shook his head, not understanding how his father could stand, let alone stalk towards the battle. Teegan took a few steps back then ran to jump the pit. Landing on the edge, he almost plummeted backwards, until a huge hand grabbed him by his leather tunic. It was Kurg, and there was nothing his son could recognize in his eyes.

"Go. Find a way to unleash our brother from his bonds." A cough came out to end the sentence, spraying Teegan with spit and blood. He dropped his son safely to the ground as the human leader shouted orders at his footmen. Kurg turned, moving towards the Roosterheads leader with death in his eyes. One would never guess he'd just had a spear stuck through his leg, as well as his stomach.

***

"Well would you look at that!" Gallus was shocked to see the mighty Tusker Chief climb from the pit.

"Unbelievable. And still Lucavion keeps his men organized! Hooray for our team! Such bravado!" Cabot was genuinely enjoying watching the other sergeant.

Lucavion was, admittedly, much better in combat situations that the master sergeant himself, and so he could now see why the man challenged Cabot's rank.

Better or not, the situation was becoming dire for the first sergeant and the other troops below. They were now nearly matched one on one, and the roar of the chief had seemed to rally the beast-men. Cabot noted one of the smaller Pigbacks running toward the Toenuk.

"How odd. What do you suppose that one is doing?" he said, pointing at the scrambling Tusker as it made its way to the beast of burden still hooked up to the wagon.

"He looks to be for a purpose, doesn't he?" chuckled the eunuch.

"That he does! I'll be a crotch wart! He is trying to unleash that Thanadont!"

"The hunter was right about these Pigbacks' respect for other creatures! Remarkable!" Gallus was amazed.

"I wonder if he realizes it's domesticated." The question as much for himself as for anyone listening. "I guess that's one more reason to vanquish the stupid savages."

"Sir, excuse me." the voice was his horn blower's. After getting the master sergeant's attention, he pointed back towards the battle, where Lucavion's troops were about to be overrun.

The first sergeant knew it, too, for he frantically looked up to their hiding place before waving a signal. The horn blower, seeing the wave from the battling squad leader, raised the horn to his mouth. As he breathed in deeply, Cabot slapped the man in the back of the head.

"I did not order the signal!" Cabot glared.

"But, sir!" The horn blower was uncertain how to respond.

"Would you rob Lucavion of his glory? Have us rush into a situation that he clearly has under control?" The question was pointed.

The man was torn between trying to use his eyes to signal Cabot to return his attention to the battle and looking his sergeant in the eye and answering his question.

"N-n-no sir? It's just...it's just...he looks to be in trouble, sir!" The soldier was truly torn.

"Did you just call me sir?" Cabot actively pulled the edges of his mouth downward in disgust.

"Y-y-yes, sir!" The soldier was confused.

"I am no sir, legionnaire. I work for my coin! Do you have a speech problem?"

Two more of the Pigbacks had fallen, but at the cost of one of Lucavion's group of five. The first sergeant and his remaining troops fought defensively in an ever-tightening circle, until the big chieftain from the pit rushed into them. The big Tusker literally picked two of the soldiers up by their shields and tossed them to the sides, as if they were a couple of rabbit carcasses.

"Sergeant Cabot, you may want to see what's happening!"

The voice was Gallus, and it caused him to look back towards the battle.

The enemy had now squared off with the lower troops one on one, and the furious blows from the savages had the men clinging to their shields with both hands in order to deflect the oversized clubs that meant death if they connected.

Lucavion, the master sergeant's unrealized rival, was crawling backwards from the still advancing chieftain. His sword, stuck deep into the savage's shoulder, had little to no effect. The giant Tusker reached down and grabbed the man by his upper arms. Lucavion winced in pain as he tried to kick at the Pigback's heaving chest.

Once again a deep breath came from the horn blower.

"Did I order the signal?" Cabot asked the man a second time.

He saw nothing but a blank stare in reply, and a quick shake of the man's head.

"I thought not!" It was a threat, not a statement.

"Cabot!" Gallus again redirected his leader to the battlefield.

He turned back just in time to see the huge Pigback holding Lucavion by the neck with an outstretched arm, slam the man's head onto his tusk. Arms that had been holding onto the beast-man's mighty wrist and waving up the hill for hopes of rescue, now fluttered about his sides. Feet followed the lead of the hands, kicking fiercely as the Pigback twisted its tusk around inside his brain. The Tusker let out a roar of triumph as it dropped Lucavion's still twitching body to the ground.

"You see what you did?" Cabot glared at the horn blower, who shook his head rapidly in confusion. "Had I not been reprimanding you, I would have seen the tide of the battle turn and ordered the charge! Now look! You're insolence has killed our beloved Lucavion!"

"Sir, I..." the soldier was wide-eyed, fearing everything all at once.

Cabot surmised the man had no idea what had just transpired.

"You what? Fool! What are you waiting for?! Our men are dying down there!"

The horn blower shook his head, looking frantically to Gallus for assistance he would not find.

"Sound the charge, you discarded cock of a horse thief!" Cabot screamed.

Too late for the valiant Lucavion, the horn sounded for his rescue. Twenty hidden legionnaires tossed aside their camouflage and charged down the hill. Twenty more in the distance lit their arrows afire and sent them raining down upon an unsuspecting village.

***

Teegan scrambled up onto the back of the wagon. It was hard for him to make out how the giant vines of steel connected to the massive harness over the Toenuk's shoulders. The bull swung its head back and forth, snorting and grunting as the battle raged on below him. Its tusks had been removed, cut off more than halfway down, and capped with large metal bowls. The bowls had rings, big enough for the boy to stand in, with a rigging like the one his father described on the Sea Tribe's boats. The hemp ropes were created by meshing together at least a dozen smaller ones-each of which were larger than any he had seen in his tribe. These ropes, bigger around than a warriors waist, led to a giant round foot of wood, not unlike those the wagon rested on, only much taller and used to coiled the rope around it. Several smaller rounded objects attached in some sort of manner that reminded him of a windmill he once explored. How angry his father had been to discover that!

Desperately, he searched to make sense of the enormous contraption.

Problems will always be. Solutions come where least expected. Remember always your place in the world around you, and any problem will find itself undone.

His father's words were always a riddle and always ended up ringing true. This time, the boy had to look at the alien bonds that shackled his four-legged brother. There, in the center of a massive wooden beam, was a steel spike holding two interlocked pieces together. That was his solution.

The steel "ropes" were made of small, solid, circular ones linked together and were easily large enough to walk on. Carefully, he rushed down one of them towards the Plainsbrother and began scrambling up the sides of the huge tackle that connected another set of steel ropes and thickened hemp opposite of the young brave. The Toenuk did not seem to notice his presence.

***

Only six of his warriors remained. They had killed all but two of the humans but at great cost. The trap had taken its toll. Then came the horn.

"Morgal!" Kurg grabbed the man and pulled him close, veins in his arms and neck fueled ferocity to every muscle in the chief's body. "Get your ass to the village! Get them to safety!" Blood covered the man's face like war paint, and gore clung to the trinkets dangling from the tusk that had ended the shouting of the Roosterheads leader.

Kurg tossed him out of the circle towards the pit. Morgal took off at full speed, dropping his club for a greater stride, he did not look

147

back. The runner leapt the pit as several of the humans' spears sliced through the air, narrowly missing him.

"Brothers! To me!" Kurg's chest swelled to add depth to his voice.

Only five Bloodthorn warriors now remained. Twenty humans rushed towards them, seeming to crawl out of the very ground. Mreggan and Yulger held bodies of fallen Roosterheads as shields to absorb incoming spears that were thrown at them in a deadly volley. Another brother was not so lucky and took one through the skull. Kurg used this fallen comrade's body as the other's did; thrown spears meant for him, sticking deep into the fleshy barrier.

Now there were only four.

***

"Look at him go!" Gallus sounded inspired as he and Cabot strolled down the hill behind the rest of the troops.

The younger of the Pigbacks was on the yoke of the Thanadont, bashing away the center pin with his crudely-carved club.

"You don't suppose he can actually break the pin, do you? That would be both unfortunate and time consuming to repair." Cabot was rubbing his chin hair again before off-handedly remembering that a battle was going on below him on the other side of the wagon.

"I want as many alive as possible!" He yelled awkwardly as gravity made his easy gate a little more elongated than he felt comfortable.

Gallus had not taken his eyes off of the Tusker on the Thanadont. "I do think he might actually break it."

Cabot sighed. "I suppose you are right. Go ahead and take the first shot." Cabot pulled his bow from across his back and readied an arrow from the quiver at his hip.

"Nice arrows!" Gallus complimented, as he did the same.

"You think? They are crafted by that fellow in the Crafting District, there in Anon."

"Oh, what was his name? Master Jul...Jullantus?" Gallus was being helpful but was more focused on taking aim. He let fly, the arrow sailing short and to the right, landing with a 'thunk' in the thick hide of the draft animal- a nuisance that wasn't even noticed.

"Master Julious. That was it. Oh! You were a bit short there." Cabot took aim, his own arrow flying high and well over the top of the both the beasts. "Goddess' cunt. Your turn." Cabot motioned with a hand and leaned on his bow while the eunuch notched another arrow.

This time the miss was very near target. So close, the Pigback looked straight at them wide-eyed, then frantically returned to bashing at the center pin with renewed vigor.

"Can you believe the tenacity of this little one?" The priest was truly in awe of their target as the master sergeant took careful aim.

As soon as he loosed the arrow he knew it was a good shot. Cabot looked at Gallus the whole time as the War Priest watched the arrow sail into the Tuskers back. He grinned at the man.

"That was a shot worthy of legend, master sergeant."

"Worthy of the heroics we have witnessed here today for certain. I was thinking 'The Battle of Lucavion Bluff' sounded the part. What do you think?"

Gallus responded to Cabot's question with a deep bow and a close-eyed smile.

This man would soon be a general, of that much, the eunuch was certain.

***

Teegan looked down at his club as it bounced off of the side of the chained Toenuk. His right hand was limp and at his side, refusing to listen to any of his requests. His left hand worked at whatever annoying bug had landed on his chest. It didn't hurt him, whatever it was, but it was causing him to bleed like never before.

He had to break this metal thing, that...

....oh that's right, he dropped his club.

What was that bug? Ouch! It had an awfully sharp shell.

Where had his club fallen?

He thought, for a brief second, maybe he was linked to it somehow, that somehow his vision seemed to follow the very path the club did. Never once did the young warrior believe it was his entire body and not just his vision that chased his club to the softened ground beneath the beast of burden.

***

Maesma looked up from the carnage about him and shook his head at the departed dancing weaver that nearly made a meal of his brains. That had been a good fight. He had not felt so alive for some time.

He patted his two hellhounds lovingly, unable to see what an odd picture it made. The dogs barked happily, licking the pieces of wet skin and bloody chucks of foe from the hunter's hands. Parts that Maesma picked up from scratching their moistened coats.

Almost simultaneously, Jove and Romule perked their massive heads up and cocked them to the side as they looked out into the distance of the moonlit flatlands. Maesma followed their alert posture to see the glowing form of one of the Plainsman running away from battle. The hunter admired his speed. There was no way, even in his younger years, could he keep up that pace for long, even if he could achieve it in the first place!

"What is it fellas?" Maesma whispered the question for excitement, which caused his hounds to stand on their feet, tails wagging with interest.

"What is it?" he asked again. This time a touch more urgently.

The two hellhounds began to growl while pulling their ears back against their heads. They crouched in anticipation for the command. Jove's front legs quivering in wait, red eyes glowing in the night. Romule licked his chops, leaning forward as if he knew what was about to come.

"*Qu da si!*" He barely finished the second word before the blurring life force of his dogs bolted off in pursuit of the fast-moving Tusker, leaving bright trails that would fade with time.

He was impressed that the Plainsmen actually increased his speed to stay ahead of the dogs, while he trotted behind the three at a decent pace.

Soon, however, both Jove and Romule began to gain on the exhausted Pigback.

Soon they began to overtake him.

Soon the three colors of blurring *joa* melded into one.

By the time Maesma approached, Jove was lying down, jaws still clamped around the runner's neck, and Romule's muzzle buried in vital groin. He could hear the swishing sounds of the Dog's tails in the grass as they began to welcome their master to dinner.

"Release," he said, and the two hellhounds rushed over to him for much appreciated praise. The beasts were so big, Maesma barely had to bend down to pet them. He cared nothing for the steel-coated teeth inside the dog's jaws. Those jaws that now tried to sneak a slimy tongue across the face of their praising trainer. He was proud of them.

When he stood up straight, he looked at the lifeless body, as he did so, Jove and Romule sat down with obedience. They did not share Maesma's respect for the dead Tusker...or Plainsman rather. When he still lived, the Plainsman could certainly move more quickly than most, at least that is what he witnessed in what little time the hunter had seen. Maesma fantasized briefly that maybe before today, running had been this one's passion.

A pain stung him somewhere in his spine, it was the price he paid because he had lived too long not knowing such a thing as passion. He looked at the dead body. This was not passion. This was just the kill, and the only thing it was good for was slating the hunger for a short time before the next.

A Boy and a Barter

You need not kick me like an idiot horse, You'Shou. I know where I am going. Solam stared up and over his shoulder at the boy on his back, who only chuckled and dug his heels in deeper.

"Oh, come on, Solam! Go faster!" Ronin was too excited to care about the lynxen's warnings. He was so happy to be out of the house that he could conquer the entire world with the child's toy sword he now held aloft, especially when he wielded it from the back of a giant feline. The healing he received from Solam's mate Sherium had done its job, aided by the quick thinking of his mother.

Shawna had given the boy some natural anti-venoms that had stemmed the ants' poison long enough for her best friends to arrive to their humble home. After a few intensive treatments, the boy had been good as new and longed for the day when his mother would once again let him leave the house. Cretus and Celeste, the Asperiis' faithful hounds, had not fared as well with the encounter of the ants. The male had perished by the swarm itself, and his mate to the Sorrow that followed his passing. Ronin had no idea about this thing they called the Sorrow, but he didn't like it one bit.

Ronin's mother had become frightfully overprotective the last several days, and the mated pair of plains cats had taken it upon themselves to get both of the humans out of the house and back to normal. Solam had offered to take the boy on a walkabout, and Sherium had convinced Shawna that she needed to make her appointment with the human merchant. One of Shawna's reasons for new-founded caution, that was not at all unwarranted, was the placement of an obelisk at the nearby village of Balanced Rock. This meant troops and patrols. It meant Sabrinian griffons hovering in the skies. It meant a whole lot more attention than she and her son needed. After some convincing, it had been decided that the Asperiis would leave their home and head back to live with their feline friends in Tor or Yukkai. Either way, the four would be joined by several more when Sherium gave birth to her first litter of cubs, and that idea made Ronin beam with excitement.

"Solam, I've been wondering about stuff. Can I ask you something?" Ronin was deep in thought.

"*Of course.*" The big cat chuckled.

It was a funny feeling for his rider who felt the odd rumble through his legs.

"When I was there, with the snake, when the ants started to get us, the snake's color never changed." the boy was puzzled. It was difficult for him to describe.

"*His color didn't change? How so? Remember, I do not see as you do, cub, you'll have to tell me more.*" Solam's patience goaded the boy to continue.

"Well, sometimes when I sneak up behind mom, and that is hard to do by the way, her colors change. She gets brighter really fast! The snake did not do that when the ants got us."

"*Oh, when you frighten her? I see. You are wondering why the snake was not frightened when it was attacked.*" The lynxen thought deeply about his answer. The boy was only about ten seasons old and probably did not need to be burdened about some of life's more gruesome content. Yet these types of questions deserved answers, and the considerable weight of those answers would be lashed on the shoulders of the boy for the rest of his days. His own first memories of life and death were much different, but he had never forgotten the wisdom in his pridemother's words that day. Perhaps his You'Shou was ready for the wisdom of such things.

"I was frightened," the boy went on as Solam made his way up the winding trails of the hill with no real effort "and I know Cretus..."

Ronin choked up with thoughts of his fallen companion. He had asked questions of what happened to his dog, but deep down, he knew that the hound had sacrificed himself for the boy. Flashes of memory confirmed the feelings, yet everything that happened that day was blurry at best. Celeste's passing had been even more difficult to fathom. Whatever had went on there, Ronin was certain that he hated this thing called 'Sorrow.'

"*There is nothing wrong with being afraid. It's all about what you do with fear.*"

They were about three quarters of the way up the hills to the north-west of the house. Soon they would be able to look across the great Sabrinian Grasslands, and sometime right near sunset. The view was sure to be remarkable, at least for one of them.

"I didn't know what to do. It all happened so fast. I just kept thinking that if I weren't I afraid I..." The boy's words were trailing off.

"You could have done something? You could not have. Life can be hard sometimes, Ronin, it puts us in hard situations. Situations that can scare us. Fear helps us know we are alive."

Navigating the terrain was not difficult, and for the boy it was a smooth ride.

"Why did the snake not fear the ants, though? Did it not know they could get him? Make him disappear?"

"Sometimes, we learn to not fear the inevitable things in this world. The snake probably knew that. It seems that coldbloods often do." The terrain was not difficult, but navigating the boy's question certainly was.

"Coldblood? What is a coldblood?" Even the inflections in the child's voice described confusion.

"Coldbloods need the sun to keep them warm, not just food like you or I." That seemed simple enough. Solam waited for another question that did not come.

"I want to be a coldblood." Solam's *Diyi You'Shou* sounded as if the sun would never rise after tonight. "That way I will not feel afraid again."

"Cub, there is nothing wrong with who or what you are, and being anything other than yourself is a foolish plight." Solam and his mounted companion made a steep switchback.

Ronin was quite adept at riding the giant cat, and a slightly tightened grip of silver mane was all that was needed to keep him in place. Clanking of Solam's jewelry seemed an odd addition to nature's symphony.

"I have walked many lands, young cub. My paws have tread upon the slippery ferns of the far jungles of the south. My claws have gripped onto the stern frozen cliffs of the north. Pounded into the dirt have I the grasslands in between, felt the warmth of the western shores soak through my toes, and scorched the tread on the burning wastelands of the east." The climb involved a couple of hops from the lynxen, both with the same results as before.

"In all of my travels, I have found but one truth. Be it paw or hoof, sandal or wheel, wing or belly, coldblood or warm; we are all

traveling towards the same destination." Keeping pace with the
sinking sun, Solam and Ronin continued to climb.

*"You cannot let the darker weather in your own journey steal
from you the fresh sent of a newborn sunrise. You cannot allow a
gasping breath, tired from racing the wind, take from you the majesty
painted upon a mountaintop's canvas."* The two rounded the last bit
to the summit of the hill.

The view was spectacular.

"What do you see, first cub?" Solam asked his passenger, while
allowing the surrounding terrain to fill his heart with peace. No
matter how many lands he travelled, such overlooks epitomized the
very wanderlust that drove him onward.

Ronin climbed down from the lynxen's shoulders. Solam watched
his strange blue eyes as they took in the marvels in a manner that the
big cat could only imagine. The hunter's vision had not seemed any
different in the small boy, even when taking into account the blue
swirls of color that seemed to flow like a whirlpool to the boy's soul.
Lynxen's historical roles as lore keepers made them incredibly
curious, and both Solam and his mate had pondered their *You'Shou's*
strange eyes since he first opened them.

"I see everything," the boy said somberly. "There is a lot of
different lights. There is also a great darkness, there." He pointed
towards the horizon.

*"Cub, there will always be darkness; with it comes all of the
things that stalk our dreams. Yet just like the night, this too will
eventually give way to reborn light."*

His single audience member was lost in translation of the big
cat's thoughts. Neither Ronin nor Shawna had points of reference
when their friends spoke to them using the mental images, so
understanding such metaphors was often like untying knots with your
toes.

*"Fate has taken you in her teeth, cub. A gentle embrace that will
tear your flesh if you struggle against it. She is the pridemother that
knows what is best for you, and rousing her hackles will surely
bloody your neck."* These were the words Solam had learned many,
many seasons ago. They were not his words, nor were they those of
the one who had spoken them to him, nor were they the words
spoken to her. These words were a truth passed down from teacher to
cub, and he hoped that somehow Ronin would find meaning in them.

"Let fate carry you, if you do so, your direction will seem aimless and without burden. You will find light, even in the darkness and fear. Just let her carry you, cub, and you will always end up where you need to be."

Ronin giggled. "What is fate?"

The lynxen rolled his eyes and thought about how to explain fate. He supposed this would be a conversation for much, much later. For now, he would have to simplify things:

"Do you see the way the grass sways across the plains below us?"

"Yes."

"Fate is like that. Like the force that causes the grass to bend."

The boy was puzzled. "I thought that it was wind that made the grass move."

"It is, but fate is like wind to the grass. The grass has no control about its own movement."

"And the wind is a she?" Ronin was trying to follow, but to no avail.

Solam thought again for a long moment, he reckoned the talk would have to wait. *"Just enjoy the view Diyi You'Shou. You'll understand some day."*

They watched the beauty of the world before them, Ronin hugged Solam deeply, whatever this Sorrow was that took Celeste, the boy knew that as long as he had Solam, it would never find him.

***

Sherium was as quiet as death's whisper, and she watched the two humans approach the secluded clearing from the opposite direction. Shawna did not see any other signs of human life in the surrounding area but, nonetheless, felt that if Filius Max saw the lynxen, no amount of animosity would be retained. Seeing such a rare beast in these lands was normal for the Asperiis, but for everyone else it would be a tavern tale passed down for generations.

Browndog the mare stomped at the tasty grasses that were slightly unreachable due to the length of the reins that Shawna had tied to a nearby branch. She nickered a bit before testing, and quickly after dismissing, a mouthful of moss growing on the side of the tree.

Shawna leaned on her tall walking staff as she watched the man approach from the distance. Her cart had been filled with rows of partially grown shoots from the Asperii garden; garlic, onions, carrots, and other crop she had planted in fall and wintered. The woman was a marvel at gardening, a talent the retired warrior would have never guessed to have before going into hiding with her son.

"Filius, nice to see you." Shawna gave a slight nod in the direction of the man's approaching footsteps.

"My lady." The merchant bowed low. Even at a comfortable distance the gardener could smell the odors of last night's adventures at the tavern. Her vision picked up a rapid heartbeat that sent his *joa* into the other organs in his body. The life-energy slowed around the liver, which after years of abuse had swollen and bloated in the man. His lifestyle would claim him before need be if he continued to indulge.

This was a normality in successful men, at least in Shawna's experience. So many times had her companions squandered their earnings for but a brief moment on a ruler's throne. She had never understood this because, after such fleeting tenure, the days following often demanded the fool carry that very same throne on boards strapped directly to the head.

"Lady, in the many years we have met, you have never once told me your name." The man took in the figure in front of him.

Shawna wore a lightweight cloak that fluttered in the gentle breeze, allowing for the man to see her too-short dress. Far from prying eyes, her farm allowed her to wear little more than her wide-brimmed sun hat, and her son's own inability to see flesh required her to don little more than what was comfortable for a summer day working in the garden. Gloves protected her hands, and sandals her feet, and sometimes a short dress to protect uncomfortable branding from the sun.

Hours upon hours of hard work kept the woman in the carved shapes of a Sabrinian Honor Guard, and the lustful stare of the sun kept her skin a deep copper. Her thin frame was well-nourished and healthy, quite the contrast to the man observing her. His arms and legs were atrophied due to lack of proper toil, and his flow of *joa* was pushed through a system of roots that seemed to have given up the taste for water.

"I do not plan on breaking that covenant, either," she said.

The man's gaze made her feel as though worms seeped under her skin. She did not have to see like a normal woman to know that he took in every inch of her, from small toe to slender neck. Her instincts were fueled by her gender and caused her to pull her hat down low and wrap her cloak around her.

"Suit yourself, then." His eyes slowly wrestled away from the mouthwatering feast and on to something that equally satisfied the man's hunger; the profit he would make from the items in the Asperii woman's cart. There were many gardeners in the area around Balanced Rock, but none as good as the blind woman; with the upcoming festival, he would be able to charge top dollar. In his own cart, he had the usual supplies, some flour, some linens, and some cheese from the Coreni farm. He began making his usual assessment of her goods, which far undercut the specimen's value.

"I will need to obtain some supplies right away, Filius." Shawna was frank and kept her head down so that the man did not see her speech as an open invitation for his too-probing eyes.

"Oh?" Her statement caused a pause in the merchant's appraisal. "And what is it that I can obtain for you?" Filius asked the question as his mind already began to formulate a way to increase the cost the woman would have to bear.

"I will be doing some travelling, and I will need some supplies I cannot acquire from my home." She was being vague.

"I see. What's the rush?" His voice was deceptively kind.

"I have a family emergency in the Capitol." The lie was full of purpose. Shawna knew the man was shrewd, and she had no intention of attempting to successfully bluff him, but she was a woman, and allowing her cloak to flutter open for a brief moment played on the primal areas of his body. This could successfully divert the attention of any man.

"What type of supplies?" He asked a question that, whatever the response would be, meant a rare and difficult to find item.

"I need my normal winter's shipment, as well as some particulars. Two sets of boots, a large water barrel, and a spare cart axel." She knew the list was suspicious, especially this far out of season. What she did not know was that the small town of Balanced Rock was bustling with activity due to the upcoming festival.

"I see." He was examining her again, the crawling feeling moving into her stomach nearly making her gag. "What is in it for me?" He dared to step closer towards her.

Shawna found the man disgusting. So much so, she almost wished he would allow his animal instinct to take control of his limbs to test her. She could see his life force flowing in excitement around both of the decision making areas of a man; though she had not known the touch of one in far too long, there was no way should could withstand the vile filth that would be his. No, if he dared to touch her, she would show him no mercy, a thought that caused her to eagerly tighten her grip on her walking staff. The fool would not even know what hit him. She could strike him in three vital areas, and then splash his brains on the ground in a blink of an eye if she wanted, but her lack of option to do so caused her to let out an audible sigh.

"What is in it for you is good, solid coin."

He was obviously not interested in her answer. He continued to advance.

Shawna now thought about the mess of disposing of his body. How she hated doing that, especially when separating thigh from shin was so difficult with but a belt knife. She supposed she could not kill him no matter how refreshing the thought.

Still the fool stepped closer.

"I would be willing to expedite your requests for a slight favor." Suggestion of the favor being something that would require her to kneel, or worse, was more than apparent.

Shawna reached down for a moment to retrieve a pouch of coin from her belt. She tossed it to the merchant who snatched it from the air as deftly as a knife master.

Filius opened the pouch to view its contents, two heavy steel coins.

"This is dwarvish steel." His words were full of awe. "Very valuable."

"There is more where that comes from." Shawna tapped her walking staff.

"I do believe we have a bargain," said Filius "I will return here in seven days with your supply."

"Three days." The woman's tone was no longer the naive witch in the woods. She knew the value of the coins.

"That may be difficult to..."

"Three days," she repeated, "and, Filius, don't make me come looking for you."

The merchant had heard of someone being 'full of surprises' before, but never so many in one glorious package. She moved over to her cart and began unloading the contents without troubled navigation of terrain or itemization. Filius watched her for a bit before moving to his to do the same.

He thumbed the coins. *More where that came from? He thought.* Adding the belt pouch to his own before he grabbed the sacks of flour.

"No way that bitch is blind," he mumbled the thought out loud but to himself, not realizing that someone as quiet as death's whisper watched him from the shadows.

Oh, Clara!

The day had been a hectic one so far, and this only made matters worse. As soon as they got into town the little ones' seemingly limitless energy compounded with the masses of people. Never before had any of the Corenis seen such a plethora of people. The festivals for the Obelisk raising at Balanced Rock had reached every small village and town from the realm; even performers had come from the capitol, fire dancers from the coastal cities, and some sort of surprise display as a gift from the Nine Kingdoms. There were so many people arriving in town that temporary housing nearly twice the size of the actual one had to be built of pole and canvas. It was unreal, a dream perhaps, and Baylee could not believe her eyes.

There were crowds on streets not made for so many boots. A perpetual cloud of dust seemed to float above the ground about shin level. The dredge goats pulling the wagon even seemed a bit agitated as they pulled into town, trumpets from unknown animals in the distance causing them to toss their head back. Locals could be pointed out by the looks of worry and distain on their faces, the creases of skin pushing eyebrows together seemed to question whether anything would ever be the same again. The general store had been torn down and moved, as was one of the linen shops. New repairs had to be made to the storefronts and taverns, all due to the desires of the new magistrate.

Baylee's younger sister had decided it would be a good idea to run off towards the fountain being built in the newly formed center of town. The well had been removed and replaced by a large pool in the center of which, the great obelisk would be erected. It had been impossible to stop the girl from taking off with the strategic timing she had used to sneak away. Baylee had been distracted while attending to Eelia. Icomus and the boys were unloading huge crates of cheese. The men had worked nearly non-stop for the last week to bring in as much a supply as possible. The fool girl had just disappeared, goaded by an excited group of children around her age.

"Where'd she go?" Icomus shouted over the back of the wagon. The noise of the crowd was unsettling. There were so many people.

"Towards the fountain. I'll take Eelia to check it out. Are you guys okay?" Baylee was the woman of the family after all.

"You guys okay?" Jacin mimicked his sister, while Jacob mocked her with a face that made him look like he came out of the womb sideways.

Baylee shook her head. "I'll be right back. Come on Eelia." Long brown waves of hair bounced as she lead her little brother quickly through the crowd, the smallest member of the family jogging to keep up with his sister, hoping to keep his arm from being pulled off
.

Baylee felt as though she were wearing a set of blinders, the sheer amount of people busily working around her was so much to take in. She searched for a glimpse of Clara's favorite gown, the very one they had crafted together as a replica of an actual High Priestess' gown. She watched for couple of bright ribbons bobbing up and down, a sign of her sister's perfect pigtails.

The construction of the new buildings, the decorations for the festival, horses, dogs, children playing, street performers, merchant's booths all seemed congested together. Where did all of these people come from?

"Clara!" Baylee called as she neared the fountain. Kids were playing everywhere, splashing around in the water. Baylee hopped up on the concrete basin that had been poured in a perfect circle. If she weren't so nearing a frantic state, she may have taken the time to notice the elegant construction, the precision. The priestess had been in town little more than two weeks, and she had changed everything.

"Clara!" Baylee glanced around, Eelia scrambled up behind her, not certain whether he should look at the other kids in the pool, or try to figure out what it was his sister was looking for.

Her vision panned around the crowd of people.

There! The last in a line of kids playing chase around the side of the building, that fool girl!

"Come on, buddy!" She jumped off of the edge of the pool, her little brother giving her a look of confusion and frustration as his head snapped backward and he was pulled into action. His little legs took three strides to her one, but he could not keep up. Baylee knew Eelia was just getting too big for her to be lugging him around on a hip. The knowledge of the dilemma, and the added time it was taking her to find her sister, was adding weight to the stick she would eventually use to thrash her little sister soundly with.

"Clara!" she yelled at the crowd and above.

"Cwar-ar-ar-ar-ar-ar-ah!" Eelia tried to repeat the call for his older sister, his trot causing his call to stutter out.

The two ran across the square towards the place the kids disappeared.

"Watch it!" Came a shout from the driver of a horse-pulled wagon; workers in the back shouted at them as well, adding to the embarrassment.

Eelia clung to her skirts as if the passing wagon were some deadly beast of legend, which was mild compared to the fit he had thrown this morning when they tried to load him in theirs.

"My lady!" the driver added with a tilted hat, the men in the back calling like buck dredge goats in the rut.

That was the last thing she needed, men looking at her in such odd ways. What did they think she was? Who did they think they were? Where was her blasted sister?

She could hear the sound of her sister's infectious laughter in the distance and getting further away. What in a Valkyr's wing was the girl thinking, ignoring her like this!

By the time Eelia and Baylee rounded the corner, Clara was nowhere to be found. Yet the elder sister felt she was at least closing in. There were less people around the back side of the shops, though there were a multitude of crates and barrels stacked carelessly about. As if the hustle and bustle weren't enough, there were enough new places to hide to keep a game of hide-and-seek or tag going for hours. She groaned. This had better not go on for another two minutes!

Baylee was angry now. Her little sister did this sort of thing all the time: running off, exploring, and being a kid. Honestly, the behavior wasn't that much different than her own. Clara did not understand. This was no normal festival. There were strange people from all over the realm. Strangers neither Baylee nor Icomus knew. Goddess knows what kind of harm could become her youngest sister without watchful eye.

Suited her right, running off like a damned dredge goat kid, Clara was just as stubborn as one and had about the same amount of common sense. She, no doubt, thought her sister wanted to be a part of this game. That could not have been further from the truth.

"Clara!" Many of the workers turned to see her, but none were the intended recipient of the call.

"Sir, did some kids come through here?" Baylee asked a man loading mead barrels into the back of a tavern, the patrons inside could already be heard at this early hour in the day.

The man grunted and pointed towards the direction of a farm house, where the front door had just slammed shut. Eelia mimicked the man pointing and grunting at the other farm houses in the area, thinking he knew what the man was indicating and was ready to show that he saw even more than the helpful workman.

Before the man stood up and put his hands on his hips, Baylee had her little brother in tow. Poor Eelia resembled an odd combination of a rag doll and a human wagon. They ran up the back porch steps of the house and began wrapping on the door forcefully.

The man that answered the door wore servants clothing. He was old enough that time had folded up his dark skin around his eyes and slightly pulled his shoulders towards his toes. His smile made his eyes disappear.

"How can I help you?" He said with a bow.

"My sister. Did she...did some kids come running through here just now?" Baylee composed herself in the middle of the question.

"Is that Baylee? Baylee Coreni?" The identification came over the shoulder of the servant, and Baylee recognized the voice as Geneeve Luena's.

"Yes, it is my lady." Baylee curtsied quickly, and Eelia did the same.

The latter causing a chuckle from the woman. The house smelled of freshly baked pie, a skill Baylee had to admit herself amateur at best.

"My lady, huh? Look at yourself! Your blossoming year is upon you, and you'll have no need for granting your equals such titles." Geneeve meant the words a compliment, but they just made Baylee blush.

"I'm sorry, Matron Luena. But did you see little Clara come through here?" She was urgently trying to look past the woman.

"Oh, Goddess! You remind more of your mother every time I see you!" Geneeve was a handsome woman, her wide smile contrasting

164

against her dark skin. Like many Sabrinians, the summer sun rapidly transformed light skin into deep coppers and caramels. Her dark straight hair and dark brown eyes were also not a rarity, nor was the kindness they showed the young woman before them.

"You must call me Geneeve, and the answer is yes, that little blonde girl came bouncing through here with about half a dozen other monsters. Probably heading out to see the soldiers and the Thanadonts." She nodded towards the front door behind her. Baylee noticed another woman behind Geneeve, Herminia Camdania. The woman wore a forced smile.

"Come on, Eelia. Let's go." Her little brother was staring intently towards the kitchen, he'd inherited his father's appetite for sweets.

"Baylee, why don't you stay here for a bit? The kids will be fine. Have some pie. This little soldier looks hungry! What is your name?" Geneeve bent down and clapped her hands together in front of Eelia, who had apparently instantly learned how to win over any woman's heart with a single, bashful grin.

"We just can't. Clara took off, and I need to rein her in for a moment. She's always doing this sort of thing."

"They are kids, and they will be fine..."

"Geneeve, let the girl go find her sister. How many children did you have before you began to relax?" The other woman was not as handsome as Geneeve. Her features advertised her long hours of sweat and flame in the blacksmith.

"Very well, but this little goat handler must stay for pie!" Geneeve picked Eelia up from his sister's skirt.

He smiled, enjoying being babied.

"Okay. I'll be back as soon as I find her." Baylee started for the door, for the first time noticing crates and straw all over the house. "Matron Luena. Sorry, Geneeve, when did you move into this house? Oh...just...I'll be right back." The latter came out only after Baylee realized that she still needed to find her estranged sister.

"Go. We'll be right here, won't we, Eelia?" Geneeve ran a finger across the boy's nose, and his laugh let his sister know it would be alright for her to go find Clara.

Baylee raced out the front door that was positioned for a nice view of the surrounding valley beyond the house's well-maintained entry area. There was a small grass field past the flowers and hedge, and further still were many temporary living quarters for various travelers that had come for the festival. This appeared a sprawling nest of tents buzzing with yet more excitement, much like the main street she and her family had come in on. Over the noise, she could hear the unfamiliar bellow of Thanadonts. Running towards all of this was a giggling group of five, no six, no seven rambunctious children. Her own sister's uniquely colored pig-tails bouncing amongst them.

"Clara! Goddess hear me, girl! Clara!" Baylee bounded off the front porch, now unhindered by her youngest sibling she could finally make up some ground. There was no way her sister had heard her over the distractions of the canvas village before them, and to Baylee's dismay the elusively quick children entered the first row of tents well before she could close the distance across the small garden area.

By the time the young woman reached full speed, the children had disappeared behind both people and housing. The whole area was alive and as Baylee approached, racing behind the children, she noticed this wasn't a place for just travelers. These people were a part of the Sabrinian Army. Armed soldiers walked about with what looked like women in simple priestess gowns and men with the golden griffons embroidered on robes even less elaborate. Baylee had never seen a full complement of soldiers before, and the sight of these men, even without breastplates and helms, spurred her into further urgency.

There were, of course, patrols. These two-by-two complements of both men and women marched casually around the outside perimeter of the camp and did not seemed bothered by the idea that Baylee and the children had invaded their living quarters. She was forced to slow as she passed the first row of perfectly aligned structures. There were several people going about their business, which seemed casual in comparison to the assumptions Baylee made. Perhaps it was due to the upcoming festivals, or distance away from a battlefield, but for whatever reason, these soldiers seemed like they were having...fun. The simple farmer's daughter always imagined soldiers as being serious even in their sleep, but this was definitely changing the fantasy.

The troops were happy, no doubt due to their ability to participate in the festivities that would be thrown the next few days. The question Baylee did not have time to answer was why they were here. She and her father had discussed, several days before, the rumors floating around the area about all of the foreign merchants that would be in town, the performers that were going to make "surprise" appearances, and the importance of the family's participation in the merchant booths. This was the Coreni chance to become known beyond Balanced Rock, a chance for a meager living to become a good one. A chance for the family business to grow, but first she had to find that knot-head of a sister.

Several passersby gave her the clues she needed to follow the children, who were racing towards the rumbling grunts of the giant beast of burden known as a Thanadont. These beasts were so big their calves were the size of a full grown draft horse. The gigantic animals even made Icomus' stubborn dredge goats look small and delicate by comparison. It was surprise the children would want to take a look at one of these legendary creatures up close, and Baylee cringed at the thought of a massive hoof crushing one of the reckless kids and teaching the whole group a lesson.

She maneuvered past several rows of tents before approaching the circular area where the Thanadont was chained, though she could see the beast above the tops of the living quarters, only the entire picture of it demonstrated any level of true majesty. To Baylee, it vaguely resembled a giant wild pig, with huge swooping teeth filed down and capped with giant metal bowls. About a dozen people crawled around it, scrubbing it down with long-handled, soapy brushes. Occasionally, It would dip its snout down into a long, wide, shallow pit that was filled with a sloppy mixture of whatever the two men carried constantly back and forth from the mess area. Contented grunts came from deep within the beast's gullet while it enjoyed its scrubbing and meal; grunts came out from other areas as well, no doubt helping the beast itself to relax, albeit at the torment of its handlers.

And so there they were, the children, all grouped around a very tall man who looked like he had somehow tightened his skin around too-large muscles. He wore white robes that nearly blended in with equally white skin. She was unsure how a man could be nearly as big as her father. He was blindfolded, taking what appeared to be no notice to the goings on around him; as if he were a sort of pale statue. To his side lay a dog, black as a cloudless night, head perked in vigilance, its dark eyes took her in with an unspoken warning. The dog was nearly twice the size of Ranger, who was no doubt at home on a hilltop awaiting their return. Standing next to the man, yet somewhat behind, was the thinnest woman Baylee had ever seen. She had few features to her body, so few she could have easily been mistaken for one of the fence posts surrounding the Thanadont. The woman carried a wooden book in her hand that somehow folded out to support writing utensils and an inkwell. It was there where Baylee found her lost sister.

"Clara! What are you doing? Didn't you hear me yelling at you?" Her shout caused the thin woman and all the children, including Clara, to jump a bit. Baylee grabbed her sister by the arm and pulled her close; only then noticing an older woman kneeling down in front of the children. The woman stood, she wore the glorious robes of the Keeper of the Doctrine, an honor given to only one elected lady at a time. The clothing meant she was one of the most powerful women in the country, and she stood there, in front of Baylee, in the small town of Balanced Rock.

"Oh, I'm so sorry, Matron. I did not see you..." the farm girl began her apology with great difficulty.

"Nonsense. I did not mind. How could you refuse such a wonderfully dressed young lady?" While she regarded the little girl's handmade robes, the priestess smiled at Clara and straightened her own gown, as if showing off what the real thing looked like. The expression of happiness looked odd on her face, as though she were not accustomed to it being there.

"So you are this little darling's guardian?" the priestess smile was gone, a thief in the night.

"I am, Matron. She is my youngest sister."

"I am her *only* sister," Clara added.

"I see." The smile was back again, but only for the briefest of moments. "You have excellent taste in gowns, an excellent way to honor the Goddess."

"Thank you, Matron."

"And you are polite. By far the most impressive young lady I have seen in this backwoods town." The priestess pursed her lips.

"She's a witch." Clara blurted it out, pride in her chest.

The statement seemed to push the priestess' head back a bit, she raised her eyebrows, and opened her eyes wide. Even the formless woman in the back dropped her quill and had to scramble to catch it before it rolled off her portable desk.

"What she means is that I can be a witch sometimes. My mother passed away several years ago. I have had to be very hard on her." Everything about the statement made Baylee sound guilty of an accusation that could not exist. Truthfully, what had happened on the farm that day still baffled her, and she had agreed with her father in that no one need know about the instance until the right time came to pass.

"Of course," the priestess replied, understanding the need for stern authority all too well.

"No. She's a real witch! Just like in the stories! My dad and my brothers said..." Clara did not like being disregarded.

"Oh, sister, there you go with that imagination of yours! She's always playing priestess, or soldier and the like, she really is quite full of spirit!" Baylee feigned a laugh. There was no way this woman did not know she was hiding something. "Come on, Clara. Let's let the lady go about her important business."

"No!" Clara was all of the sudden much younger than Eelia. "Not until you tell her you're a witch!"

"You are being embarrassing, young lady. If you keep this up, you will feel the back of my hand." Baylee was serious about the threat.

Clara crossed her arms in defiance, but she knew her place.

"There's no worry, miss...?" the priestess drug out the last consonants to form a question.

"Coreni, Matron. My name is Baylee Coreni." The farmer's daughter was proud of the way that sounded.

"The goat farmer's daughter. I have heard of you. Best cheese in all the lands, I do believe." The compliment was sincere.

"Thank you, Matron." Baylee bowed in acceptance of the praise. "Please, come by our booth later, if you have time of course. We have an amazing berry-wine batch made with some perfectly aged, flavored vinegar. It's simply delightful. We would be honored if you would take a sample into your lovely villa." She was a bit amazed that such mercantile words had escaped her mouth. Perhaps this was why her father always had her doing the talking with the town merchants, trading for needed supplies and the like. Goddess knows her father had not the tongue for such words.

"I will certainly do so, Lady Coreni. After all, I would enjoy a break from planning this cursed parade." The priestess grinned at her again, an awkward, misplaced twist of her lips.

"Then if you will excuse me. Come, Clara." She pulled her sister backward and turned to leave.

"Just one more thing before you go, Miss Coreni. This is my guardian, Bo'Ah." She motioned to the blindfolded man, who still looked like a statue. "He can see things most others cannot. The Goddess has blessed him, you see."

"I see that he is blindfolded, Matron. What can he see like that?" Baylee tried for a bit of charm, but there was fear in her voice.

"These are special blindfolds, made with thin golden discs sewn into them. Just over the eyes. Hunters, like Bo'Ah here, need them when they are around so many people, like hoods over the head of a falcon." The matron looked at the man as if he were a well-bred hound.

"Hunters. Oh, I see! He is a trained hunter! What does he hunt?" Baylee was curious, as were the slack-jawed children who did not know who to be more intrigued by or frightened of: the pale man, the black warhound by his side, or the giant animal in the background.

"He hunts whatever, or whomever, I want him to." The priestess approached the man, her hand drawing a seductive line up his carved arm towards an oversized shoulder.

One of the most powerful women in all the land or not, it was clear this man could snap the matron like a twig if he so desired. His arm below the shoulder was bigger than the matron's waist.

"The thing is, Miss Coreni, hunters tend to get excited around Otherbreeds and the like." She moved over to the other side of the man, dragging a fingernail, as before, across the exposed part of his chest with the same hand she had, no doubt, used to trace on him many times before.

"Otherbreeds, like the Pigbacks we have here in camp, look different to him, so he can 'see' them even if they are mixed into a crowd of people just like you and I." She continued her lecture slowly, enjoying the sound her touch made on his skin.

Baylee was openly confused. So much so, she did not notice the growing groups of people that were stopping to hear the woman speak.

"But aren't the Tuskers ten feet tall? With huge fangs and cloven hooves? That would look different to any of us, wouldn't it?" Baylee thought the answer was obvious, but it clearly wasn't.

"True enough," the priestess agreed. "Stunties, Tuskers, or Pigbacks, Tyrians, Taurans, all look very different than all of us. But do you know what does not?" This question was meant for the children, soldiers, and servants gathering around, all now paying close attention to the speech. "Well, Miss Coreni? Do you?"

Baylee had been taunted by her brothers before, but never had such a seemingly innocent inquiry made her feel so small.

Baylee was no fool. She knew where this was going. She pulled her sister close with both shoulders, so close it hurt the little girl, who was confused at both the priestess' strange speech and her sister's palatable fear.

"Answer the question, girl." The gaze set upon Baylee by the priestess was a wolf crouching before the pounce. Her tracing hand went up the back of the pale man's neck and began to slowly tug on his blindfold.

"I would suppose that something like a witch might appear similar to us...not that I..." The gaze turned her blood icy. There was no escaping this wolf.

The black dog stood and looked at Baylee, her pounding heart causing its ears to twitch. Everything was quiet for the longest second ever.

"Exactly. Witches look exactly like you and I, to you and I. But to a hunter like this one, they are a giant trying to hide in a chicken coup. They are a special type of Otherbreed. And they get hunters oh so excited! Sometimes the lust of the hunt overtakes them, and they can ravage one of these evil creatures in but a moment..." Her hand toyed with the ceremonial knot that tied the blindfold on the man.

"But for people like you and I, Lady Coreni, we have nothing to fear from hunters like Bo'Ah. They are as well trained as the mongrels by their side. They will protect all of us that are Righteous in the Doctrine. Do you understand?" the Matron began to pull loose the knot.

Baylee worked her mouth to respond but could only nod. As she did so, a tear fell down her cheek. She was no witch.

The blindfold fell off of the hunter, and for the first time the stone statue moved. His head looking down and sideways, immediately towards the two girls. His eyes locked onto Baylee, his milky white eyes without color or distinction, his dead eyes saw into her, through her. Those dead white eyes saw exactly what happened that day on the farm, and he instantly knew more about her than even she did.

With a snarl he stepped through the group of children who squealed in fear of being trampled, his hound on his heels. Baylee shook her head, unable to turn away from his stare. Clara, at last, saw the seriousness of the situation and let out a scream, just as a muscled arm grappled a hand of stone around Baylee's neck. In a moment, the vice-like fingers were extinguishing any cry for help. She could not move on her own accord, her hands giving up protecting her sister in an instinctual, yet futile, effort to dislodge the hunter's fingers.

He picked her up, still snarling, still staring through her. Clara spun around and tried to jump on Baylee's legs as she was lifted up from behind her, the weight of which seemed to only affect the rapidity in which Baylee lost her breath, something that was happening all too quickly.

"She does not defend herself?" The matron sheathed a dagger she had pulled from somewhere within the revealing robes.

The statue spoke, gravel in his throat. "Perhaps she cannot. She has awoken...but...perhaps...she does not know yet how to use it." He tilted his head from side to side, the veins in his neck bulging with anticipation. Those dead, colorless eyes still staring into her.

Clara let go of her sister's feet; it did not relieve her struggle for breath, the hand that held her squeezed tighter. Baylee's face began to lose its color, as if it moved into her rapidly reddening eyes and flushed down her checks as tears. Clara began to punch and kick at the hunter screaming for him to let her sister go, until a black dog almost tore the girl in half with snapping steel-coated teeth. Clara fell backwards crawling away from the beast as quickly as possible. The hunter downed the mongrel with a simple finger pointing towards the ground with his free hand.

People all around were watching, soldiers and servants alike. Silence ruled the moment, the very long moment that allowed the priestess to approach the dangling girl, whose eyes were starting to roll backwards into her head.

"Let her go, Bo'Ah." the Matron ordered her guardian.

The man hissed at the space between dangling prey and commanding master, clearly unsure if instinct to kill or to obey would win his internal conflict.

"I said release her!" it was a firm statement, louder than the first. It caused the man to follow instruction.

Baylee fell to the ground without strength in her legs to stop her. Clara fell on top of her sister, sobbing uncontrollably. The older Coreni gagged and choked in an attempt to get breath past her violated throat.

The priestess knelt down, inspecting both of the sisters as if they somehow made a very shoddy-looking throw rug.

"Clara, you need to get up. You two will be coming with me back to my villa. We have a lot to understand. Come. I will not let Bo'Ah hurt her again." The priestess' words were soft and kind.

"W-why d-did... he... h-h-h-hurt her..... in the f-f-f-f-irst p-p-p..." the little girl's words could barely be made out between sobs.

"Witches are bad, Clara. We have to be very careful around them."

"N-n-n-not hu-hu-her..."Clara's small frame was barking for air nearly as bad as her older sibling's.

"Oh, Clara, that remains to be seen. That remains to be seen. Pick her up." The priestess began to head back towards her villa, holding the hand of a very sad little girl. Behind them came a pale man holding a near lifeless form with his black dog in tow.

"Enjoy the show, everyone?" The shapeless woman snapped the crowd back into focus. "Get back to work. We still have a party to throw, a parade to plan, and a raising to put into motion."

The Keeper of Doctrine took Clara's hand and kept her at pace behind the pale-skinned man who carried Baylee over his shoulder, his big black hound sniffing from behind as if she were a treat for good behavior. The crowd began to disperse, with a few lingering stares at the two little girls.

Dwarvish Steel

"What do you see out there, Tuskslayer?" Cabot didn't bother looking up from his game of bones. There were only two men at the table with him, the eunuch Gallus and a merchant they had met the night before in the local tavern. The three men had been playing all night long and were heavily infused with spirits from the night before.

"Tuskslayer?" Maesma turned from his post at the flap, on the outside of which sat Jove and Romule, his faithful hellhounds. He started heading towards the table inside the officer's tent. The place looked as if a hurricane had been through it. Broken bottles, food baskets, and even naked people were strewn all about. There had been legendary debauchery the night before, and the foggy memories of it would surely be someday blown beyond proportion.

"That one not good either?"

Cabot was only half paying attention to his question, focusing on his tokens and how they would fit in with the rest of the board.

"Marcus, maybe you should call him by his name?" Gallus was a war priest and, as such, was assigned to the young sergeant as an advisor and medic, one of the many roles the priests play in the Sabrinian military.

"I'm getting sober, Gallus, you had best watch your informality." It was difficult to tell if it was an idle or actual threat.

"Bah! Both of you had better watch your game or Filius is going to own all of your shinies!" He gave a maniacal laugh.

"Tuskslayer...Shaman killer...Drumstopper." Marcus let out a sigh.

"What is wrong with his own name?" Gallus asked again.

"Goddess's cunt, man! I don't know his real name! Take this!" He slapped down his playing piece on the table, nearly too hard, causing the other bones to rattle around. It was a good play. He could tell by the groans of his opponents.

"What do you mean you don't know his name?" It was Filius' turn.

"He is no servant," Gallus said. "He is untouchable. Therefore not given a name amongst citizens of the empire. Only his priestess gives him a name."

"I know what an untouchable is. I just figured he was a soldier like the rest of you. BOOM!" The last word came down with a playing piece. It was a decent move as well. The turn now went to Gallus.

"Nonetheless, he does have a name. You should ask him." Gallus tapped his pieces together.

"So what is your name?" Filius asked Maesma the question, but tipped his head back to look under the table "Ouch! What the hell was that?"

"Sorry, sir." Came a woman's voice out from under the table.

The other two men at the table laughed.

"See! That's why I never let a woman suck my cock. They are terrible at it! You want a good body shake? Start being nice to Gallus here, he's the best!" The sergeant laughed heartedly.

"Well, you're just lucky mine's been removed because I think this..." he played his piece and both men cowered under his boast, "...allows me to fuck you both!" Gallus sat back with his arms folded after the play.

"Shit. Nice move, Gallus." There was a genuine level of respect in Cabot's defeat.

After groaning and double checking the last play, Filius pushed at the girl giving him pleasure. He was no longer in the mood. Meekly, she crawled from under the table to stand in the corner. Her acolyte robe and hair were disheveled, a tell-tale sign that she had spent the evening at the whim of these men.

"I've got to piss." Filius pointed at the girl. "Don't think you are done counting chickens, bitch? When I get back here you are going to finish!"

Gallus and Cabot laughed. Neither Maesma nor the girl found the statement funny. The merchant left to relieve himself.

"So what is your name?" Marcus asked Maesma the question, but Gallus held just as much curiosity towards whatever the answer may be.

"My name is Hunter, sergeant," he answered with a slight bow.

Cabot laughed. "Very well, very well. What were you looking at just now...Hunter?"

"The Matron Raen. She has captured a weaver." Maesma folded his hands together casually.

"A weaver? Right here in town?" Gallus was taken aback.

"Don't act so surprised Gallus, weavers can be anywhere, our friend here showed us that even the Pigbacks have them! I would not have believed it had I not seen the survivors' wills crushed at the sight of their shamans' severed heads. Didn't even have to chain some of them, they just walked right into the cages. Never seen anything like it!" The sergeant was lost in memory.

"The last few days have seen many surprises," Gallus added.

"True. I could not believe the Tusker leader pulled through those wounds," Cabot stated.

"Aye. And the young one has yet to succumb to your arrow," he said, nothing short of astonished.

"The Goddess favored our journey, for certain. Does that Eagle still fly overhead?" The sergeant realized he had not seen it since they arrived in town.

"You should have killed that bird." Maesma vomited the sentence.

"Nonsense." Gallus defended an earlier argument. "Our symbol is the gryphon, and a gryphon has an eagle's head. The eagle was no doubt a symbol of our success and good fortune."

"Indeed. The raptor is one of the many forms of the Goddess and a blessing to us all." The sergeant was a true believer.

The hunter openly scoffed. The other two men exchanged baffled looks.

Filius reentered the tent. His head was soaking wet as if he had dunked his head in a water trough, or forgot where it was he was supposed to relieve himself.

"Alright! One more game, then!" The merchant was full of renewed vigor. "I'll not be tricked into that same move again!"

He moved across the tent, searching for something to drink. Both Cabot and Gallus watched the man, intrigued by the sense of ferocity in his search. He moved sleeping bodies, thinking each one was hiding the last bottle of spirits and looked under beds, tossing blankets aside, To no avail.

"What are you doing, man?" Gallus said.

"Looking for something to drink." Filius looked around for where to search next.

"You cleared us out an hour ago," Cabot said, a slight chuckle accompanying the response.

"Oh, just send the girl." Gallus stated the obvious, "It's your money anyhow. Come here, girl. Take this..." He grabbed some of the money from his side of the table. "Take this to our new friend's wife. Tell her he would like her best."

The acolyte nodded quickly, grabbed the coin, and ran out of the tent.

"Don't forget to mention to the woman what his cock tastes like!" Marcus was joking, of course, yet for some reason only Gallus and the sergeant laughed.

"One more game, eh? What do you think?" Filius was speaking from the inside of an ale barrel. He had lost much coin to the war priest, and had nothing visibly left to offer in what would surely be a sacrifice to the more skilled player. Such is the folly with drink and gambling; courage to take risks rarely comes with the skill to capitalize on them.

"I think you have nothing left to wager." Marcus said, looking at the merchant with a raised eyebrow. "Unless, of course, you'd like to call in your wife to give you a loan. Tell me, Filius, how did you land a gem like that?"

The merchant started towards the table, as he did he took in a fist full of his own genitals. "It's because I'm hung like a damned Thanadont!"

"Oh, please." Gallus was clearly not taken by the bluff.

Cabot burst out in laughter.

"What?" Filius let go of himself to open his arms wide as if to expose a wounded heart.

"That poor acolyte has not so much as made a gasp for breath, let alone a cough or gag, *and* once we got back here you had difficulty keeping your robes from over the top of your head! None of us here have ever seen such a deprived field mouse!" Gallus' insult was dry but caused a snicker from the sergeant.

"That's right, Gallus, I think even the mice stand a bit taller around this merchant's wares!" Marcus enjoyed a hearty guffaw.

"Hunter, can you see the man's sorrow? We truly are mystified...maybe with your vision..."

"Oh, knock it off." Filius was defeated. "Besides, it is not the size of the beast, but rather the might of its roar that counts!"

"A beast only roars when it seeks its way home. Are you suggesting you are lost?" Maesma wasn't really paying attention, nor did he realize that his statement had silenced the sergeant and his advisor.

Both Marcus and Gallus looked to the hunter, then towards each other before laughing so hard the two nearly fell out of their chairs.

"He has jokes!" Gallus said, holding his stomach.

"That he does! Perhaps we should wake the acolyte and see if Filius here knew his way around...oh, hunter! You truly are a marvel!" Cabot was having a hard time recouping his breath.

"Actually, I think any man could get lost around that one, did you see the size of her forest? A man must need a hatchet and flame to reach her dripping cunt!" The eunuch now had Filius joining in on the laugh.

"You know," Filius sat down, leaning in to the others, "I heard Tyrian women have no hair down there."

"No, really? That's disgusting! How do you separate them from their young?" Cabot sounded curious.

"Perhaps they have no need. Perhaps their men have the same affliction as our merchant friend here!" Gallus was smiling wryly.

"Oh! Enough about my cock! Let's play another game already!" It was plain to see the martyred man was frustrated with his newfound 'friends'.

Marcus sat back in his chair and intertwined his fingers behind his head. He plopped both of his feet up on the table and tipped his chair back on the hind two legs.

"We are back to the original problem, Master Filius Max. You have nothing left to gamble. Now I am certain that when I speak to my colleague here, he would be more than happy to take whatever it is you wish to lose. I know I would. We are at an impasse. What do you have left to lose? Gallus has already cleared you out!" He untwined a hand from its resting place to offer the merchant a rebuttal. Gallus folded his arms across his chest.

"He hasn't cleared me out. Not completely. I still have this!"

The merchant slid his hand into a boot and pulled out a small leather pouch. When he opened it, he pulled out a large steel coin. The coin shined as if it had been polished, and reflected light off the many candles inside the officer's tent. Marcus put his feet down, and the chair fell back into position with a slight clunk.

"This is Dwarvish steel, boys. Rare and valuable. How about this to get me into another game?" Filius knew the answer, the widened eyes of his perspective opponents told him such.

"Let's have a look at it." Cabot nodded his head slightly as if to tell the man to toss over the coin.

Filius obliged, pinching his thumb under the coin and in between his middle two fingers, he gave it a flick. The sound that filled the air came from the strings of solid purity. The coin tumbled through the air like a trapeze artist flipping towards the outstretched hand of the catcher.

It never got there. Without warning, or without seeming to have the need to move from one part of the tent to another, the hunter was there at the table. He caught the coin several inches from Cabot's awaiting grasp. The interception was so shocking it caused the sergeant and Gallus to jump backwards. Gallus so much so that the man tipped over backwards into his chair. The eunuch's rogue foot kicked the underside of the table sending coins and glassware up in the air.

The calamity did not detour the hunter who now studied the coin intently, holding it between thumb and forefinger. He slowly spun it in the light, as if he were appraising its value.

"Goddess' cunt, man! You scared the shit out of me!" Cabot was not the only one.

Gallus was already scrambling back up to the table still clenching his chest.

"Where did you get this?" Maesma asked the question to the coin, but it was meant for Filius.

The other two men turned to look at the merchant. They had been in the field with this hunter for several weeks now, and though neither knew the nature of the man's vision, they definitely did not doubt it. Maesma saw things that no one else did. If it had not been for him, they would not have come across an entire tribe of marauding Tuskers. If not for him, they would not have been able to stop the shaman that cast dark magick upon their troops. Now the aimless hunter saw something in this fool merchant's rare coin, and neither Marcus nor Gallus hadn't the slightest clue as to what that might be.

"I...I won it in a game of bones a few weeks ago."

179

Three sets of eyes turned from the coin to him. Not one pair lacked scrutiny. It was Maesma's, however, that looked through the skin of the man, behind his bones, and into his blood. It was here where he could see the energies around his heart speeding up, the flush of fear moving into his muscles. Maesma hated liars.

The hunter knocked the table over with one hand, striking it so hard it nearly landed upon its own legs after spinning entirely around. The three men seated could barely react before Maesma was inches from the merchant's face. Fear pounded through the man as the hunter pressed the coin against the man's forehead. Using a single finger, he held the coin above his eyes in the center of his skull. Maesma put so much pressure on the fellow, that Filius' head was tilted awkwardly backwards. The man whimpered with cowardice as he held his hands up in surrender.

"Will this help you remember?" Maesma spoke to an idiot child.

"I...I...swear. I mean...I do gamble all the time...I am bound to win at least some times! Come on, guys! What's the big deal about a coin?" His heart beat faster again, and Maesma could see it.

Filius did not know. He did not understand that the blind man in front of him was not blind at all. He had no knowledge that hunters could see the life force of all living things. He had no idea that *joa* left trails, and that trained eyes could see these. He was naive to the fact that once a hunter was familiar with someone's *joa*, it was like recognizing a familiar face. Filius certainly did not know this hunter recognized the trail left on this coin, and that trail would lead him to someone from the hunter's distant past, the woman that broke his heart.

Maesma pulled out one of his crooked blades and pressed it against the man's throat, the faintest line of crimson drawing down his neck. Gallus and Marcus exchanged looks of concern, yet it was a motion from the sergeant's hand that let Gallus relax his grip from the hilt of his own dagger. Untouchables were not to behave as such but, apparently, Cabot wanted to see this play out.

"Where did you get this? I will not ask again." Maesma gave no bluff, and Filius knew this was no game.

"From a woman in the woods. A gardener. I trade with her twice a year. She gave the pouch to me. She...she...she said there was more where that came from. I...I can take you to her."

"Why would you not just say so?" Gallus asked the obvious question.

"Yes. Why protect her?" Marcus added.

"Profits man. Profits. This woman gives me her produce for next to nothing, and she's the best I've ever seen. Look. Like I said. I'll take you guys with me..."

"There is no need. Just point the direction," the hunter spoke through his teeth, his blade scraped on the man's neck.

"I can only tell you where we meet. It's south and east of here. About a full day's ride..." If the merchant had not just relieved himself, he would have at this moment, but his heart rate did not spike. He was not lying.

"Not good enough," Marcus said.

"It will suffice. I can pick up her trail from there." The hunter was already beginning to calculate the methods he would need to stalk the prey.

Maesma let up the pressure on the coin and pulled back his blade. Filius now had a red imprint of the coin's intricacies on his forehead, dwarfish symbols and a great mountain in the distance, crossed hammer and pick axe, all in rich detail on the man's skin.

The commotion awakened the naked servants sleeping on the floor of the tent, they were attempting to back into the safest corners they could find. Both Cabot and Gallus looked at the hunter, quite curious about what had transpired. Marcus had no idea of the significance, yet the pure ferocity inspired by the coin intrigued him.

"Sergeant, we must go to this meeting spot. I will find wherever her dwelling place is from there. Bring five of your best skirmishers. We will need them." Maesma was gathering his meager belongings.

"Wait a second here, hunter. What is so damned important about a gardener that lives in the woods?" Gallus had a knack for stating the communal interest.

"The question you should be asking, eunuch, is why does a gardener in the woods have dwarvish steel?" Maesma began to roll everything into a pack.

"Leave us." The sergeant ordered the servants gone. "Not you." The last order was for Filius. "You sit there."

He stood and walked over to Maesma. "Valid point. Why does a gardener have a rare coin? But do I care enough to take five men

181

with me and leave this festival on the whim of a hunter? You have to give me more, man." He whispered to make the statement direr.

Maesma shook his head. He hated entitlement almost as much as he hated liars. Yet, he supposed he needed the man at least as a distraction.

"The woman that handed him that coin is Shawn'Athasia. She and I trained together for Her Own Voice. Shawn'Athasia defected during a mission and became an enemy of the state. She protected some dangerous Otherbreeds and helped them to flee our great nation. If we were to retrieve her, your name would echo among the singers in the temple halls. You're first command mission scrolls would be written with the blood of villains..." Maesma narrowed his eyes for emphasis.

"I like the sound of that," said Marcus.

"Come." Maesma was urgent. "I will tell you more on the way."

"Why do you need so many men for just this one woman?" Gallus interjected the question that was forgotten in the excitement.

"Shawn'Athasia is formidable and, last I saw her, she had formidable allies as well." Maesma did not need his words to twist the man's arm; promise of battle was always a suitable motivator.

"Gallus, order ten of our best skirmishers to the ready. I will take no chances. Come, tell me more, hunter..." Cabot followed Maesma out of the tent, and Gallus slipped out towards the skirmisher district of the camp.

Filius still sat inside.

"Oh, hunter, what was the command for your dogs to attack?" The two hellhounds looked up as if they knew he was talking about them. Jove and Romule seemed to be fully capable of understanding the common tongue.

Filius, overhearing the question from inside the tent, began to look around, realizing he was the last one in the tent.

"Why do you want to know that?" Filius had panic in his voice, the idea of being torn to shreds by steel-plated teeth did not sit well.

"Don't you know, merchant?" the sergeant put his hand on Maesma's shoulder, a tone of camaraderie in his words. "We hate liars."

Maesma gave the command and the big dogs bounded into the tent. Screams and snarls came from the inside as well as the sound of tumbling chairs and bodies. The noises were horrendous, causing passersby to stop and stare.

Marcus simply smiled and waved. Nodding to the soldiers and servants he recognized. He was so focused on pretending a man was not being torn apart inside his tent that the onlookers seemed to question their own sanity. He smiled at the hunter and patted him on the shoulders.

"We leave before midday," he said to Maesma. "I'm going to go get some food, you coming, coincatcher?"

"Coincatcher?" The hunter chewed on wax.

Marcus did not like the nickname either.

"I'll figure one out someday, you just wait." He slapped Maesma on the back, and the two headed off to breakfast.

New Perceptions

"Sister, she truly is amazing."

"I agree, sister. Her skills are just...well...unbelievable."

"She even left her boots on!"

"And her corset!"

"The men can barely control themselves...even with the threat of priesthood!"

"The way she looks up at the ones in front of her!"

"And over her shoulder to the one in back."

"When she does that they almost lose their mind!"

"I think that one is about to!"

Agytha worked the man in front of her taking him into her mouth so completely that she could feel him in her throat. She shook her head back and forth as if she were a she wolf shredding a rabbit. All the while, she stared up at him, ignoring the man who thrust himself behind her. Abruptly, she pulled him from her and began working his cock with a vice-like grip. The man began spraying his essence everywhere. As if they were somehow linked, the guard taking her from behind let out a groan of pleasure and pushed deep inside her, Agytha looked back to watch him, moaning as if she had just taken a bite of something deliciously forbidden.

The twins watched in amazement, they were moistened by the picture in front of them. The two guards had been defeated without sword or arrow, exhaustion somehow making the back of their heads heavier than the front. Tremors of the lust they just felt took over the knees of one, and he had to brace against the wall for risk of toppling over. Agytha sat up and pulled each a bit closer, telling their smaller selves intimate secrets with her tongue, reassuring their performance with her lips, all between smiles that started in her eyes. The two priestesses applauded and squealed as if they had just watched Matron Cynthia appear in front of them with a bag full of wrapped presents.

Agytha stood up and gave a deep bow for the applause.

"Bravo!" said one of the twins.

"Encore!" said the other.

"Ladies, ladies!" Agytha used both hands to fan down the cheers. "I have no problem giving you another show, but first, allow me to freshen up, and for Daemon's sake allow me to get some water!"

"Of course, of course!" the first twin exclaimed.

"You two, be gone!" The second ordered the guards.

"You, get us some fresh water!" the first barked at the quiet chamber maid, who jumped at the chance to leave the room.

Agytha slapped one of the guards on his backside, as both left the room half-dressed. The playful slap almost caused the man to trip over his one good sandal and half buckled sword belt. She gave him a signature smile and bit her bottom lip, one causing him to blush, the other to redden. The twins both laughed.

"Girl," Agytha stopped the chamber maid from leaving. "Fetch us a bottle of strawberry wine. If that isn't too bold a request, mistresses?"

"Not at all!" said the first.

"By all means! Fetch two," said the second.

Agytha walked over to the cleaning basin, her high-heeled boots making distinctive sounds. The design of the shoes required a deft balance, and the way she stepped with one foot in front of the other caused her hips to sway in a well-practiced saunter. As she crossed the room she used both hands to pull up her hair to allow the nape of her neck to be kissed by the light summer wind that blew in from the open window above the free-standing basin.

The room was grandiose. Originally just containing a large fireplace and chandelier of crystals, both powered by the Great Pyramid, the young women seemed to add to it with every passing visit. The cleaning basin, for example, was an elegant and delicate work of polished steel, craftsmanship that, no doubt, came from hands of passion. The large bowl, hand thrown porcelain, fragile and precise. The tapestries that hung on the wall depicted the use of the room, various positions of lust depicted from texts of old. The bed on which Agytha preformed was more expensive than Agytha's Inn, framed, as the wash basin, in polished steel with intricate carvings of intertwined bodies. Two statues of paired lovers watched from the corners of the room, and an ornate serving bar rested in the corner opposite the door, made of a solid piece of well-oiled wood, carved by someone with unbridled devotion to perfection. Long lounging chairs and a beverage table finished out the room, marking the favored positions the voyeurs watched from.

Agytha stood at the wash basin and began to use a damp cloth to wipe herself clean of the remnants of the recent most performance. She could feel the eyes of the twins boring through her shoulder blades. She decided to take a risk.

"Would one of you be willing to give me a hand here?" She turned her head so the question would reach her audience but continued to stare out the window, waiting in silence for a response. Agytha hoped that curiosity would be on her side, this could be the doorway into discovering the whereabouts of her brother.

The two twins exchanged a look, a strange hybrid offspring of excitement and caution. Neither wanted to move, yet both had a tension inside them, not unlike that generated while watching their favorite entertainer.

"I apologize for asking, mistresses. Sometimes I forget my place." Agytha acted as if she could not reach a spot on her back with the moistened cloth. She waited in silence for a moment before she heard the sounds of footsteps approaching behind her. One of the twins had let curiosity take over. The other still sat on the bed, astonished that the first had made her move. Her hand covered her mouth in a wide-eyed expression of admiration of her sister's courage.

"You were pretending..." said the first twin as she took the warm cloth across Agytha's back. "You could have easily reached this spot." For a beginner, her voice had taken on a masterful level of flirtation.

"You got me." Agytha admitted as she turned around. Their eyes danced with one other, hinting at more.

"Sister, are you going to kiss her?" The interruption made the twin closest to Agytha jump back, as though she had been entranced by the red district woman.

Agytha smiled in victory. It was time to move forward with her plan.

"Apologies, mistress. I did not mean to offend."

"I took none." The girl closest to her was on fire.

Agytha had seen the look a thousand times. She stoked the flames by pressing her index finger against the priestess' lips. "Not you, sweet one." Agytha turned to the twin still on the bed. "I did not mean to offend you." She directed the statement towards a now perplexed young woman across the room.

"Oh, do not worry yourself, Miss Agytha." She stood up to approach the other two, obviously an observant student of the walk the red district woman thought she had locked away the secret to.

The three made a triangle of primal connection that was both very real and much forbidden. They inched closer and closer, three sets of lips dampened by desire. The closeness was such that each shared the other's breath. Agytha traced a jawline on each girl to pull them both in, a predator readying for the killing bite.

"Oh, sorry!" The chambermaid came in too quickly, the second interruption in Agytha's maneuvers. She had the water and the wine, and was short of breath from the rush to retrieve the requested items.

"Fool girl!" said the first twin.

"Guards!" called the second. Two guards from outside the door came bursting in. "Slit her thr..."

"Wait!" Agytha urged the priestesses. "There is no need for that. She got us what I asked for, and I don't want to wait for a cleanup before we start the next show." It was the quickest excuse she could come up with.

The servant cowered in fear, and the two guards grabbed the hilts of their swords, attack dogs waiting for the right word.

"She saw nothing." Agytha tried to sound nonchalant. And walked towards the bar towards the newly placed beverages. "Besides, I was hoping this one could join me next time." she used the knife of laughter to slice the tension in the room.

"This one?" The first twin was shocked. The servant was not attractive, in fact for all of the beauty in the room, both alive and crafted, this servant was an unfortunate contrast.

"You must be joking!" The second was disarmed, exchanging her rage for disbelief.

"Of course! Come now. You know my tastes!" Agytha poured three glasses of the strawberry wine. "You three can go, now." She added to the interlopers.

None moved until the twins waved their hands in agreement, then all three left the room, the chambermaid wiping tears from her eyes. Agytha watched as the three servants left the room. When the doors closed, both twins joined her at the bar. She handed each a glass, then reached down into the side of her custom boots to retrieve a pouch tucked in the side. Producing it, renewed the other girls' admiration for the craft.

"I so love your shoes." The compliment was reflected with Agytha's own admiration for Yurri's work.

"I have got to get a pair." Both nodded in agreement.

"I'll introduce you to my guy, he would be honored to make the high ladies a pair of boots I'm sure!" The red district woman made a purposeful pause. "You know, now that I think about it, it would be hard for me to introduce your ladyships, beings how I do not even know your names myself..." Agytha untied the knot synching closed the small leather pouch, still selling the casual nature of the conversation rather than the dangers of the potential social intimacy. Playing with the twins was playing with fire. The High Priestess' daughters looked at each other, each working out in their own way how to move forward. They both knew this simple exchange of names meant breaking the invisible barrier created by caste. Both also knew that, oddly enough, this red district whore was the closest thing they had ever had to a friend. As pathetic as it seemed, neither of the twins could remember having a playmate that did not wear acolyte robes, or an instructor that did not define life through the pages of scripture. All of this was a cookie jar on the shelf guarded by scorpions.

Silently, both decided to shatter it for the taste of now-hidden contents.

"Flynne."

"Aernne"

"Agytha."

The three giggled, the twins smiled at each other, proud they had done something that would infuriate their mother. Agytha was several years older than the girls, at lead six winters, if not more. Though this age difference meant little towards credibility of influence, the fact that those years were spent outside of the confines of a temple did. The two girls were as beautiful as the gemstones lodged in the hilt of a sacrificial dagger, and just as deadly as the dagger itself. Platinum hair flowed down shoulders, framing skin that shied away from the sun. Pouting lips that got their way, could be narrowed with a remorseless tenacity that had literally destroyed people's lives. This close, the red district woman could see their fragmented eyes, partially hazel and partially blue, they seemed as if they had seen into dreams, or maybe even well beyond. It was hard for her to not be intimidated, because she did indeed stand on a cliff and her shoes, no matter how popular in current company, took practice to balance.

"What is in the pouch?" Flynne asked while licking her lips.

"Yes, yes! What is this you have?" Aernne bit her bottom lip and stood on tippy toes to try to see inside.

"This, ladies, is the second part of your entertainment." Agytha took a pinch of the contents and dropped it into her own wine glass. She mixed it with a finger, and then slowly sucked the remnants off her makeshift stirrer. In one swift gulp, she downed the mixture; squinted a bit at the tartness of it, then over exaggerated the audible sound of slating her thirst.

Her captive audience raised eyebrows at one another.

"Want some?" She looked back and forth.

"Yes." Aernne was quick to offer her glass, and Agytha obliged. This time she offered the damp stirrer to the holder of the cup. Aernne did not miss a beat and took the finger into her mouth so deeply that Flynne blushed with an open mouth smile.

"Don't even think about leaving me out." The process was repeated for Flynne, right down to the oral fixation of mixing tools.

"Now what did we drink?"

"Yes, what was this poison you have given us?"

"Poison? No." Agytha smiled. "You just drank my favorite mixture of mushrooms and ground lotus leaves. We are about to see the world through different eyes."

The twins glanced at each other, grins growing from someplace hidden.

"We can relate," stated one.

"Definitely," agreed the other.

"You have done *Hanjue* before?" Agytha was intrigued to say the least. Nobility continued to baffle her.

"Not exactly." Flynne motioned to refill her wine, and the red district woman used it as a cue to complete the task for all three of them.

"We have seen the world in different ways than most." Aernne added to the mystery.

189

"Well, regardless, you are in for an adventure. This will be unlike anything you have done before." Agytha sipped her wine, aware that they were about to go on a mind's journey of altering consciousness.

"What can we expect?" Aernne rubbed her hands together while waiting for the answer.

"I'm so excited!" Flynne used her eyes to help draw out the vowel sounds.

"You can expect to be out of your mind in about a tenth cycle. When that happens, I will guide you. *Hanjue* cannot be taken lightly. Some say the Plainsmen use it before a battle, the Cliff people before a drop, and the people of the Nine Kingdoms...well, they take it before their first time."

The girls stared at her, taking in everything she said, gulping down information like starving Thanadonts.

"No matter *why* you take it, or where you are from, there is always a guide. Someone you trust to show you the path. Someone to lead you through the journey. This journey is ours, and I will take you through it. Then, someday, you will take someone on their first journey, understand?" Agytha was in control of the room, the statues, the wash basin, and the bar. She was in control of the bed, the soft lounging chairs, and the double doors. The red district woman was in control of the twins before her.

"How will we know when something is happening?"

"Will it make our skin tingle?"

"Each journey is different. Special. Yet preparation is always the same." She looked around the room and motioned to the girls to follow her to the wash basin where the windows were still open to the summer night's air. "For example, windows are bad." She let the girls look outside, at nearly a hundred hands up, the fall would be fatal.

"We will undoubtedly want to go outside at some point, but trust me, this will not be the right way to leave." She laughed, but the twins did not.

"You never know," said Flynne, "maybe the Goddess will help us fly?"

"You can never be certain!" added Aernne. The girls seemed to know something Agytha did not.

She could tell they wanted to play this game with her. They wanted to see just how far they could go.

190

"This room will undoubtedly get very small soon, we will want a way to get out to the courtyard. Do you know of a way to get around without being seen?"

"Whether we are seen or not, we can go where we want." Flynne sounded arrogant, but the other two knew she was plainly stating a fact.

Servants and guards were too afraid of the little daemons to make mention of their tomfoolery, let alone their late night comings or goings into the courtyard.

"As we start feeling it, we need to just sit and talk about the sensations, then if we go out to explore, we will all be able to experience the *Hanjue* in our own way. Just remember that no one else knows we are under its spell. It is our journey and our journey alone. I, hopefully, do not need to remind you how furious your mother would be if she discovered our indiscretion tonight."

Agytha smiled to mask her true trepidation.

"Do not worry, Agytha. We shall protect you from mother." Aernne placed a hand on her new friend's shoulder.

"Besides, mother's pet has been away for some weeks now, getting away with whatever we want has been incredibly easy," reassured Flynne.

"Good, I suppose that works to our advantage. I also advise that we get together some items of interest; mirrors, candles, and the like." Agytha walked back over behind the bar area where she had a large pack. The pack's normal contents included several outfits for her demonstrations and had been modified to include some of the previously mentioned items, as well as a specialized outfit for her journey, and some delicious candies stashed away for just such an occasion.

Agytha also had two special gifts for the young women, delicately wrapped in ribbons and special cloth, she would present these to the twins when the *Hanjue* was in full effect. The items were a woman's secret in many places, a proud badge in some, and the bringer of comfort on a lonely night in all, taking the place of absent male companionship. Over the last several weeks, the girls' sexual curiosity had been a source of income for the red district woman, tonight she planned on taking that curiosity to the next level. She left the gifts wrapped up, a surprise for later.

She began to change into her outfit, a loosely tied top replaced her corset and pants with wide leggings took the vacant positions left by stockings and boots. Both garments were made from fine silk and were the most expensive items in Agytha's wardrobe. She tied sure-footed sandals on her feet and pulled her hair into a single ponytail. Agytha had not yet bore a child, careful use of herbs had prevented this. Nonetheless, her curvy hips were an added bonus to her trade, especially when accented by a tight stomach forged from the mastery of those hips. As it turned out, her bosoms had no need for the corset in order to mesmerize the eyes of onlookers. The woman was truly gifted. Her dark hair was a precursor for butterscotch skin, her long eyelashes framing eager and inviting eyes.

"I feel we are under-dressed, sister," Flynne said, placing a portion of Agytha's blouse sleeve in between her thumb and forefinger. "This is fine silk! The touch is amazing! It's unlike anything I've ever felt!'

Her sibling joined her. "You're right, sister! This is amazing, we must both get an outfit like this."

Agytha laughed, excitement came with it. "You both are starting to feel the effects. Your robes will be just fine! Here, help me with these!" She gathered up some candles she had set on the bar, a hair brush, and a hand mirror. She passed some of the items off to the twins and headed towards the small beverage table between the lounging chairs.

She put the candles down and motioned for the girls to sit. They obliged and placed their items on the table.

"Smell these." The candles were all made with different scents, one vanilla, one of honey, and the last of wild berries. "Let me light these."

Agytha hopped up, and moved back towards the fireplace to light a stick for the candles. As soon as she turned her back, Aernne smiled at Flynne. Glancing towards the back of their favorite celebrity, Aernne let her vision slip away to become open. The feeling was intoxicating as never before, coursing through her veins as if it were the first time she had channeled the flows. With a wave of her hand the three candles lit, and Aernne released her state-breathless. Flynne noticed her sister's elation, and her wide eyes suggested her sibling tell her more, yet all Aernne could do was smile. As the red district woman turned around the twins put on the faces of innocence, a ruse that might have worked on anyone other than a fellow expert.

"How did you? What did…?"

The two allowed only for grins and wiggling feet in response.

"Never mind, I forget everything in this palace is powered by the pyramid, you must have some lighting stone or something. I'll just lower the other lights now. Let's see, where was that dial? Oh! Yes! Over here…" Agytha went on describing her actions, only realizing as she dimmed the lights, it was the effects of the *Hanjue* that had her tongue wagging so, not her forgetful nature. The twins watched her every move, abnormally large smiles inviting her to continue rambling on.

"It's starting to happen, can you feel it?" Agytha sat down in front of the candles. Just watch the flames. The seasoned journey guide took a hand of each of the twins, and the three stared at the dancing flames. Her touch sent an invisible feather across the outside of the two girls' arms, under their gowns, up their necks to finally bore into their cheeks with a newfound warmth.

"I feel it." said Flynne.

"Definitely," Aernne concluded with a sigh.

"Watch the flames, here it comes. Just relax and let it happen." Agytha could not help but smile, her body tingled with every inch of fine silk brushing against it.

The three flames danced in seductive sinuous form. The girls watched as the light created by them began to extend out, refracting beams spreading across the room. Then the room shrank down-down and down-until only one flame could be seen at a time. The wick, black towards the base, became a vast hue of color ranging from oranges and reds to blues and whites where the flames embraced it. Reflections of the dance could be seen in the rapidly growing pool of wax as it pushed its way down the sides of the column-like ballroom, reserved for its sole performer. The flame was like the fire inside their hearts. They understood it. They relished it. The smells from the candles, too, had a life all of their own. They hit the women's nostrils but seemingly dug into their minds. Never before had such an odor been so intense, so real. Shifting gaze from one of these miraculous torches to the next merely started the process all over again, from refracting light, to shrinking room, to glorious fragrance.

"Well, what happened next?" Yurri sat forward, his teacup shaking from either anticipation for the continuing story or too much tea.

"For a while, we mostly just talked, brushed each other's hair, you know. Girl stuff."

"Don't be a bitch. You know I would brush my hair if I had any." The craftsman ran a hand across his bald head.

Agytha reveled in her teacup, taking in the steamy aroma along with the overwhelming smell of leather in the cobbler's shop.

"We spent quite some time in the viewing chamber before we went out into the inner courtyard. The twins were right, no one even questioned our going outside. It was as if the girls did this on regular occasions." She sipped her tea.

"Well, how were they doing? Were they rabid rats or perfect princesses?"

"They were professionals. Like they had done *Hanjue* a hundred times. It was unreal how well they handled themselves."

"Nobles. Lies born right into them." It was not the tea leaving the bad taste in Yurri's mouth.

"You have no idea." Agytha's gaze went into the fluid of her cup to recall more of the story.

***

The three lay on their backs in the grass of the inner courtyard. The beautiful flower and hedge arrangements coupled with the pyramid-powered outside lights had captivated them for quite some time. The eldest, and leader of the journey they were on, lay between the younger twins. She pointed out the stars above them.

"We could probably see them better if the outside lights were not so bright, is there a dial out here?" Agytha did not know if the outside lights could be controlled as they could indoors.

"Of course there is, right over there." Aernne pointed near one of the exits.

"Okay." Agytha began to get up when Aernne grabbed her hand.

"What is that star, right there, it seems brighter than the rest..." the twin cared nothing for the answer, she merely used the question

194

as a distraction for her sister, who now had eyes lacking both pupil and iris as they worked to manipulate the flows of wind.

Flynne's mind and body raced with intensity as she formed an invisible hand that wrapped around the dial. It was her first taste of chocolate, her first time watching a man and a woman, her first time using the flows, all over again. The glowing crystals in the light poles around the courtyard dimmed to a dull pinpoint, giving way to the black canvas on which the Goddess herself hung millions of sparkling diamonds. Agytha was unaware, trying to remember the name of an irrelevant ball of twinkling distraction.

With the lights dimmed in the courtyard, the Goddess showed the three her majesty. Above them the stars swam in clouds of color, the light of each one stretching out to touch another. Somehow each one was alive, and the streaks of light intersected to form a web of brilliance, trapping their imaginations. Summer winds pulled clouds across the shimmering backdrop, and those were the shape changers of legend.

An old man's face became an old woman who smiled and laughed at them, just before she turned into a rabbit to race away. Some sort of dragon flew in chase of the rabbit before turning into an ornate basket of fruit. Dancers and jesters, soldiers in chariots, maidens with flowing gowns, all made a trek across the sky. And then came the lovers, all shapes and sizes, moving into each other, changing positions with twisting bodies never before imagined. The three laughed with one another as they took turns pointing out various depravity that only they seemed privy to. It was an unfathomable vastness above them, milky rivers of stars made small again by the reminder that they were in a small courtyard in a gigantic world.

It was only then when Agytha remembered she had not turned down the lights.

"Hey, who turned down the lights?" Agytha asked.

"I think only the Goddess can do that, dear." Flynne smiled, that devious visage of hidden knowledge.

"Not the stars, you shit. The courtyard lights."

"Did you just call me a shit?" Flynne was still grinning.

"I believe she did, sister." Aernne's own expression of approval pushed her lips forward.

"I'll call you a shit again, if you are hard of hearing." Agytha joined in with the two sisters in a chuckle, not knowing that none before her had ever survived such an insult.

"Oh, sister, let's show her!" Aernne was overly excited.

"We mustn't!" Flynne was not as firm as she could have been.

"Show me what?" Agytha was lost.

***

"Show you what?" Yurri sipped at his empty cup, before making the realization and moving across the room for a refill.

"Will you stop interrupting me, bootmaker? I swear!"

"It's not my fault, you are terrible at telling a story!" Yurri hustled over to refill her cup.

"What do you mean I am terrible at telling a story?" Agytha was not amused.

"I mean you ramble on and on with insignificant details..."

"Example?"

"Okay look, I don't care about the rabbits in the sky or the ornate wash basin, just get to the point!" He was teasing of course, but Agytha went forward with the man's torture.

"I am getting to the point. You see, they took me back to the viewing room and had me sit on the bed, while they each sat on the edge of their chairs..."

***

Aernne held her palm towards Agytha, the *Hanjue* causing its smooth edges to appear sharp and angular. Her vision focused on her fingers and her palm so intently that the few lines, on youthful skin, seemed to wave and fluctuate. Then, where there was only an outstretched hand, a bright flame appeared. It was as if an invisible wick grew from the center, giving an anchor to a dancer twice the size of those still performing on pools of wax on top of the candles. Never before had *Hanjue* been so intense for her that it caused such an illusion to appear, morphing and changing things that already existed, yes, but never was there a manifestation of something.

The flame began to rise above Aernne's hand, floating in the air towards Agytha, who gave it wide birth as if some force pulled her eyes wide and her scalp backwards. Another flame appeared in Arenne's hand and again started to move towards her, then a third, and then a fourth, all floating-all dancing.

***

Yurri dropped his teacup, pieces of it clattering across the floor.
"Mother's cunt." Yurri looked down at the mess then across to his friend. "You're fucking with me, right? You don't mean to tell me that..."
"That's exactly what I'm telling you." Agytha was on the edge of her seat, goose bumps taking up residence on her arms. "The floating fire was one thing, Yurri, but their eyes...their eyes..."

***

Agytha watched the floating flames circle around the room, they flew in patterns, weaving around the chandelier and dancing about the statues. There was nearly a dozen flying around the room now, groups of two and three chasing each other about. Trails from behind made them look like flaming snakes. More appeared, and more joined in the mesmerizing game.
"How many can we control, sister?"
"I do not know, but it seems easier, does it not?"
"Oh, yes, it does!"
The *Hanjue* enhanced the show beyond imagining, Agytha was mystified, a child watching a magician's routine- if that magician could materialize serpents made of flame flying around the room. Pulling her eyes away from the blurs of flames was difficult, but when she did she found herself staring at two wide-eyed girls with gaping smiles that showed awe and concentration. It was their eyes that captivated the red district woman now. No odd colored irises, rather, a milky white surface that seemed to glow with the powers they controlled. She could see her own reflection in them, and the reflection of the entire room. Platinum locks seemed to swirl with a life of their own as the two girls manipulated the energies around the room.
Watching them was terrifying. Unnatural. Pale skin protected from the sun, flushed with reds of forbidden desires. They were

197

drunk with a power Agytha couldn't possibly understand. She slowly shook her head, unwilling to believe what she saw. Abruptly, the light show winked out, snakes of flame disappearing in an instant. The heat of the room calming with the outside breeze. The summer's breath hit her face, cooling the damp streaks that had found their way from her eyes to her chin during the display.

"Oh, Agytha, did we scare you?" Flynne was in front of her, a concerned stare in her half-hazel, half-blue eyes that seemed normal, comparatively.

"We would never hurt you!" The voice was Aernne. She, too, seemed back to normal.

***

"You blew it? You blew it!" Yurri was flabbergasted.

"I didn't blow it. You have no faith."

"Oh, contraire, I'm a picture of faith. The Goddess herself hath blessed me with mad skills and great taste." He exaggerated a victorious laugh, inspiring a grin from his best friend. "Well then, how did you get out of this pickle?"

"I did what anyone would have done...I rolled with it..."

***

Each twin used a thumb to wipe a tear away. They were sad, and yet fascinated by the feel of her skin. The effects of the drug still going strong.

"We're sorry," said one.

"We did not mean to frighten you," added the other.

"You did not frighten me." Agytha stuttered a bit, the combination of the lie, the drugs, and the visions she saw.

"We just wanted you to know who we are."

"We just wanted to show you."

"We got carried away."

They looked at one another then back to her, strange words forming in their mouths. "We are so sorry."

Agytha looked at them, regaining her composure. "I was not crying out of fear, I was crying because...I was crying because..."

She took a breath, getting ready for the ruse, she told herself she could do it. She remembered her first time with a customer, she made him believe she liked it. She could do that now. She had to. "I was crying because... it was so beautiful." The twins exchanged a confused stare. It was in that moment they battled between doubt and belief.

Agytha pressed her advantage.

"We all have...things...that make us special. Things that make us...beautiful." She took each girl by the tender place where back of the head meets top of the neck, and pulled them close to her. Their lips touched.

Agytha continued. "Let me show you what makes me special." With that, she kissed them.

All right and all wrong, the three kissed, tongues dancing, hands grasping, and hearts pounding. It was the beginning of much, much more.

***

"You are fucking kidding me. You slept with both of them?"

Agytha looked up at him, seeking approval.

"You dirty, dirty old woman!" Yurri slapped her playfully on the knee.

"Oh, please, those two had been aching to get close to me for weeks, and they were innocent in touch. Their minds had already completed deeds far more... intriguing."

"I can't believe you fucked the twins! You slut!" Yurri was rubbing his chin, his brows squishing together.

"We have more important things at stake here." Agytha was looking at her friend when a third voice spoke up, one quietly waiting during the entire story.

"The twins are weavers." Koll'Ynn addressed the looming shadow darkening an otherwise pleasant tale.

"That makes them witches, does it not?" Yurri stated the obvious.

"That it does," Agytha said. "And it means we can use it against them."

"It also means they are more dangerous than we imagined, Aggie." Koll'Ynn's worry was visible. "Maybe we should rethink what we are doing."

Agytha stood to meet her lover, embraced him in a way that he knew all too well. It was why he loved her, and why he could never refuse her.

"We keep on this path. My brother needs me, and I'll not leave him to rot in some cell under the palace, or temple, or whatever. We have to finish putting things in place." She looked into his emerald eyes and waited for a 'no' that, surprisingly, didn't come.

"Very well, then. Let's talk about the next stage."

Koll'Ynn pulled up a chair and motioned Agytha to sit. Yurri refilled teacups and then leaned into the conversation. Koll'Ynn spoke fast, and thought faster, with a devious mind only the foolish disrespected. If anyone could tear down a thousand year-old government, it was him, and both Yurri and Agytha knew it. He was a viper no one saw until it struck.

He was the Treesnake, and he played a deadly game.

***

The three breathed with the heavy etchings of exhaustion as they lay on the bed, staring up at the crystal chandelier. The summer air chilled the sweat that soaked their hair. All three were silent, though the twins were so because of the infant moments of a new age. The night had been altering in so many ways, it was hard to fathom just how much. The effects of the red district woman's mixture had begun to slip away, leaving detailed memories of a night that words would never do justice. Simultaneously, the twins snuggled up against her, as if they were connected by the night. The after effects of ecstasy still making the slightest touch turn into an earthquake. Their platinum covered heads came to rest on each of Agytha's arms in such a way their eyes could send secrets to the others. She took turns kissing each of them on the forehead.

The twins knew it would truly be a shame when the day came that they would have to kill her.

The Comforts of Power

Baylee sat at the long table, she could feel the man's presence behind her and still imagined his grip around her neck. He was a *mangmu lieren,* a hunter for the great Sabrinian Empire, more than that, he was the guardian for the woman across the long table from her.

Baylee was not certain which one of them made her feel less comfortable, the man who picked her up with one arm of carved stone by her throat, or the woman that held her fate in her hands. Those hands, folded into fists, allowing a place to rest her chin. Apparently conserving the energy required to hold her head up in order to power the way her eyes bored into her soul. Occasionally, her index fingers would create a triangle that pushed her lips together in quiet contemplation. Silence lingered, broken only by the uncomfortable shifting of Baylee in her high-backed chair. The food on the plate in front of her had not been touched, not due to lack of desire, but rather a defiance spawned by the young woman's worry for her family.

Baylee had not seen her sister Clara, or her brother Eelia, since the priestess took her into custody two days before. Her father had to be worried beyond understanding. Last he had seen, his eldest daughter had been running off to chase after his youngest, taking along his smallest son with her. Baylee had left the youngest with a family friend, and she knew Geneeve was more than capable, but her father Icomus was not known for his ability to keep a level head when it came to the safety of his family. It was this that made Baylee the most afraid. She had not been mistreated after the initial arrest, they offered her food and a room, albeit, under the watchful eyes of this Bo'Ah, the priestess' protector. Icomus did not know this, however, and with the influx of strangers in town, his imagination would be creating all manner of torturous visage of his missing children.

Yet she had not been mistreated. That is, if one would define being denied access to her family as humane. She had not been tortured other than this deprivation. She had been asked many questions, questions about herself to which she did not know the answers. The nature of these questions also meant Clara was somewhere in the house, for they were getting stories that mimicked the child's wild imagination.

"You will not eat?" Raen was a powerful woman. It showed in her transformation of the small town of Balanced Rock. She had literally moved buildings to make its very shape suit her needs, despite the cost to the local residents. Her motivations were unknown to all but, perhaps, her clerk, a serpent of a woman whose personality was as plain and shapeless as her body.

"I am not hungry, Mother." The lie was easy to discern. The young woman had not eaten since her discovery.

"I am surprised by your polite nature, given your breeding." Raen meant to insult Baylee, a futile attempt for a young girl so proud of her upbringing.

The Keeper of Doctrine had pressed the girl from every angle in an attempt to get her to channel, the unfortunate result being nothing but a blank stare coupled with frustration. The problem wasn't in her method of interrogation, it was the fact that Baylee, truly, did not know what she was capable of. There had been a discussion about 'the incident' with her father, a discussion that had been finalized with an attempt to keep everything quiet. A decision unraveled by something as simple as a child's game.

"Thank you for your kindness, Mother." This was a plea as much as a compliment, not seeing her little sister had been like holding her heart hostage from her lungs.

"I have sent for the rest of your family. They should be here shortly, your two brothers and your father." She let out a deep sigh when Baylee looked at her hopefully. "You are peculiar for a witch, Miss Coreni."

"I am not witch, Matron." She sounded defeated, as if she had carried on the same conversation with a dredge goat. "I told you I..."

"I have heard you!" She slammed her fist on the table, causing Baylee's dishes to rattle. "Bo'Ah can see your power, and you yourself have admitted to saving your sister." She smoothed her robes in an attempt to regain her composure. "You are either oblivious, or are the best liar I have seen. We shall see when your family arrives." The word 'family' came out as if it had sprouted wings and antennae and flown into her mouth in the first place.

As if on cue, the clerk entered the room from behind the seated priestess, Clara in tow. She had been given a new dress, one that was made for servants, and probably a material more fine than the girl had worn before.

"Baylee!" Clara squeaked out her sister's name but was silenced with a harsh squeeze from the clerk's hand.

"Don't you dare hurt her!" Baylee stood and was abruptly reseated by the blindfolded man behind her.

"Sit, Clara." the priestess spoke with an open-palm motion towards the chair to her right, which was pulled out by the clerk. The little girl did as commanded, and the serpent-woman pushed the chair in to proper distance.

"Sister, I'm so sorry! I did not mean..." Clara was crying, traumatized by the evening in isolation.

"Hush, Clara," Baylee said. "You've done nothing wrong. The Matron Raen is just worried about you is all."

Clara looked at the Keeper of Doctrine with a puzzled look, who quickly covered her own look of bewilderment with a smile towards the little girl.

"Your sister is wise, Clara. She knows just how worried I am over the safety of all of our people. Even your sister's. We have to be extra careful around people who can do the things Baylee can do."

If she had not been interrogated all night, Baylee would have believed the woman.

"My sister is good, Mother. I promise! Can we please go? I want to see my daddy..." Clara barely got the last word out before starting to cry, the sound was such that Baylee found tears bubbling up from the knot in her stomach.

"Oh hush dear, your father is on his way. I have sent for him, and your brothers." the woman was clearly out of patience with the tears.

Raen looked back to Baylee. "What to do with you? Well? Have you a thought? The doctrine is clear on what to do with a witch, yet here you are, lacking any spellcraft or enchantment. You are deceived by your little sister, dressed in the handcrafted robes of the chantry. You utter no curses and seem to present no threat to us. Yet, clearly, my hunter sees the taint within you."

Baylee had no chance to retort, the doors to the dining room crept open and were met by the clerk, who took a whisper from the invading servant and gave it to Raen in similar manner.

"It seems your family is here, Miss Coreni. I hope you will behave yourself." She clapped her hands, and a flurry of servants entered.

Men and woman sat at the long table with enough glassware and pitchers of water and wine for twice the number of people in attendance. One scooped up her untouched plate, another the utensils, a third replaced them with new items. Platters and fruit and bread befitting a late-morning meal were placed in the center of the table. Four well-dressed servants remained in the corners of the room awaiting command.

The doors opened and four topless guards marched into the room, posting against the wall at each corner of the table. Following them came Icomus, dressed in his nicest jacket (which meant he wore the one with the least holes) and had what was left of his hair combed to the side. Her brothers followed closely behind him, looking equally dapper. All had concerned looks on their faces, but none equaling that of the master of his family, who literally vibrated with the adrenaline that filled his veins. He had clearly not slept, and the twins, miniature versions of himself both had eyes reddened from the recent drying of tears. Between them was Eelia, best dressed of the family, no doubt due to the request of Lady Geneeve.

"Daddy!" Clara leapt from her chair and raced around the table to the arms of her father. The rapid movement caused the nearest guards to stiffen, then relaxing with a quickly-raised hand of the priestess, who rose with practiced grace.

"Beebottom!" The big man took his youngest daughter in his arms, kissing her several times before allowing her to burrow between his neck and shoulder. He looked over at his eldest daughter, who had also risen from her seat with precision and control lead by measured breath that counteracted a pounding heart.

Icomus took a step towards his daughter, and Baylee could hear the blindfolded man behind her shift.

"Please sit, father." Baylee was surprised that her voice was steady, as she motioned towards one of the open seats at the table. The tension in the room was thick. None in the family were fools, and causing a ruckus in this situation would not befit any positive outcome. She locked eyes with Raen and, for a moment, thought she saw a brief nod of approval. Icomus looked at both of them and back to his daughter, who worked herself into a smile without meeting his eyes. She could not hide her fear from him if she allowed him a direct observation.

Icomus pulled out a chair and motioned to the boys to do the same. In the meantime, the Keeper whispered to a servant who quickly darted into the door behind her. In an instant, the servant returned with a small wooden chair meant to be placed on a bigger one to allow Eelia his own place at the table.

"Water?" asked the priestess. "Or wine? I think I will have a glass of wine."

Icomus was awkward in the tall-backed seat, in the setting of the room, in his own skin. However, he, too, took up a glass of wine.

"There is food, please eat. I know this situation is awkward for you all." Raen smiled. No one moved to eat. Silence held the room. "Suit yourselves." She began to load her small plate with some bread and fruit, paused a moment after it was full, and then took a bite of the warm bread. "Delicious."

Baylee realized she was staring and quickly began filling her own plate. Gingerly, Jacin and Jacob did the same. Icomus did not move.

"Why have you taken my daughter prisoner?" he asked plainly.

Dabbing off her mouth with a napkin, the Matron finished chewing and swallowing before looking towards the man.

"She is no prisoner...yet. Are you Lady Coreni?" The title was meant to put the farmer in place, though it seemed to only redden his face. When he looked at Baylee, he only saw his baby girl stuck in the cold of the world, no matter how much of her mother's appearance she grew into.

"What mean you by yet?'" It was a demand from a protective parent.

"Father, your tongue." Baylee had no desire to correct the man, but she had seen the woman at work. Disrespect would not be tolerated.

"Remarkable young woman." Raen smiled at Baylee, aware of the conflict. "Remarkable in that she understands the way of things. You wish me to speak plainly? Very well, I shall."

She took another bite of fruit, staring for a moment, as if to find words to properly define the predicament. Baylee knew better. The pause was a control mechanism, a tool to remind Icomus where the power in the room was.

"The only reason your daughter still lives, is due to her respect for the Doctrine. Truthfully, had little Clara not been wearing her make-believe priestess robes, yesterday would have gone quite differently for your family." She continued to chew her food, almost obnoxiously. "We would have killed the little witch here on sight, then hunted you down and had you crucified for not turning her in the moment you suspected her abilities."

Icomus stiffened, as did the guards in the room. Jacob, who had been eating a bite of bread swallowed so loudly someone back at the dairy could have heard him.

"So, odd as it sounds, the reason for your discovery is also the reason for your salvation, Lady Coreni. My predicament is twofold. What can this witch do? And will this witch be a danger to the empire? The doctrine is clear. All witches must be cleansed with fire." She popped a grape into her mouth.

"You'll not be setting fire to MY girl!" Icomus stood up, slamming his chair against the wall with the same movement. Instantly, swords were drawn by the guards, all pointing them at the nearest child.

"FATHER SIT!" Baylee's voice boomed across the room, unbelievably forceful for her size, and caused the big man to look at her. "Please, father. Sit. If the Honorable Matron wanted to burn me at the stake, she would not have arranged this meeting." Icomus looked at his daughter, trying to get a read. "Sit."

Reluctantly, he looked back for his chair and, with the help of a servant, sat down at the table. Raen casually waved her hand, and the guards sheathed their weapons.

"Matron, how do you propose we proceed? I trust your wisdom to guide us." Baylee was asking for the priestess to spare her family's lives, she simply used different words.

"Remarkable young woman." The priestess was definitely amused, if not impressed. "How I think we shall proceed is up to the word of the Goddess. She has not spoken to me of this issue, and likely will not until her will is announced at this evening's festivities. Tonight we raise the Obelisk in her name. Tonight the true followers of the Scriptures will be rewarded with Her Own Light. In the meantime, young Clara and Lady Coreni will not leave my side."

Icomus squirmed in his seat.

"You will be my honored guest at the Raising Ceremony at dusk, Lady Coreni, and I will be assigning a special guard just to keep an eye on young Clara. The rest of your family may return to business as usual. Now, please, since we have worked out the matter at hand, won't you eat, Master Goatman?"

It was an insult that cut Icomus deeply. He looked to his daughter who nodded somberly.

This might as well be a meal of thistle, cactus, and roasted quill-rat.

***

"I hate the way they speak," he mumbled through his tusks. Kurg was enfeebled by his wounds from the battle and amazed that he still lived. He was able to keep down a little water now, a gift from the Sky Father that had not been his greatest. Teegan still lived as well, albeit, he was in a dreamer's sleep from which few ever woke.

Kurg did not know of this gift, but from what he was told after waking, both he and his boy had been visited by the Eagle Shaman after the battle. The shaman's magick had been so strong it not only healed some of the wounded, it was praised by some of their human captors for doing so.

"They squeak like rat dogs fucking." Mreggan managed to make his chief laugh a bit, which pulled at his wounded insides.

"If we could only get at those shiny fingers hanging off that one's belt." Yulger had lived too, though now had only one arm left to use.

"Have you seen Teegan?" Kurg sat up, looking around at all of the cages.

"They moved him, and some of the others earlier this morning. All looked ready for the long..." Mreggan trailed off, remembering who he addressed, with the added help of his leader's glare.

"He took an arrow straight through the back, chieftain. It is a wonder he has lived this long." Yulger was not proud of the words he spoke, but they rang true.

"He is watched by the spirits, and I believe the shaman has a plan for him." Kurg was weakened, but pride strengthened him. "It will be many winters before someone sings that brave the long song." Kurg felt the scar on his own chest, one from long ago.

"I hope you are right, chieftain. Some of the others said when the take them away like that..." Kurg gave Yulger a look that warned of a loss of his remaining arm.

Mreggan diffused the situation, "Bull killer is strong, no matter what they have in store for the lad, he's sure to prevail."

Kurg barely had the strength to turn his head towards the distance and hope for the best.

***

Baylee stared at herself in the mirror, never before had she worn such a beautiful gown, had servants to dress her, or even put on fine makeup. She looked a woman for certain, one ready for her own betrothal. Yet Baylee did not recognize the woman before her in the mirror, for all that glamour that should fill her with joy, it actually stole happiness away. She walked in a den of starving lions, chained to the lioness, one having a most insatiable hunger. Whoever Raen was, her need for control was absolute. She was drunk on the power granted by her title. Baylee despised her.

"The gown looks lovely. You and young Clara will make a fine addition to my entourage, and show the people of this hole of a town my generosity." The Matron made adjustments to Baylee's hair from behind. "You are a beautiful little witch, aren't you?"

"Thank you, Mother." Baylee met her eyes in the mirror.

"You have freckles. Do you know where they come from?" Raen ran her hand over Baylee's shoulders, tracing the faint dots with her finger. The priestess was indeed an attractive woman, the type that any girl would like to grow gracefully into, but her touch felt like a violation. An intrusion.

"I do not, Keeper." Her lips quivered, she closed her eyes to hold back tears.

"It is said that long ago, there were many different types of people, different colors." She brushed Baylee's hair over her ear so she could whisper into it. "The fairest of which stayed beautiful and pale, even in the sunlight."

"They did not darken?" She stuttered a bit, feeling the woman's breath on her neck.

"Only in small spots. Only with these... freckles." She smiled, knowing how uncomfortable the girl was. "They are a sign of your rare heritage, Lady Coreni. They are a gift from the Goddess."

"I am fortunate, Matron."

"That you are." She sat down on the bed and motioned for a servant to bring her wine. "Do you like this room?"

Baylee looked around, the room was nearly the size of her family's entire ground floor. The bed had four large posts and a canopy, there was a large armoire, a dresser with a grand mirror, a standing wash basin with another mirror, *and* the full-size one she stood in front of. There was more wealth in the room than the farmer's daughter had ever seen in one place, wealth that, in her opinion, could be better spent elsewhere.

"It is an amazing room, Matron." Baylee forced a mousey smile.

"I'm glad that you like it, because it is yours."

"Mine, matron?" Something narrowed her throat and turned her stomach at the same time.

"Yes." The priestess sipped her wine. "I have decided to keep you. You and Clara, of course."

"Keep us?"

"For such a remarkable young woman, you have a great deal of trouble hearing." She waved at the servant for another glass of wine and walked it over to the petrified farm girl. Baylee took the wine down in a single drink.

"My, my! Careful now, we have a long night ahead of us. Tonight we will bring the town of Balanced Rock into the fold of the Goddess. The people will see her gifts and her mercy."

"Her mercy? Wait. I thought we were already in her fold?"

"Much has been forgotten in this town, like that dog-loving heathen. We will offer up the souls of the wounded Plainsmen to Her Embrace, so they may no longer suffer the wounds of battle. Is that not mercy?"

"It is what you say, Mother. How many will you offer?" Baylee shuttered to think what this woman was capable of. She did not know what heathen the priestess spoke of.

"Just the weak ones, I think there is a half dozen or so. Those that will soon die of infection and the like. I'll not risk any slave stock good for service or the games." She studied Baylee for a moment. "I take it you do not agree with the offering?"

"I do not have the luxury of your wisdom, Matron. I have no opinion of my own."

"You see! You are a true joy! My own little Valkyr! The truth is, the offering will serve to remind the people that I am here to protect them, and the nature of the offering will remind them what costs I am willing to incur for that protection. It has been too long since this town has seen a Cleansing."

"Matron, what will become of my family?"

"That all depends on you, my dear. If you continue to behave, then I don't foresee anything bad happening to them at all. Especially if we can figure out what this power is inside of you, and how we can use it to our advantage." There was a smirk on her lips, one that betrayed Baylee's value to her.

The door came swinging open causing both women to jump. It was a handmaiden leading Clara, dressed in an adorable outfit with embroidered griffons and symbols of the church. She ran up to hug her sister but stopped abruptly.

"Wow, sis! You look like an Angel!" She was in awe of her older sibling.

"That is exactly what I said, Clara. Isn't she beautiful?"

Baylee knelt down, tears filling her eyes, she pulled Clara in close and squeezed her with all her might. "I love you, Clara." Baylee pushed her out to arm's length to get a good look at the little girl. "Come on now, let's go watch them raise this Obelisk!" She pulled her sister in close once more, closing her eyes with the hug. She could feel Raen watching them with her victorious little smirk, one that only Baylee might someday be able to wipe away.

***

The center of town was a mass of people. There were street jesters, performers, painted men and women on stilts, merchant booths, and children's skill challenges. There was a large temporary platform built with a thick canvas top and two rows of padded chairs. Many of the town's councilwomen sat with their husbands, awaiting the arrival of Priestess Raen and her entourage. The town well had been removed, a large concrete pool in its place. This pool would serve as the base to the Obelisk that lay on the ground. A large wooden crane-pulley had been erected and several ropes attached to the stone monument ran to a harness that sat on the ground. When it was time, the harness would be attached to the Thanadont that brought the object to town.

Musicians played on a second platform, one built with a much more sinister purpose. A table in the shape of a wooden cross had hinges on the bottom, so whoever was tied to it could be raised for the scrutiny of onlookers. Behind it was a cage with several dark shapes moving about inside it. Baylee knew these shapes would be the entertainment prior to the raising of the golden-topped symbol of faith.

Baylee had no idea how the Obelisk worked. All she knew was as soon as it stood on end, it would somehow power all the lighting crystals in the town. Its power could be used for anything properly attuned, and that was the science for which Sabrinians were famous. The Keeper of Doctrine, constantly complaining about all the walking she had to do, was relieved the Obelisk would alleviate the limitations of the Goddess Carriage, enabling its use outside the proximity of Mother's Yarn. She said it would also allow the town to have access to Sky Chariots and Strike Griffons for added defense. In short, bringing comforts to the people of Balanced Rock that they had never before seen. Unfortunately for Baylee's family, the arrival of the Obelisk brought nothing but discomfort.

The topless guards did not have to push people out of the way as the priestess, her guardian, her clerk and handmaidens, and now Baylee and Clara, made their way towards the covered platform. The swarm of bodies cleared the way in front of them, inspired by both fear and respect.

"Glory of the Goddess!" The shout came from the crowd, and in a few seconds the entire group was cheering in the Keeper's name.

The councilwomen stood, applauding her as she walked up the stairs to the platform. Baylee had never seen such a gathering of people, and all of them had their eyes on her. Her heart raced, and her knees wobbled. She clutched her sister's hand, who stared open-mouthed at the sea of people. With a squeeze, she signaled Clara to take her seat, praying she did not trip and fall whilst in such plain view. Ambrosia Max was there, wearing the traditional robes of mourning. She had lost her husband the same day Baylee had been detained. Herminia, the blacksmith, (Baylee could not recall her last name), Dana Travenore, Tanya Daisee, and Geneeve Luena were there as well, all welcoming the Lady Coreni with warm smiles. Otillia Mialka was also present, though she seemed as if her mind drifted upon a distant ocean.

Raen did not sit, rather she stepped forward on the platform, her arms wide and her palms down, she motioned to hush the crowd. Her priestess robes were flashy and revealing, the pinnacle of Sabrinian fashion. Baylee may not like the woman, but her 'presence' was undeniable.

"People of Balanced Rock! Neighbors and Travelers! Tradesmen and Entertainers! Thank you for coming to this day of great celebration!" Cheers required her to repeat the visual command for quiet.

"Today, we celebrate the gifts of the Goddess! We raise up a symbol of her love, and in return she will bring us all into her warm embrace! In that warmth, she will bring us light without torches, carriages without wheels, and a life without fear!"

More praise exploded from the onlookers and, for a moment, the priestess reveled in it.

"It is the fear we have of our enemies that we will destroy today, and it will start right here, in the shadow of our Goddess! As many of you know, our brave Sergeant Lucavion died while fighting the Otherbreeds we now have in proper chains. These beastmen slew him without a second thought, one driving his teeth into the brave warriors head. But it was his sacrifice that allowed the trap to be sprung and our soldiers to prevail! He shall not be forgotten! Join with me in prayer, and help me to call Valkyr to take his soul to the Goddess."

Baylee found her mind wandering during the prayer. She found herself staring at Otillia, wondering what the small, round woman was thinking. Otillia sat in her chair, staring at the cage behind the adjacent scaffold. It was a blank stare from a defeated woman. Did she know someone in that cage? The familiar sounds of the ending of the divine entreaty brought her back to the moment.

"...may you forever walk with the Goddess, peace and good will to your children, may you show no mercy to our enemies. Amen."

The crowd echoed the final word before looking up to the Keeper.

"The Scriptures demand justice by blood. The purity of our ways must prevail. As it states in the Book of Titanius, chapter two, verse twelve, 'The righteous have fallen and it is we, the still-standing, that will bathe in the blood of those that fell them'."

The crowd mumbled approval in various levels of praise to the Goddess.

"I draw your attention to the instruments of our vengeance, there on the Scaffold of Purification!" The crowd followed her signal to three men wearing pure white hoods, the golden symbol of the Griffon embroidered on the forehead. The men were gigantic. Though not carved like a work of art like Raen's hunter, Baylee observed that each had arms bigger than her waist, and by the looks of their round, bare stomachs, the men had never before missed a meal. Each stood in front of the cross-shaped table. One held a wicked two-handed axe, its polished face was curved and cut with jagged teeth. The second had a long hammer, blunt on one side and narrowing to a thin point on the other. The third had a pair of swords, gleaming, hooked blades, cut and curved in places that made her shutter to look upon. Each raised their weapons one at a time, displaying them for the mob. Cheers filled the air.

"Before we show the Goddess' will to our enemies, we must also understand the nature of our Doctrine. One of your own has willingly accepted the aid of some of these creatures. She has allowed them to live amongst her freely." Distasteful murmurs filtered through the crowd, as they tried to figure out who the offender was. "Fear not people, for this woman has come to me in repentance. She has seen the error of her ways. Lady Mialka, please. Step forward."

Baylee's eyes widened when Otillia stood and stepped next to the Keeper. The farmer's daughter inadvertently placed her hand over her heart. This woman, a criminal?

"Lady Mialka, have you not given shelter to our enemy, the Dogmen of Man'Antas?"

"I have, Mother."

"And do you see the error of your ways?"

"I do, Mother."

"Then you know what you must do." The Keeper placed her hand on the woman's shoulder.

Four blindfolded men, each followed by a soldier dressed in ceremonial armor, were led on to the execution scaffold.

Baylee recognized them right away as Ottila's guardsmen. In all of her years, she could not even recall the men speaking; let alone

213

doing anything that would define them as enemies. In fact, their good behavior often made her wonder why people talked so poorly about them. Certainly, their elongated noses and ears gave them an almost comical appearance, but they had never done anything wrong in her recollection. She did recall that when the general store caught fire two years previous, the four men had been instrumental in saving two children trapped inside. The Village Council had commended them. Now they were being pushed to their knees in front of a bloodthirsty crowd. The soldiers standing behind them raised their sharpened swords and waited.

"I do, Mother." Otillia raised her hand, and the town went silent, the locals all knowing what was about to happen, and all knowing it was wrong.

Her hand dropped, and with it the four swords in unison, blades being driven directly into each man's heart for a merciful death. Baylee could hear the sounds of the blades sliding into the men and out of the bodies as they fell, merciful or not, the twitching Dogmen wiggled unnaturally, so much so, one of them fell off of the front of the scaffold. Someone in the crowd laughed. Someone else cheered. Baylee's hands covered her mouth, she was horrified at the vision, at the sounds, and now at the mob who was shouting for more.

After a few moments the bodies were dragged off, and Raen was again motioning for silence. When the crowd obliged, she turned to Otillia, whose tears cut into her best makeup, causing the darker lines around her eyes to spill down her cheeks.

"You have done the right thing, and for that the Goddess shall show you mercy. Kneel." She did so, though she visibly shook with a vain attempt to retain some form of dignity.

"You will wear the robes of the Acolyte for five years."

Otillia looked up, for all of her sacrifice, she appeared even more wounded. Baylee surmised that this was not a pre-negotiated portion of her punishment.

"Use this time, to reflect on the Scriptures, to reflect in the teachings of the Goddess. The church will seize your businesses during your penance until you are deemed worthy of reintroduction. The Goddess is wise and forgiving. Go with Her Own Grace."

Otillia was visibly stunned, as two Acolytes helped her up and walked her down the stairs of the covered platform. The other councilwomen were a greenish white. None had guessed the outcome.

"The Goddess is wise. In that wisdom, she has made us all strong. Stronger than the Otherbreeds. Stronger than the Dogmen. Stronger than the Tuskers. These Pigbacks loom in the plains not far from here. They attack trade caravans, kill our settlers, rape our woman, and steal our children. Her Own Grace has seen us victorious in the recent Battle of Lucavion Bluff despite the legendary sacrifice of our heroes, our soldiers overcame extensive numbers and even the Pigback's pagan magick. Share with me now the vengeance of our fallen! Share with me the demand of the Goddess!" There was no doubt that the priestess was fueled by the captivation of the crowd, that and the power of manipulation. The woman was capable of anything, and to the mob in front of her, she had the written word of the Goddess on her side.

Baylee followed her gaze back to the execution scaffold. Chanting pounded in her head as the townsfolk and travelers demanded justice for the soldiers that fell in battle only days before. Watered down blood dripped from the front of the platform, diluted by the servants' poor attempt at mopping up the mess. Her stomach turned. She had seen animals butchered, chickens prepared for plucking, fish cleaned before the pan, but never before had she seen something like this. So much blood already, and Raen demanded more.

Nightmare coming true, two soldiers dragged one of the Tuskers from the cage. The man tried to struggle but was powerless to his escorts. They lay the struggling man on the table, synching down his arms and legs. He growled and cursed at them. The man with the axe moved towards a crank in the back of the platform, and with a victorious roar, began turning the handle. With each turn came a loud click, and the cross began elevating until the man tied to it faced the crowd. They cheered as the man spat curses at them. They threw rotten vegetables and fruits at him, as well as vicious insults. The three executioners began walking around him in circles, while in front they rose their weapons high in the air for approval. The mob was in a near frenzy.

The man with the hammer stopped circling the tied Plainsman. The other two stepped to the side. He held the hammer aloft, inciting a higher level of noise from the audience. The Plainsman growled at

215

him, trying to defy the weakness caused by previous wounds inflicted on him. The executioner swung the hammer into the prisoner's mid-section, the thud blasting the air away from him in a spray of blood. Baylee put a fist against her lips and a hand over her sister's eyes. The hammer swung again. Cheers switched to sounds of condolence mixed with laughter. Baylee was going to be sick. Again the hammer struck the man, this time in one knee, next in the other. Each causing the condemned Tusker to scream in pain. Soon, the man spun the hammer round and struck the prisoner in the head with the spike. Hands and feet twitched, and shit fell down the table to rest in the rapidly growing pool of blood.

The Sabrinians loved it. Baylee fought back vomit. She tried desperately to search the crowd for her family, but there were just so many people chanting and cheering for more. Even the faces that had seemed disgusted at Ottilia's loss were part of the diseased herd, shaking their fists in eerie unison.

A second prisoner was being drug up to the table, this one easily as weak as the first, if not more so. He, too, was tied down and cranked up to face the rabid congregation. This time it was the man with the hooked swords that performed the show. He stood in front of the plainsman, so only his exaggerated arm movements could been seen from behind. When he stepped away a slight bulge of crimson grew on the prisoner's lower abdomen. It grew quickly until it burst, the poor man's entrails spilling out and onto the platform. The Plainsman tried to scream but only gagged, the splotch of his insides on the platform preventing him from doing so. Even the faces of the crowd reflected his pain, some even pointing out the obvious pain caused by being disemboweled. The man with the sword then cut the bonds of one of the prisoner's arms, knowing it would be his natural instinct to try to pull some of his intestines back into his own body. It was, of course, futile.

No one cheered, and Baylee could not hold back her natural instinct to puke. She covered her mouth and raced off the back of the platform. Delirious, she looked for a private place to release the contents of her stomach, hoping some of the visions she saw would go with it. She braced herself upright and began to heave.

Raen whispered discretely to the clerk, who in turn went over to the hunter and removed his blindfold. The clerk then passed on the order given by her master, and the man casually hopped off the back of their covered scaffold in pursuit of the sickened girl. Clara moved to follow her sister, but her hand was caught by Raen, who sat the girl on her lap as yet a third prisoner was being mounted onto the cross-shaped table.

Baylee threw up three or four times, before she realized she held onto the cage of doomed prisoners for balance. Through spectacles made from her own tears, she saw its contents. There was a boy in there, perhaps her age, sleeping at an unnatural depth. There was a peace about him, and that peace told her he was even less deserving of such an undeserving fate.

Why all this death? Why such cruelty? Images raced through her mind, specific flashes of the executions. Why did they have to hurt these people? There was a heat in her forehead, in her heart. Why did that bitch have to ruin everything? Baylee felt weightless. He was just a boy!

A man yelped in pain behind her, she turned towards the sound- her vision blurred. She could make out the shape of Raen's guardian on his knees, holding his eyes. Other shapes came up behind him, as dizziness swirled around her. Then she felt a touch on the hand that gripped the outside of the cage. It was a kind touch. A concerned touch.

There was a warmth in her head. She felt weightless. As the blurry visions approached her, Baylee collapsed to the ground.

***

It was warmth that woke Teegan from his sleep. He had no idea where he was, or even who he was for that matter. All he saw was the spirit before him. A light shown from the center of her forehead, but she did not look well. He sat up and rushed to help her, but his legs did not want to cooperate. He pulled himself up with the bars of his cage, fighting to make it to her. His hand touched hers and she looked at him. Her eyes were those from his dreams, glowing like a shaman's. She smiled, and slumped to the ground.

Four Roosterhead guards raced up, spears drawn. Two pulled the girl away from the cage while the other two thrust their weapons between the bars, forcing Teegan to back up. There were two other Plainsmen in the cage with him, both recovering from what Teegan assumed was a similar sleep.

Two females in strange clothing looked at a pale-skinned male (warrior by the looks) who held his hands up to his eyes in pain. One of the females, more ornately decorated than the other, moved over to check the collapsed girl. She looked up into the cage at him, then called over another man not dressed as a Roosterhead.

She spoke to him in their squeaky tongue, often motioning to Teegan and his companions. The man shook his head and shrugged his shoulders in disbelief. The woman abruptly approached the cage again and looked at the three of them. She then barked orders at the two guards that had threatened him earlier.

If a few brief moments, guards were shackling the three of them, and they were being led down the road towards one of the biggest human shelters Teegan had ever seen. His stomach growled with displeasure, Sky Father he was hungry! The guards pulled the three along in a jog, away from the strange cheering and chanting. The pace was not a tough one, in fact Morgal would have laughed if he saw the Roosterheads trying to run.

Teegan just hoped that wherever they were going, he could learn the words for food and water.

***

The final blows were being struck by the axeman when Raen returned to her seat. She was outwardly flustered.

"Where's Baylee?" Clara asked.

"She's fine dear, just a bit sick. She'll meet us back at the house soon enough." The other women exchanged concerned glances, but none offered an opinion. They had not seen what had happened by the cage, but all were shrewd businesswomen capable of doing math. People once sitting with them were there no longer.

Raen took a breath to regain her composure, she smoothed her gown, and painted on her face of dignity.

"Her Own Grace has spoken. Her blood debt has been paid."

There was a unanimous grumble of approval. Most of the onlookers had barely made it through the third execution.

"Now, our Benevolent Mother will grant us her light! Celebrate with me as we raise the Obelisk!" Her arms went up, and people cheered.

Down the street, the newly harnessed Thanadont (done so during the executions) began to prod forward under the specific commands of its handlers. The pulley crane creaked under the strain. The ropes went taught under the tension. Thirty men on each side used a guiding rope to ensure that the base would fit into the pre-poured foundation. The crowd watched in awe as the golden top pointed higher and higher into the sky. It did not take long before the Obelisk was firmly in place, waterproof sealant being poured into the seams. The last bits of sunlight fading from the sky.

Raen again addressed the crowd. "Let this be a testament to your faith, good people. Let this be a symbol of the change we will see in the future! Goddess, give us your light!"

Like the words to some magick spell, Raen's last command seemed to call upon a miracle. The newly placed light poles that spanned from her villa to the town square and down the main street to the edge of town, all lit up. Decorated trees and houses lit up, all to sounds of astonishment from the people gathered. They cheered for their Goddess, they cheered for her Keeper of the Doctrine. Raen held her arms up, appearing to praise Her Own Grace, and as people joined her, fireworks began to light up the sky.

The spectacle was complete.

The councilwomen feigned the fervor of those under the spell of the priestess. People would talk about this to the far reaches of the kingdom, and that meant Balanced Rock would never be the same, especially now that they had power and all the comfort that comes with it.

Just a Sword

The last bits of sunlight were disappearing in the distance as Maesma approached the farmhouse alone, leaving the four skirmishers in the small courtyard. There was no need for stealth. Besides, she would have seen them approaching for the entire last league or more.

He could see her inside the building through the dull grey walls and shadowy foundation. Her energy was just as vibrant as always and decidedly calm. She sipped on a cup of tea, and a second cup waited across from her, energies of fire and water rising as steam into the air.

He neared the farmhouse, passing by the shapes that made up a packed horse cart. Apparently, Shawn'Athasia had been planning on taking her leave of this place. Maesma did not blame her. Now that Balanced Rock was actively 'on the map' so to speak, it would only be a matter of time before she would be brought to justice. He sought justice of his own accord, vengeance for the most horrendous of crimes-the breaking of a heart.

He entered the farmhouse cautiously, one of his curved swords leading the way, not knowing if his old friend planned some sort of welcome gift in the form of a trap. She had not, and he proceeded through the atrium into the room where she sat, awaiting the uncomfortable reunion.

"How did you find me?" Shawna asked as Maesma entered the room.

He noted her sword resting on the table, perhaps the memory of their last meeting was not so far from her mind after all.

"It's been a long time, Shawn'Athasia." Maesma sat down in front of her, after burying the tip of his sword into the wooded surface of the table so it stood straight up.

"I haven't been called that since...I...I never thought I would see you again, Maesma." She took a sip of tea.

"I know you did not. Not with the way you left."

"That was so long ago, tell me you do not still carry that angst." She looked at his *joa*. It beat wildly in his chest, so much so, she did not need to hear the answer.

"Carry it? Carry it?" He spoke through his teeth. "I sleep with it every night. It is my only real ally."

"That is an alliance signed by your own hand, Maesma. You could have left with me."

"I had my duty."

"You had her."

"...and you had him." He tasted the words, and they were bitter.

"Do not pretend to know my mind without first breaking bread with your own. You were content as long as you had your queen and your warrior girl. You chose your path, one I do not hold against you. You chose the life you knew, not the one I offered." She took another sip from her cup.

"You offered that I share you with another man."

"At least I offered, you forced me to share."

He slammed his fist on the table. "Like we have a choice! We are dogs to them. You know this!"

"Oh, Maze, why do you hate me so?" She shook her head, staring at the swirling energies in her cup.

"Do not use that name, wench! You have lost that privilege. You left me there to rot!" growled Maesma.

"You left yourself there to rot. You knew my mind! I was not meant to be in a cage!" Shawn'Athasia was still calm. It was clear there were no remnants of the times they once shared together, and seeing it filled the emptiness in Maesma's chest with a strange concoction of loathing and sadness.

"No one is meant to be in a cage..." he continued, "...no one is meant to be treated like an animal. Like a dog, thrown a bone every now and again, patted on the head for good behavior."

"Then you should have left with me. Besides, if I recall correctly, I don't think you ever minded the way Her Own Voice pats you on the head.'"

"You used me as a distraction. You used me so you could leave with him. It was a lesson in misdirection I will never forget." He alluded to more hidden meanings.

"Listen to yourself, Maze. You sound like a spoiled noble boy who has lost his toy soldiers. I was never yours. You liked being on the wall. You liked getting the lady on Firstdays and the 'wench' on Thirddays. Don't give me the 'puppy left out in the rain' routine.

Speaking of puppies, don't you usually run around with a pair of those steel-toothed daemons?"

Maesma sneered. "Jove and Romule. My best trained thus far. They are... indisposed at the moment." He swelled with pride...or guilt.

"Maze. What have you done?"

"I told you to STOP CALLING ME THAT!" His command was a roar.

Shawna moved backward, sliding her chair a safe distance from the table while drawing her sword. She readied a stance from the seated position, the long curved portion of the sword arching over her head.

Maesma slid his chair backwards as well, pulling his curved blade out of the table and a second one from its sheath behind his back. Both sat staring at one another, every muscle a condensed spring.

"I see you kept Longku safe and sound." Maesma observed her weapon.

Most swords were like any other piece of steel, the dull grays of unliving objects, but some weapons held onto the elements used to craft them. A hunter could see the remnants of fire or ice crawling through etched runes. Other weapons were crafted with such precision, such perfect technique, they flowed with the living energies of the stars. A hunter saw these like a beacon in the night. Then there was Longku, the Dragon's Tear in the old tongue, a sword made before known history, a sword that's method of creation was a complete mystery, a sword that's very presence showed there were forces of evil at work in the world.

"I don't want to use her on you, Maesma, but I will if you press this..."

"Press this, Shawn'Athasia? You are wanted for desertion from twelve years ago. I have come to bring you in."

"Those deeds are as long forgotten as that name, hunter, and I am certain I am far removed from the bounty boards of the empire."

Only lips moved, both ready to strike. This was the place where a battle would be fought and won, here, in the seconds before a strike. A warrior's enemy was not just an opponent but a strange sort of confidant. Maesma was arguably the greatest warrior spawned in the Dark Beneath, and Shawna knew this. In contrast, the Asperii woman had the Dragon's Tear, and with it the reach and style of the slashing weapons of the North.

"On the contrary, Shawn'Athasia, not a moon passes when I am not made to remember the cost of my failure. That and, of course, the company you keep makes you a traitor and a compassionate." The statement was a direct admittance that the woman's sacrifice had not worked. He knew about her son, her friends, and their plan of escape.

Shawna's head turned towards the outside. The skirmishers were gone. She stared out into the distance through the walls, their trails went off in a direction that made her heart sink.

"Goddess, Maesma? What did you do?"

"My duty..." The self-reassurance was the only warning for his attack as he leapt into the air.

***

"*We must hurry, oaf. What are you doing back there?*" Sherium moved through the tall grass at the edge of the field.

"*I just think we should go back. There cannot be more than a small flock of them.*" Solam picked up speed to a trot to catch up to his mate, Ronin clutched his mane and hugged the big cat's shoulders with his knees.

"*We stick to the plan. You saw the look on her face when she recognized that hunter's life force. He will never stop looking for Ronin. If she is successful, we meet her at the place of peace.*"

"*When she is successful,*" Solam corrected his mate.

"*Where's mommy?*" Ronin trembled. Fearful pictures rolling through his head.

"*She's coming, cub. Do not fret.*" Solam did his best to comfort the boy.

The two Lynxen moved forward, heading toward the hills that created a natural barrier to the plains.

"*Do you think he will listen to reason? Shawna said they had history.*" Sherium did not know what type of history.

"*Shawna has many tools at her disposal. Human males react to her, her shape is most pleasing. If that fails, she always has her skill as a warrior.*"

It was true Shawna had seen much more than her fair share of combat; but unlike her two friends, her days of battle had been long absent. Unfortunately, the hunter she recognized had probably been slaughtering people only days before. The thought made the male nervous.

They hadn't far to go to get to the base of the steep hill, when both Solam and Sherium heard movement to their right. With the sound of oxygen being sucked from the sky, a flame erupted in front of them. Sounds to the left preceded flames igniting over there, as well.

"Run!" Solam's thoughts were escorted by a roar.

Sherium, up ahead, began to race towards the narrowing gap in the flames. It was clear that only one of them would make it. This fire was no accident, and being trapped in a burning field was the last thing either of the Lynxen wanted.

The flames came together well before Sherium approached the line, but the pregnant cat was not deterred, she soared through the air, breaching the flames. Solam had to make a decision, he could pick up speed and follow his mate easy enough, but he could easily loose his passenger in the jump. If Ronin fell into the flames, there would be no way to get him out. His mate safely on the other side, he banked quickly to his right where he saw another gap in the flames closing rapidly.

Sherium made a wide turn shortly after landing beyond the rapidly growing wall of flame. Right away, she saw the gap her mate was heading towards and redirected her course to meet him. It was then a solid wall of black muscle slammed into her flank, steel teeth tearing into her shoulder. The attack was foolish. Momentum causing Sherium to topple to her side, she used her hind legs to vault her canine attacker into the flame she had just crossed. The smell of burning hair hit her nostrils almost instantly, and snarls and yelps could be heard from the flames. The queen got her feet under herself quickly, and pain shot through her shoulder.

Sherium turned to resume her gate when the burning hellhound leapt back out of the flames to attack.

"Kill, blood, kill!" it called as it barreled towards her. It was the last attack the war dog would make. Sherium was a Pridemother, she killed to survive at least once a week. The blind rage of a burning foe only made her more desperate. And the attacker more vulnerable to a massive claw-filled paw. She timed her defense perfectly, batting the hound to the ground in a cloud of burning embers, its lower jaw

barely attached. "*Kill, blood, kill*" its last thoughts lingering in her mind.

She looked towards her mate. "*Run, you oaf!*" She thought as she changed direction yet again. Those that sprung the trap would be after her, and an injured shoulder would slow her down, she needed to make higher ground. Sherium turned to head toward the safety of the steep slope of the hill, a movement that inadvertently caused a well-aimed javelin to miss its mark. She flinched at another as it grazed the top of her back. Two men stood at either of her flanks, shields up, and each readying another deadly missile.

***

Fool woman! Shawna scolded herself for letting her guard down. Maesma attacked with a textbook strategy that meant she had to choose which blade would hit her. There was no good outcome. Both knew she would choose the non-fatal blow, while defending against the one that would kill her. This would, undoubtedly, leave her vulnerable to a flurry of bloody options that would bring the melee to an abrupt end. What Maesma had forgotten was Shawna never did like playing by the rules, and practiced attacks rarely had the intended effect on someone so adept at using her surroundings.

In the same instant he leapt into the air, Shawna was moving. She rolled off to the side, grabbed the edge of the chair with one hand and flipped it around to us the legs as a four-pronged shield. The killing blow had been dodged, and the less fatal one had been deflected by one or more of the chair legs. She continued her roll, adding a swipe of her sword that her opponent had to hop to avoid being permanently hobbled. She used her legs like a windmill for the momentum needed to stand in an instant. She faced her opponent, changing the grip of her sword to a reverse position, and held her open hand out straight, two fingers in the air slightly hooked towards him. Her heart was beating hard now, and she was off balance from the assault. Maesma sneered at the woman, even though he admired her skillful recovery. They slowly circled each other, keeping the dining room table between them.

"Nice move. I'm glad my first attack did not kill you." There was a truthful irony to his taunt.

"Where are your dogs, Maze?"

"I told you. They are indisposed."

"What do you mean by that? Where did those soldiers out front go?" Shawna knew the answer.

They still circled the table, one foot crossing over the other like deadly mirror-images of each other.

"Rarely do men impress me, if you'll recall. But the sergeant I've been assigned to-he's different. Brilliant, actually." He made a quick move, the woman counterbalanced. He would not catch her off guard again. He would have to use another ally-rage. "You should see how adept he is at coming up with traps. Why, earlier this month, we ambushed an entire tribe of Plainspeople and, thanks to his little trap, suffered minimal losses." He had her, her heart was racing, and his story a clue as to what happened outside. What she thought had been a noble time-buying sacrifice, had separated her from her friends and her son. He had needed that extra push.

"We took many prisoners, Shawn'Athasia. We made them all slaves." The last word was a slit across the neck, truth spilling onto the floor. He did not have time to savor his success.

With a cry in the name of her son, Shawna cut the dining room table in half, she followed through with the swing in a flawless motion arching downward, a slice that intended to make two parts of her opponent as well.

Shawna heard the sound of clashing steel as Maesma's hooked blade intercepted the Dragon's Tear, but she did not hear the sound of his second blade entering her abdomen just below her ribcage.

* * *

Solam and Ronin raced for the gap in the roaring wall of fire, the boy buried his face in the Lynxen's mane and hugged his back. Solam pushed his muscles to abnormal exertion, trying to outrun the flames.

He had it, the flames barely touched when he reached the edge. "*Hold on cub!*" he said with a growl.

Solam leapt into the air-the opposing body of a hellhound leaping from its intended direction. The collision was a near miss, the hellhound had leapt too high. Solam landed outside of the ring of fire safely.

Albeit, now he lacked a passenger. Solam roared at the realization that his rider had been plucked from his back, and slid to a stop to turn around. When he did so, he momentarily lost his footing and rolled to a stop. He twisted his legs back under him and immediately headed back towards the blazing wall that separated him from his cub. He dashed forward and pounced into the fire without a second thought.

Though he could literally feel his whiskers melt away and smell his own mane catching fire, he powered through, just as steely teeth were about to clamp down on the helpless form of his cub. A blur of fire and cat plowed into the dog, taking it off the boy so swiftly it was as if it had never been hovering over him in the first place. His front paws dug in deep, as did his teeth, and when the two rolled across the ground some distance from the motionless boy, Solam was already raking out the dog's insides with his hind legs. The roll extinguished the flames on the Plainscat as he once again righted himself. He raced over to check on Ronin, sniffing deeply.

"Yi'Shou! Are you okay?"

Ronin moaned, his head was trickling blood, but he was alive.

With a thud, a javelin struck Solam in his side. It was right behind his front shoulder-the soft spot all hunters seek. Another Javelin hit him in the opposite side, then a third.

The trap had been complete.

Solam looked at his first cub and felt no pain. He remembered the baby Shawna nestled into his mane for the first time. He lunged forward, movement faster than the soldier could have realized. A swipe of his paw took the man's head from his shoulders. In a spray of blood, Solam saw an exit, he could see a way to say a last goodbye to his mate.

He felt her snuggled up to him, felt her warmth, and snuggled up to her was a little boy with swirling blues eyes.

The one that lay on the ground behind him. There was no pain. He pounced toward a second soldier, who managed to raise his shield in a feeble attempt to stop the big male. The tactic was futile, the weight of the cat blasted the breath from his lungs, crushing ribs, and sending the worthless handheld barrier sailing. Solam did not bother searching for his throat, his mouth engulfed the man's head, teeth penetrating helmet, skull and brain.

Another missile hit him, causing him to turn slowly.

A little boy, barely walking, called his name as he ran clumsily towards him. The laughter was infectious, and it brought sunlight with it.

A third soldier fell, now lacking the arm that threw the last short spear.

Shadows were closing in on the big cat, not just those in the shape of the soldiers closing in, but those of the direst in nature. He sought out the bleeding boy. Another soldier took a swipe from Solam's mighty paw, but his helm protected him. He screamed and fell away, holding his face.

Solam wanted to smell Ronin one last time, he lay on his belly and crawled over the top of him. It was Solam's last attempt to protect him. He closed his eyes with love and took a deep breath, as more javelins hit their mark.

The Lorekeeper would breathe no more.

***

The wound was deep, and both of them knew it. Soldiers need not fool themselves when exposed to so much death. Her arms were going numb, her hands unable to grip her sword. Shawna brought her knee up into Maesma's chin, a blow that stood the man up.

With a clatter of steel, the Dragon's Tear fell to the ground. Shawna staggered backwards, trying to hold in the blood seeping from her side.

Maesma was enraged. He shook off the dizzying effects of his opponents kick. He stepped forward and grabbed the back of her head, viciously twisting it back with a fist full of hair. Savagely, he struck her in the face with the hilt of his hooked blade. He did not let go. Rather he used his grip to ready her for another crushing blow. Then a third.

Only after her body went limp did he stop. She slumped to the floor, her *joa* fluttered. It would not be long now.

***

Sherium hopped sideways and bolted towards the hill, she used the body of one soldier to block the line of sight of the other. The warrior nearest to her hurled his javelin too hastily and missed, while the second had to hold his attack for fear of friendly fire. By the time he had an open shot, Sherium was at full speed. Even favoring a leg the speed made for a near impossible throw. The soldier missed, and the pregnant lynxen bounded up the hill.

The two soldiers watched in awe as the cat displayed her grace, making flawless switchbacks and leaping terrain-all while favoring a wounded leg. Sherium made her way up the hill in no time and turned back to look towards the farm. The flames were spreading, lighting up the darkening sky. The wind had switched, and soon the fire would reach the farm. She dared not let herself be open. Channeling now, even to heal her wound, would surely be seen by the hunter below, and she had no idea how many men he had with her. She needed to gain more distance to meet her mate and her friends at the agreed place of peace.

Sherium thought of the cubs growing in her belly. She thought of the one she had left in the care of her mate. She had to have faith they would meet her, it would be too risky for her to go back for them right now. Get to safety, heal, and wait for them at the rendezvous point. That was all she could do for the time being. Fates willing, they would not be delayed.

***

Maesma walked out of the farmhouse and into the field to meet the returning soldiers. He held the *Longku*.

Two of the soldiers carried the massive head of the lynxen by its mane, mouth open and tongue dangling. Its jewelry and jingled as they labored towards the house. There were only seven soldiers left and no sign of Jove and Romule. One of the skirmishers helped Cabot walk, he had taken a nasty blow to the head. Another carried a bundle, a little boy whose limp arms and legs bounced up and down with motion of the movement.

"We got the male lynxen. It was as you said. The female escaped." Cabot was labored.

"The child lives. That is good." The hunter had distance in his voice. Due, in part, to the loss of Jove and Romule.

"One of your dogs almost took him, but this fucking cat was unreal! Damn near took my eye out with one hit." Marcus checked his wound. He was still drunk from the excitement of the fight, the days to come would surely find a curse rather than praise to the beast's assault.

"You're lucky it didn't take your head off like it did Thratus'. Poor bastard." One of the skirmishers was helping clean the sergeant's wound.

Some of the other troops were meandering around, looking for things of value.

"Take what you want," Cabot ordered, "but get it done. The fire has changed direction, and it will be here soon. We'll all be roasted cow balls if we stick around. You two, clear out that cart! We can load it with whatever's valuable."

"What about him?" The skirmisher lifted the unconscious boy up as if he would float away.

"I'll take him," Maesma said, moving over to Ronin. Throwing the boy over his shoulder he began to walk away, still able to hear some of the soldiers talking.

"Sergeant, come take a look at this! That is a dwarvish made cast-iron stove!" The man whistled, an audible testament to the value of the object.

"These tapestries are worth a pretty penny, too," said another.

"What the fuck are you two doing?" Marcus inquired of two skirmishers he noticed hunched over Shawna's body.

"What do you mean, sarge? There's still a little life left in her," one responded.

"She's still warm!" said the other, as he started the act.

"You want a turn, boss? I mean look at her! She's a real beauty!"

"Goddess's cunt, no!" Marcus was not amused. "I only fuck women out of duty, and when that calls, I expect them to be a little more willing."

Those that were not otherwise distracted by lust, began loading the stove and other valuables.

The sergeant stepped out front, heading over to the cart to inspect his trophy. The sounds of the troops' vile deeds seemed part of a dark orchestra, supported by the crackle of the approaching fire and the frenzy of the farm's livestock.

The headdress of the Plainscat would certainly make him rich. He touched the bloody wounds on his face-yet it would be this scar, this scar that would make him famous.

He looked over to the hunter that was walking away, calling loud enough to stop him: "Nice sword! Did that belong to the gardener?"

Maesma stopped but did not turn, the sounds of men cheering each other on inside the hut turned bile in his stomach. "What sword?" he called back.

Marcus did not pursue the matter, he supposed he owed the hunter that. After all, his assignment to Cabot had led to wealth and, undoubtedly, power and fame. Why not let him have it? After all, it was just a sword.

Bound For Anon

They had been three days on the road to Anon, the capitol city of the Sabrinian Empire. Already on the horizon was the massive mountain where the city rested. It was said that the Goddess built the city in the heavens, then sent it down to the earth with such force it destroyed those that sought to kill the devout. The blast not only acted as a weapon, it gave them a home while causing a massive crater, whose natural walls were impossible to scale. The Goddess, in her benevolence, wept for those enemies that died with the appearance of the city, and her tears filled it with the life-giving waters of Crystalline Lake. A pair of natural waterfalls relieved the massive reservoir known as the Mother's Tears. They, in turn, fed the mighty Winged River that now ran parallel to the cobblestone road the caravan travelled upon. Every now and again a trade barge navigated down the river, operators staring at the extensive caravan.

Legend of the Scriptures or no, Baylee had always wanted to see the famous city, however, under much different circumstances. Wearing the robes of an Acolyte was not what she had in mind. Baylee really had no idea what to expect for her term as an Acolyte, but it definitely meant she would be restricted to the temple grounds rather than exploring the marvels of the ancient city. Otillia wore the robes as well, but did not have the luxury of Baylee's naivety. The woman sat beside her in the Goddess Carriage, holding her hand tightly, and smiling when she could-a smile that never replaced the worry in her eyes. Baylee had no real experience with Acolytes, the last few weeks had been all she had seen of them, and she felt the tasks of servitude were somewhat romantic. She would get to see things she never dreamed possible back on the dairy, and her family would be looked after. She was also rid of the Keeper Raen, the conniving woman intimidated Baylee nearly as much as a charging Dredge Goat, and any distance from her was a good thing. She would serve her time, a year or two at the most, and return home to Balanced Rock to look after her family. She smiled at these thoughts, and tried to silently sooth her worried friend with that same smile.

The caravan was large, guarded by nearly fifty highly trained warriors, and a speechless hunter that cradled a strange curved sword as if it held the secrets of life's meaning. A small boy, between her age and Clara's, was chained with cuff and collar and walked behind him. For three days the boy had been forced to keep a marching pace outside of the converted wagon of slaves like a puppy too small to be taken on a walk by its master. The hunter did not even slow when the boy tripped, he would yank him up to his feet and continue on. The boy's freshly shaved head was bright in a hue of red in the summer sun, an odd contrast to his tanned skin. It was the boy's eyes, however, that captivated Baylee's imagination. She had only caught a glimpse of them, but in that brief moment, the swirling blues drowned her in their whirlpool. They were unlike the dead eyes of Bo'Ah, the Keeper's guardian, who sat in the Goddess Carriage with them, still unable to see after Baylee's second incident at the Raising Ceremony. The Keeper's clerk was there as well, and for the last three days had done little besides glare at Baylee, and look at the wounded hunter with all too intimate concern.

Blinding the hunter had been as accidental as healing the wounded Tuskers. Twice now, she had left the Goddess Carriage at a stopping point to relieve herself, and twice the young Tusker she had saved had raced to the edge of the slave wagon to get a glimpse of her. He did not know it, but healing him had saved her as well. Raen had decided to send Baylee to the capitol as an Acolyte, a place where the many scholars and theologists could discover the nature of the gift the Goddess had given her. Jacin and Jacob would go to the city to begin their service in the army, while Icomus, Clara, and Eelia would be moved to her Villa. The Keeper of the Doctrine had said it would be easier for her father to advise her on a new business venture without the travel time from the dairy. Baylee really had no choice but to go along with the lie, the woman had come to Balanced Rock and changed-no, ruined-everything.

The twins were in high spirits, there were a few other boys their age starting their service as well. They were already set about to light duties and being integrated into the brotherhood of soldiers through a bit of mocking and teasing. Baylee imagined the teasing would grow more intense once they reached the city, but for now, the harmless jokes just added to the good mood of the young recruits. Jacin and Jacob stopped by several times, introducing her to some of the other soldiers, even higher-ranked ones. Who knew that having an acolyte as a sister would mean such rapid acceptance for them?

The rest of the Caravan was made up of merchant carts, entertainers, priests, acolytes like herself, and the large cage full of Tuskers. The slave wagon was made from converting the oversized flatbed cart pulled by the mighty Thanadont and was used for the delivery of the Obelisks. The mission was led by a very successful young sergeant who, despite a grievous head wound, had been the topic of conversation around the entire population of the cavalcade. Baylee had seen the man once, but was made uncomfortable due to the way his eyes seemed to remove her robes. More and more often men were looking at her that way, a look she did not find flattering in the slightest.

Every night the caravan became a tiny town, its inhabitants continuing the celebration from Balanced Rock. Soldiers passed coin for entertainers and merchants, the wine flowed like a river. Acolytes and Priests did any deed commanded of them, as deemed by the laws of the empire written in the Scriptures. The entire concepts of these two factions of servitude were part of a much bigger machine. Control and fear were used to keep a culture in lawful order. Convicted women were made Acolytes for a time, nameless servants and handmaidens who were required to follow the orders of whomever they were assigned. This meant, more often than not, they would be subject to the requisites of men: lowly, single-minded dogs, usually too long without affection. Being lowered to this level often calloused the Acolyte during her tenure, bringing her closer to the word of the Goddess, arming her with the distain needed to keep the men in line.

The Sabrinian Priesthood embodied this distain. If the requirements of the Acolytes were degrading, they were a picnic in a field of flowers compared to the priesthood. A man condemned to this was stripped of everything, including the very parts of the body that defined him as a man. His name was forgotten, even to the extreme that families had funerals and periods of mourning. The sentence would be passed to the next of kin in the event of one taking one's own life, so the penance was complete.

The closer one got to the capitol city of Anon, the more rigid the laws became. Partly because the capitol was the traditional home of the High Priestess, Her Own Voice, and Protector of the People. And the capitol was home to the Great Pyramid of Anon, the source of all Sabrinian power. Its massive golden top was attuned to the pinnacles of all the Obelisks across the great nation, and it allowed for the energies of the Earth to be utilized by their builders. Building and street lighting, water pumps, and stoves all calibrated to the energies provided by the pyramid. Even city defenses and flying crafts like Sky Chariots and Strike Griffons, floating ones like Goddess Carriages and Wag Barges, could move seamlessly in a defined radius near the structures. The technology purposely described as a miraculous gift from the Goddess, hidden from the minds of the common folk as yet another method of control.

Tomorrow, Baylee and her brothers would be close enough to witness some of these miracles. The blue-eyed boy and the Tuskers would be new to the sights as well. She'd heard stories as a girl. Many times had her mind already made this journey, and tomorrow she would finally see it with her own eyes. Soon thereafter, however, both Baylee and Otillia would be assigned to someone for theirs tenure as Acolytes. She had no idea what that meant, but based on the reactions she had seen from the other woman, it could not be too enticing. Baylee hoped she was wrong, she had to hope-to do otherwise would surely drive her mad.

***

Teegan had only seen the girl that saved him twice. Whoever she was, she had the powers of creation; the ability to heal a wound that even the Eagle Shaman could not. There had been no sign of the shaman that had bound him to the spirit of Halftooth, the slain Toenuk bull of his first hunt. He wondered if he would see the wise woman again, especially after some of the others told him of her presence after the battle. He had questions for her. For example, what was the strange dream he had before the binding ceremony? Why did she follow him? Oddly, Teegan felt like he could feel the Eagle Shaman. He felt as though she were thinking of him, or watching him for some strange reason, and that she waited for him someplace safe to the east.

None of the Bloodthorns could speak the language of the Roosterheads. As such, there was much debate among them as to the fate of the tribe. Tauka'Aun and Lu'Kall, Teegan's two wives, were not members of the captives. This meant they had either escaped or perished. He chose to believe the former, primarily because he knew how resourceful the two women were, but also because the young Plainsman did not have the heart to swallow the possibility of the latter. Kurg felt the Roosterheads would make use of the majority of the tribe. The grown men, strong enough to work or fight would be taken to a labor camp or the pits; the more fortunate option granting a warrior's death in battle. Young men would, undoubtedly, be sold to the keepers of the human games who were known to seek them in order to train them for sport combat. As for the old and the women, Kurg was unsure. Humans had no desire for the broad hips and ivory tusks of a Plainsman female, and often had to crane their necks in order to look up at them. There had been talk of a plan to retrieve one of the metal 'fingers' held by one of the Roosterheads, but as of now, there had been no action based off those words.

Teegan shared in his father's concern. The braves he occupied the cage with in the human settlement had told him of the atrocities during the executions. The savage murders of his brothers had been worse than tales told to scare children. These murders were stalled due to the magick of the human girl that had healed them. Knowing people would be willing to commit such acts was nearly incomprehensible. Yet here they were, in a cage made of the humans' metal, being pulled by a beast that was meant to be as free as they were. The whole situation was beyond understanding.

To make strange matters even more bizarre, on the fourth day of their journey away from the human dwellings, carts with bird wings soared down out of the sky, pairs of Roosterheads riding on their backs. They flew down close to the slave cage, peering at the contents. The Bloodthorns' reactions (including Teegan's) were as expected. They were terrified. Some even thought of them as great Spirits, floating on the Skyfather's wind. Wherever they were being taken, it was certain to be as unfamiliar as all of this human magick. Teegan was forced to endure the thought that they might be going to a form of the vile executions he had survived only days before.

***

On the fifth day, Ronin's blistered and bloodied feet could take no more. Five days of walking, falling down, and being jerked around had taken its toll.

"If you do not get up, I will tie you to that wagon, and you will be dragged the rest of the way. Your skin will peel off over time, but you'll not die. No, we are too close to our destination for that." Maesma looked down at the boy, unaffected by the intricate orbs that were his eyes. His hunter's vision could only see the remnants of his own past swirling in the boy's life force. A memory of the child's mother that made up half of the boy's *joa*.

"I can't." Ronin spat the phrase through his teeth.

The hunter looked down on him, distain in his eyes. "You can't. Why? Because of your feet? Your feet are no longer your own, boy. Nothing is your own. You belong to the Goddess now. You are a little dog, a pet for Her Own Voice."

He leaned down, only inches away from the little boy's face. "Get up."

Ronin gritted his teeth and with as much effort as he could muster, he stood up, knees quivering with the pain that started at his feet.

"Good, now come." He turned away.

As Ronin took a step to follow him, he fell down, unable to get through the anguish.

"You are worthless." Maesma spat on him.

"Where's my mom?" Ronin yelled at his captor, tears giving him strength.

"She's dead, boy. Dead. Because she was weak. Like you."

The statement hollowed out his insides, picked his bones clean like a buzzard would a carcass. His mother was dead? Like Cretus? Like Celestte? Gone forever?

"Yes. She is dead, boy."

Ronin did not realize he spoke his thoughts out loud.

"You know something else, boy? I killed her." He was proud of the effect the words had on his prisoner. His tongue was a whip, and it tore at the boy's very soul.

Ronin looked up at the man, hatred in his heart, he allowed it to fill his veins and harden in his lungs. He lunged forward in an assault on Maesma's forward most leg, sinking his teeth into a meaty calf. His victim did not so much as flinch. Ronin bit down with all his strength, a muffled scream giving him added ferocity, and still the man did not react as expected. Truth be told, the boy had no real idea how he was supposed to react, he just thought it would be more than this. He could taste salty blood in his mouth, and it made him squeeze even harder. Only then did Maesma react.

The man's calf began to harden as he flexed it. The muscles were so solid they forced the boy's jaws apart. When his mouth wide open, the hunter popped his knee, causing the boy's head to snap back. It the same motion, he kicked Ronin in the stomach, sending the boy into a fit that was a hybrid of coughing and vomiting. Maesma watched as the boy fought his weakness, as rage battled fear and pain. His young heart pulsed with a newfound desire, a sort of animosity born of loss and heartbreak.

Ronin stared up at him, a look most men would see for what Maesma could not; it was a wish of death-a very painful death. Yet the hunter could only see the *joa* flowing through the boy, vibrant and full of renewal, no matter what the motivation.

"Good," he told the boy. "You will need that if you are to find the strength to avenge your mother someday. Now get up."

Somehow, Ronin did so. Yet, in the act, he did not realize he had just been placed into a different type of shackles. These ones he would fashion on his own accord, at the cost of his own innocence.

One foot plodded in front of another, and in a few hours they started passing the outlying farms and ranches of the capitol. The sight of these, as well as the frequent Sky Chariots and various passersby allowed for a further distraction to his crippling blisters. River boats were frequent here, and the town at the base of the Southern Barrier Ridge could now be seen. Pale streaks that would turn into two of the tallest waterfalls in the empire when distance was exchanged with proximity towered over the town like some sort of exposed vein of precious stone on the mountainside. The mist from the waterfalls seemed to sooth the air, not quite to the point of dampened humidity, but still palatable to those not acclimated to it.

"Tie this on." Maesma ordered as he tossed a blindfold to the boy. Had it not hit his hands, he may not have caught it. "You will see too many people otherwise. Too much energy in one place will sicken your mind."

Ronin did not argue. He was already made dizzy by the sea of life force. The town at the base of the barrier was ten times as large as Balanced Rock, even at the height of the festival, and the caravan had not even made it to the great lift yet. Ronin had not seen this many life forms since he stumbled into a sea of stinging ants just weeks before, and that was a sight he need not be reminded of.

***

It was unreal. Baylee stared out the windows of the Goddess Carriage to try to see everything she could. So many people were in the streets! Columned buildings with signs depicting their purpose were several stories taller than the largest inn in Balanced Rock. The cobblestone street widened and marvelous arched bridges spanned the river, connecting a second street of equal size.

"So this is the capitol?" Baylee asked, almost breathless for all of her excitement.

"Oh, no, dear." Otillia answered her with a chuckle. She took Baylee by the shoulder to direct her attention. She used her fingers under an eager chin to gently guide the farmgirl's gaze upward. "We are going up there first."

Baylee did not notice the caravan splitting up. To many of its members, Durromay, or simply Durro, was their final destination. The slave wagon headed off to the west. One of the Tuskers staring at the Goddess Carriage as it disappeared in the opposite direction. Baylee, Otillia, and the others continued towards the base of the roaring waterfall. The wounded sergeant and his war priest, the hunter and his poor, leashed, little blue-eyed boy, many of the soldiers, priests, and acolytes, all waited in line for their turn to get on the lift.

The sound of the falls was deafening. They emptied into a large pond surrounded by handcrafted, large, marble blocks-the weight of each too much for her to calculate. It looked as though giants had built the pool rather than the natural forces of the waterfalls. Trimmed grass and flowers covered the peaceful edges around the barrier stones, forming a large area of unrivaled beauty. Children played in the park, lovers kissed on benches or beneath cherry trees. It was a sight from a fairy tale, peaceful and serene. How she wished Clara could see it!

Lost in the images around her, Baylee lost track of the time they waited in line until, finally, the all too quiet clerk finally spoke.

"Try not to puke." It was more than a suggestion. The woman had barely spoken in five days, and this was the most pleasant of the few words she had uttered.

The carriage driver maneuvered the Goddess Carriage into position after some sort of traffic guard with a perfect uniform, a shiny whistle, and too bright white gloves began to give him the proper signals. It was only then that Baylee realized the entire portion of the lift area was a statue of two Valkyr, winged warrior-women that carried the spirits of the dead to be with Her Own Grace. With a lurch, the carriage, its passengers, and all of the people standing around it, began moving upward. The entire ground around it was some sort of platform attached to invisible rope. It was a miracle! The hand of the Goddess herself raised them to the top of the lift.

She realized right away what the clerk had meant. The waiting area disappeared quickly, full-sized people turning into dots beneath them. The buildings even shrank down to small squares as the platform rose into the air. It happened so fast part of Baylee's stomach must have been forgotten at the base of the waterfall, and she found her fist adding to the support of her lips to keep back anything that dare try to escape from her insides.

As they approached the top, she realized the meaning of small. She could see the river they traveled next to for the past several days. It had become a small blue string fading off in the distance. The sprawling fields of farmland became a blend of squares and rectangles across the countryside. The sprawl of Burro was hidden by clouds that were made from mist rising from the Mother's Tears. The view was a delicate dessert she had never before seen on a plate, let alone tasted with her own tongue.

Then she turned around.

If the countryside below the lift was a dessert, the capitol in the center of Crystalline Lake was a feast for someone starved of all things fair in the world. Baylee's eyes had beheld many things over the last few days, sights that her small town mind never could have imagined. This view took her breath away, literally. (Well, it was either the view or the height she had just spanned so quickly that did the deed.) She found herself lightheaded and dizzy.

"Plug your nose, and close your mouth, and blow. Like this." Otillia demonstrated the action for Baylee to repeat.

240

When she did so, her ears let out a series of 'pops'. The relief of air pressure seemed to make the world stop spinning.

The edge of the body of water known as Crystalline Lake started down the slope a ways. Housing dotted the inner edges, as well as terraced fields. There was a large town, nearly the size of Durro at the base of the slope. Busy docks trafficked boats from the town to the center island wherein lay the capitol city of Anon. The island in the center of the lake looked like a manmade isle of marble and polished granite. From the lines of docks stretching into the water to the massive Great Pyramid of Anon towering from the middle, there was nothing that was not placed in an orderly, mathematical fashion. Even trees, flower planters, and hedges were all balanced to precision. The Temple of the Gospel, nestled against the Great Pyramid, held a beauty that was truly a present to mankind from the hands of the Goddess. It was no wonder the visage removed all doubt for its onlookers. Baylee realized, in that moment, the Scriptures had to be true. All of the legends of the Goddess creating the City of Anon in the heavens were fact, because there was no way such perfection could be achieved on this earth. It was only by Her hand, Her invisible touch, the lifts could bring a young farm girl to such a conclusion.

She was again lost in the moment, so much so that the Goddess Carriage had left the lift area and began its descent into the town below without her noticing. There was still quite an entourage surrounding the carriage, and it caused many of the people passing by to look inside at her and her fellow constituents. The driver smiled pleasantly, either due to the same views beheld by Baylee, or the proximity to the end of his charge of driving the passengers to their destination. Even the lower class on this side of the lift seemed to be cleanlier than anyone Baylee had known. She had heard that near the city, every house had a bath in it, filled magically by the hand of Her Grace. All doubt had been banished as soon as she reached the top, and so she could not wait to see a table that made its own food, as well.

They would be taking a floating barge from the town docks into the main city. There was a steady stream of floating platforms that ran in tight patterns, on structured schedules. Good old fashioned boats also ferried across the lake, carrying small groups of passengers, fishermen, and other cargo. There was no bridge spanning the distance from the slopes edge to the center island. Baylee surmised this was not due to a lack of engineering capability. Lifts without rope or chain and floating carriages seemed to make bridge building a task fit for a toddler. Baylee imagined the lack of water spanning structure was probably specifically chosen for defense of the capitol. It was no wonder the Sabrinian Empire was said to be unconquerable, an army would have to take the Lifts of Durro, if the invaders knew how to operate them, and then traverse a near bottomless freshwater lake, all the while being harassed by flying chariots, floating war barges, and Strike Griffons. It would be impossible for an opposing general to get into this place without careful and imaginative planning and the ability to sustain a great loss of his own troops' lives.

Yet to all of this splendor, Baylee was too filled with awe and inspiration to realize this impenetrable design; this majestic conglomeration of polished stone, sparkling pillars, and gleaming statues; this serene place of solitude for the Goddess' chosen, unable to be broken by her enemies, would be equally impossible from which to escape.

One of Those Days

The summer had been full of excitement for Marcus. His mission had been such a success. Not only had he been made Captain and given his own command, he was also granted a small apartment for Gallus and himself on the Center Isle. He had dreamed of such an honor as a boy, yet still he wanted more.

His eyes were now set on the next rank up, and everyone knew it, including the generals that held the precious seats. Becoming a general for the Sabrinian Army was the highest rank a man could achieve without marriage. It was respected by everyone, from untouchables to the High Priestess herself, and he would be sure to have it. Competition was fierce, however, and Cabot was aware the legend of his deeds, which gave him a shot at a higher rank in the first place, faded with every passing day.

Luckily for the young Captain, his raid on the small farm had given him two very important things, a lot of money from his share of the spoils, and an ally within the temple very close to the ear of the High Priestess herself. On a few occasions, a random warning sent through very strange channels had reached him of some political maneuvers that may have dropped him out of favor in the eyes of Her Own Voice. But, thanks to his sightless ally, he was able to thwart them.

The wealth he obtained was a different matter altogether. Cabot's mind was all strategies and trickery and, oddly enough, did not span into the realm of investment and gain. Again luck was on his side, as Gallus had history with the subject. As the Captain learned over several defeats at the gambling table, the eunuch merely calculated possible outcomes of the situations, then bet either heavily or lightly as the math saw fit. So, as it turned out, Gallus new even the most brilliant strategy could fail, and once one knew how to figure in the odds, he would always walk away victorious.

The slave trade and, more specifically, the portion associated with the games, was one such gamble Gallus could calculate the odds on. Coupled with the Captain's devious skills at manipulation, the pair could literally bathe in coin won with the strategic and calculated rise and fall of proposed champions. They just needed a champion.

It was this need that led them to the Inn in Durro. They were there to meet a slave trader that had just prepared a new shipment of stock from Brenbay, the north easternmost port of the empire. Her name was Glenda Randulf, and she was well known across the empire as the best slaver around. It was she who purchased the Tusker stock several months before, and after proper conditioning, resold to the highest bidder. Though Cabot's commission had not been nearly as much as he expected, communiqué expressed she would discount the stock to any of those responsible for the capture. Marketing ploy or not, Marcus and several other of the troops had bitten on the offer and prompted the woman to make a special trip.

The Inn was called 'Agytha's', and it had grown in reputation almost as fast as the captain's. The owner was apparently a business woman of good repute. She ran a tight ship, and all of her employees were clean. The Inn was larger than many in Durro and had a large common area with a sizable stage. A balcony lead up to the rooms, which were always in good order and well kept. Customers were treated with top priority at the Inn that prided quality over quantity. The prostitutes were also picked from top stock and were paid better than most at other places on Durro. The end result being, the working men and women at Agytha's were top of the line.

Right as Marcus and Gallus entered, they were greeted by a man and a woman, both entirely too beautiful and too scantily clad for confusion of purpose. They seated the two and offered drinks and companionship. Right away, Cabot vowed to return, but ordered only libations for the upcoming negotiations. The Captain knew little of Glenda Randulf other than her name and occupation, but being a successful businesswoman meant she undoubtedly shook hands with her right and held a deadly viper in her left. He only hoped the woman tried the usual seduction techniques on him. Feigning weakness to this had served him well in the past, and judging by the amount of prospective customers, any tool he could use would be of value.

Luckily, several of the soldiers that hoped to purchase one of the Tusker fighters were under his command still, and would not dare outbid him. Just to insure this common courtesy took place, both Marcus and Gallus made their way around the room greeting the fellow men, all of which looked forward to making it rich by sponsoring their very own arena champion. There were, however, a couple of well-dressed women in the room, neither of which did Cabot recognize. This proposed more than a slight problem, especially due to the size of each woman's entourage. Marcus was not the only one intimidated by the pair, who now took turns complimenting each other's choices in the latest late-summer fashion. Some of the soldiers were even grumbling about whether or not to stay and try picking up a gladiator. The task seemed futile at best if bidding against those two.

It drove the captain crazy to watch the women talk, the way they exaggerated their vowels and giggled between casual insults of common acquaintances. It was no doubt that Cabot was respectful of his place as sub-servant as defined in the Doctrine, nor was it one that the captain feared the wrath of the Goddess; yet he honestly felt soft lips were best placed around a cock, rather than parting to vomit such rubbish. Even then, Marcus' own taste for oral pleasure brought to question the value of such lips, finding none more skilled than his fellows'. Such thoughts were interrupted when the doors to the main area opened for a group of six soldiers to enter.

They filed in, looking as if they had just survived a battle of epic scale. This was not the case, however. It was the will of their commander, who believed that polishing armor was as futile as training a recruit with a wooden gladius. The men looked ready to fight everyone in the room, all at once if need be, and dared the occupants to try. Glenda soon followed her troops, and Marcus nearly mistook the woman for one of her own men. The woman was as large around as she was tall. She was so intimidating to the eye that Gallus tensed up, fearing retribution from even a glance.

"Drinks fur me men!" Her voice boomed across the room, thrown out by a huge smile that lacked the majority of her teeth, parts of the final word causing her tongue to roll with her strange coastal accent.

All at once Agytha's place became a hustle of bodies, servants and bartenders snapped into action. Glenda smiled and laughed; a jovial soul that had seen many of the pleasures of wealth in her line of work. She took a big handful of a waitress' bottom as she passed, an action that both confirmed Gallus' suspicions and disarmed one of Cabot's hopeful weapons of trade. Expectedly, she barely gave the two a glance as she approached the two noblewomen. They would be her best customers today, not just because of their social status, but because of the apparent lack of exposure either woman had ever had to battle. It was almost certain they had been to gladiator matches, that being the most common form of entertainment in the capitol. But to be able to appraise the caliber of a soldier up close was another matter altogether. Then there was the idea that these slaves were Pigbacks; each and every one of them half again as tall as a human, and equally proportioned in breadth. The weakest of the stock would, no doubt, appear just as fierce as the strongest. Marcus knew this, and he was absolutely certain that Glenda did as well. Maybe there was hope after all.

After tipping back a mug of ale (and a second) Randulf began making small talk with the noblewomen. Based on the captain's observations, Glenda's frequent crotch-touching was like biting into a poorly made dessert. Only through sheer will did the high ladies manage to hold back complete looks of distain. As she spoke to them, two of her soldiers flanked her at either side, oogling the two ladies with a daring that openly shocked the captain. Eulacians were a strange lot.

It wasn't long before the titanic woman thundered towards the two men, complete with raining ale and ear-plugging laughter. Gallus reckoned there was no way this human could stop her momentum as she made her approach and, therefore, visibly took a step back in defense.

"Awe, 'loky dere. I skurd eem!"

Cabot nodded in response.

"I think you did, my lady." He did not mean to hesitate on the last word, but it happened.

"Guess dat sneep ee got wiff doze robes made eem all joompy! Yer not all joompy, are ya?" She placed her hands on her hips.

The guards with her eyed the captain up and down, either determining how long he would last in a fight with them, or in the bedroom with Randulf.

"No, my lady. I'm not jumpy at all." Marcus managed a smile and a bow of his head.

"Dat is a good thing!" She swung one of her hands between Marcus' legs, powerfully cupping his manhood. Oddly enough, the force of the swing did not deal a painful blow and was somehow oddly comfortable. The giant woman was proficient, he had to give her that.

"I like dis won! Heem a looker!" Never in his days had Marcus ever been called a looker, but he supposed he would take it where he could get it. There was definitely hope in the transactions, after all. The two men looked at him with-jealousy-in their eyes. Jealousy?

"Wait on there!" Glenda took a step away from Marcus to look him up and down. "Yur da mon een charge of geeting me oll of deese Pig-a-backs, be ya not?"

She was hard to understand, but Cabot nodded.

"Dat one elle uv a find, mon! Yur a good one, ay!" She patted Marcus on the back so hard it nearly knocked the wind out of him. She pulled him close and whispered something in his ear he did not understand. When she let him go, she gave him a wink that only he and Gallus saw. It caused the eunuch to mask a chuckle with a cough.

"Come now! We go to see da Pig-a-backs!" Glenda made the announcement for everyone in the common room (and whoever might be wondering as far south as Balanced Rock). Randulf led the way out of the Inn and into the warmth of the day.

Out in the street, the cart that brought in the potential slaves had been cleverly converted to a temporary showcase, the sides folded down and two ramps on either side. The Tuskers were in a row behind the cart, being assembled into marketable condition. Marcus, Gallus, and the others all gathered around waiting for the auction to begin.

"Well, would you look at that, Marcus?!" Gallus was careful to hold back his excitement from the others.

"Isn't that the..."

"It is! That is the chieftain! The one that plunged his teeth into Lucavion's skull." Gallus was certain of the identification, despite the severed tusks.

"He looks defeated." Cabot noted.

"They cut off their tusks, it makes them placated. Destroys their will to escape. They only then seek death in battle." Gallus imparted his knowledge through guarded hand, but his eyes never left the chief.

"How dreadful." Marcus was sincere. "Is that not the one I shot in the back?"

"Oh, that it is! He lived, too! What a remarkably strong people."

"You sound as if you respect them, Gallus. Mind that tongue." Cabot respected them as well, the scornful statement almost sounded facetious.

"Captain, the chieftain is mighty. If...Lady (he had a hard time with the title) Randulf is on your side, then perhaps she will dissuade bidding from the others."

"Perhaps." Marcus was in deep thought.

The bidding began with one of the Tuskers. People were conservative at first, as with many auctions, until the thrill of the moment took over. It became suddenly very clear as to why Glenda's men looked so rough. The Tuskers, despite being chained, ankles to waist to wrists to collar, took at least two of the men to handle. It was also apparent, very quickly, that very few new slave owners would be leaving Durro today with a slave as long as the two noblewomen were there. They seemed to have little cause for a bid yet little regard for cost. Though they did not win every purchase, it was as if they simply wanted to see who could end up with the most new playthings. Marcus did bid on (and win) a one-armed Tusker. He had seen the ferocity of that one in battle, and no one seemed to think a second thought about the foolish captain's meager bid. Even Gallus seemed a little taken aback at what appeared to be a foolish decision, but to Cabot, that one was one of the two in the line-up that had not yet been robbed of spirit. That one wanted revenge.

It then came time for the sale of the chief. He was the biggest Pigback there, and truly intimidating, even with the slumped shoulders of lost dignity. When he got to the center of the platform, Randulf gave Marcus another discrete wink, causing Gallus to poke him in the side. The Captain shooed his warpriest's hand in annoyance. Boldly, Glenda began checking the inside of the chief's mouth, and even raised his arms and let them drop down to the sides. She shook her head at him, and turned with a look of disgust to the crowd.

"Dees wun not fer sale. Dees wun too seekly. No gud fer the byin!" She motioned to send him off the platform the direction he came, when Marcus stepped forward.

"Ladies and Gentlemen, perhaps I can be of help to you on this purchase." Glenda stopped the men from ushering the Tusker off and looked at the captain in a most confused manner. "Sick or no, I feel it is of utmost importance that you know this particular Pigback is responsible for killing our own Lucavion. The fallen hero the battle was named for." A hush came over the crowd, and the noble women (and even some of their entourage) openly gasped. "Now I could allow this Pigback to be taken back to his cage and try to negotiate with this fine, reputable woman, who unfortunately, has no idea of the real value of this beast. Nor does she know that it was he who took his once sharpened tusks, and holding our out-numbered hero aloft with savage arms, slammed his tusks into the poor man's face- just so he could taste his blood and brains!" His arms shook with passion. He walked the length of the captured audience. "It was this savage act that rallied our troops to victory! It was this noble sacrifice that won us the battle! What would it not be worth to see this one punished for this atrocious crime? What would you pay to offer this treacherous beast up to the Goddess herself for public display and sacrifice, knowing her blessings would then be upon you? Or better yet, would you nurse him to health and plot him against the vengeance of our own noble breed, knowing the price you could charge for someone to slay the slayer of mighty Lucavion? How much would a warrior pay you, the master of this daemon of the plains, for a chance at immortality?" The captain was animated. Rage was in his heart, greed was in his eyes. Gallus had no idea what the man was doing, but the speech was so moving that the warpriest would have sold his own cock all over again for a chance to buy the savage, and that was an item he direly missed.

The bidding frenzy began. Even passersby that heard just part of the speech drove the price upward. In no time, Gallus had calculated that the value of the Tusker exceeded the value of all the others combined, and still the bidding rose. A few of the participants dropped out, but stayed to watch intently. Still the price for the Tusker rose, now three times the value of all the others combined. As Marcus suspected, the remaining two citizens battling over the Plainsman were the two noblewomen, whose prior sly cordialness had turned to open scoff, finally pushing the bids to four times the combined amounts of the rest until, at last, a victor emerged. The crowd cheered the purchaser, who looked flushed with either excitement, or the vast amount of coin she had just offered for a single slave. The runner-up glared with such ferocity she might have slain a charging Thanadont with only her eyes. Marcus smiled. Both women would be taken out of the rest of the bidding.

He returned to his place while the excitement calmed. There were only three Tuskers left, two of which he did not care about, and the one he had shot in the back with the arrow. When he returned, Gallus looked at him with wide eyes. The eunuch had no idea what Cabot was planning, but could not wait to see it come to pass.

Offers started going up on the first Pigback, Marcus was careful to help drive the price up high enough to knock out another bidder. This was not difficult. Those that remained were so excited at a chance to own a gladiator, due to the two women no longer participating, that they quickly overstepped their boundaries. Similar to the first, the second's cost soared too high, no doubt knocking out a second competitor for Cabot's wanted prize.

There wasn't as much excitement for the Tusker Marcus shot as he suspected, still he had to pay more than he wanted in order to win the bid. All in all, he was proud of himself. One by one, the owners were allowed to approach their prize, each given a special paint brush and unique color to temporarily mark the property until a permanent brand could be properly placed. It was as he suspected, the one-armed Pigback made a lunge at the captain when he approached him. Cabot did not flinch, he was battle hardened, but he did add rage to the beast by smiling. It took two of Glenda's burley guards to put him back into place. He painted the Tusker on the stump just below his elbow, then again on his good arm in the same place. He did not have to speak their language to drive home that threat. Still the beast-man was fiercely defiant.

The younger one he had shot was not nearly as hostile as the one-armed soon-to-be champion. It looked at Marcus with a sort of stern inquisition that, oddly, made the captain less comfortable than the rage shown by his other fighter. Brute strength was important in battle and won out against brains more often than not, but if one could harness both, as this younger one seemed to have done, then one could be unstoppable. He painted the scar on the Tusker's chest, then slowly walked around and painted the one on his back. It was as he suspected, the arrow had stuck him clean through- and in the lung. It was a fatal blow for certain. He circled back to the front.

"How did you survive that, eh, little one?" Cabot asked the question to the Tusker, who in turn looked at him with his head cocked sideways.

"Strong." the Pigback replied. It actually answered him!

To add to Cabot's suspicions, the other Tuskers looked at him with confusion, and then looked to the chieftain who grumbled something to Marcus' newest purchase. Marcus smiled, he had been right.

"What is going on here?" Gallus had been holding in his questions since the speech. Now the anxiety was simply too much for the warpriest to handle.

"Come." Cabot put his hand on the eunuch's shoulder and guided him towards Glenda. "I will tell you on our way home." A smile barely touched his lips. He paid the woman, who shook her head, still confused by his strange speech that undoubtedly cost him the best warrior in the group.

"Eer," she said. "Thank ye fer wat ye spook back theer." She tossed him a steel talon back. "Ye maed me far moore than I bargained fer!" She shot him a wink as he smiled at her, shaking the coin at her in thanks. With that, the two men turned and headed away from the crowd, shaking hands with other proud owners in both congratulations and farewell.

As soon as they covered some ground, a smile split Cabot's face from ear to ear. Gallus was still puzzled, but seeing the captain in such a mood passed the same smile on to the eunuch like a contagious cough.

"Okay, okay. Now will you tell me? What were you thinking? She was going to practicality give you the chief. Instead, you made the woman rich! In return, you bought a gimp and a child that won't be ready for the ring for at least two snows!" He gathered up a bit of courage. "Not very sound investments, Marcus."

"Gallus, Gallus, Gallus." He smiled as he shook his head with slight disapproval. "I'm baffled you did not pick up on it before."

"Pick up on what, pray tell!" the warpriest was perplexed.

"Well, the obvious purchase of the one-armed Tusker was a bargain in and of itself."

"True, we did see his ferocity in battle."

"Yes, that and a spiked shield, or...or...better yet, an oversized ball and chain could be grafted to the stump simply enough." It was clear the captain had already begun spinning fantasies of glory in his imagination.

"And I suppose we saw the tenacity of the little one as he refused to give up on his task." Gallus found his muse with the possible outcomes.

"True and, of course, his miraculous survival, but our inside knowledge of the product is not why I did what I did!" He was still excited with himself, and savored that the eunuch was still clueless.

"Then what?"

"You really didn't see it?" He stopped the man in the street.

"See what? Oh, come out with it, you're killing me!" He sounded a bit irritated at his metaphoric torture.

"The Tusker I shot is the chieftain's son. The resemblance was uncanny." Marcus paused at Gallus' furrowed brow.

"They all look the same to me," Gallus stated dryly.

"I'm sure they'd say the same about us, dear Gallus. Yet this is definitely not so. Even here, under the fold of the Goddess, we see variations in color and hue."

"I have read there are northern groups of humans that even have fair skin and green eyes! Wait, you are getting me sidetracked." The two resumed walking towards the falls. "So what if the two savages are related? I don't see the point...how do you know their relationship is father and son?"

"Simple, during the battle, the boy was given a task that took him out of the direct melee. Afterwards, the chief never left his side, even when his own wounds seemed near enough to claiming him. They are father and son." He had made his point to the warpriest, who was once again intrigued by the thought process.

"Nonetheless, I fail to see the significance..."

"The point is, with the atrocious price that idiot (he looked around to see if his insult was too loud) woman paid, she will have to keep him alive for several seasons. Time enough for our young soldier to train."

"Train for what?"

"A challenge, Gallus. A challenge I will propose in honor of the fallen hero of Lucavion's Bluff. When that happens we will pit my champion against hers in a fight to the death!" The captain was animated again and nearly lost in fantasy.

252

"Even if all of that comes to pass, which is very unlikely, what makes you think our fighter even has a chance? I mean, you saw that chief fight! He has no equal!"

"Exactly the point, Gallus, and that means not only will the Tusker survive the seasons we need to train, but when the time comes, all of the odds will be against our favor. We can bet the entirety of whatever wealth I have accumulated at the time! We will become the richest men in all Sabrinia!" He was selling the daydream to his servant as deftly as he had sold the chief's value to the crowd.

"What makes you so certain of victory in the near-improbable battle?" Gallus was being the cynical adversary.

"Because, my dear man, no father, despite race or tone of skin, could ever bring himself to kill his own son. He will, however, give his own life to ensure his child's survival."

The plan stopped Gallus in his tracks again. He truly was mystified by the captain's unconventional thinking. The man would definitely be a general someday.

***

The High Priestess hated the Dark Beneath, but she had put off her *mangmu lieren's* request for her presence long enough.

"Hold the light higher guards, should I slip and fall I would have you both report to the priesthood."

Instantly, the lanterns were raised to provide wider circles of light for the three of them to navigate the spiraling stairs.

They would continue down past the dungeons, the storage place of those criminals and Otherbreeds not suited for servitude or slavery. The Dark Beneath was deeper still, for below the discarded miscreants and condemned scum was the housing for the Sabrinian Hunters. The assassins and trained murderers that kept the country safe from those that would seek to destroy it. The Dark Beneath was more than simple dormitories for the *mangmu lieren*. It also held many training arenas of various types, and dog kennels for the notorious hellhounds. She had even heard there was a sort of forge somewhere down here, but she herself had never been.

Hunters only emerged from the dark for three reasons: the Choosing, a Hunt, or the Will of their priestess. The annual Choosing, held in the coldest months, was really nothing more than an exhibition of the hunters' battle prowess that became a mass orgy of wine, opium, and sex for the priestesses privileged enough to have earned an invitation. Like sharks to a school of mackerel, the hunters were devoured, each priestess making her choice of morsel as she went along. After several hours, or sometimes several days, slated of desire and ecstasy, the women would each be granted the protection and control of one of the deadliest creatures in all the lands. Earning an invitation to the event was based on the sole determination of the High Priestess herself who, in turn, was showered with any imagined manner of bribery to grant such favor. The latent function of such a popular festival, was that it caused a tremendous amount of slander amongst the priestesses of Sabrinia, as each jockeyed for higher position and esteem. All was a part of the unspoken game that nearly every flesh-and-blood woman born to this world enjoyed to play.

Soon she was there, the place where the prizes of the games were created. Hidden from the sunlight they did not need, and kept secret from all but the highest nobility and the warpriests that helped to maintain the order of things. She nearly jumped out of her skin at the presence of Maesma, waiting silently with his arms behind his back like a ghost on the darkest of nights. The light almost glimmered off of his skin, and his pale white eyes were like bowls of milk that reflected the images of the three. The High Lady's escort had partially drawn their swords when they saw the man, not realizing that had they done that, both would have done so for the last time.

"My Lady." Maesma bowed low, an action made by a deadly viper, too close for comfort.

"*Shui Nan'de*. You look well. It is good to see you." She greeted him with grace, but her touch did not mask the long intimacy the two had shared.

"The boy is this way." He turned away from the priestess and into the darkness.

The two guards had to hustle to follow her hurried steps. The hallway was lined with hunters on each side, as a sign of both honor and loyalty. They were so motionless, their pale skin such that every muscle could be seen and appeared to be made of marble, perfect constructions of artwork, worthy of the statues in the temple above. Each pair bowed their heads in unison as the priestess approached. To them, she was the Goddess Herself, each and every one of them willing to give her their lives in any way she deemed fit.

They neared the kennels, oddly, the area was not as odorous as she suspected. The hunters and priests kept the area immaculate. She resolved to tell some of the temple servants to redouble their efforts. There was also not the suspected whining or barking associated with dogs, though there was the occasional growl, silenced by the loud snap of a hunter's fingers. The new recruits were kept here, forced to live, eat, and sleep with the dogs; a difficulty not fully realized until competition came during meal time.

Maesma paused before opening one of the doors, "Be wary. The child has a way with the dogs I do not understand. I had to kill four last week, he had somehow commanded to turn against us. I made him watch the first three, then beat him until he did the fourth himself."

"You taught him attack commands, already?" the High Lady asked.

"No, Mother. That was what was odd, he didn't say a thing." The hunter had a hint of confusion in his normally stoic tone.

"Interesting," she said as he cautiously opened the door.

When the lights of the crystalline lanterns flooded the room, she could see the naked boy huddled in the corner alone. The half dozen or so hellhounds in the room did not attack, but growled openly, hunkering down in defense of the boy. She could see his entire body was covered in bruises.

"Goddess, *Shui Nan'de,* do you think you could have beat him further?"

"If you wish..." Maesma began to enter the room, until her delicate hand seized his arm.

"I do not wish. Look at him! Oh, daemon's filth!" The sound of her voice seemed to revive the boy a bit. He lifted a weakened head to see her with his one eye not blocked by swelling. Right away, she noticed his swirling blue orbs.

The sight almost made her forget the dogs, whose hackles rose as she knelt down to get a closer look. They all growled at her in unison, a phenomenon that all noticed. Her guards began to unsheathe swords until she stopped them with an outstretched hand.

"I'll not harm you, boy." Her voice was butterscotch taffy. "You can tell your friends that I vow it so."

The two guards looked at one another, openly confused.

255

"Are you suggesting he can speak to the dogs somehow?" Maesma spoke plainly.

"I'm not entirely certain. Yet those strange eyes are unlike any I've ever seen. Does he see as you do?"

"It appears so, Mother." replied the hunter.

"He was the one you found with the Lorekeepers, was he not?" Even to Maesma, her tone was soothing.

"He was, Mother. Could they have taught him something?"

"I do not yet know, my pet." She waved a guard closer. "More light." The illumination lit the boy's features, and she was able to look at his strange eye. The snarling rose with the soldier's movement.

"I won't let him hurt you either, boy." It was fresh butterscotch taffy, straight from the oven, sticky on the tongue. Candy or no, the dogs did not seem to listen to the boy. That or he did not yet trust her.

"I suppose I will have to put him down." Maesma did sound slightly disappointed.

"I do not think that is the required route, my pet. Besides, with his unique eyes I'm certain he will be a hit with my daughters. Though I suppose he is a bit too young for a Choosing. I wish he was not so badly bruised, I cannot tell if he is of fair breeding."

"Some of the men said the boy's mother was quite fair." Maesma did not like the memory of the skirmishers, so he swallowed deeply when he finished the sentence.

"The boy's mother? Why, *Shui Nan'de*, you never before made mention of the boy's mother."

Maesma cursed at his mistake. His run in with a woman from his past had clouded his mind in many ways, but he had not reported that Shawna was the mother for a vast number of reasons; wrath of the jealous Matron being but one.

"Apologies, Mother. I did not think it important."

"Oh course you didn't. And usually you aren't supposed to think, so usually that is a good thing." She spoke the words aloud to the man, looking over her shoulder at him. When she looked back to the boy, he seemed a bit livelier.

"*He's just a big bully, isn't he?*" She spoke without words to the boy.

"*Yes,*" he said to her, thoughts and memories of his beating flooding her mind.

"*You can tell the dogs I won't hurt you. I promise I will not.*"

There was a moment of pause, as the three men watched the priestess stare intently at the naked child. Then all of the dogs simply laid down, almost in unison. Some panting from the strain of being so close to attack from the moment the door opened.

"*Thank you,*" she said. "*I have to go now, but I will be back to check on you soon. Do what this big bully says for now, okay?*"

"*He killed my mother! I hate him!*" Horrors of the child's loss affected not only her mind, but her heart.

"*I understand, and I will return, I promise.*" She allowed herself to think of the boy as valuable, a thought that was not untrue, though the means to that purpose were probably somewhat less personal than what she would have him think. She stood and quickly left the room.

"I have seen enough. Come. Walk me out of this place."

The four started towards the exit, repeating the same head bowing process of the statue-like pairs of men in the hallway. It was not until they nearly reached the stairwell that she dare speak.

"That boy has a rare talent, pet, you must break him."

"I will, Mother."

"You must make him one of us."

"I will, Mother."

"And let his face heal, I want to see if he will be a match for one of my daughters."

"I will, Mother." She turned again to start up the winding stairwell.

"Oh, and one more thing, who was the boy's mother?"

"I do not know, Mother."

"You did not come across her along with the Lorekeepers?" She raised an eyebrow.

"No, Mother. The young sergeant found her."

"Captain."

"I'm sorry, mother. Captain?"

"Cabot is a captain, now."

"I see, Mother. Apologies." Maesma gave more care for a bucket of hellhound shit.

"So...You did not slay her?" She was testing him, and he knew it.

"I did not, Mother." Maesma was the same stone as his men.

"I see...interesting..." She turned to leave, deep in thought and slightly taken aback. It had been a long time since the man had lied to her, and there had always been only one reason: her.

***

"Oh, we love them, don't we sister?" Flynne was clapping her hands excitedly.

"Oh, yes! We most definitely do!" Aernne was already trying to get the right one onto her foot.

"Yurri has literally been slaving day and night to complete them for you before the autumn festival. I'll have to teach you how to walk in them, of course, but you're certain they please you?" Agytha found she did not have to feign interest in their response. The twos' approval could very well make Yurri, and herself, a comfortable income due to a growing waiting list for the style.

The bald craftsman performed marvelously, as usual, and the twins' boots had been made to Agytha's specifications. He had refused to deliver the boots to them in person. He had opted to drink away any trepidation caused from a phobia of rejection, and now lay in a wine-induced coma in the back of his shop. Agytha assured him she would make a timely and respectful substitute for the delivery and had done what was asked, as promised.

Her friendship with the twins had grown into more in the past several months. Rarely was there any more of the shows in the Viewing Room. Instead, the meetings were reserved for just the three and were beginning to take up a lot of the businesswoman's time. Luckily, Koll'Ynn had picked up much of the operating stress, a strong supporter of the red district woman's seduction of the two noble girls.

"Here, let me help you." She leaned over to help Aernne put on her first boot and then the second. She helped the young woman stand, holding her hands up high in order to balance properly.

"Oh my, I am so much taller! I love this!" Aernne attempted to walk across the room in the same sensual manner she had already mastered, after about three steps she wobbled, tripped, and fell on her hands and knees. The fall sounded like it hurt, and the squinted eyes of the prone twin seemed to verify this. Agytha, Flynne, and their newest handmaiden all waited in silence.

At first, it sounded as if she were crying. Agytha's heart stopped beating. If the girl was hurt, she could order Agytha into Acolytes robes by the end of the day. That would sabotage everything she had spent the last several months working for. Her head was bobbing up and down as if she sobbed uncontrollably. It wasn't until the three onlookers where jolted by a primal snort from the prone one that they realized her reaction had been quite the opposite. She was laughing at herself!

She was laughing so hard it caused the other girls to laugh as well. Even the handmaiden had to cover her mouth with a fist to avoid detection of her own amusement in the picture.

"I want to try!" Flynne was slipping on her boots, while Aernne was trying to gather her feet beneath her for a second attempt.

The young women digressed to clumsy, giggling toddlers for the next several hours, several glasses of wine adding to their lack of maturity. After a while, they could cross the room without stumbling, and Aernne even had a bit of sway to her hips towards the end. Soon, it came time for Agytha to leave, to return to her place of business with a brief detour to Yurri's shop to tell him the good news.

On her way out the door, she stopped at the handmaiden to introduce herself. She had noticed the young girl enjoying herself several times during the 'walking in heels' lesson. She was a stunning little thing with cute little freckles, about the same age as the twins.

"What's your name, girl?" Agytha asked, to which the handmaiden merely blinked in astonishment.

Unsure what to do, she looked to the heiresses.

"Well, answer her," Aernne said.

"Yes. Speak, girl," Flynne urged.

"It's okay," the eldest woman said. "We won't tell anyone you told us." She smiled and looked over her shoulder to the twins. "I like this one. She's cute."

"Thank you, my lady," the handmaiden said.

"You're welcome. But seriously, what is your name?" Agytha restated the question.

Both twins were now filled with curiosity.

"They called me Baylee back home, my lady," the girl responded, to someone apparently very small and very invisible, living in the rugs beneath Agytha's shoes.

"Very well, Baylee. It is nice to meet you!" She touched Baylee on the nose before waving goodbye to the sisters. "You two take care of this one, she looks like she might have potential!"

The latter statement was filled with so much innuendo it actually made the servant blush. Nonetheless, it was not a statement without truth. There was something about this young lady that the red district woman liked right away.

The twins said their goodbyes by blowing Agytha kisses and thanking her, many times, for their new shoes, as she turned and strolled down the hallway of the temple, and out into the fresh late-summer air.

***

Dana walked with her arm through her son's. Her pride in the young man was the morning sunshine that broke over the horizon, bringing an entire countryside to life for the coming day. They approached the newly completed house after his tour through the small town he no longer recognized. Everything in Balanced Rock had changed.

"It looks nice, mom," the young man said, tipping up his wide-brimmed hat to get a better view. Yet as he looked over his parent's newly built home, it was his mother's gaze that took him in. It had been far too long since she had seen him, so long a face-splitting smile helped to gather tears in her eyes.

"You look so amazing, son."

He had his father's emerald green eyes and was developing the same weathered stare, and even though he had often complained of getting her husband's height as well, she saw nothing but perfection. The young man was frightfully handsome.

"Mom, stop," he said, squeezing her hand to kneel down to inspect the buildings foundation. When he crouched down, the motion caused his riding cloak to flutter, exposing a holstered crossbow and several sheathed blades, the tools of a fighter.

Dana put her hands on her hips, a posture that still made the young man instinctually weary, though now she was easily disarmed with his suave sideways smile.

"This is that new style of foundation. Dwarvish, I believe. Looks sturdy!"

"It is, and costly." She was not to be dissuaded from concern with small talk. "What in the world do you need those dreadful things for?" Dana motioned towards the weapons.

"Snakes, mostly," her son joked, and she knew it, but rather than pushing the issue, he moved close and comforted her with both hands on her shoulders. "Mom. It will be fine." He kissed the woman on the forehead.

"Oh, I know, It's just everything is changing, and in order to afford these new housing structures, many of us have become indebted to the Keeper. Your father and I haven't had debt since you were a boy! It's just..."

"Here. Take this." He pressed a purse of coin into her hand. It was nearly bursting.

"What? Where did you get this?" There was enough coin in the purse for a season's worth of living.

"Mom, don't worry about it. You know I work very hard in Durro. I do very well. Please, you and dad have done so much for me." There was that smile again.

"Stole it from a poor noblewoman you ravaged, no doubt?" The woman's voice came from behind them, startling them both.

Dana merely gasped, but in one swift motion her son had spun round to meet the intruder, flourishing a hand crossbow in each hand, mechanical gears whirling and spinning as the prods snapped into position and mechanized rollers pulled the string back. With a deadly click, two bolts snapped into position from a magazine attached to the base. By the time he turned to face his foe, the interloper had two sharp ends of very pointy sticks pointing at her. It was hard to tell who was more surprised, Herminia, who made the mistake of spooking the young man, or his mother, who's hand went slowly from a fluttered heart to a gaping jaw.

"Don't shoot me for fuck's sake!" Herminia shot both her hands up in the air.

"Goddess' cunt, woman!" the young man said with a sigh. Gears ratcheted and ticked as he put the crossbows back into their holsters.

Dana stared at them both. "Wow! That got me all wet! Look at how sexy your boy has become!" Herminia slowly lowered her hands before sauntering up to the green-eyed rogue.

"You stay away from my son, trollup." Dana and Herminia were great friends, but her boy was way off limits to the blacksmith.

"Oh, fine," Herminia said in defeat. "He's not wide enough for my liking anyhow." It was in a jest, and all present knew the woman would make an exception given the chance.

"You'll never know how wide I am, if you keep on like that." Those eyes and that smile together-he could have her in a drop of his wide-brimmed hat.

"She'll never know anyhow! What?! Oh just stop, you two!" Dana was a teakettle gone too long on the fire. "Get inside."

Herminia took the handsome man's other arm, despite a warning glare from her friend, and the three entered the home. Dana toured her son around the home. It was significantly smaller than the one he had grown up in, but more than adequate for his parents. Still, he could tell this home did not hold the memories of the one she had been forced to tear down. After the tour, she led the boy to the small wine cellar, where she walked over to the northernmost wall. It was time to get to the reason he had ridden all the way here.

Cleverly hidden behind one of the shelves stocked with wine barrels was a freshly dug passageway. It resembled a newly created mine shaft, complete with wooden timbers for support. His parents had been busy. The tunnel system was poorly lit with a few crystalline lanterns hung on the wall, part of the luxury added by the obelisk raised earlier in the season. It was a less than gentle downward slope that continued for several hundred feet, about halfway down, he could hear the sounds of voices. The conversation became more and more audible until a hush came from the direction of their destination.

"It's just us." Dana said as the three entered the meeting room.

Ambrosia, Geneeve, and Tanya were all in the room, all but Tanya standing alert until they were assured no one else was coming. Tanya helped a woman who the young man did not recognize, who apparently had difficulty standing. She sat on one of the overturned buckets surrounding a table that must have been assembled in the room, for it was far too big to have been carried down the shaft. Opposite the corridor he entered was a second, and he could here sounds of footsteps coming down it.

"You ladies all remember my son, Koll'Ynn, don't you?" Dana spoke as if they did not expect his arrival.

"Of course they do!" Came a man's voice from the opposing hallway. It was the young man's father, but the only resemblance not hidden by a layer of dirt was two piercing emerald eyes.

Koll'Ynn moved in to embrace his father, oblivious to both the filth and the placement of his wide-brimmed hat. A second man retrieved the hat and waited for his turn to hug the newcomer, before returning it to his head like he must have done a thousand times before.

There was a brief moment of simple celebration as old friends reunited, yet before long, Koll'Ynn drew the room's attention back to the seated woman.

"So you found her, dad?" His eyes regarded the woman with concern. She did not look well.

"Sure did, on the road almost a day's journey from here. Down over by Marmot Hills. She was in rough shape, man."

"She's still in rough shape," he spoke the truth. "Has she spoken?"

"Not a word." Tanya was the nurse of the group and had tended to the woman for some time. "She barely eats or drinks."

"Tell him what I saw!" The other man was clearly excited.

"You tell him what you saw, goat cock, you got a tongue don't ya?" Koll'Ynn's father was just fooling around with Tanya's husband, the same way he had done since the young man could remember.

"Well, you see, we comes around the corner there, to see if the fire had burned out or how far it had went."

"Fire?" Koll'Ynn asked.

"Oh, yeah! Half the damn range went up in flames the last day of the raising festival!" His dad seemed impressed. "Blackened up the southern sky like a damn storm cloud."

"Anyhows," the man went on, "there on the road there, I sees this huge silver-ish cat the size of a damned horse standing over this pile of rags-course, turns out it's this lady here." He motioned to the woman seated at the table. "Anyhows, the damn cat dashes off while shithead over here is still staring at the sky."

"Yeah, yeah. This horse-sized cat sure as shit didn't leave no tracks." Koll'Ynn's dad certainly didn't believe his buddy.

"So we grabs the lady, and she's beat up somethin' fierce, and we gets her back here to Tanya for fixin'."

"So why send for me? She was probably just mugged or something."

"She was burned badly, too. She came from the fire." Tanya said. "But it's her eyes. They're like that pale man's eyes that Keeper Raen had here. And she's painted. She's got all these symbols on her body and one here on her cheek. Look up, dear." Tanya asked in a gentle voice, and the woman slowly complied. The sight was tragic. One side of her face was badly scarred, a severe contrast to the other that was a picture of beauty and perfection, and her eyes were a milky white film. They looked like death.

Koll'Ynn did not falter. He could not imagine what the woman had gone through, nor did he want to. "I have seen this mark on her cheek. This is a Tyrian Tear. It means she has fought for the Highbreeds in the lands of Tear. She was a hero once."

The woman looked at him, looked into him. He had played games with many different people, he knew a look of defeat when he saw it.

"This one is beaten, Mother. I don't see how she can be of use to our cause." He pursed his lips and began to walk away from the table. "It's too bad." He addressed the other people in the room. "So many slave caravans have come through Durro, lately. That poor child." His last sentence was bait, true enough. He had seen many children come through in chains, but he had no idea if one was this woman's, or if she even had any for that matter. He got his answer soon enough.

"They took my son." The woman stood, quiet as a final breath. Her conviction of tone startled everyone.

Koll'Ynn smiled inwardly. "They took many sons." Koll'Ynn turned and met the woman's stare. "The question is, can you help us take them back?"

Shawna looked down at the table, her hands shook with weakness. The entire room was silent, wide-eyed children. When she looked up there was no rage, no fear, and no trepidation; there was only resolve.

"By my last drop of blood, I swear it. Each and every one of them will burn." The icy tone of her words froze their hearts, even the Treesnake, who elicited the vow, gave time to pause.

They could now have their revolution.

Sometime in the past, during the Age of Aquarius

Halfway There

The wiry man's shoes squeaked with every step as he walked down the polished floor of the entryway. Four men in suits formed a boxed pattern around him as they escorted him towards the elevator. They seemed to scan in all directions at once, looking for possible signs of an ambush. The uniformed marching of designer dress shoes was a stark contrast to the man in the middle's obnoxious, high-pitched sneakers, and to make matters worse, he whistled a tune from a previous decade's spy movie, so far off key he was the only one who recognized it. While he attempted to destroy the other four's eardrums, he added an off rhythm tap with both of his hands on a briefcase that he clutched to his chest, opting to disregard the obviously ingenious handle that had been invented.

Before reaching the high-ceilinged hallway, they had to pass through a security area, just like the other visitors to the business complex, but these five had special access through the use of cards that could be slid through special readers. Security guards watched them carefully, as they made their way past the checkpoint and up to the nearest elevator.

The wiry man was dressed as a man would for success, true enough, but it looked as if he had stored his clothing in the trunk of a car and hadn't the inclination to take it to the cleaners to get it pressed. Both visual assumptions were true. He wore canvas sneakers with mismatched shoelaces, and only stopped his tapping long enough to push up his thick-rimmed glasses when they slid down his nose.

The other four looked dangerous, right down to the semi-transparent wireless transmitters that clipped cleverly behind their ears. One man was a giant, having to be some sort of athlete in the past or even in the present. His opposite was a man of below average height, with eyes that seemed to bore right through you. The third team member came from the hard concrete of some rough city. He wore dark sunglasses even in the comfortable lighting of the building. The fourth team member looked a little out of place, perhaps due to his recent entry to the team. He was a clean-shaven bald man with a square jaw that looked as hard as a cinder block, and tattoos on his neck and cheek that were a tell-tale sign of a past spent behind bars.

The five entered the first elevator, square shoulders taking up the majority of the room, forcing the wiry man to clench the briefcase even more tightly. A pair of well-dressed women attempted to join them, not taking them into full account due to the distraction of some juicy morning office gossip.

The giant man merely held up his hand, an object bigger than either woman's head. "Take the next one ladies." His voice was deep and full of warning. The women took a quick assessment of the other occupants and wisely decided to move on, leaving the men with the light echoes of clicking, business-appropriate heels on polished floors.

The doors closed with a peaceful sigh, and the smaller man near the control panel slid his access card through a reader hidden in a compartment beside the obvious user controls. A strange voice that failed in its attempt to sound either sultry or comforting due to its robotic nature came over the intercom:

"Welcome, private contractor number 469862. Access granted. Thank you for your patience."

The room began to soar upward, a speed that could even be considered nauseating. There was little choice however, there was no way the men had any intention of taking the stairs, even if the tapping and whistling trumped the pleasant stringed quartet playing in the background.

The elevator doors opened into a carpeted hallway with extended ceilings. Powerful pieces of artwork hung on either side of the hall bragging about the wealth invested in the skyscraper. The men proceeded into a waiting room with an entire wall of glass that allowed them to look out across the city below. In front of this wall was an oversized desk, sinuous lines carved with the custom intention of giving the viewers the subconscious impression of solidarity. Business deals made on this floor left little to chance.

A beautiful man sat at the desk. His name was Dominick Theodore Schneider, a name given to him by a mother who placed way too much emphasis on tradition. He absolutely hated his middle name, but as every boy in his family had a middle name the started with a "t", he was stuck with it. Dominick did not do well in school, dropped out of his first year of college before realizing his calling as a hairdresser. Unfortunately, that turned out to be a job he actually had to work at too, so several thousand dollars in loan debt later he found this job. Working for his boss was perfect, aside from sending the occasional e-mail or running the occasional errand, all Dominick had to do was take phone messages, and enjoy his extensive social networking. The pay was good, too, good enough that he never really considered pursuing cosmetology again. He was far too pretty to work hard anyhow. He needed as much free time as possible to spend his many hours in either the gym or the tanning beds (or both) rather than search for any real level of self-importance. He was a sign of changing times-a shift in the old ways of corporate power distribution. Dominick greeted them with a perfectly bleached smile that made all four of the wiry man's escorts want to cause him pain in one way or another.

"Ah! Mr. Griffon, was it?"

"Please, please, call me Bartholomew." The wiry man replied with an exaggerated aristocratic air.

"Yes. Very well. Mr. Bartholomew. This way. Miss Mei is expecting you." Dominick looked like he was either hurt or trying to avoid flatulence when he responded.

"Wait here, gentleman." The wiry man had apparently discovered a British Accent in the last few seconds. His squeaky shoes contrasted his pretentious gate, as he mimicked some sort of historical English fop.

The pretty man led his guest down yet another hallway to a pair of ornate double doors. A solid gold dragon circling a yin and yang split down the middle to allow him access to the room inside. The wiry man proceeded in alone, with an awkward handshake to his greeter.

To say the room was boastful, grandiose, elegant, or even overly-godly would be an understatement. Decorations of solid gold, statues of precious stone, and ancient long-extinct wood all carried the heritage and success of the building owner's Chinese heritage. Two walls were glass and externally accented by an infinity pool. A lounge area accompanied by a solid bar topped with crystalline bottles of the finest spirits dominated one corner, and ornate doors dominated another. The centerpiece of the room was a desk, with a surface made of polished jade that spoke of a price tag no one could possibly afford. Foo Dogs made up the base of this priceless representation of the success of the family throughout the generations. Behind the desk, a three dimensional wall hanging showed a panorama of some sort of ancient battle between men and demonic creatures; monstrous beings with the heads of beasts and bodies of men wielding terribly oversized weapons. Dragons fought from the clouds in the sky, soaring down to destroy an alliance of humans and their Foo Dogs, bitterly resolved in their defense against such foes.

A woman stood in the corner of the two windows staring out into the distant thoughts that plagued her. She did not seem to notice the entrance of the man who, in all strangeness, did not seem to be affected by the sheer amount of priceless artwork and decorations in the room. He merely whistled and tapped, waiting for his chance to be addressed by the woman.

The woman wore a dark, business skirt slit high so on one side it almost hinted at the presence of the intimate stockings of fantasy. Her heels were lithe and stylish, enhancing the grace required for her to navigate in them helping her to both curve her calf and look her constituents in the eye. A rounded backside met the end of a tailored blazer which covered the fine silk blouse underneath. The outfit was finished by black pearls and a thin watch worth as much as an exotic sports car.

She was in her forties, but had taken this with a grace that most would pay large sums to mimic with surgeries. The exotic woman hadn't even bothered to dye the streaks of silver that framed her seemingly ageless face, to jet-black like the rest of her silky, straight hair. When she turned to the wiry man, her stunning appearance actually caused him to stop whistling for a brief second, and wave at her awkwardly with his fingers rather than tapping with them. She floated past him with a style all her own, so quickly her hair wisped around her back.

"Would you like a drink?" she asked while she moved to the bar.

"That would be nice, Miss Mei. Thank you."

"What will it be?" Her voice was sultry. Hypnotic.

"Scotch," he said.

She poured the drink and walked it over to him. He thanked her, and the two exchanged awkward pleasantries.

"Let us cut to the chase," Mei said after a brief silence. "I am concerned about our time frame. Have you discovered the source of the pathogen?"

"Honey, let me tell you, I have spent so much time with rats the past few weeks, I have discovered a new way to make cheese." There was silence. "Get it? Because rats like...ANY how. Moving on...yes. I have discovered the source of the pathogen, but I have some bad news."

"What is that?" She was not amused at those two words together.

"There are some latent functions with this that we didn't expect."

"Such as?"

"Well, with lack of aging comes with a greatly slowed cell synthesis."

"And...?" She was clearly a woman who liked to focus on results.

"...and every rat I gave the virus to became sterile."

"But it worked?" Apparently this side effect meant little to the woman.

"Oh, it worked. Cell regeneration increased so dramatically that in every case study..."

"Aging stopped." She wanted to say it herself.

"That's right, aging stopped."

"How long before we can market it?" She was hungry, almost eerily so.

"I have to engineer one that will take to humans. Six months? One year?" He shrugged, time was of little importance to him.

"That long? Let me guess, it will cost me another hefty chunk of change."

The wiry man smiled in acknowledgement. "All of the data is here." He popped open his briefcase and pulled out its only contents, a single flash drive that could have easily fit in his pocket.

She took the small data container, and turned it over in her fingers like a gambler would a golden chip.

"Alright. Six months. No more." She stared at him, hawk-like eyes daring deception.

"You got it, love." There was that British accent again. He smiled at her and finished his scotch. "Thanks for the drink! That was absolutely delightful!"

She did not look amused.

ırned to leave and heard her start walking towards the
again, this time powering on her cell phone to make a call.
ꜱed the doors behind him and met up with his escort of four,
staring at poor Dominick so intently he was frozen in fear at his
desk. The squeaking and whistling started up to break the
uncomfortable silence.

"Let's blow this popsicle stand, gentleman!" The men moved into
position around him, and they moved towards the elevator. As the
five men entered and turned to face the door, the smallest turned
partially toward the wiry man, who was waving two unwarranted
middle fingers at the pretty office assistant as the doors closed, while
wagging his tongue out in the air. Dominick looked at them in
absolute horror.

"So it's done?" Caine asked.

"Three down, three to go," he responded while pushing his
glasses up on his nose. "We are halfway there."

Caine nodded, a silent contentment easing over his soul. Soon all
these greedy, bureaucratic fucks would watch their world crumble
with the promise of immortality. Soon it would happen, and they
would be the ones that did it.

About Jade Jesser

My Dad is a well-spoken, creative, and intelligent person who is capable of achieving anything he puts his mind to. Owning his own business, acting, writing, doing standup comedy, and being a great father are just a few of my dad's many talents. Being a single father, Jade has never decided once that his personal life is more important than spending his time with me. This is one of the most admirable traits that makes me proud to call him my dad. Always giving me great advice, inspiring different ideas and perspectives throughout my life, and teaching me countless life skills, I couldn't ask for a better father. Aside from being one of the most social people in existence, an intellectual genius, he is one of the most creative people you will ever meet. Drawing, painting, and writing are some of his favorite things to do. With hard work and dedication my dad wrote a book. Never once sacrificing time with me, he created a great piece of art and a new universe that you, the reader, will immerse yourselves in throughout the time you enjoy this book. I Love You Dad!

-Collyn Jesser

Made in the
USA
Columbia, SC